Acclaim for Thomas Sanchez's

King Bongo

"[*King Bongo*] swims with revolutionaries and corrupt police, American gangsters and debauched Hollywood movie stars, Cuban showgirls and rich American tourists. Its colors are lurid, its tropes ambitious, its narrative piled high with upholstered imagery. . . . Sanchez presents this rich gumbo with an assured showmanship."
—*South Florida Sun Sentinel*

"Imagine that the styles of Raymond Chandler and Graham Greene eloped and ran off to Havana in 1957—Sanchez's *King Bongo* is their love child. . . . A beautiful book." —*San Francisco Examiner*

"Gripping . . . Sanchez is a marvelous writer. He creates startling images of worlds unknown to the average reader. Then he propels his stories at high speed. Once you are launched into *King Bongo*, you must keep reading to find out what happens."
—*Houston Chronicle*

"Seduction and betrayal . . . a classic noir style that dances to a '50s beat . . . rich pop culture details and political reverberations. . . . [Sanchez's] Havana is a lavish and menacing dreamscape."
—*St. Petersburg Times*

"Sanchez has exhumed a lost moment in time—the last days of a Caribbean Pompeii." —*The Oregonian*

"Colorful, vibrant and pulsing with life. . . . Havana in the '50s . . . [the] territory of alcohol-drenched tropical noir tales of Graham Greene, Malcolm Lowry and W. Somerset Maugham, gets a strong jolt of Cuban coffee and good old American rock'n'roll. . . . Sanchez manages to evoke a rich, vibrant Havana with its magical dreaminess fully intact." —*The News-Press* (Florida)

"The writing of Thomas Sanchez is a lush display of the pain of truth and the power of integrity. *King Bongo* is a lyrical masterpiece of such potency that no glass bottle of 'genre' could ever contain its impact. Not to read this book is to suffer a self-inflicted wound of irreplaceable loss." —Andrew Vachss

"Begins . . . with a real bang. [Sanchez] knows how to ignite a story and keep it burning." —*Detroit Free Press*

"Intricately-plotted . . . full of surprises and vivid, often bizarre characters. There are echoes here of Dashiell Hammett and Graham Greene, but the music is Sanchez's own, and a captivating music it is, moving with the swift, syncopated rhythms of an Afro-Cuban dance." —Philip Caputo

"Sanchez ably constructs a layered mystery. . . . [He] most successfully and sensitively evokes Havana when he probes the racial dynamics of pre-revolution Cuba." —*The Miami Herald*

"Nasty cool. A terrific read—swift and grotesque, bursting with dark magic, humor and design." —Joy Williams

"On the brink of revolution [Havana] proves as sinister a crossroads as any . . . each twist and turn introduces a new set of characters more outrageous than the last." —*San Antonio Express*

"Powerful . . . spectacular . . . amazing." —Howard Norman

"A surrealistic fairy tale of Havana, filled with strange and diverse characters. Sanchez's novel can be read as a contemporary Shakespearean tragedy, and provides insight into a place and a time that is forever lost." —*Pittsburgh Tribune-Review*

"Sanchez's sleuth follows in the noble line of detectives in Dashiell Hammett's and Raymond Chandler's fiction. [*King Bongo* is] savvy and unsentimental, but he's vulnerable and highly emotional, a real Latin lover." —*The Press Democrat* (Santa Rosa, CA)

THOMAS SANCHEZ

King Bongo

Thomas Sanchez lived for many years in Key West, Mallorca, and Paris, where the French Republic named him the Chevalier des Arts et des Lettres. He currently resides in San Francisco. He is the author of *Mile Zero*, *Day of the Bees*, *Zoot-Suit Murders*, and *Rabbit Boss*, which was named by the *San Francisco Chronicle* as one of the most important books of the twentieth century.

King Bongo

King Bongo

A NOVEL OF HAVANA

Thomas Sanchez

VINTAGE CONTEMPORARIES
VINTAGE BOOKS
A DIVISION OF RANDOM HOUSE, INC.
NEW YORK

*To the guiding dove
who flew over my life
her spread of wings
forming a perfect A
for Astrid.*

Contents

9/09

King Bongo

tropical lies

1.

White Spider Dancing

King Bongo drove along the Malecón. All his troubles slid right off his shoulders and out over the ocean.

The canvas top of his Oldsmobile Rocket 88 convertible was down and oversized fuzzy dice hung from the chrome stub of the rearview mirror, swaying to a rumba throbbing from the radio. He loved this drive out of Havana headed for the Tropicana, past the centuries-old mansions facing the sea; fanciful three-story palaces with gaily colored facades of pillars and balconies, cheek by cheek with each other, like old tarts posing for a group reunion shot in the glare of tropical sunlight, shining with a glamour that refused to fade away. One after another these gaudy palaces preened along the curve of the Malecón, with its high stone seawall backing down the ocean that lapped against it. Perched on the seawall were perennial love-birds, men and women, boys and girls, lovers all, sitting and swoon-ing, holding hands, faces nuzzling necks, shoulders being caressed, lips kissing, and all the while waves crashing below. The moon shone down and the stars led the way along the Malecón as the road curved. The grand old mansions gave way to modern high-rise apart-ments, hotel towers, and sprawling shopping galleries. Bongo loved it all, old gods and new money, yesterday's dreams rubbing shoulders with tomorrow's promises.

The radio blasted out a hot new tune. Bongo beat its rhythm on the steering wheel as he picked up on the lyric and sang along. *"Lazarus rose from the dead and walked the dog. Do your hips shake when our lips kiss?"* He gunned the engine and the Rocket flew along the edge of the ocean.

Yes, old Saint Lazarus walked the dead walk with his ghost dog, leading the way between two worlds. Bongo felt that his own spirit dog was running loose, luck was headed his way.

The palms swayed along the Malecón like soft skirts rustling in the breeze; horns honked hello from carloads of females passing by, the women leaning from windows, blowing kisses.

Bongo punched the car radio button and the music of a Miami station came on loud and clear: "*I found my thriiilll on Blueberry Hiiilll.*" He tapped out the beat with two fingers on the dashboard.

Tomorrow morning would be good for Bongo's business, because tonight people having a good time would do bad things—crash cars, walk through plate-glass windows, fall into swimming pools and go to sleep underwater. Mistakes everywhere, blame to be assigned, value to be appraised, damages to be calculated, claims to be made, demands to be filed. All the things Bongo needed to make his up-and-coming one-man insurance office succeed. And that billboard looming ahead at the side of the road where the Malecón swooped in a ninety-degree left turn—BACARDI, THE FAMOUS RUM THAT MAKES THE WHOLE WORLD HAPPY—that billboard would one day be replaced with a new declaration: KING BONGO'S GREAT TROPICAL LIFE INSURANCE, WHERE EVERYONE IS ROYALTY.

Elvis Presley's lip-lashed words jumped out of the radio speaker: "*You ain't nothin' but a hound dog.*" Even Elvis across the water in America had his spirit dog, walking to hell and back, paradise and beyond. Bongo glanced up at the moon over Havana and a sky full of stars. Before him the fuzzy dice dangled from the rearview mirror, fate swinging in the balance, the fate of all lovers, politicians and assassins, puckered up and waiting for a lucky kiss at the stroke of midnight.

Martin Fox was a giant of a man and his Tropicana was a giant of a place. The nightclub was New York's Cotton Club, Paris's Folies Bergères, and Monte Carlo's Grand Casino all rolled into one in a jungle on the outskirts of Havana, far enough out of the city so that the pleasures it offered didn't offend the faint of heart. The idea of the Tropicana was that you might lose your money, but you'd do it in an exotic setting while rubbing elbows with the highest rollers and getting an eyeful of the world's most beautiful showgirls. It was a world-class idea, and the world beat a path to Martin's door.

King Bongo hoped to meet the giant Martin and sell him some insurance. Even though Martin was already hooked up with the orchestrators of the biggest protection racket in Havana, Bongo figured he offered something more legit—real payoffs for real losses. There were things that even the world's biggest bad boys couldn't protect you from. Acts of God, for example. Just thirteen years ago, in 1944, the Tropicana's roofless paradise got smacked by a hurricane that tore through banyan trees, uprooted palms, and stripped the earth down to its red dirt hide. Who better to pay off and help rebuild after that than those who had been hit by it too? Great Tropical Life was a homegrown company backed by local agricultural banks, eager to prime the pump of the economy in order to save their own financial skins. As Great Tropical Life's only insurance agent in Havana, King Bongo knew he was a little man, but he had a big plan. Tonight his plan was to finally get Martin to sign a multimillion-dollar policy insuring the world's most beautiful nightclub against any and all tragedies that could possibly befall it.

King Bongo aimed his speeding convertible at a concrete arch spanning the entrance of a long drive. Colorful blinking neon lights on the arch spelled out TROPICANA. Driving through the arch always gave Bongo a jump of anticipation, the excitement of entering a jungle governed by different rules. He drove up the road lined with royal palms, their silver trunks shimmering in the car's headlights. Suddenly the road cut through a thicket of ferns and vines intertwined in a green mesh through which he could glimpse eight voluptuous bodies in a tropical mist. The famous Tropicana muses. The life-sized marble nymphs were circled around a fountain; colored lights shooting up through a watery spray animated their frolic.

Bongo drove past the fountain and pulled to a stop underneath a swooping fan-shaped canopy dominating the entrance to the Tropicana. Other cars were arriving and being greeted by uniformed attendants. Bongo loved this social dance, the attendants helping elegant ladies in cocktail dresses out of their cars, then handing them off to a tuxedoed escort; a guy who might be a politician, a high-stakes poker player, a made man from Chicago, or just a regular Joe who had saved it all up to make the show, play the role, and wearing the best damn shoes money could buy.

"Hey, man! Love those kickers!" The parking attendant whistled, looking down at Bongo's black-and-white patent leather shoes as he stepped out of the Rocket.

Bongo reached into the inside pocket of his wide-lapeled powder-blue tuxedo, pulled out a folded peso note, and slipped it to the attendant with a wink. "These are the same kind of shoes Carlos Guardel danced in. Handmade in Argentina."

"You don't say! Guardel, the greatest tango man of all!" The attendant peered closely at Bongo. "You look like Guardel. Same killer Latin-lover looks. Hey, maybe you *are* him. All the big stars come out to play at the Tropicana."

"Especially the dead ones." Bongo winked, and walked through the double glass doors swung open by two doormen who saluted his entrance into the foyer as if he were a true king.

If a man can be judged by the way he walks, then maybe Bongo *was* a king. He walked to the *beat,* not arrogant, not strutting, not threatening. He had a natural rhythm drumming in his blood. People noticed his walk because he always seemed balanced, like a guy poised high up on a tightrope while the earth spun out of control below.

Coming across the red carpet, beneath the sparkling overhead chandeliers, was a seven-foot-tall man with muscles bulging beneath his suit. His shaved head glistened, his mouth was a huge gash beneath a once bulbous nose flattened by battles both in and out of the boxing ring.

"Do you have a ticket to tonight's show?" the man demanded. He stared hard at Bongo, then laughed and threw his arms around him in a bear hug, lifting him off the ground and giving him a swift kiss on each cheek. "Bongo, my brother! The first show is already over. Why so late?"

"I took the scenic route. I drove along the Malecón." Bongo smiled. "Let me down, Fido."

Fido lowered Bongo to the ground. Then, like a gorilla with the nimble feet of a ballerina, he did a dance as he sang a mock tune. *"Fido, let me down, I drove along the Malecón. Got my pay today, hoping tonight to get some play."*

"I wouldn't mind getting lucky."

"Lucky! What luck do you need? You've got the moves. You could steal the nipples off a nun while she said her rosary."

"Yeah, I could add that to my collection."

"Collection? You call that parade of puff and powder that goes through your bedroom a collection? That's a harem."

"I gave up the harem. Got a steady girl now. Say, is the Giant here?"

"You mean *me*? Of course I'm here. I'm always here."

"I mean *Martin*."

"Around somewhere. You know, keeps the roulette wheels greased and the dancers' G-strings in the right crease. We're sold out tonight."

"As usual."

"The most beautiful girls."

"And the highest gambling stakes."

"Forget the dough, the girls are the highest stakes."

"Is *she* here?"

Fido's enormous mouth opened in a grin that exposed a mouthful of gold-capped teeth large as piano keys. "She's here. When she came out of her tree earlier the joint went wild. There was such a roar that even the five-thousand-dollar-ante gamblers in the private poker room upstairs stopped playing."

"In the jungle, the mighty jungle, the Panther stalks tonight," sang Bongo.

"She sure does. She caused such a commotion I'm sure it could be heard even by those bearded rebels hiding out in the mountains, jerking off their rifles instead of enjoying the Havana high life."

"If the Panther is ready, so am I."

"Let's go."

Fido led the way across the red-carpeted lobby, past open doorways leading to gaming rooms where the excited talk from people crowded around the tables rose in a crescendo that gave way only to the deeper throb of music coming from the cavernous cabaret ahead.

The entrance to the cabaret was blocked by a velvet rope and guarded by a stiff man in a tuxedo standing behind an imposing wooden podium. He had all the good humor of a judge about to hand down a life sentence, which was why everyone called him the Judge.

When Bongo and Fido stopped in front of the Judge, he didn't crack a smile, nor did he take down the velvet rope. He ran his finger across names written on a list. "You're not here," he told Bongo without looking up. "No reservation, no entrance."

Fido placed his huge paw over the list of names and glared into the Judge's face. "Let him in. You know who he is."

"He's the king . . . King of the Bongo," the Judge replied sarcastically. "But as an insurance man, he's a big nothing. I filed a claim on that fender bender I was involved in last year. The grille of my Chevy Bel Air was punched out. Do you think I heard from the King here? Do you think he went down to the police station to explain on my behalf that I was *not* over the center line when that collision happened? Do you think he called to tell me my claim had been accepted? Do you think he raced over to my house with the check I was entitled to? That's what a good insurance agent would do. That's what an agent from an *American* company would do. I'm telling you, Cuban insurance is worthless. The phone company is just as bad. You might as well go up to your rooftop and shout out your message instead of trying to get a telephone connection in this town."

Bongo smiled. "That's why you didn't hear from me. I was phoning all the time. As usual, no ring."

The Judge tightened the velvet rope closing off the cabaret entrance. "No ring, no admittance."

Bongo reached into his tuxedo pocket and pulled out a pen and checkbook. He filled in a check as he spoke. "Here's the money, your claim is paid in full. You didn't get paid earlier because of the holidays. You know how it is, the mail is slower than usual."

The Judge took the check and shoved it into his pocket. "That's another thing. Mail doesn't move, water doesn't flow. Cuba is getting to be a banana republic."

"I wrote the check for more money than what you claimed your losses were," Bongo said. "A holiday bonus."

The Judge grudgingly unhooked the velvet rope. "I still wouldn't buy insurance from you again, even if you unzipped my pants and smoked my cigar."

"Keep your pants zipped." Bongo winked. "There's only a few puffs left on your tiny cigarillo. You don't want to deny your wife her once-a-year smoke."

Bongo stepped past the podium and into a vast amphitheater magically illuminated by colored lights in towering trees. With no roof overhead, it was a paradise under the stars. Down in front, on a raised dance floor, festive revelers shook their hips to the blasting rhythm of a twenty-five-piece band perched high above in a giant bamboo cage.

Bongo felt the beat pulsing up through the soles of his feet. His two-toned shoes kept time to the music. He strode past tables of excited people. The blue mist of cigarette and cigar smoke made the women's clinging dresses sparkle and the men's white dinner jackets shine. The moon overhead beamed down.

"Hey, Bongo, Happy New Year!"

Bongo heard the words shouted as he glided onto the dance floor and into the gyrating crowd.

A young woman danced up next to him, her hips swinging in

rhythm with his. The sweat on her face made her glow, as if she were one of the muses from the fountain outside, miraculously come to life. Her satin dress was as slick as her skin.

"Mercedes!" Bongo took her by the waist and floated with her across the dance floor through waves of dancers. Together they were a ship at sea, bow and stern taking the swells of syncopated notes.

"Lose yourself, Bongo! Go, King!"

Bongo felt the beat, felt it the way he had as a boy, standing naked before his father, his head shaved, while his father slapped his skull with his open palms, slapping the beat into him, tattooing his memory.

"Hey, King!" came a shout from the bandstand. "Come on up and join us!"

Bongo danced up to the bandstand with Mercedes at his side and they shimmied through the wide bamboo bars into the cage. The band members grinned with expectation. One of them stood, and over the heads of the others tossed a set of bongos. Bongo caught the drums and ran his hands over their skintight heads, taking the beat. His sound soared across the crowded dance floor and swirled up into the night sky, punctuating a note for every star above.

The band stopped; they knew Bongo was sailing. The dancers stopped; they knew Bongo was in orbit. His solo had everyone gasping, his lightning moves had the monkeys chattering, his beat had the saints smiling and the dead dogs walking.

His furious drumming stormed to a climax. Thunderous applause washed over him.

He rested his hands on the bongos and looked out into the crowd, searching for one special face, gazing into all eyes, trying to find his father. *Daddy, did you hear that? I got the beat you pounded into my head! Damn you and praise you for beating me into deliverance!*

"You're soaking wet!"

Bongo glanced up, still in a daze.

Mercedes wiped the sweat from his forehead with a handkerchief.

The band blasted into a new dance tune. Bongo smiled at Mercedes. "Would you like a rum and Coke?"

"Yes," she sang back to him, "rum and Coca-Cola!"

Bongo made his way to a palm-thatched bar. Revelers patted him on the back, congratulating him on his playing, shouting above the music to buy him drinks. Cold glasses of rum and Coke were shoved at him and he grabbed as many as he could.

Mercedes sat calmly at a table on the edge of the dance floor. Her black hair was piled atop her head in an elaborate braid that made her appear to be crowned royalty. Laced through the braid were bright stars of jasmine blossoms. She took the drink offered by Bongo, then waved to three young women at another table. The women giggled and waved back. They were thrilled that one of their own had snagged Bongo. They had all seen him dance or play the bongos in clubs around town. He was a hard one to catch, half Cuban and half American. Just when a girl thought she understood him, had him nailed to the floor with a wedding ring ready to be slipped onto her finger, one half of Bongo would escape. A girl couldn't chase him because she wasn't sure which half to chase. He was fifty percent enigma, a man who knew the darkest secrets of the seedy back streets of Old Havana yet also knew the swankiest people in the country clubs. A girl had to accept that Bongo was black and white, yes and no, tonight but not tomorrow. All of this made him more attractive, the handsome fox, the swift fish, the drum-playing, dancing fanatic with a great grin, ready to defy the odds and stay single. And tonight one of their own had triumphed. Mercedes was next to Bongo, coolly sipping a rum and Coke as people cleared the dance floor for the next fabulous cabaret extravaganza.

Bongo slipped his arm around Mercedes' bare shoulders and embraced her affectionately.

The lights went out. The crowd hushed. Everything was black.

A voice boomed from the darkness with the melodrama of Moses coming down from the mountain.

"Laaadieees and Gentlemeeen, the most famous cabaret in the world offers the fiesta of women, the show of shows, a true paradise under the stars!"

A spotlight pierced down from above, illuminating on a vast stage a master of ceremonies in a white tuxedo.

"Behold now, the Queen of the Jungle, the black pearl of the Antilles, le chat noir, the rarest of the rare, the seldom seen, the one and only . . . Cuuubaaan PANTHER!"

The master of ceremonies disappeared in a swirl of mist.

The crowd gasped in a collective *"aaahhhhh!"*

From the lush jungle backdrop, six-foot-tall female bird creatures magically appeared in the trees, slowly spreading their wings to reveal nearly naked bodies. Glittering bits of jeweled costumes clung to their breasts and formed tiny strategic triangles between long legs and the thrust of buttocks. Iridescent feathered headdresses adorned the fabulous birds of paradise. They stood poised, wings outspread, ready to soar over the audience.

The sound of a single drum rose up.

All eyes were fixed on the stage. Shafts of blue, red, and yellow light shot through the slowly dissipating mist, revealing at the back of the stage the skeletal steel form of a monstrous white spider. From behind the spider, a dark creature slithered down the thick trunk of a banyan tree to the beat of the drum. In syncopated movements, the creature made its way from the base of the banyan into the maze of the giant spider. The spider's spiny steel skeleton lit up in a gaudy flash of lights.

The deep voice of the master of ceremonies breathed from hidden loudspeakers: *"The Panther."*

A shudder went through the crowd.

The Panther leapt from the steel spider. On all fours, she arched her glistening back, her satiny black skin shining. She shook her head as if trying to free herself from a leash tight around her neck. She strained against the force, digging the red claws of her fingernails into the floor.

The cheering audience stood up from their tables and threw white gardenias onto the stage.

The band blasted into a conga that raked the cat's back. She prowled to the fierce rhythm. On her black feet were strapped gold high-heeled shoes. She rose, a glorious Panther, naked as the day God made her. Her feline body vibrated with menacing sensuality. The thunderous conga shook her world. The audience screamed, caught in the titillation of the prey being set upon by the predator.

The muscles in the Panther's sleek shoulders twitched. A melodious, murderous purr ripped from her throat, joining the howl of up-tempo music.

The tall birds of paradise descended from high in the trees and surrounded the Panther in a pulsating swirl of flesh and feathers. The Panther burst through the birds and for the first time showed her face. It was black, and her short hair was white: God's panther angel on the prowl. From her lips flamed a volcanic tirade.

> *The dead wander in the canefields.*
> *At night dragging chains are heard.*
> *Lightning flashes like a razor blade*
> *Slitting the flesh of the conga night.*

Many in the audience did not understand a word of the Spanish being sung, but were dazzled by the sizzling syllables exploding from an exotic world exposed for their entertainment. They thought they were listening to a passionate love song. Some knew the difference. They understood this was a chain-dragging scream of suffering, a cry for emancipation.

The Panther gyrated across the stage in a frenzied conga trance, her blood stirred by ancient longing for salvation from cruelty and starvation.

Bongo felt a heavy hand on his shoulder. He turned to see the grinning face of Fido.

"She's here! Outside!"

"Okay. I'm coming."

Bongo turned to Mercedes. "I'll be right back."

Mercedes didn't hear him. Her eyes were transfixed, but not by the wild antics onstage. She was staring straight up.

A glistening silver thread hung down from the branches of a banyan tree. At the bottom of the thread dangled a white spider, its crooked legs moving frantically, like a marionette suspended on a string.

The conga music on the stage grew louder. The spider dropped lower, hanging directly over Mercedes' head.

Bongo reached up to grab it.

"No." Mercedes pulled his arm down. "Don't kill it."

The spider swung back and forth, wriggling, then dropped to the table in front of Mercedes.

A fist slammed down and crushed the spider before it could make a move.

Mercedes cried out, startled.

A black-skinned woman, in a traditional white Santera dress with a white bandanna wrapped around her head, leaned over Mercedes and scooped up the dead insect. "White spiders are bad luck," she hissed. "Especially tonight. You'll see."

"It's worse luck to kill something harmless."

"Dancing white spiders are not harmless. Leave, if you don't want to end up like this." The woman opened her fist, showing the crushed spider.

Mercedes was terrified.

Bongo confronted the woman. "*You* should leave."

The woman put her face close to Bongo's. "You might look white, but you're as black inside as I am."

Mercedes was confused. She asked Bongo, "What does she mean?"

Bongo didn't answer. He took the woman by the arm. "You should go. I don't want them to throw you out."

"Will I be thrown out because of my color? Or because I tell the truth?"

"I don't make the rules."

"It's all right to be black if you're naked and on the stage, but if you're not they don't want you. Even President Batista couldn't get in here if he weren't president."

"That's not the issue," Bongo said sternly. "You're frightening the lady."

The woman screamed, "I know who you are! *You* are the one in danger! *You* are the one who must leave!" She continued screaming, but the conga music drowned out her words. She turned in a swirl of white, evaporating like a cloud.

Bongo sat down. Mercedes was trembling. He put his arm around her.

"Excuse me," he said in an apologetic tone. "I have something I must do, but I'll come right back."

Mercedes grabbed his wrist. "Please don't leave!"

"There's nothing to be frightened of."

Mercedes looked skeptical.

"Don't worry, we'll ring in the New Year together."

"What's so important that you have to leave?"

"Just for a few minutes."

"Promise?"

He kissed her cheek.

Mercedes reluctantly let go of his wrist, then smiled. "Hurry back if you want that special midnight kiss."

Bongo got up and pushed through the crowd. He made his way along the center aisle, between the tables occupied by high-roller gamblers, swanky socialites, rich foreigners and the political elite.

At a table big enough for twelve sat three men. Two of them, Pedro and Paulo, were heavyset, their holstered guns bulging beneath their suit jackets. They guarded a slight man, Humberto Zapata, seated between them. Zapata wore a creamy linen suit, a red bow tie, a sharply creased Panama hat and silver-rimmed sunglasses. He peered intently at the stage through a pair of opera glasses, as a pencil-thin mustache twitched on his upper lip.

When Zapata angled the opera glasses higher, Bongo knew he was gazing at a man in a banyan tree towering above the stage. The man was on a wooden platform painted to look like part of the tree. He crouched behind a cannon-sized spotlight that kept the Panther in an ethereal glow wherever she moved.

Without shifting the opera glasses, Zapata spoke to Bongo as he passed.

"A man doesn't ever have to be alone. Why? Because there are more good women in the world than there are bad men."

Bongo stopped. His response was quick. "I despise you."

"And then what? Do you have a life after that?"

"You stole my life."

"Well, then, you'll just have to save up your pesos and buy her back."

Zapata lowered the opera glasses. "Here," he offered the glasses to Bongo. "Have a look at what you lost."

The idea of what Bongo had lost suddenly filled his head with images: dogs tumbling underwater, crabs flying through the air, a girl cocooned in mud like a mummy, mud being washed away from her nine-year-old skin by coarse male hands, on one finger of the man's hands a gold ring, a ruby-red eye shining from its center.

Bongo looked at the hand holding the opera glasses. On the third finger was a gold ring set with a blood-red ruby.

"What's wrong, Bongo? Cat got your tongue?"

"You won't always be able to keep the Panther in a cage."

"Tut-tut, my pet, hurry along. Mr. Wu is waiting for you outside."

"I'm not your goddamned pet. How did you know Wu was waiting?"

Zapata raised the opera glasses, his lips creased into a smirk. "I know everything. It's time for you to go. You shouldn't be here."

"Don't tell me when, where, or how to be. I'm not a child anymore."

"You are to me."

"It's not *my* skin you own."

"Don't get personal."

"Personal? You don't know the word. You only know—"

"—*power*. But don't you see? Power *is* personal."

Bongo noticed that Zapata was not drinking. This was not a party to him. The only festive note on the table was a basket of flowers.

Zapata sniffed disdainfully. "If I were you, I'd walk out of here right now and never come back."

"You don't give me orders. I'll do what I want. This isn't a communist country."

Zapata set the opera glasses down with a *thump*. His voice had a raspy edge. "It's not a communist country, *yet*. And it's only because of men like me that it isn't."

"To hell with you and your kind." Bongo turned and headed for the foyer, where the Judge blocked his way with the velvet rope.

"C'mon, Judge, unhook this damn rope and let me pass."

"You were in such a hurry to get in, what's your hurry to get out? You should stay."

"Unhook the rope, or I'll wrap it around your neck."

"Baby boy's got to run home and get his beauty rest? Too bad, the Panther's not finished yet."

"She's none of your business."

"She's got her biggest conga number coming up. You should see her in that one, her lovely papaya ripe and wet, waiting for the monkey to slip the banana in. Oh, my, more sweets to eat than on Carmen Miranda's fruit hat. Stick around."

Bongo grabbed the Judge by the throat.

"Watch it," the Judge choked. "I've got insurance."

Bongo tightened his grip. "I sold you the insurance!"

Fido yanked Bongo's hand away from the Judge's throat. "My friend, you don't want trouble here. You should go."

"Why the hell are so many people telling me to leave?"

Fido smiled enigmatically at Bongo and shrugged his huge shoulders.

Bongo crossed the red carpet and stepped outside through the glass entrance doors. The uniformed attendant gave a slight bow, murmuring, "Mr. Wu is waiting by the muses."

Bongo walked up the drive under the palms. A canary-yellow 1936 Packard Victoria limousine was parked next to the naked muses frolicking in the spraying fountain.

A Chinese man stepped out of the Victoria. He was square-jawed, stocky, wearing a purple suit and a wide tie with a snarling dragon embroidered on it. He poked a finger into Bongo's chest. "I've got to frisk you."

"Come on, Ming, you know who I am."

"No one gets to Mr. Wu without the frisk."

Bongo raised his hands in the air.

Ming patted him down from the ankles up. He felt the holstered gun under Bongo's armpit. "Jackpot!"

"Don't take my gun. This is supposed to be business among friends."

"How do I know what kind of business it will end up being?"

"Are you kidding? What did your mother put in your tea this morning?"

The rear window of the Victoria rolled down. In the shadow of the backseat, in the far corner, glowed the red tip of a cigarette. A cloud of smoke floated from the open window. A voice came quietly through the smoke. "It's okay, Ming. He has a license to carry the gun."

"I thought he lost his license."

"What is lost once can be bought twice."

"But he's no longer a private dick, is he? The President said there would be no more private dicks. No guys can carry guns except police and soldiers. The President suspended all the licenses."

"Suspended some, stretched others," the voice corrected. "Sometimes there's a state of emergency, sometimes not. It all depends on how the children behave."

Bongo interrupted, "I'm in the insurance business now, Mr. Wu. It's simpler. The only way to make a living with a gun these days is to be on the side of the President, or with the bearded boys in the mountains."

Ming finished frisking Bongo. "Shall I unlock the door for him, Mr. Wu?"

"Listen," Bongo said with irritation, "I was told she was here. That's why I came out."

"Unlock it for him," commanded Wu.

Ming dug a key out of his pocket and opened the back door. Bongo got in and the door slammed behind him. The key clicked and locked the door again.

The air was filled with cigarette smoke and a distinctive perfume. Wu sat on the far side of a plush leather seat, reclining against silk pillows. Bongo's attention was caught by a creature balanced on Wu's knees. She was fragile and wispy, with an inviting flowered face and a sulky pout.

"Thank you for bringing her, Mr. Wu."

Wu's cheeks hollowed as he inhaled another drag from the cigarette smoldering at the end of a carved ivory holder. He let the smoke leak slowly from his nostrils. He was not a man to be rushed, always speaking with measured care; words were not random noises to be shot haphazardly out of one's mouth. Havana was a town of fast-talkers, but if you were Chinese and your people had come here as nothing more than yellow slaves to replace black slaves, you kept your own counsel. You listened. If you were smart, you kept on listening. You let the other guy blab away so you could read him. You could read his whole life in less time than it takes to boil a kettle of tea if you just kept your mouth shut.

Bongo inhaled the smoky perfumed air. He had never smelled anything so delicious in his life. "I didn't think you would really bring her."

Wu said nothing.

"How much will she cost me?"

Wu remained silent.

Bongo shifted uneasily. "I didn't mean to insult you by talking money. It's just that I've never seen one this beautiful, and you have brought me so many beautiful ones."

Wu sank back deeper into the pillows. He spoke in a soft, conspiratorial tone. "A Chinese emperor used to travel in his golden carriage through the countryside holding one this beautiful on his knees. Her perfume filled the carriage. Her perfume was so heavenly it made everything outside, no matter how rancid or ugly, seem *beautiful*. This one is fit for such an emperor."

"Can I have a closer look?"

Wu didn't answer. His cigarette was finished and the perfume was even more overpowering, a syrup that a man could swim in.

"If you won't take money from me, Mr. Wu, what do you want?"

"One thing not yet done. One thing promised."

"What do you want done? I mean, you know me. I keep my promises."

"Promised now, done another time. Always something to be done in time."

"That's true. So I owe you one. What's the promise?"

"Will you love her?"

Bongo was caught off guard, fearful of giving the wrong answer.

Wu sighed. "She traveled all the way from China to be with you. Do you know how difficult a journey that is? Can you appreciate her effort? Do you know how big a risk she took, a risk that could have spoiled her beauty, ended her life? Do you know how fragile she truly is?"

Bongo knew, Bongo appreciated. He wanted to show proper respect. "May I have a closer look at her fragile beauty?"

"Ming!" Wu commanded his bodyguard in the front seat, "Fire!"

Ming leaned over from the front seat, where he had been watching everything in the rearview mirror. He flicked a Zippo lighter and its flame fully illuminated Mr. Wu.

Wu wore a long blue silk tunic with gold thread woven through it. His face was a tea-stained porcelain color and a satin skullcap fit tightly on his head. Balanced on his knees was a sight that made Bongo inhale sharply.

From a clay pot, a splendid orchid's shiny stalk shot out of a green spray of leaves, culminating in a lavish display of a purple-tongued bloom taunting the air around it.

As discreetly as he could, so as not to disturb Mr. Wu's reverential gaze, Bongo asked, "May I know her name?"

With a long, mellow sigh, Wu released the precious syllables: "*Vanda dearei.*"

"*Vanda dearei,*" Bongo repeated in a whisper. "I already love her."

Wu gazed fiercely at Bongo. "You're not just saying that?"

"Of course not. You know me. I'm one of your best customers. May I smell her?"

"Yes." Wu gave the orchid a little bounce with his knees.

Bongo leaned over, his nose close to the inviting bloom, but not touching it. He didn't want Mr. Wu to think him capable of anything improper.

"She's not a little hooker," Wu emphasized.

"You're right, but she does have a kind of promiscuous dazzle."

"What does she smell like?" Wu's question had a challenging edge. "What is the perfume of her essence?"

Bongo closed his eyes, concentrating on the heavenly scent without being distracted by beauty. "Sticks of cloves burning. Vanilla steaming."

"Is that all? Can't you do better?"

Bongo opened his eyes. The taunting purple tongue was right before him. He inhaled deeply, afraid to venture an answer for fear it would be wrong and Mr. Wu would not let him take her.

"Let's say you just got married," Wu prodded Bongo. "You married a girl from Camagüey in the center of Cuba. Those girls are the blackest coffee on all of the island. Let's say you married one of those beauties, you had your honeymoon night, it was bliss, and the next day your wife disappeared. You had to search for her because she betrayed you, or maybe she didn't betray you but was kidnapped. You searched and searched but couldn't find her. You were going crazy, you couldn't sleep, you couldn't think, you wanted to kill yourself. Finally the police called and they said they had someone who might be your wife at the morgue and they wanted you to come and identify her. So you go there. It is a depressing place. You go into a cold room. The police roll out a cart with a body on it covered by a sheet. They begin to peel back the sheet and you close your eyes, because you don't want to see her once-smiling eyes now lifeless. You keep your eyes closed and they ask, 'Is this your wife?' And you just stand there, you don't want to know. 'Yes or no?' they demand. You keep your eyes closed and lean toward her. She's not breathing; she's dead. You are afraid to inhale her scent, afraid to breathe. But you must know the truth. What do you *smell*?"

"Cinnamon! Goddamn it, *cinnamon*!"

Bongo pulled back from the flower and jolted upright.

A knowing expression spread across Wu's face. He passed the plant to Bongo. "She's yours. The only one in all of Cuba."

Bongo felt the weight of the treasure in his hands. "I can't thank you enough, Mr. Wu."

"Oh, I will find a way for you to thank me. Something to be done, a promise to keep."

"I already paid you the final installment for the *Broughtonia ortgiasana* I bought last month."

"That orchid *was* a little hooker. She was shameless with her blossoms."

"I'm giving her a chance to reform." Bongo winked. "So far she's behaving."

"You have a hothouse full of wayward girls," Wu scolded.

"That's how nature made them."

"I should never have got you started."

"You told me it was a noble addiction, a vocation for royalty."

"Expensive."

"I'm willing to pay."

"Now that you have dear *Vanda,* you will be a changed man. More virtuous, less promiscuous. You run after life too much. You should slow down, let it come to you. Everything good will come to you if you have the patience to wait."

"It's a modern world we live in, Mr. Wu. Every year faster cars, more television channels, faster girls."

"Girls go faster, but they are still going to the same place, the husband-man. When they get there they stop."

"That's why I stick to my orchids."

"They can betray you too, don't be too sure."

"I've got a good girl waiting for me inside the club. I'd better get back to her." Bongo slid over to leave.

Wu pulled Bongo back. "Don't go in there. Don't take *Vanda* inside. Take her home. She's too innocent for what goes on in the Tropicana. Take her home and be happy."

"Sorry, Mr. Wu. I want to take *Vanda* in and show her to that special girl I'm with."

"Both girls might not be safe in there."

"They'll be safe. They'll be with me."

Wu sighed. "Go back inside if you must."

"Happy New Year, Mr. Wu."

"It's not *my* New Year," Wu said. "Ming, let him out."

Ming unlocked the back door and swung it open.

Bongo stepped from the car and someone slammed into him so hard he almost dropped the orchid.

The woman who had knocked into him threw her head back and laughed. She wasn't much of a woman, more like a girl, a tall girl with a short haircut and dressed like a boy. Atop her head was a white U.S. Navy sailor's cap cocked at a jaunty angle. She was never without the cap, and never without her odd laugh, a kind of heigh-ho cackle, like wind rapping across the tin roof of an abandoned barn on the American plains. She had two Cuban sailors at her side, black men in white uniforms. She liked navy men, regardless of nationality. That's why she was called Sailor Girl, and that's why she always wore her sailor's cap; she never left home or walked into a bar without it.

Sailor Girl grabbed Bongo's hand and shoved it inside her shirt and over her breast. It was a small breast, not much meat to it. The nipple was hard with excitement.

"What do you feel?"

"Your tit."

"Don't be so explicit!"

"Hmmm. I feel your heart beating."

"It's the beat of all Havana fucking on New Year's Eve."

"Sounds familiar."

"Yes!" She let go of his hand and laughed. She hugged her two sailors closer. "Bongo, do you have any idea how much I like this crisp bacon in a white uniform?"

"I've noticed your appetite over the years."

"Well, those Tropicana bastards won't let me bring my bacon into their cabaret. They say it's because these boys are *burnt* bacon. What kind of crap is that? This bacon is from their own navy!"

"Don't feel bad. The President's bacon is burnt too."

"That's why he's the President, so he can slip his burnt bacon into all the places normally forbidden to him."

"Some say that's one of the reasons."

"What do you say?"

"I'm not political."

"Don't go into the Tropicana, then. Come with us. Help me sneak these boys into Sans Souci. I'm going to rip up the dance floor."

"They won't let you in with these gentlemen. You know how it is."

"Fuck how it is."

"That's the American way."

"I thought you said you weren't political."

"I'm not. Just realistic."

Sailor Girl turned to Ming. "What about you, chopsticks? You want to go to Sans Souci?"

Ming silently stroked his dragon necktie.

"Come on, sticky rice," challenged Sailor Girl. "You're not afraid to go where your yellow ass isn't wanted, are you?"

Ming glared at her. "Like Mr. Wu said, it's not *my* New Year."

"All of you Chinese boys are the same, afraid to make a move, just sticky rice." She kicked the back door of the Victoria. "Hey, Wu, why don't we all go over to your laundry and smoke a magic pipe? Every night there is New Year's Eve."

"Ming!" Wu's voice commanded from inside the car. "Drive!"

Ming jumped into the Victoria, the twelve-cylinder engine growled and the car roared away.

"Everybody on this island is chickenshit!" Sailor Girl shouted at the disappearing Victoria. "The only ones who aren't chickenshit are those bearded boys fighting up in the mountains."

"If that's the way you feel about it," Bongo advised, "why don't you go to the mountains and find yourself a bearded boy?"

"I will." Sailor Girl threw her head back, her mouth opened in a laugh, her white teeth gleaming in the moonlight. "You just keep your eyes on me, Mister Drummer Boy. I'll fuck one of those rebels so hard his beard will fall off. I swear I'll do it."

"Good luck." Bongo turned and walked toward the Tropicana.

A white Cadillac Eldorado convertible careened around the circular drive, headed straight for Bongo. He jumped aside, landing in the flowered arms of a hibiscus bush. He caught a glimpse of the driver inside the speeding car.

The driver wore a white tux and his blond hair was slicked back from his tanned face. It was Guy Armstrong. Such an American name. A name like that didn't come from a mother, but from a vote by a Wall Street brokerage house. Seated next to Guy was his wife, a haughty beauty with cool blue eyes in a marble-white face. Elizabeth was her regal name, perfect for someone who appeared to be above the commoners of the world, speeding past in her Cadillac chariot.

As the Armstrongs raced by like they had just robbed the casino, Bongo thought that either they had not seen him or they didn't give a damn if they ran him down. The odd thing was that slouched in the car's backseat was Hurricane Hurler, the Havana Sugar Kings pitcher. Like Bongo, he was half Cuban, with an American father.

Bongo got up from the side of the road and dusted himself off. Nothing broken, and the orchid was safe. He walked up to the glass entrance doors of the Tropicana. The uniformed attendant snapped to attention, saluted, then threw open the doors to the paradise under the stars. Inside, at the velvet rope, the Judge smirked disdainfully before letting Bongo pass.

The tables were crowded with people and covered with buckets of champagne, party hats and whistle poppers. Bongo passed where Zapata had been sitting, but he was gone, and so were his two goons in their cheap suits.

A fierce conga beat blasted from the orchestra on the elevated bandstand. The Panther pranced onstage, leading a high-kicking line of nearly naked beauties with outlandish headdresses of glittering glass beads and blinking lights.

Mercedes was seated at the table in front of the stage, right where Bongo had left her. She turned with a smile and a wave, calling for him to hurry before the hour struck so they could have their midnight kiss.

Bongo clutched the orchid to his body, protecting it against the bump and push of the crowd as he struggled toward Mercedes. The crashing sound of tape-recorded thunder broadcast from loudspeakers, a rain of colorful confetti showered down. The booming voice of the master of ceremonies announced that it was only seconds until midnight. The crowd took up the gleeful countdown to the New Year:

> Five
> Four
> Three
> Two
> One
> HAPPY NINETEEN FIFTY-SEVEN!

Mercedes raised her hand to her lips to blow Bongo a kiss as a bomb exploded.

The force of the blast hurled Bongo back. In a flash of blue light he saw Mercedes, her flesh disintegrating, her bones shattering, her body flying apart.

Bongo fought his way up from the floor. Screaming people stampeded for the exits. He looked back to where Mercedes had been, but there was only a red vapor in the air and a circle of burnt people covered by blood.

Then another fear overtook him. What about his sister, the Panther? He fought harder against the surrounding panic, desperately trying to get to the stage. He couldn't make any progress. Dancers on-stage were screaming in shock, the flesh of their exposed bodies pierced by shards of glass, blood streaming from their wounds. Bongo kept struggling. The tide of the crowd surged against him.

The conga night had been split wide open with the tick of a time bomb. The world had been blasted to hell.

2.

Sinners and Saints

*O*klaaahoooma, *where the wind comes sweeping down the* plain. Oh, the air so sweeeeet—"

"Would you stop your singing?"

Leaping Larry Lizard glared across the bar counter at Broadway Betty. The narrow slits of his scowling eyes dared her to make another peep, just one itsy-bitsy peep and he was going to smack her silly. Except he couldn't bean her in front of her husband, Johnny PayDay, a bald little schmo whose muscles bulged and twitched beneath his discount-store suit that was nine fashion years behind the times. The bald schmo even wore a tie with a hula girl in a grass skirt and bare tits on it. Guys like PayDay, who had been in the war out in the South Pacific, they always had to wear some sort of badge saying they were there, fought the big one and banged all the local tail.

"Don't be so hard on her," Johnny PayDay said. His voice was like a letter sent by ship, arriving way too late to have any impact on Lizard.

"You shut your trap, too," Lizard snarled. He was the boss here. He wasn't about to let things get out of control. Just because everybody was hungover didn't make it a holiday. "Don't think the meter stops running the first day of the New Year. No free rides in this town. This is Havana."

PayDay tried to mollify him. "I know I wasn't flown here for no holiday."

"Then if you're such a bright bulb, why did you bring your wife with you?"

"It's family time, Christmas and New Year's stuff. And she's never seen the Caribbean."

"How many times have I got to tell you that ain't the Caribbean?" Lizard hooked a big thumb over his shoulder, pointing out of the Hotel Nacional's Terrace Bar through the huge plate-glass window, where the sun's high-noon rays smacked the surface of the glittering water beyond. "It ain't the Carib, it's the stinking Atlantic. Same god-damn piece of water that the Statue of Liberty pisses in. Same goddamn piece of water they dump all New York City's shit into. Don't be a romantic sap. This is Cuba, not Hawaii. By the way, you dress like a sap, except for that tie, it's a killer. Those hula girls must have been some hump. Tell me, did you ever get one to—"

Broadway Betty cut Lizard off. "It's pretty water," she cooed.

Betty rubbed Lizard raw. If she wasn't asked a question she talked straight. But if you asked her a question, she answered by singing you a line from some Broadway musical show, like that *Oklahoma* shit. It drove Lizard crazy. He knew these two from before, in Atlantic City. PayDay was always dragging his wife along on business. It was a good thing PayDay was recommended from the top, and got the job done—slit a man's throat, put a bullet in his head. But Lizard was top dog here, PayDay had to answer to him. That was the way it was. If you were underneath you got the abuse shoveled onto your head, because if you didn't like it and squawked, they'd be shoveling dirt into your face as you stared up dead-eyed from your grave.

Broadway Betty continued her rapture. "It's such a beautiful sea here. It looks like . . . melted peacocks."

"Melted peacocks!" Lizard choked on the Manhattan he had just raised to his lips. He spluttered the booze back into the glass. "That's probably something you read in a goddamn tourist guide. 'The waters of Havana are pretty as melted peacocks.' Yeah, sure. And the pretty rain is as slick as the sweat on a gorilla's balls."

Betty looked down. Her dress was halfway up above her knees. She liked looking at her knees, round and plump as two peaches in a basket. Maybe she could get a suntan on them if she and Johnny stayed here long enough. Sometimes their stay was long, sometimes short, she never knew in advance. That was one of the exciting things about her husband's job; he wasn't a nine-to-fiver. Her knees were nice, but between them was another lovely sight that intrigued her. The top of the barstool was upholstered in bright raspberry-colored

Naugahyde. Shot through the raspberry were flecks of bright glittery stuff, like flecks of real gold. She liked the idea of it, a raspberry-gold sherbet. She wished she could get a lipstick that color, she already had every other shade. Maybe she could get that color in the hotel gift shop. She should ask them if they had "hot raspberry–gold swirl." She couldn't stop staring; she liked the idea of sitting on something that looked good enough to eat. Everything in Cuba was so colorful. She wanted to stay.

"What are you gawking at?" Lizard cut into Betty's thoughts.

She turned her eyes up to him and sang. *"Chicks and ducks and geese better scurry, when I take you out in my surrey, with the fringe on top."*

Lizard was fuming. He hated these Broadway lyrics.

PayDay tried to head off more trouble. "You were asking Betty another question earlier. What was it?"

"What do I care what it was? Yeah, I remember, I was asking if she wanted another drink. Then she started singing about the fucking Oklahoma plains. Now she's going on with more Broadway sissy stuff. You should stop taking her to those musicals, that's how the queers in New York brainwash people. That's how they make you a fairy boy."

Lizard shot both of them a sour glance. He swore to himself if this Daffy Duck dame popped off with any more pansy song shit he was going to whup her. To hell with business propriety and trying to be a good boss. Goddamn crazy, these two were. If he had to bet, he'd bet that every time this dame clammed her big red lipstick–coated Daffy Duck kisser on PayDay's pecker she was probably humming him off with *"I'm gonna wash that man right outta my hair."* Goddamn perverts.

"To answer your first question"—PayDay tried to calm the big man—"Betty will have another Banana Banshee."

"Banana Banshee," Lizard groaned. "That's not a cocktail, that's a milk shake. That's the fifth one this morning. Was her mother a monkey?"

Johnny PayDay pushed his cocktail napkin around on the slick varnished mahogany of the bar. He admired the picture on the napkin, the whole big beautiful Hotel Nacional, as if it were a Spanish palace or something, seen from the towering front with a line of palms leading right up to it. He thought of the briefcase of dough in his room. It was safe there. All these fancy hotels in Havana that were owned by the Right Guys from America were safe, because if you stole from the Right Guys and got caught they would make your mother eat a jelly donut with your tongue stuffed in the donut's hole.

PayDay looked back at Lizard. He noticed all the angry red spider veins covering Lizard's fleshy jowls. Those spiderwebs had been created over a lifetime of boozing and smoking and being pissed off that among the Right Guys he wasn't the top dog. PayDay thought again of the briefcase in his room stuffed with C-notes. It represented only half his pay; half now, half when the job was done. He had come to do a job, so he had to bide his time. He watched the red spider veins jump on Lizard's cheeks as his teeth chomped the ice from the glass of liquor he had just sucked dry. Those spiderwebs gave PayDay an idea. Maybe he could do two jobs down here; one for pay, the other for pleasure.

"No more Banana Banshees," Lizard moaned. "I'm banning Banshees before your wife pops out monkey twins right here on the floor."

PayDay quickly filled Lizard in on the medicinal side effects of the Banana Banshee, a blended mix of bananas, crème de cacao, rum and sugary coconut flakes. Banshees were hard to get in big northern cities; most bars didn't have bananas or crème de cacao. If Banshees were made with bananas just starting to overripen, getting black spots on their yellow skins so they had that squishy sweet jungle taste, well, then, they were tops with his wife, kept her happy. This was one reason he always accepted jobs in tropical climates. He could get paid and make his wife happy too. There was nothing he liked better than to watch his wife poolside at a hotel, sun-tanning in her bathing suit, sipping a Banana Banshee out of a glass with a straw as she bent over to paint her toenails from a bottle of fire-engine-red polish. That was the best.

"What was that you just mumbled?" Lizard barked.

"I said the Banana Banshee is healthy for you and it's a hell of a hangover cure, especially on New Year's Day."

"Women and business, shit, they don't mix." Lizard nudged Pay-Day. "And how about you? You going to have some goddamn girly-girl drinky-poo? Maybe a Pink Cadillac Fart, a Grasshopper Turd, or a White Russian Hemorrhoid?"

PayDay didn't answer. Out of his jacket pocket he pulled a candy bar in a bright white wrapper across which was printed in bold red letters PAYDAY. He flipped the candy bar over and carefully peeled back the wrapper so as not to make a ragged tear. He finessed the peanut-coated caramel bar out without spoiling the wrapper. He flattened the wrapper on the bar, smoothed it with the palm of his hand, and folded the edges back in on themselves so that only the name PAYDAY showed.

Lizard watched the ritual. This was maybe the eighth PayDay candy bar this bald-headed shorty had gobbled up since he first got here; he was always smoothing the wrappers down when he was finished and placing them carefully back in his jacket pocket. But Lizard knew that PayDay was good at what he did, and that he always left his calling card. No matter who the guy whacked, he always stuffed a PayDay wrapper in the stiff's mouth. That way the Right Guys knew who'd done the job. Johnny PayDay was a good take-out man, smart with a gun or a knife; he asked no questions, was obedient as a dog, and kept his trap shut. You could kick the shit out of him, but you couldn't kick the secrets out of him.

"You know," Lizard ventured a professional opinion, "you keep on eating that kiddy-shit candy and it's going to give you diabetes. Your legs are going to fall off at the knees."

PayDay ran his palm thoughtfully over the slick candy wrapper without saying a word.

Broadway Betty lifted her head up from staring at the shiny seat between her legs, still dazzled. "How do they get those gold specks in there?"

The bartender handed her a big frothy Banana Banshee, then shook his head; he didn't know how they got the specks in there.

"*I* know." Lizard smiled smugly.

"Really?" Betty sat up straight and crossed her legs. She had good legs, like her knees, smooth white skin, plump in all the right places. She thought her patent leather peach-colored high heels made her legs even more tempting.

Lizard gave her the once-over, a dishwater blonde, a ditsy dame. Normally he liked this kind, big tits, small brains. But Betty's brain was so tiny it could fit into a fast-melting ice cube. "I'll tell you what that gold stuff is. It's nauga shit. Naugas shit out little gold metallic nuggets."

Betty gave Lizard a blank look.

Lizard wondered again why PayDay didn't keep this looney-tunes dame at home where she belonged. Just because a guy is hired to do business in Cuba doesn't mean he can slack off. Lizard had never brought his own wife to Havana, not once. He kept her up in Tampa, pure squaresville. He liked that idea; him in Havana with the rackets while the wife and kiddies lived in a suburban tract, where each house had the same fried brown lawn out front with runt palm trees sticking up and a couple of kids' bikes lying on their sides. If anybody came looking to clock him there they wouldn't know which door to knock on, since each house was indistinguishable from the others. The sameness of the middle class was perfect for a guy like him, everyone was invisible and zombied out from watching shit TV. The worst TV was the Lucy show. Lizard hated Lucy, a whiny, clown-faced, redheaded bitch. He didn't have an ounce of sympathy for Desi, her rumba-assed Cuban Pete husband. Desi always played the injured party, but everyone in Havana knew he was a schlong man who stuck it to every chorus girl in his nightclub act. Not that Lizard had it in for a schlong man; he himself was famous for that. Matter of fact, people didn't know whether he got his name from *his* lizard, which would leap out of his pants whenever a broad-assed babe was around, or from the fact that at the least slight, his black snub-nosed lizard of a revolver would leap out and blow the offending party's brains through the roof.

Lizard continued his natural science lesson to Betty. "And another thing about naugas, they ain't gonna be making car seats and bar-stools out of them much longer."

"Why?" Betty asked wide-eyed.

Jesus, she really was dumb to buy into this one. "Because"—Lizard winked—"Ford Motor Company has nearly killed off the last of the herd to use their hides for that new car, the Thunderbird."

Betty frowned. "Do naugas exist, or are you just pulling my leg?"

Yeah, Lizard was pulling her leg, in fact he wanted to pull her legs open and plug her right there, just to see if he could fuck some sense into her. He leaned his red spider-veined face up close to her peachy complexion and bragged, "Take it from me, naugas exist. Great herds of them."

"Where?"

"New York City."

"New York City? I've never seen them there."

"You weren't looking in the right places."

"What do they look like?"

"You can't mistake them. They have big heads and tiny dicks, just like the Jews. Their skins make great seat covers." Lizard threw his head back and roared at his joke, foam frothing in the corners of his mouth like a rabid dog.

PayDay pulled another candy bar from his pocket. He carefully undid the wrapper as if it were an ancient shroud wound around a mummy.

"Come with me!" Lizard barked to PayDay. "We've got to talk business."

PayDay slipped the candy bar back into his pocket. Already the sugar from the last bar was making his ears ring in a sugar rush. He was feeling twitchy.

Lizard led the way across the vast tiled floor to the plate-glass window facing the ocean. Through the window, looking directly down, they had a good view of the hotel's VIP swimming pool. There was another pool on the other side of the hotel for the regular guests, but this one, reserved for the special few, was just outside the private cocktail lounge downstairs. People were splashing in the pool and others sunned themselves in deck chairs. A middle-aged man hefted himself out of the water and trotted over to a redheaded teenage girl splayed out on her back in a lounge chair. She was nearly nude, except for two narrow strips of a bikini. Around the crotch of the bikini bottom wispy feathers of red hair peeked out. The man stood over her, grinning and dripping water. She handed him a towel and he started to dry off, laughing down at her like a department-store Santa Claus patronizing a kid on his knee.

Lizard's lizard got hard watching this. He wanted to lick the red hair in the crotch of the girl's bathing suit.

PayDay watched dispassionately. He wanted to know what the business was.

Lizard panted, "Do you recognize them?"

"No." PayDay shook his head.

"Shit, man, those are famous people. She's too young to have hummed off enough dick yet to really make it in Hollywood. She's only had a bit part in one movie, a kid movie about a boy who loses his dog. She's gonna be a big movie star. You don't recognize the guy?"

"No."

"Don't you ever go to the movies?"

"No."

"You've probably got a goddamn TV."

"Yeah. Betty likes the Lucy show."

"Shit, I should have known. Well, if you knew the movies, you'd know that guy down there is Robin Hood, he's General Custer, he's Captain Blood."

"Means nothing to me. That's kid stuff."

"Yeah, that's funny, because that guy likes kids too. I heard he once had two twelve-year-olds at the same time. Someone asked him what kind of fuck that was and he said well, if you add their ages together, it's like being with a hot twenty-four-year-old." Lizard paused. "Movie stars can get away with all kinds of shit. Look at him, out of shape, potbelly, skinny legs, dyed hair. Tan as a nigger, though."

"Is he the guy?"

"Of course not. He's not the guy we brought you here for."

"What guy is that? I thought you said we were going to talk business."

"It's all business in Havana. Even when it's pleasure, it's business."

"So why are we watching a bad actor?"

"You're right about that. On the screen he's a good guy. But in life he's a bad actor."

"A lot of guys like that. Good guys in public, bad actors at home with their families."

"So you've got morals?"

"I've got standards."

"Never mix morals with business."

"I don't. So let's get on with it. What's the business?"

"That guy down there is important. He's with the Right Guys here, but he's also in bed with the bearded boys."

"So make him my business and your problem is over."

"You can't shoot a movie star! You can't shoot General Custer, for Christ's sakes!"

"Okay, then, I'll stab him in the heart."

"No, no. I just want you to keep an eye on him. Watch him like you would a puppy with no sense who might run out into the street and get himself run over."

"You brought me all the way from Detroit to baby-sit a bad actor?"

"He's so famous that fans are always mobbing him. Especially the Cubans, they idolize this guy. He's like one of their own. He lives here at the Nacional while in town, but the real action is over at the Hotel Capri, where he keeps the penthouse. That's where he does his serious play. It's a stabbin' cabin in the sky."

"He's doing teenage girls?"

"There's talk about boys too," Lizard added, looking to see if PayDay seemed shocked. "He's got a mirrored bedroom wall in the penthouse."

"He likes to watch?"

"Likes to film. That mirror is a two-way. On the bedroom side it reflects the action, but from the other side you can see right in without anybody knowing you're there. He's got a camera on the other side, films everything. In his Beverly Hills mansion, he's got tape recorders in all the johns. You know how dames are always in the john at parties, putting on their lipstick and talking about how big one guy's wallet is and how little another guy's dick is. After the parties, he plays the recorded girl talk back to his pals and they have a real hoot."

"So okay, I watch him like a puppy. But that's not serious business."

Lizard put his arm around PayDay's shoulders and turned him sideways, looking straight out the window. "You see down there across the lawn, at the bottom of the garden where the Malecón is?"

"What's a Mealycomb?"

"It's the stone seawall that the Cubans brought Chinese coolies here to build at the turn of the century. It starts at La Punta fortress, the entrance to Old Havana, then curves along the oceanfront, past here to the Almendares River. The Malecón is both a seawall and a highway, a seven-mile run."

"These Cubans are clever."

"Not that clever. I heard a guy in the bar at the dog track, he bet another guy that the Cubans never designed the Malecón. It was designed by *American* architects."

"You think that's true?"

"I wouldn't bet a thousand bucks against the guy who said it was."

"So what am I looking at the Mealycomb for? Just some cars whizzing back and forth on it in front of the ocean."

"I'm trying to give you a little history. It's important you know where you are in the scheme of things."

"Where am I?"

"Look carefully through that bunch of palms down there."

"I see a big bird out in the middle of the Mealycomb or whatever you call it."

"Good boy. It's a giant bronze American eagle with a wingspan of twenty feet, perched on marble columns. It's facing across the sea to the U.S.A., ready to fly home to the land of liberty."

"Why do I care?"

"You'll care soon. The eagle is a monument to the *Maine,* our ship that was blown up by the Spanish in the Civil War or something. During the Big Race coming up, the President himself will be sitting in the place of honor under the eagle. He'll be watching cars from all over the world zip by. This race has a richer purse than the one in Monaco. The course follows the Malecón past all the casinos."

"What's a Monaco? Am I supposed to know that too?"

"Monaco's a place in Switzerland or something, where they race Ferraris, Porsches, Jags and stuff."

PayDay watched the eagle flick in and out of view through the waving palm fronds. His mind was getting too stuffed up with all these history lessons. He didn't come here to go to school. "What's the business?"

"Johnny boy," Lizard whispered into his ear, "the Right Guys want you to do a hit involving the President."

"They want me to shoot the President of Cuba in front of a crowd of people?" PayDay couldn't believe what he was hearing. "That's just suicide! Besides, you can't get a clean hit from here, too far."

"Not so loud. Calm down. From up above us, in the VIP suites, there's a view clear as the dawn of creation."

"I don't know. I've whacked a lot of important guys, but no politicians. That's trouble, shooting a president. I thought he was on our side."

"It's not us that's doing the hit."

"I don't get it."

"His own enemies are doing the hit."

"And you're going to let it go down?"

"We'll be heroes in the right places. Many favors will be owed if we tag the assassin."

"So I'm not the one who actually sticks the candy bar wrapper into the President's mouth?"

"No. Shooting presidents is not our business. Shooting the person who shoots the President, *that's* our business."

Johnny PayDay had a lot to think about. He watched the eagle, its wings spread, flickering in the distance. It looked like it was flying. He glanced over at the red spider veins jumping on Lizard's flushed cheeks. He gazed down at the swimming pool. The bad actor was rubbing suntan oil above the small breasts of the teenage redhead in the lounge chair. He had a visible hard-on in his skimpy royal-blue nylon swimsuit.

PayDay had survived by seeing all the angles and mapping them out ahead of time. If his business was to shoot the shooter, then somebody would eventually be gunning for him too. Who was going to hit him? The bad actor?

Sweet Maria was a maid with a mission at the Hotel Nacional. She considered herself smart and lucky to be a maid. It was a well-paid job, difficult to get. Lots of competition. Girls would do anything, stand on their heads, go down on their knees in front of anyone who could put a good word in or get an interview. The Nacional was a glory of a hotel. Maria liked everything about it, its long Spanish-tiled corridors, its high-ceilinged, air-conditioned rooms, its swanky bars and lush gardens, its deep-water swimming pools, its sophisticated restaurants.

Famous people from all over the world stayed at the Nacional. Maria knew all the guests were famous, they had to be; one night at the Nacional cost more than Maria made in three months, working twelve hours a day, six days a week. But it was the highest-paid maid's job in all of Havana, most maids made one-fifth the money. Another thing Maria loved about the Nacional was the uniforms: cute powder-blue dresses that fell just below the knee, with white aprons that were tied in a fluffy bow at the back. Very stylish, very French. Maria knew this because she had seen, in one of the magazines left behind by a guest, a splashy photo layout of the Ritz Hotel in Paris. Those pretty Ritz maids had similar dresses, and they got to wear the same style pretty hats as the girls of the Nacional. This made Maria proud. In their matching uniforms, they were like girl soldiers in the same elite housekeeping army.

Maria gazed out the window of the room she was cleaning. The room was high up so she had a good view. She could see the private pool area down below, and the guests in bathing suits, talking and laughing, drinking colorful fruit concoctions served on silver platters by waiters. All rich people down there, all white people, even the waiters. She sighed. It was pretty to think of their lives.

It was always a thrill when Maria got to open the door of a just-vacated room. The hardest part was waiting until the guests had left. Sometimes she held her breath, her heart pounding, watching as the uniformed bellhop rolled his luggage cart down the hallway and knocked softly on a room door. The guests would walk out, the woman fashionably dressed for the airplane or cruise ship, the man in a suit and tie. They would disappear with the bellhop and the luggage into the elevator. Finally, Maria had the room to herself. The scent of the departed guests was heavy in the air, the woman's perfume, the man's aftershave lotion. Sometimes Maria heard conversation the guests left behind. They were talking about what to have for dinner, steak or lobster? What wine, red or white? Where to dine, the Havana Yacht Club, Chez Merito, Castillo de Jagua, La Zaragozana? What cabaret show after dinner, the Sans Souci or the Tropicana? Where to go dancing, Mocambo Club because it's air-conditioned, Bambú Club at Rancho Boyeros because its music is hot? Where to have a nightcap, Montmartre in Vedado or Morocco Club on the Prado? What a feast Havana is! Back home it's raining or snowing and sure to be boring. Aren't we the lucky ones!

Maria's father was a sugarcane cutter and her mother had nine kids to care for in a two-room, palm-thatched, dirt-floored hut with no toilet, no running water, and no electricity. Maria ran away when she was fourteen and fell in love with a handsome man who drove one of the ox-drawn carts loaded with cane from the fields to the mill. She learned early on that if you were a girl, compliant and cute, well, then, the saints would hear your prayers and the gods would accept all those songbirds you strangled and placed as offerings on the sacred altar of your Santera. The souls of those birds would wrap around you in a good-luck halo and stay with you long after the oxcart driver tired of you and handed you over to another oxcart driver. But Maria also knew that sometimes luck, if it couldn't be bought or stolen, could come with a little assistance from the gods. All a girl had to do was push her luck right to the edge.

Maria looked beyond the hotel pool, past the tropical gardens laid out in stately grandeur, down to the Malecón. Such a lovely parade of cars on the Malecón: Fords, Chevrolets, Buicks, Packards, Pontiacs and Oldsmobiles. What colors they flashed! Beyond them, on the stone seawall, lovers snuggled, body to body, gazing starry-eyed across the ocean's sun-reflected golden skin.

Maria sat on the edge of the bed and waited. She knew if she watched long enough she would see the lovers on the seawall kiss. Sometimes it was a first date for the lovers so they just held hands, but then at the end there had to be a little kiss, even if it was only a peck on the cheek. Others were bolder, they crushed their mouths together with a soul-suck wonder, oblivious to the crashing waves below them, the honking cars and catcalls behind them.

So many men kissing so many girls. Maria thought, Heaven. Those men were bus drivers, or shirtless dockworkers, or factory workers in blue coveralls, or shopkeepers in white shirts and neckties. So many different types of men with only one thing on their minds. How Maria wished to be sitting on the seawall, her eyes closed, her moist lips poised. She was a good girl. Her house was painted pale blue and pink to please the saints. Everything in her life was kept cool with blue, and pink was the spirit of love. The pink gloss she wore on her cocoa-colored lips was the same triumphant color of love worn on the face of Queen Erzulie, the black Madonna whom Maria adored.

Like Erzulie, Maria wasn't refined and didn't go for fancy lace. But black lingerie was another thing altogether; a girl had to make exceptions. Like Erzulie, Maria smoked unfiltered cigarettes, drank young rum that burned her tonsils, and ate roast pork greasy enough to slip down her throat without swallowing. Like Erzulie, Maria was a splendid commoner with exceptional appetites.

Maria let her gaze drift farther along the Malecón, where the road widened around the *Maine* monument with its immense American eagle. She knew her history. The American ship *Maine* was blown up in Havana harbor by the Americans themselves in order to blame the Spanish and start a war at the end of the last century. The Americans had wanted to get their hands around Cuba's waist and hold her down to get all her sweet sugar. The Americans were shameless. Now they had their hands up Cuba's dress, on her breasts, they were raping her.

From way up where Maria watched, the *Maine* monument was in clear sight. When the moment came and the President was on the grandstand during the Big Race, Maria would go into the closet of the room and find the rifle left there for her. She would come back to the window and, with the marksmanship she had learned in a rebel camp, she would take aim and get the job done. One shot and Cuba would become a free country.

Maria got up and went to the bedroom closet. Not to find the rifle, it was much too early for that, but to look for anything the rich guests might have left behind. On the floor of the closet she saw a white glove with shiny buttons up the side. She tried to slip the glove onto her hand, but the threads of the finger seams began to split. She pulled harder, forcing the glove to fit. Then she peered under the bed, searching for the matching glove. No luck, but at least she had half a pair. Last month she had found another glove, a pink suede one. The pink and white gloves worn together would make a statement, show people that she had so many gloves that she got bored wearing them in matched pairs and mixed their colors and styles just to keep life interesting. All the girls would appreciate her daring.

Finding the white glove gave Maria hope that there might be more treasures. She went through all the drawers in the Italian Baroque–style dresser. Nothing. She pulled up the cushions on an imitation Louis XVI sofa, slipping her fingers into crevices, feeling for coins. Nothing. She removed the silk-covered seat of a sleek lounge chair. Payday of the gods! American money! A two-dollar bill! This was huge magic, the lucky number *two*. A big reward in life was coming her way. A two-dollar bill was so powerful it shouldn't be spent, it would just keep giving and giving, pouring honey from heaven. She folded the bill carefully, unbuttoned the top of her maid's uniform, and tucked the bill safely beneath her bra against her skin.

Such a lucky day. Maria began to strip the king-sized bed in order to make it up fresh with the clean sheets she had brought. She pulled the blanket off, exposing the top sheet twisted into a knot. She knew what that meant; two lovers caught in a hurricane of passion the night before. She unraveled the sheet and from it fell peach-colored silk panties trimmed in creamy lace. These were the kind of panties Maria had seen Marilyn Monroe wearing in a double-page photo spread in a movie magazine. Maria plucked the panties up between thumb and forefinger. They were new, with no stains or wear, used only for the act of seduction. Maria visualized the blond woman from up north, there on the bed, wearing nothing but these. And the man, naked, except for a starched white shirt he didn't want to waste time taking off. Maria imagined the man pulling the blonde's panties down, sliding them off her alabaster skin and raising them to his nose, inhaling her intimate scent.

Maria held the delicate silk to her own nose and inhaled. A faint female perfume wafted up. She looked at the label sewn into the waistband: NEIMAN MARCUS, DALLAS, TEXAS. The two-dollar bill tucked beneath her bra was already bringing her luck.

Maria always left the exploration of the bathroom for last; that was where the biggest treasure might be, but she didn't want to rush in. After she had the bedroom vacuumed and tidied up, looking as if no human had ever spent one minute there, she allowed herself to open the bathroom door.

The bathroom suite was grand, all marble, mirrors and gleaming chrome fixtures. There was even a crystal chandelier. The toilet lid was up and a used condom floated in the water. Maria quickly made the sign of the cross three times, flushed the toilet, and banged the lid down. She glanced around. A pile of used towels lay bunched up in the corner on the floor. She shook out the towels but found nothing left behind. On the long marble counter was only a half-empty cobalt-blue jar of face cream that said CHANEL on it. Now, that was something a girl could use. Maria's luck was growing. She set about scrubbing the bathroom and, when she had everything glistening like the fronds of a palm tree after a quick rain, she slid back the glass door of the shower stall.

There, side by side in the center of the porcelain tub, with their sharp toes pointing toward the drain, was a pair of high-heeled shoes. The shoes were made of glossy flame-red patent leather and stood high on stiletto heels. What a strange but miraculous vision, the bright red surrounded by a sea of white! Who would have left shoes in a bathtub? Did the owner's man dislike them because they made his woman look too desirable to other men, so he hid them while she was packing in the other room? Or perhaps the woman was spiritual and had left the shoes behind as an offering to Queen Erzulie. It was impossible to tell. But one thing Maria knew, the magic two-dollar bill was burning a lucky hole right through to her heart.

Maria cautiously lifted the shoes. She gasped, marveling at ribbon-thin ankle straps with dainty metal buckles. Inside the narrow insteps were identical labels that read: CHRISTIAN DIOR, PARIS, FRANCE. She didn't know who the Christian in Paris was. She thought the shoes looked like the ones Dorothy wore in *The Wizard of Oz*. She had watched a scratchy old print of that movie in the theater of the sugar mill town where she had grown up. She had had to work a week just to buy the ticket to get into the theater, where she sat in the balcony because her skin was too dark to sit up front with the white people.

What if these red shoes were Dorothy's shoes? If so, it meant bad witches were flying around, that the gods would have to be appeased and the saints fed. This was a big responsibility. Maria sighed deeply. She needed an arsenal of witches to fight witches. She had to be brave. She decided to keep the shoes. She clutched them to her and wept with joy.

Maria thought she heard witches whispering. She held her breath. But the whispering sound was only water running in the sink. Someone had forgotten to close the faucet. She turned the water off, then went back into the bedroom with the shoes and face cream. She sat on the edge of the bed, kicked off her own worn shoes, and put on the red ones. What a marvel! The shoes were tight, but they fit her feet, and her feet were not small. She didn't have the courage to walk in the shoes yet. She bent forward and looked at her face in the dresser mirror. She unscrewed the cap from the face-cream jar. A heady scent of mint and aloe vera rushed up. She studied herself closely in the mirror as she applied fingertip dabs of white cream to her dark face. She was such an African princess, such a Spanish seductress. She batted her long eyelashes. She smoothed cream around her mouth, thinking about Esther Fernández, the brilliant and brave Mexican movie star with the perfect nose and flowing black hair. What a hard life Esther had lived, especially in that movie *Flower of Blood,* when her tender heart was betrayed by the suave actor Víctor

Junco. No woman deserved to be treated like that. Víctor was a man who could steal any woman's heart. He looked like a Latin version of the dashing American star Errol Flynn. Víctor had the same kind of seductive mustache above voluptuous lips, the same slicked-back black hair, high cheekbones and broad shoulders. Maria fell back on the bed, not thinking of dark Víctor but of white Errol. She wanted Errol to treat her the way Víctor treated Esther when he was seducing her in the movie. Maria wanted it rough.

The scent of face cream and the tight magic of the red shoes were making Maria delirious. The soft pink roses on the wallpapered walls floated around her. She had seen Errol Flynn in that other blood movie, *Captain Blood,* filmed right here in Cuba. Errol swung by ropes from the mast of a pirate ship that he sailed on the high seas. He was like Tarzan, swinging on vines through the jungle, shirtless, a huge knife dangling at his belt. Errol swung through the roses toward Maria. She heard the other pirates shouting threats, trying to stop him from rescuing her. Errol swooped her up. He kissed her and his hands moved over her breasts and between her legs. The other pirates were closing in, shooting their long pistols.

No, it wasn't pistol shots. It was loud knocking.

Maria leapt up from the bed. "Mother of God!" She prayed it wasn't the floor manager knocking at the door. The manager would fire her. Maybe she was going to be punished by a bad witch for being a black Dorothy in a white girl's red shoes. The *shoes*! As she opened the door she remembered she was still wearing them.

Standing in the doorway was Leaping Larry Lizard. He looked Maria up and down, his eyes stripping off all her clothes, everything except the shoes. A big grin flashed on his face and a hard-on bucked at his pants zipper.

"Where the fuck did you get those shoes?"

Maria's eyes widened. She was afraid to blink for fear it would open up the dam and tears would gush out.

"Don't be afraid, my coconut meringue." Lizard reached his arms around her waist and put his big hands on her bottom. He pushed her into the room and kicked the door closed behind him as he held her in a tight embrace. "Open up your legs and give me your Cuban banana split."

3.
Shark Bait

Orchestra Kubavana Viva was on the radio playing "Tropical Lies." The music was a hit because it used only two rhythms, the slap of waves on the beach and the wind-scrape of swaying palm trees. Bongo drummed out the simple percussion on his desk. His fingers wanted to go somewhere else, find another beat, feel a different pulse. He had a pounding headache, a deep and insistent throb in his temples. He took another swig of rum from the glass on his desk, more hair of the dog. He wanted to douse that dog with rum, throw a lighted match on it, and watch it run burning through hell.

He felt responsible for what had happened in the Tropicana the night before. Maybe if he hadn't been away from the table getting the orchid, he would have been sitting in Mercedes' place at the stroke of midnight. He would have been the one blown to bits. It didn't seem fair that she had died and he hadn't. Somewhere in him was a Spanish streak of chivalry that decreed it was the man who should suffer for the woman.

The up-tempo notes of "Tropical Lies" swished through the air. The music's mood was the exact opposite of Bongo's. He poured more rum from his bottle of Bacardi. Tropical truth? What the hell was the truth anyway? The morning newspapers were full of the Tropicana bombing. Of course the speculation, if not outright accusation, was that the bombing was the work of revolutionaries. Hadn't they been setting off bombs all around the city? Nothing new in that.

It was Bongo's job to be skeptical. He was an insurance investigator and, for the right price, a private dick. Stenciled in bold black letters on the frosted glass of his office door was KBII, which stood for "King Bongo Insurance and Investigations." Above the bold initials was also stenciled GREAT TROPICAL LIFE INSURANCE COMPANY. It was common sense, you had to insure it to investigate it. So the investigator in Bongo got to thinking, between the drumbeats on the radio and the throbbing in his temples. In fact, that bomb could have been planted by rebels, or by those who wanted everyone to *think* it was the rebels, or by the Giant of the Tropicana to collect the insurance money. Tropical lies, tropical truth. Who was to know? Who was to care? Bongo cared. Mercedes was dead and his sister was missing. He blamed himself.

He heard high-heeled shoes on the staircase outside the door. It sounded like Mercedes when she came to visit him. He must be hallucinating. He took another swig of rum and let it burn a little reality into him, but he still heard the footsteps. He could always tell the footsteps of a woman in high heels, his ears were tuned to that. As a percussion man he knew the distinctive beat of each female, for each laid down a different beat as she walked, each had her own rhythm. This rhythm sounded like Mercedes. But Mercedes was dead.

Bongo got up and switched the radio off. The refrain of "Tropical Lies" abruptly stopped, and so did the footsteps outside the closed door. Maybe it was just the damn pounding in his head. He was sorry the footsteps had stopped. Could it have been Mercedes? Could last night have been only a nightmare? Perhaps he was just waking up. Then again, maybe last night really did happen and Mercedes was miraculously alive, Mercedes was walking.

He forced himself to think about something else. Had the Giant of the Tropicana bombed his own club to collect the insurance, knowing the rebels would be blamed and nobody would suspect him? Not a bad scheme; many businesses were using it during these unsettled times. But if the Giant was responsible it meant he was also placing his greatest assets at risk—the dancers, especially the most famous of all, the Panther. Whatever the truth was, the Giant's insurance company would have to pay him off, and after it did it would drop him. Insurance companies play the odds; after one loss, they cut and run as standard practice. Which meant Bongo could sell the Giant a new policy. It would have to be a very expensive policy, given the recent history, but that was justified considering the risk. To have the world-famous Tropicana as a client, now *that* would provide some good word of mouth, some serious stature, which was what Bongo needed. He liked this line of reasoning, and the rum helped him along with it. The rum made him think that fairly soon now the bearded boys in the mountains would all be shot, the bombing would stop, and things would go back to cockeyed normal.

The footsteps began again.

The sound of high heels clicking on the tile floor outside was different this time. Maybe it was because the sound was closer, coming from the hallway just beyond the door. Bongo stiffened and the hair on the back of his neck stood up. The different beat he heard was imprinted in his blood. It was the beat of the Panther. He leapt up, raced to the door and threw it open.

But it wasn't his sister. The beat of his headache had thrown his timing off. Or could it be that the woman standing before him now moved to the same beat as his sister? Impossible. This woman was white, white as a hen's egg, white as a fish's belly, white as a lily. White, rich and American. She was dressed from head to toe in such an up-to-date style that it looked like someone had ripped a life-sized page out of *Vogue* magazine and propped it up. What was she doing here on New Year's Day, or any day? She belonged across town in Miramar, in the Country Club district, the Beverly Hills of Havana, where the gardens were the lushest, the mansions the fanciest, and the sun always shone gold. But here she was, in a white linen suit, crowned by a white mohair hat with a white peacock feather. Even her voice sounded white.

"Are you going to ask me in?"

Bongo was immobile, like a fly just zapped by the tongue of an albino lizard.

"Are you the insurance agent? The sign on the door says 'Great Tropical Life.' "

He felt his senses returning. *Bam-bam* went the headache throbbing between his ears; *boom-boom* went the rum drum in his brain. Usually he made the first move with females, led the way, danced the first step, but not this time. She gave him a smile that gleamed as big and bright as the chrome grille on a Cadillac Eldorado.

"Are you open for business or not?"

"Sure . . . yeah, well, come in."

She walked in and imperiously sat in the shabby rattan chair in front of his desk.

Bongo closed the door and sat down behind the desk. Self-consciously clearing his throat, he slipped the half-empty rum bottle off the desktop and into a drawer. He knew who she was. "What can I do for you, Mrs. Armstrong?"

She crossed her long legs. Her silk stockings were white; her high-heeled shoes were white suede. "Tell me, exactly what line of business are you in?"

"I'm, uh, an insurance salesman, an insurance adjuster, an insurance investigator. Property, fire, theft, accident."

"You must be very successful. The roads of Cuba are simply murderous. You can make a tidy living on auto accidents alone. There are more automobile accidents per capita in Cuba than in any other place in the world. People are just crazy on these roads."

"You're very knowledgeable about the conditions of our roads and drivers."

"I have to be. I'm paying a fortune to insure my three cars here. More than I pay for my five cars in Newport."

"Let's just say that in Cuba driving is considered a sport."

"A blood sport. Spain has its bullfights, Cuba has its highways."

"So you want to switch insurance companies?"

"No."

"Maybe you're in the market for home insurance? You get a discount if you have a police panic light on top of your house."

"You mean those lights outside on your roof that flash when you push a button next to your bed if you're being robbed at night?"

"Robbed or . . . anything."

"I've got five of them."

"Must be a big house."

"Depends on what you're used to."

Her thin nostrils pinched in as she took a deep breath. As she exhaled, the linen fabric of the stylish short jacket covering her breasts rustled with the sound of leaves caught in a breeze. "Is that vanilla I smell?"

"Could be."

Her eyes swept the desktop and she saw a small potted orchid. She got up and came toward Bongo at the desk, bent over and put her face close to the flower. Then she sat on the edge of the desk as if sitting sidesaddle on a horse, an aristocratic pose. She reached up and removed her hat, then unpinned the diamond clip in her blond hair and shook her hair loose.

Bongo could smell her perfume. It was distinct, like crushed roses and leather, with the same exciting rush as the scent of a new car's interior.

He could swear she was jealous of the orchid, competing with its beauty and fragrance. Nothing, *nothing* in the room was going to be more sublime than she was.

"What variety is this?" she asked.

"Just a small Madagascar baby. Vanilla is made from its pods. I once had a different orchid with a powerful cinnamon perfume. No one could compete with her."

"No one? What was her name?"

"Vanda dearei."

"Is that the one I saw you carrying into the Tropicana last night?"

Bongo was surprised. He hadn't been certain if she had seen him when she and her husband nearly ran him down in their Cadillac. So much for Cuba's murderous roads. "You saw me last night?"

"I most certainly did." She leaned closer, her blond hair framing her face. "And I saw you earlier, playing the drums."

"Bongos. Playing the bongos."

"You were good. Do you often get up and play with the band?"

"When the music moves me."

"The crowd loved it."

"And you? What kind of music do you like?"

"Love songs, like Peggy Lee and Johnnie Ray sing. You probably haven't heard them."

"I might. We get the American stations here."

"You would know them if you heard them."

"So what do they sound like?"

"A warm bath. A warm bath filled with tears."

"And what does my music sound like?"

She gazed down at his hands, where his fingers had been tapping on the desktop the whole time they had been talking. "To me it's not like music when you play. It's like . . . *urgency.* As if you've got something important to say but you're not quite certain how to do it. You're searching, sending out a signal, trying to connect."

"That's quite an analysis. I was only playing the bongos."

"You were doing more than that. I could see it."

A familiar image flashed through Bongo's mind. He was seven years old, standing next to his sister, both nearly naked. Their father stood behind them, slapping the beat onto their shaved heads with his open palms. *Whack-whack-thwack-thwack-thwack!* All the neighbors gathered around, fascinated, passing the rum bottle back and forth as his father sang, *"The Bongo has two heads, man and woman, hate and love, war and peace, Christianity and Santería! Those heads are always at odds, tricking you into thinking they are two and not ONE! It is up to you to communicate the message of unity, so the body can dance and the spirit come! The Bongo is the same drum!" Thwack-thwack-whap-ditty-do-dap-whack!*

Bongo looked into Mrs. Armstrong's blue eyes. "I'm not certain whether I'm playing the bongos . . . or they're playing me."

"It really is exceptional." She pressed her hands over his to stop his incessant drumming on the desktop.

"Not so exceptional here. Cubans are very musical. It's in the blood. Some people say it's even in the food."

"If it were in the rice and beans," she laughed, "then all of Latin America would be musical."

"We have a few more things on the menu than that."

She arched an eyebrow. "Is that so? What? Pork and fried bananas?"

"I don't think you're able to *taste* what we cook."

"Don't get testy. Be nice." She removed her hands from his. "Sometimes I have my maid cook Cuban dishes."

"That's the problem. She's cooking for you, not her family."

"You seem so sure of yourself."

"I'm certain about food and music."

"I'm not so sure, if you haven't heard Peggy Lee or Johnnie Ray. And have you ever eaten anything other than Cuban food?"

"My father was American. He met my mother when he was stationed at Guantánamo Bay. I went to college in America."

She seemed amused. "Where would someone like you go to college?"

"University of Miami."

"That's not exactly Harvard."

"I didn't exactly want to go to Harvard."

"What did you major in, sunshine?"

"Sunshine with a minor in gangsters."

"My, you're good."

"If you want to check out my credentials, there's a diploma behind me."

She gazed at a framed document on the wall. "An English major! My God, now that's flying with the eagles. You know, I never understood how people in America could major in something called *English;* it's what they already speak and know. It would be like someone in China getting a major in Chinese. Does that make any sense?"

"I take it you don't have much use for colleges."

"My people *founded* them. Why should I *go* to them? There's too much life to be lived."

"You're right, there's too much life to be lived."

"Why did you leave Miami?"

"Miami is dying. The great hotels are being turned into old-age homes, or worse, catering to families with kids. The suburbs are bigger than the city. It's not like Havana. Havana has history, five hundred years of history. Havana has a center as elegant as any city in Europe. It has a heart, it has an identity. It's booming with new businesses, new hotels. Grand boulevards are being laid out, grand schemes are in the works. There's opportunity here. Havana is the future."

"A future with broken sewers," she said sarcastically. "And water that's unfit to drink and phones that almost never work."

"You take the good with the bad. Havana has opera, it has theater, it has glamour."

"So do London, New York, and Paris."

"London, New York, and Paris don't have sun twelve months of the year."

"You sure are a cocky boy."

"I just have my own way of seeing the world."

"So what are you seeing now?" She laid the gaze of her blue eyes on him, a haughty challenge.

"I see that people walk into my office for all kinds of reasons. Some want to insure their business, their car, or their life. Others want me to do a little investigating on the side, since that's part of my business too, though it's hardly enough to pay the bills. People walk through that door when they need help. They've lost their pet, their money, their—"

"—husband."

For the first time she looked vulnerable. All that pale white skin didn't look so plush now, merely common.

Her voice started to tremble. "I was told I could trust you. You sell insurance mostly to the Americans, British, and Canadians, the ABC community; the country club set, the foreign movers and shakers. You're the only one in Havana who specializes in that world, knows its secrets, all its little nooks and crannies. More importantly, you're part of the Cuban world. You are unique. You are the only one I can come to."

"If your husband is lost, he must have gotten lost between last night and today, because I saw him at the Tropicana last night in the Cadillac with you."

"I didn't say we weren't still together. But he's gone, gone from me, gone from the marriage."

"I can't help you, then."

"I want you to find out *why* he's lost to me. Then I can work on getting him back."

Here it comes, Bongo thought. She wants a tail on the husband to find him cheating, then, *bam-bam*, Bongo takes the incriminating photos, she sues for divorce, and the rich get richer.

"I know what you're thinking." She placed her hand over his again to stop his fingers from tapping on the desk. "But this isn't some simple divorce case. My husband *did* go to Harvard. But he's not the one with the money. I'm the one who pays all the bills. It's not money I want, it's answers."

Now Bongo got it. Simple, really. It was about pride. She couldn't imagine any man walking away from her body, her position, her dough, the whole perfumed aura of her life. He didn't like the deal. It stank.

She got up from the desk and sat back down in the shabby rattan chair, exasperated. "Are you going to help me?"

Her husband, Guy Armstrong, had walked through Bongo's office door no more than three months before, had sat in the same rattan chair. He had negotiated a very substantial policy on his own life with his wife as beneficiary. If Armstrong wanted money he would have taken out a large policy on *her* life with *himself* as beneficiary. Bongo remembered asking Armstrong, an athletic man, a picture of American health, "Why take out such a large policy?" Armstrong had smiled at him, with that big American car-grille smile he and his wife both had, and answered, "Life is a game of polo."

Mrs. Armstrong snapped her alligator purse open and pulled out a checkbook. "I can make it worth your while."

Maybe she was on the square. Maybe he was being too harsh. After all, these Americans celebrated Christmas just like Cubans, some of them, anyway.

She wrote out a check. Her fingers were slender. Her perfectly polished fingernails were the same pink color as the throat of a lovebird when it lifted its small head to preen for its mate. Her handwriting was as elegant as the amount she wrote down on the check—*five hundred dollars.*

"This should cover your time and expenses." She slid the check across the desk.

Bongo saw himself paying his rent. He saw himself betting on baseball, the horses, the dogs, the lottery. He saw orchids. Fields of orchids. All *Vanda dearei.* Precious *Vanda dearei.*

He grinned. "I'm your man."

"I'm not looking for a man. I'm looking for a service."

"That's the American way, isn't it?"

"You know"—she uncrossed her legs and stood to leave—"you'd better be careful that the American half of you doesn't get the upper hand."

"I'm watching that."

"I'm sure you are." She went to the door and opened it, then turned to him. "By the way, how many languages do you speak?"

"You know the answer to that."

"Two?"

"Three."

"Spanish and English. What's the third?"

"*Music.*"

"My, my." She smiled. "Aren't you the one-man band." She closed the door behind her.

Bongo pulled the bottle of rum from the drawer and took a good stiff belt. The sharp afternoon light shot down through the slats of the window louvers and cut across his desk. The scent of Mrs. Armstrong's perfume lingered in the air, faint but insistent, a competitive reminder. He recalled the scent of the *Vanda dearei* he once held in his hands, now blown away in the Tropicana blast. The big-band rhythm of "Tropical Lies" came back to him, reverberating in his mind. He drummed the music's percussive beat with his fingers next to the orchid on the desk. The rum was busy with its buzzing performance in his head. He drummed harder. He inhaled the scent of the orchid mixed with Mrs. Armstrong's lingering perfume; tropical truth tangled with tropical lies.

The sound of footsteps was outside the door again. Was she coming back? Or was it the sound of his own drumming?

Humberto Zapata lived in dreams and slept with nightmares. Everywhere Zapata went dreams followed.

It is one thing for a man to be trapped by his past, but another to be caught in a net of dreams. To be trapped in the past means a man can't move forward. To be ensnared by dreams means that a man lives a suspended life, as if in a bubble. Zapata was in that bubble with his hands and face pressed to the transparent membrane that held him prisoner as fate took him, tumbling the bubble up and over like a giant beach ball in a hurricane, spinning out of control. He compensated for this by walking slower than other men, taking on an air of exaggerated gravity, always flat-footed, sure in his actions. Deliberateness was his game, the sober face he showed to the world; always the stalwart citizen, keeping the peace by keeping the secrets. But inside his personal bubble Zapata was in turmoil, trying to keep from puking because all his dreams were the same, always of her, his sweet pet, his sleek Panther.

His nightmare? That in the end he would lose her.

Zapata walked down a long hallway. The old tiles on the floor were worn and cracked. He stopped before the door at the end of the hallway and knocked with a hard-knuckled rap. No answer. He tried the door. It was unlocked.

Bongo was behind his desk as the office door opened. In one hand he held a revolver.

Zapata stepped into the room and stood motionless. In the dim light his linen suit and straw Panama hat were the color of dirty honey. His sunglasses were so black that his eyes were hidden, and below his sharp nose was the straight line of a mustache dyed black, like a bold exclamation mark lying on its side. He spoke in his usual mock whisper, like an executioner offering a man facing a firing squad a last cigarette. "And how is my favorite gunslinging insurance hustler?"

"What took you so long?" Bongo aimed the revolver higher.

"Tut-tut, you knew I'd be coming."

"Where are your two bodyguards?"

"Outside. So you can put your popgun away."

"I figured you'd be getting around to me."

"My dear, a horrendous crime has been committed. A girl was killed."

"I noticed you left before the bomb exploded."

"I was called away on other matters."

"I've already made a report of what I saw to the police."

"I've read it."

"Of course."

"I'm more than the police. I'm . . . special."

"Secret, you mean. Secret intelligence."

"Oh, I don't think intelligence is ever secret. Take yourself, for example, everyone can see you're intelligent. It's no secret."

"Since I'm so intelligent, I should tell you something I didn't tell the police last night?"

"That would not only make you intelligent, that would make you wise."

"Here's what will make me wise. Where is my sister?"

"She's safe."

"Many of the dancers onstage were hurt when the bomb exploded. Was my sister hurt?"

"She was behind the first row of dancers. Those in the front were badly cut by shards of glass."

"Yes, there was a lot of blood."

"Blood spattered everywhere. You saw it. I wasn't there."

"Where were *you*?"

"I can't divulge secrets."

"You left before the explosion. What secret intelligence did you have about what was going to happen?"

"I'm here to ask the questions."

"I want answers. Where is my sister? I went to her house last night. She wasn't there. I made the rounds of all the hospitals; there was no record of her. I slept in my car outside her place. She never showed."

"I've told you what you need to know. When there is more, you will be informed."

"Was she cut up?"

"I want you to answer *my* questions."

"I will. Answer mine first."

"Superficial wounds."

"Her face?"

"Not a scratch."

Bongo exhaled a sigh of relief. "Thank God."

"Do you know who might have planted that bomb?"

"No. Who would do such a thing? Killing and maiming."

"Nothing is fair."

"What happened last night wasn't unfair, it was politics."

"Then you do know who did it?"

"Hell, no!" Bongo banged his fist on the desk.

Zapata was silent, then continued in his emphatic whisper, "Over *one hundred* bombs have gone off in Havana just in the past week."

"Some say the government is behind the bombings, that it's a counterrevolutionary move."

"Don't be naive," Zapata said curtly. "Those who are doing the bombing are not naive."

"You're right. And those who set themselves up as judge and executioner, nightly assassinating so-called terrorists, are not naive; they're monsters. As you said, nothing is fair."

"Unfortunately so. Tell me, how well did you know the girl who died?"

"Well enough. Mercedes was a sweet girl, a university student. I should say, she *was* a student, until your people closed the university down."

"I know she was a student."

Bongo shot Zapata a look of disdain. "You have a dossier on every student in the country."

"We have information. And her three friends? The ones who were seated at a table near hers. What were their names?"

"I don't know. I never really paid that much attention. It was Mercedes I was interested in."

"Did you know her friends were university students too?"

"If you knew that, why ask me?"

"They've all disappeared."

"Like my sister."

"That's a different matter."

"Not to me."

In the enclosed room the humidity was intense. Zapata took a handkerchief from his pocket, removed his Panama hat, and wiped sweat from his forehead. "There were bombers all over Havana on New Year's Eve, targeting politicians, soldiers, police, government buildings. Fortunately none of them was very successful, except at the Tropicana."

"None of that was in this morning's newspaper."

"My dear Bongo, we don't want to wake the babies."

"What makes you think they're sleeping? When the public is being bombed nobody sleeps."

"It's a terrible thing. Innocent people. Your girl was innocent. I want you to help me stop these murderers. I want you to think hard about every move you made last night at the club; what everyone said to you, what everyone did, how they acted. Was there anything . . . anything at all the least bit suspicious?"

Bongo didn't want to help. He had wanted to kill Zapata for years, but he couldn't because of his sister. But he also hated those who set off bombs, those who were as vicious as Zapata and his kind. Bongo had to help one enemy in order to stop the other, those who blew up innocents. He said under his breath, "Tropical truth, tropical lies."

"What?"

"I was just thinking."

"Take your time."

Bongo didn't want to name names. Damn, he didn't want to, but someone was responsible for killing lovely Mercedes. "There were people last night who were acting strangely."

"In what way?"

"Not really *so* strange."

"Tell me. Remember, your sister could have been blown to bits."

Bongo repeated the words in a hushed voice, "Blown to bits."

"Yes. *Our* Panther dead."

"Dead." Bongo could hardly say the word.

"Speak up, man. I've got to investigate every scrap of evidence. Whoever it is, on the far right or the far left, it makes no difference."

Bongo went back in his mind to the white spider dangling from the branches of the banyan tree above his table at the Tropicana. He saw Mercedes' expression change from gaiety to fear as she watched the insect drop lower on its silver thread until it hung directly above her. She asked him not to kill it. He saw the spider land on the table. He saw a fist slam down.

"There was a spider and a woman who killed it."

"Good, you're thinking now. Why is the woman important?"

"She said, 'I know you. You should leave here right now.' "

"She knew the bomb was going to go off and she was warning you to get out?"

"Maybe."

"Did she say anything else?"

"She said, 'You might look white, but you're as black inside as I am.' "

"She certainly did know you, then."

"Apparently. But I'd never laid eyes on her before. Odd that they didn't stop her from entering the club because of the color of her skin. Someone must have slipped her in."

"What happened next?"

"She disappeared."

"Can you describe her? Her clothes, her age?"

"She was wearing, hell, what was she wearing? A traditional white Santera dress and a white bandanna wrapped around her head. She looked poor, about thirty, maybe younger."

"How dark was she? Brown butter?"

"No, darker."

"Coffee?"

"Tar."

"That's very black. It's rare to see one that black; in the country, yes, in the city not so much."

"I remember thinking she was pretty, but spooked out."

"How so?"

"When she killed the spider on the table she said, 'White spiders are bad luck, especially tonight.' Scared the hell out of Mercedes."

"What else do you remember that seemed unusual or suspicious?"

"*You*. You said, 'If I were you I would walk out of here right now and never come back.' And you knew that Mr. Wu was waiting for me outside the Tropicana."

"Did anyone else tell you to leave?"

"Fido."

"What about the Judge at the rope?"

"The Judge said I should *stay*."

"Any others who told you to leave?"

"Well, Mr. Wu told me not to go back in, to go home and be happy."

"That's all?"

Bongo thought for a moment. "Sailor Girl."

"That trashy American who likes rough trade and queers?"

"She happens to be very rich trash."

"That's the worst kind."

"She walks on the wild side, it's her choice."

"What did she say?"

"Sailor Girl wanted me to go to Sans Souci with her and two Cuban sailors she had picked up. She couldn't get the sailors into the Tropicana because their skin was too coffee."

"Can you think of anything else out of the ordinary?"

There was one more thing, maybe the most illuminating jigsaw puzzle piece of all. Just moments before the bomb exploded, the Armstrongs had sped away from the nightclub in their Cadillac with Hurricane Hurler in the backseat. But, as much as Bongo wanted the person found who killed Mercedes, he still couldn't trust Zapata with this information.

"Let's have it," Zapata urged. "There's more."

"I'm cleaned out."

The real reason Bongo had taken the money from Mrs. Armstrong to spy on her husband was that it would give him a chance to spy on them *both*. He needed time and a cover to find out if there was

any connection between those two social birds of prey and the bombing. If there was, he would right that injustice, and soon.

Zapata stiffened and demanded, "Come with me."

"Where to? The Pineapple Field, or your personal house of tor-
tures, the Blue Mansion?"

"Two good choices, but I'm saving them for a special occasion.
Right now we're going to the morgue, so you won't need your
popgun."

"Why the morgue?"

"No more questions."

Bongo and Zapata stepped out into the bright sunlight. Narrow Obispo Street was crowded with shoppers cruising the stores. In the shadows of some doorways loitered people dressed in ragged clothes, watching good fortune pass them by. The street had once been the most elegant in Havana, with everything refined that money could buy. But Obispo was *Old* Havana. Time had moved on. Districts like Vedado and Miramar now dominantly prevailed with their grand boulevards and glass-fronted, air-conditioned showrooms. Obispo still had a touch of class, but it was fading fast.

The swank Floridita restaurant was at one end of Obispo. Behind the Floridita towered the enormous edifice of the national Capitolio. The bottom half of the Capitolio was obscured by other buildings, its disembodied white dome appeared to float, like a giant flying saucer attempting a landing in downtown Havana.

At the other end of Obispo was the Ambos Mundos Hotel. Its twenty-foot-tall windows were open to catch the breeze. Inside at the bar people sipped iced drinks beneath the heat-beating swoosh of overhead fans. Parked in front of the hotel was Zapata's black Plymouth, its chrome grille and bumpers glinting in the sun.

Leaning against the Plymouth's long hood were Zapata's two ever-present subordinates, Pedro and Paulo. It didn't make any difference which one was Pedro and which one was Paulo, because whenever Zapata issued an order in his mock whisper both men snapped to attention; then each performed the same ritual, first patting the front of his trousers, just to reassure himself that he still had balls, then patting the bulge under his jacket, to reassure himself that he still had his gun.

"Pedro," Zapata ordered, "to the morgue."

Both men straightened to attention, patting their balls, patting their guns. Pedro saluted and jumped into the car behind the steering wheel. Paulo saluted, opened the back door for Zapata, then jumped into the front on the passenger side. Pedro and Paulo adjusted their neckties as if they were snapping on airplane seat belts to prepare for a bumpy ride.

Bongo slipped into the back of the car next to Zapata. He looked through the window into the Ambos Mundos Hotel. A sleek young white woman swung around on her stool at the bar and gazed at Bongo. Her glossy red lips sucked on a blue straw that poked out of the green mint leaves floating on top of her icy mojito. Bongo knew where female tourists like her came from by the way they dressed. If they were from the States he could even tell which city they were from by their accents.

"Pedro," Zapata's mock whisper inquired, "why aren't we moving?"

Pedro ran a hand across his sweaty forehead and looked over to Paulo for backup.

Paulo squirmed. "Captain Zapata, we had a radio message while you were gone. It was urgent."

"Why didn't you come and get me?"

"Because our orders were to stay here until you returned."

Zapata looked at Paulo like he was a slow greyhound that had just lost its ninth dog race. "That didn't mean that urgent messages shouldn't be delivered."

"Sorry, Captain." Paulo wiped sweat from his forehead the same way Pedro had.

"Well, then?" Zapata glared. "What was the message?"

"Another dead body, Captain."

"That's not my concern."

"Excuse me, Captain, headquarters says it is. They say this one is not the usual fruit for the Pineapple Field. They want you to check it out."

"You have the address?"

"Yes, sir, just like you instructed us. It's written down."

"Let me see it."

Paulo reached into his pocket, fished out a piece of paper, and handed it over.

"I can't read this. I told you, let Pedro do the driving *and* the writing. You do the other stuff." Zapata handed the paper back to Paulo.

Paulo squinted at the handwriting on the paper, confused, then understanding dawned. "I know where it is. Should we go?"

"Of course. It's urgent."

Pedro started the engine and the Plymouth shuddered to life with a muffled roar.

As the car pulled away, Zapata glanced through the window to see what Bongo had been looking at inside the hotel bar. He saw the woman on the barstool. She had cropped blond hair. She looked like that movie star, what was her name, Grace Kelly? Could be. They were all coming to Havana now, blondes, redheads, brunettes, wearing tight skimpy pants called Capris, or toreador pants, or some stupid thing. When these women sat on barstools the pale skin of their naked midriffs was exposed. The waists of the pants fit low around the swell of their hips and pulled up tight in the crack of their asses to show off the split of two plump papayas. They were a dime a dozen, these good-time girls, flying in all day long, sailing in on cruise ships and private yachts. Zapata had no need for foreigners.

The Plymouth pulled away from the hotel, snaked through the narrow bustling streets of Old Havana and onto broad Ejido Avenue, passing the Central Railroad Station and turning right in front of the shipping docks, speeding by passenger and cargo ships, past industrial yards and factories, then continuing through towns that had long since been swallowed up by the city's sprawl. Eventually the pavement ended and the Plymouth wheeled along dirt streets lined with shacks built of rusted tin and salvaged lumber. No electricity or sewers existed here. Tattered clothing was drying on ropes in the dust. Silent children stood outside the shacks, their bellies ballooned from malnutrition, as if they had been eating air. This was not the glamorous playground of the rich. This was not a Technicolor travelogue shown around the world to lure tourists to carefree Cuba, the Pearl of the Antilles.

As the Plymouth whizzed by, Bongo knew that the squalor he

saw out the window was reality for the majority of Havana's popula-
tion. He himself had lived this reality. He understood those who tried
to crawl out of it by any means possible, to claw their way to a wage
one inch over the poverty line. This was the tropical truth for most of
those whose skins were black—African black, slave black, bondage
black, sugarcane-cutting brute animal black, disposable black. Bongo
knew the scent of rank, sweaty desperation. He knew the smell of
fear and defeat. It wasn't just the stench of shit that got to you,
though it seemed to rise up from the ground whether the wind was
blowing in your direction or not, but the shoeless feet, the despairing
hearts, the hopeless, scabbed faces.

Bongo also knew the lush smell of success, the fragrant scent of a
new stack of peso bills. He knew the look of well-fed cologne-
slapped cheeks, the faces of those who held those stacks of cash in
their tight fists. Cash was piled up in the Capitolio, in the casinos, in
the fancy Art Deco office buildings and banks of Vedado, in the
beach mansions of Miramar, in the four-hundred-year-old palaces of
Old Havana. Bongo understood: A man was either a prince or a pig,
born on the right side or the wrong side of the law. A man was either
holding the shit end of the stick or someone else was.

Shielded by the Plymouth's windshield, Pedro and Paulo didn't
give a thought to the fact that they were passing through one of the
worst slums in the world. It was nothing unusual to them; even rich
countries have poor people. Why scratch your ass about it? Why go
up into the mountains and fight to change it? In the end it was all
going to be just like it was in the beginning, haves and have-nots. So
thank the blessed Virgin if you had a little of the action. And if you
had a lot, thank God you didn't have a conscience.

Inside the Plymouth it was hot. Outside it was hotter. The car
made an arc around the southern neighborhoods of Havana Bay,
then turned east through the colonial town of Guanabacoa, a former
center for trafficking in African slaves. As the Plymouth passed
through the town, holy women, dressed in white with white bandannas around their heads, stood guard. They tossed water from pans
onto the street where the car had intruded, magic intended to cleanse
away the evil spirit passing by and to keep it from setting its evil eye

on the locals. The women were responsible for stopping the evil from breathing its malignant fire into houses, preventing it from forcing worms into children's bare feet; worms that would eat through hearts and explode livers, blast the eyeballs out of heads. There was no evil that the people of these humble homes hadn't witnessed or suffered over the generations. Strangers had invaded their family villages in Africa and sailed their ancestors here in chains. This time the women had the protection of the gods, the magic water of the Orishas.

The Plymouth kept going, making for the open road, then picked up speed and crossed the Rio Cojimar bridge toward the Atlantic. The road swerved, following the shoreline past bungalows bunched at the sea's edge, and finally ending at an ornately tiled bathing pavilion aspiring to be a Cuban Taj Mahal. A festive crowd of people in bathing suits milled around the pavilion among stalls where hawkers called out delicacies for sale, deep-fried churros, cold colas and syrupy pineapple chunks.

Pedro and Paulo in the front seat of the Plymouth were rubbernecking in all directions, trying to take memory snapshots of every shapely girl they passed. The car pulled to a stop in front of the bathing pavilion. A crowd gathered around it, admiring the svelte American lines and heavy chrome fixtures flashing in sunlight.

The men got out. A uniformed policeman appeared, saluted Zapata, and requested that he follow.

Zapata immediately gave orders. "Pedro and Paulo, stay with the car, in case I get any more urgent messages."

"Yes, Captain," barked Pedro and Paulo in unison. They were happy to be left alone with the pretty girls in the crowd who might happen to think it was they who owned the Plymouth.

Bongo followed Zapata and the policeman to the back of the pavilion, where the sea licked the shore with lazy waves and a rickety boat had been pulled up onto the sand. The boat's once brightly painted hull was chipped and sun-faded. The letters across its prow half spelled out the name of a woman.

Next to the boat was a scrawny fisherman wearing a pair of ragged shorts. He appeared to be an old man, but he was no more than thirty, a man who had been fishing for a living under the broiling sun since he was old enough to crawl to the sea. He feared Zapata, a suit-wearing city man with a hat and dark glasses who walked with the self-righteous air of an executioner.

The policeman pointed at the fisherman. "Show the Captain!"

The fisherman started trembling, then stepped up to the boat. Inside were two battered oars, a rusty bailing bucket, a crumpled casting net with bits of glistening sea slime clinging to it, and an old piece of canvas.

The policeman demanded, "Go on!"

The fisherman reluctantly reached a trembling hand inside the boat. His fingers touched the edge of the canvas.

"Pull it back," the policeman ordered.

The fisherman was sweating. He pulled the canvas away.

At first, in the glare of the sun, the object in the hollow of the boat looked like an odd-shaped fish that had been yanked up from the depths. Then it seemed to resemble a grotesque sea monster, like those drawn on the edges of ancient mariners' maps, bizarre creatures that rose up from below to scare the sea biscuits out of a sailor.

Zapata bent over the hull and looked closer. He could make out a large rectangular piece of flesh. It was the torso of a man but without head, arms or legs. A pair of underpants, once white, now a putrid gray, clung to what was left of the torso's mauled lower half.

The fisherman lowered his eyes apologetically. "It came up in my net."

"When?" Zapata asked.

"Near noon."

"You reported it then?"

"Yes, sir. I rowed to shore and reported it right away."

Zapata gazed at the torso's chest; an iron bar pierced straight through it.

"Where were you fishing?"

"Up by Cojimar, below where the river comes into the sea."

"Somebody chopped him up good," Zapata whispered.

"No, sir," the fisherman meekly disagreed. "He was held underwater by the weight of the bar, then the sharks got to him. I know how sharks eat. They rip at the flesh. Everything was torn off. You can see the teeth marks."

"Shark bait," Zapata whispered. "Maybe this is the beginning of a new Pineapple Field."

"Pineapple field?" The fisherman shook his head. "No, sir, I'm a fisherman, not a farmer. This came from the ocean."

"Of course it did." Zapata knew the fisherman didn't understand what Pineapple Field he meant.

Zapata nodded to the policeman. "Wrap the victim in the canvas and put him in my trunk. I'm headed to the morgue, I'll give the stiff a lift."

"What about him?" The policeman grabbed the fisherman by the arm. "Should I throw him in the slammer?"

Zapata ran a finger over his mustache as he contemplated the fisherman's fate.

Bongo looked at the fisherman's terrified face and said to Zapata, "Let this poor fellow go."

Zapata swung around and turned the glare of his sunglasses on Bongo. "Stay out of it."

"If he'd killed the other guy," Bongo said, "he never would have brought the body in and reported it."

Zapata sneered at Bongo. "Little fish don't eat big fish."

"Damn right," Bongo said.

Zapata ordered the policeman, "Let the little fish go back to the sea." He turned and walked away.

The policeman wrapped the body in the canvas and carried it off. The fisherman was still too terrified to move.

Bongo took a five-peso bill out of his wallet and offered it to the fisherman. "At least you can go home to your family with something."

The fisherman shyly took the money. A grateful smile spread on his sun-blistered lips as he mumbled, "Strangest day of my life."

4.

Rhythm in the Rain

The Plymouth headed back to Havana with four men inside and half a man in the trunk.

When the car crossed the bridge over the Rio Cojimar, Zapata ordered, "Turn off here and go into town."

"Okay, Captain." Pedro wheeled the Plymouth off the highway onto a narrow road.

The town of Cojimar was on a small bay where a sluggish river reluctantly gave up the fight to the much larger ocean. It was a simple place where women and children huddled in the shade of wooden houses waiting for the men to come back from the sea. Piers poked up from the water where fishing boats moored. At one pier there were big, fancy boats, vessels not meant for those who worked the sea for a living, but for those who made a game out of fishing, measured their prowess by how persistent they were in plowing through deep waters hoping to blindly snag a big fish. To them a fish was a trophy to hang on a wall, or a reason to buy another self-congratulatory round of drinks.

Most people from Havana took their holiday farther up the coast, in the resorts of Playas del Este, where the beaches were broad and sandy and the water gentle. Cojimar was a working fishermen's refuge, but it had a few places where visitors with limited means could stay. And there was La Terraza, a no-nonsense fishermen's restaurant at the edge of the bay.

The Plymouth pulled to a stop outside La Terraza. The four men got out.

Zapata pointed at Pedro and Paulo. "Stay here with the car."

"Please, Captain," Pedro complained. "It's hot out here."

"We need a cool drink," Paulo whined.

Zapata turned the glare of his sunglasses on Pedro and Paulo. They lowered their heads and resentfully slumped back to the Plymouth. They didn't like this. When they had stayed with the car at the bathing pavilion, they got to be big shots from the city, flirting with giggling girls in skimpy bathing suits. One of those girls had a broad sugarcane-fed bottom and she was eager to let the sun shine on it. They got her phone number. Now they had to wait in the hot sun with no human in sight, standing guard over a rotting, half-eaten corpse that was starting to smell fishy.

Bongo and Zapata walked into La Terraza and sat down at a table. They were the only customers. There was never much action in the late afternoon. Late afternoons were for siesta; a person didn't want to move much, it was too hot and sticky. Finally a waiter appeared through a beaded curtain that separated the main room from a back kitchen. He took their order and quickly brought the drinks, long-necked bottles of Hatuey beer accompanied by glasses of dark rum. Outside, through the open window, the flat ocean was turning from blue to white, more like the surface of a mirror than water. On the mirror was reflected a pile of dark clouds getting ready to rain.

Zapata took a sip of rum, running his tongue along his lips to savor the sugar-tart taste. He pulled out a cigar, bit off one end, and put the cigar in his mouth. He struck a match and held it to the cigar. As he sucked, the flame fired up the cigar's tip in a red circle. He leaned back in his chair and exhaled. A plume of smoke rose into the thick humidity, hovering above him like an improbable halo.

Bongo drank his rum in silence. He'd be damned if he was going to be social with this man. He turned away and watched through the window as the clouds ganged up on one another.

Zapata puffed on his cigar and drank his chaser of Hatuey. He had come into La Terraza to reflect. Having Bongo across from him jarred his memory. He let his memory flow, fluid as a river of rum, drifting away to twenty years before.

Back then Zapata was a young policeman in Havana, a real green yucca. He was the lowest man in the pecking order, and having a rough go of it because he believed policemen should be good guys.

Most of his cohorts were stealing from parking meters, shaking protection dough from small businesses, or taking bribes from busted pimps. These cops had an easy life on the sugarcane train of corruption. They were promoted while Zapata was passed over. One day, he decided to get away from the grind where everybody was taking a bite out of everyone else's ass. He had to find a cheap place, since big money was for the higher-ups who got their split of payoffs and kickbacks. So he went to Cojimar. He wanted to fish and think.

The place he rented was in a group of five tiny bungalows gathered around a patio that sprouted a straggly, sunburnt palm. From the window of his bungalow Zapata could see around the curve of the harbor to the old stone Spanish watchtower on a hilltop.

Zapata's first day was relaxing. He had time on the water in his small rented boat to think while his fishing line bobbed. He wondered whether he could make it as a policeman. He wasn't naive; he knew the game. Did he want to play it?

By the second day of his holiday, Zapata decided to turn in his badge. He had a friend who was an accountant at the Coca-Cola factory. His friend told him there was big opportunity at Coke. Cuba had the sugar, Coke had the formula.

On the third day of Zapata's vacation, everything changed. A woman with two children checked into the bungalow next to his. Something about the trio compelled him to figure out their story. As a policeman, he was trained to discreetly observe.

The woman seemed happy enough, always fussing over her children. The girl was the same luscious licorice color as her mother, but the boy was white. Different fathers? But how could that be? They appeared to be exactly the same age, about seven, a black-and-white photo of identical sexual opposites. Except that the black girl had white hair; not blond hair—*white*. She also had the feline grace of her mother, moving with the agility of a jungle cat. Her brother never left her side. He always had a big grin on his face, as if he had just been given a birthday present.

The children loved to swim off a little fishing pier. They kept each other happy and amused. On hot afternoons idle tourists would stroll by, usually Americans who had stopped at La Terraza for lunch. For fun, the tourists would toss a coin off the end of the pier and the children would immediately dive for it in intense competition. They would pull themselves back up onto the pier, gazing raptly at the coin held out in one of their open palms as they laughed and water dripped down their bodies. Their bathing suits were identical, just white cotton underpants. The boy's minimal maleness was outlined at the center of his wet underpants when he stood up. When the girl stood, her white underpants clung to her wet black skin, making the cotton material transparent in the bright sunlight. When Zapata watched her he couldn't help but see, through the soaked cotton stretched around her waist, the pout of the budding flower between her legs.

The girl had no inhibitions. The very first time she saw Zapata watching her on the pier she waved back at him and laughed, then dove into the water. At that moment it was as if an arrow shot from a bow flew up from the sea where the girl disappeared and struck Zapata in the heart. When the girl resurfaced, his world changed forever. How carnal she looked, beyond her years, already aware that she was the stalker, a stealthy jungle cat, the Panther.

Zapata tried to grasp the meaning of the arrow that had pierced his heart, to pull it out before it did fatal damage. He recalled the words of a Spanish poem he had memorized years before:

> *Nobody understood the perfume*
> *of your belly's dark magnolia.*
> *Nobody knew how you tormented*
> *a hummingbird of love*
> *between your teeth.*

After this Zapata became restless. At night he couldn't sleep, for which he was thankful, for if he had not been awake he would not have witnessed what he had.

Zapata had wondered for some time why the woman with the radiant licorice skin was always alone. Was her husband dead? Was she divorced? On the run from a wife-beater? Then one night Zapata heard a loud racket from the bungalow next door. He went to the window and peered through the wooden slats. He could hear the voices of a woman and a man arguing, followed by the sound of things being thrown. Should he intervene?

The noise and shouting intensified. Zapata opened his door and walked out, but just as he did the door of the other bungalow banged open. A man staggered backward out of the doorway, as if drunk or reeling from a punch.

Zapata quickly slid into the shadows.

The mother of the children chased after the man—a white man, dressed in blue jeans and a rayon shirt printed with Hawaiian hula girls. The mother wore a clinging red dress. She moved steadily ahead on high-heeled yellow shoes. She raised her hand and smacked the man across the face. He lurched backward, banging up against the pathetic little palm tree in the center of the courtyard. He rubbed his hand across his mouth where she had hit him and stared defiantly back at her. She smacked him again. Blood trickled from the corner of his lip.

He grinned. "That was nice."

"You bastard!" She charged, slamming into his body.

The man threw his arms around her and she leapt up, hooking her legs around his waist. Her red dress rode high, exposing her smooth black bottom in the moonlight. With one hand she reached down and unzipped his pants, grabbing his stiff member as deftly as a black eagle snatching a white rabbit that had popped from its hole. He groaned while she moved furiously up and down, determined to break his manhood. She rode him as tears flowed down her cheeks. He crushed her lips with a tongue-ramming kiss. Their bodies banged against the pathetic palm. His manhood was planted in her center; she was going to tear it out by its root, or they were going to rip the palm tree out of the earth. Gasps of exasperation burst simultaneously from their lungs as they slid down the trunk of the palm, entangling at its base like writhing black and white snakes.

The next morning was very quiet. Zapata was surprised to find himself waking from a sound sleep. It was noon. The blades of the fan over his bed made the humidity worse, thwacking away at the salt-heavy air until it dripped in a light perspiring rain down onto

him. Groggy, he staggered to the washbasin. The heat was so oppres-
sive that even the cold water tap was spewing hot water. He remembered the night before. Did that really happen? Or was it one of those
dreams he had when the heat and humidity were stifling, dreams that
were like startling hallucinations?

Zapata quickly threw on his clothes and opened the front door,
half expecting to see the two lovers from the night before coiled at
the bottom of the palm tree in spent ecstasy.

The palm looked more pathetic than ever in its solitude. Its sunburnt fronds hung down in utter dejection, not even an idle breeze
was interested in touching it. Zapata walked over and stroked its
trunk. Last night had been only a dream, gone now.

It was the last day of his vacation. Zapata decided to treat himself to one final day on the ocean. Maybe this time he would catch a
good fish for dinner.

He went down to the water's edge. At the end of the rickety little
pier poking into the bay were the two children, clinging to each other
desperately, as if the wind of a hurricane were trying to tear them
apart.

A middle-aged white woman in baggy Bermuda shorts and a gar-
ish flower-splashed tunic walked out to the end of the pier and stood
behind the children. Her head was shaded from the sun by a straw
hat that declared on its crown, "Havana Olé!"

"Hey, kiddos!" the woman shouted in a jolly American accent.
"Let me take your picture with my new camera. You're both so
cute."

The children did not respond.

"Come on, don't play so hard to get."

The children did not turn around.

"What's wrong, kids? Cat got your tongue?"

No response.

"Oh, I get it." The woman dug a hand into the pocket of her
baggy shorts. "You cute seals aren't going to perform unless you get
paid for it." She pulled a coin from her pocket. "Here goes, kids."
She tossed the coin over the children's heads and it splashed into the
water.

The children did not move.

"Hey!" The woman was irritated. "That was two bits American! That's more than your daddy makes in a day."

The children remained silent.

"Have it your way," the woman snapped. "I'm not diving in after small change." She stomped off the pier.

The children remained motionless. Finally, they turned around, tears falling from their eyes.

Zapata suddenly had an intuition. "Jesus," he hissed, and ran back to the bungalows.

He raced into the patio with its pathetic palm. The door to his bungalow was closed, but the door to the one next door was wide open and sun was streaming in.

He could see into the front room. There was some cheap bamboo furniture and a faded maritime poster on the wall. A few children's items were scattered about, a sandal, a straw donkey, a plastic beach bucket.

Zapata knocked on the side of the door but got no response. He knocked again. Still no answer.

He stepped into the room, careful not to move too fast. What if his intuition was wrong? He would look like a fool. What if the mother suddenly appeared? How could he explain? Worse, what if the guy from last night appeared? Zapata knew about this kind of crew-cut ex-military American. They had fought in the jungles during the last World War. They had climbed over the bodies of their dead buddies with flamethrowers to burn Japanese soldiers out of hidden caves carved into coral rock. Zapata could imagine the guy shouting from the back bedroom, then stalking up the hallway out of the darkness. He would be naked, with only his dog tags dangling on a chain around his neck, a flamethrower gripped in his hands, and with a deep *whoosh* the orange flame would leap out, searing off Zapata's flesh.

Zapata took out his police identification badge and held it before him, as if it were an asbestos shield to protect him from the fury of hell as he headed down the hallway.

"Humberto Zapata, Havana police!"

No response.

He walked to the end of the hallway. The bedroom door was open. He cautiously peered in.

He was relieved to find no one. The bed was unmade. A few suitcases containing neatly folded clothes lay open on the floor.

The sound of running water came from behind the closed bathroom door.

"Excuse me," Zapata spoke softly. "Havana police. Don't be alarmed."

The water kept running. A slow, steady hiss.

He knocked lightly. "Pardon me, I came to tell you that your children are down by the pier. They're very upset. Perhaps you should attend to them?"

He put his ear to the door. Water continued to hiss.

He tried the doorknob, expecting it to be locked, but it clicked open in his hand.

He could see the sink, its faucet running water. He pushed the door open further.

Across white floor tile was a bathtub with a plastic curtain hanging in front of it.

"Don't be alarmed. Havana police."

No sound from the other side of the curtain.

Zapata placed his hand on the edge of the curtain and gently pulled it back.

What he saw was a sea of red.

Floating in the red sea was the woman in the red dress, adrift in her own blood. Her throat had been slit and a straight razor lay resting on her breasts. Zapata knew from the pallor of her face that she had been dead for hours.

The intuition he'd had when he saw the devastation in the eyes of the children at the end of the pier was right.

Zapata swung around. Where was that white son of a bitch that had killed the children's mother?

He yanked his gun from its holster under his jacket. He leveled the gun before him and walked back out into the hall.

Zapata remembered the night before, the man against the palm, his pants around his ankles, his muscular arms supporting the weight of the woman in the red dress as she wrapped her legs around his waist.

Zapata checked the closets. He looked under the beds. The tough guy wasn't hiding inside. Zapata went outside and stood on the cracked, sunbaked cement of the patio. Oh, God, he thought, the kids might have seen the murder. If so, they were the only eyewitnesses. The guy might come back to shut them up.

Zapata ran to the pier. The children still sat at the end of it, clinging to each other.

What could he possibly say to them? To comfort them, to win their confidence? He cleared his throat.

"You've been sitting out here for a very long time. Would you like to get out of the sun? Maybe come to the restaurant for some churros and a Coke?"

The children didn't turn around.

"I'm a policeman. Don't be frightened."

Without a word the children stood up, never letting go of each other's hand. Then, in a flash, they dove together into the water and disappeared beneath the surface.

Zapata hurried to the end of the pier. The children didn't come up.

He ripped off his jacket, unhooked his holstered gun and dove in.

He swam deep into the blue. How could they have gone down so far so fast? He kept swimming, his lungs beginning to burn. Then he saw them. Their legs and arms were intertwined to form one creature huddled at the bottom of the sea, sucking water into their open mouths to fill their lungs.

Zapata grabbed them both by the hair and yanked, swimming up with their already limp bodies. He broke the surface of the water, gasping for air, pulling the children with him to shore.

He lay on his stomach, coughing up water with the children. He heard a rough voice from above.

"What the fuck do you think you're doing?"

Zapata looked up.

It was the tough American. His big fist clutched the neck of a rum bottle as if it were a club.

Zapata thought of his gun on the pier, too far away. He was helpless.

The man fell to his knees and gathered the children up in his arms.

"I'm police," Zapata said. "Havana police."

"I don't give a fuck if you're the Texas Rangers," the man snarled. "What are you doing to *my kids*?"

Zapata had to think fast. This guy was the *father*. What if he was *innocent*?

"Your wife," Zapata said, his throat raw from coughing water.

"What about her? She's none of your business."

"In the bungalow. The children—"

The man's bloodshot eyes suddenly registered comprehension. "Goddamn! Don't tell me!" He let go of the children and ran to his bungalow.

Even as far away from the beach as the bungalow was, from inside could be heard the agonized howl of the man, who had come upon his wife with her throat slit by his own razor.

If the man was the killer, Zapata thought, he was also the world's greatest actor. Then again, maybe the man had been so drunk the night before that he had no memory of what he'd done.

Hearing the bloodcurdling cries, the children suddenly clung to Zapata as if he were still swimming with them in the depths of the sea.

The howling brought the whole village to life. People, including the police, came running from every direction.

Zapata quickly took charge. He was from Havana, he knew how to handle a crisis of this magnitude.

He ordered photographs to be taken of the victim and the bungalow's interior. He had everything dusted for fingerprints. Then he had the bungalow roped off against the morbid curiosity of the locals, some of whom had even tried climbing through the windows.

Zapata attempted to interview the stricken father, but the man gave him knife-throwing scowls. Zapata wanted to separate the man from the children. What if he was the murderer? But there was no proof. It could be a suicide as well as a murder. Zapata had to let the family be.

That night, after the photographers and fingerprint dusters were gone, after the ambulance had come and the woman's blood-soaked body had been raised from its sea of red, wrapped in a rubber sheet and driven away, Zapata returned to the deserted bungalow. He went through all the closets and dresser drawers. In one of the suitcases he found a note twisted up in a pair of ripped, child-size cotton underpants. It read: "I will kill your black magnolia."

Zapata thought of himself as a good policeman who could make connections and beat down doubts to get to simple deductions. How curious it was that the note had used the word *magnolia*. It was as if someone had read his mind when he saw the young girl on the pier, glistening in her wet underwear, and he recalled the poetic line: *"Nobody understood the perfume of your belly's dark magnolia."*

Was it just a coincidence? Zapata didn't believe in coincidence. He was determined to unravel this mystery.

The morning after Zapata found the note, he jerked awake from a deep sleep on the floor of the death bungalow with the magnolia note in his hand. He stared up at the ceiling fan. The monotonous whir of the blades was not what had awakened him. He heard the patter of rain striking the wooden window shutters outside. The raindrops were fat and tropical, whacking the wood with juicy splats. But that was not the sound that had awakened him either. There was another sound, a rhythmic slapping in the distance. He pushed himself up from the floor. The thought crossed his mind that he should have found a way to hold the father for suspicion of murder last night. The guy had probably taken the children and was halfway back to the United States by now. Zapata would never see them again. Good-bye to the mystery of the dark magnolia.

Zapata stepped outside the bungalow into the warm rain. What was the sound that had awakened him? It wouldn't stop. He walked toward the beach. The sound grew more insistent.

When Zapata came into view of the pier where the children usually were he stopped in surprise. They were there, standing stiffly, clothed only in their white cotton underpants. The fat drops of rain hit their exposed skin. Their heads had been shorn of hair. The white boy's black hair was gone, the black girl's white hair was gone, shaved clean. Behind them was their father. The man's muscled arms rose in the air and his big hands came down onto the children's heads, slapping their smooth skulls as if they were a pair of bongo drums.

Zapata couldn't intervene; the children weren't being hurt. The whole tableau seemed to be some kind of ritual. The nearly naked children standing in the rain looking out to sea as their father tried to communicate with his dead wife, using the only medium he thought she could hear. The sound of drumming traveled to the gray smudged horizon, where the water of the ocean met the water of the pouring heavens.

Zapata stood transfixed, carried away by the incessant rhythm. He listened to the percussive bongo beat, deep into it: if dark magnolia had a sound, this was it. But Zapata's mind didn't stop there. He thought of something that being a cop had already taught him. A wife would not normally harm herself if her husband cheated with another woman. But a hysterical wife might kill herself if her husband was cheating with his own daughter.

Zapata listened to the rhythm in the rain.

Pedro and Paulo were pissed off. They had stood out in the sun guarding a corpse in the trunk of the Plymouth and had never even been offered a beer. Now, on the drive back to Havana, they were sullen. What could the Captain and Bongo have had to talk about that was so important it kept them in La Terraza for so long?

Pedro wanted some rumba action to put him in a better mood. "Can I turn on the radio, Captain?"

"No."

"But, Captain, maybe some Beny Moré?"

"Yeah," Paulo chimed in. "Beny might even cheer up the stiff in the trunk."

Pedro and Paulo laughed in unison at the joke.

Seated in the backseat with Bongo, Zapata said nothing, which meant there would be no music. He was brooding about bigger issues. He felt that he alone knew the truth of life, the bribes from all sides, the triple-dealing and backstabbing. He had a pain in his heart for the country that he loved so much. There was a party going on, but on the edges of everyday life dark forces were gathering to stop the party and turn it into a wake. There had been a jailbreak the night before, two revolutionaries had shot their way out of prison. Sooner or later they would be caught and brought into the Blue Mansion, and then dumped in the Pineapple Field. But there would be others after these two, that was the real problem. Cut off two heads and five more popped up. He knew that the bombs going off at night in the city were not going to stop. A dog is never rid of fleas.

He didn't want the radio on because even on the airwaves there were little rumor bombs. The government did a good job of censoring out what the public didn't need to hear, but the government also slipped in rumors they wanted spread. A recent one was that Fidel Castro hadn't been on the leaky boat that chugged over from Mexico and landed a pathetic invasion force of eighty-two men. Most of the sons of bitches had been stuck in a swamp, cut off from food and supplies, and killed by government troops. The rumor had it that the great revolutionary had stayed behind in Mexico with a whore; this was based on a signed confession from a captured rebel. But Zapata knew confessions weren't worth the paper they were written on. Confessions could be beaten out of a man, or pulled out of him with his tongue. True lies. In fact, President Batista announced that Castro had been killed in the swamp after deserting his men. Lying truth. Zapata's own informants, those he pulled the truth from by letting them keep their tongues, said Castro was alive, and that there were enough hidden arms on the island for the rebels to fight a protracted war. Who was the cat and who was the mouse in this game?

Zapata spoke in his hoarse whisper. "Okay."

"Okay what, Captain?" Pedro asked.

"Okay for Beny Moré."

"Thanks a million, Captain." Pedro flicked on the radio and a silken stream of music wafted through the car.

"It's not Beny," Pedro said, hoping Zapata wouldn't make him turn it off.

"Leave it," Zapata answered. "It's María Teresa Vera."

Of all the songs to be playing, of all the little radio bombs that could be going off, none of them could have affected Zapata more than this one, a personal one, the song "Twenty Years." The song exploded in his heart like tiny pieces of memory shrapnel.

Pedro and Paulo in the front seat felt better now. At least they had music, even if it was woman's stuff; I lost my love and he's never coming back stuff.

"Say, Captain," Pedro asked with newfound enthusiasm, "do you want us to swing by and dump the stiff in the Pineapple Field?"

"I already told you, no." Zapata spoke low and even. "It's not that kind of situation. It isn't political. I want this one taken to the morgue. I want a full autopsy."

"You're not going to get a full autopsy"—Paulo scratched the stubble of his beard as he smirked—"because there's only half a man left."

Zapata didn't smile or answer, which meant Paulo had better be quiet. Paulo started humming to the tune on the radio. It was distracting Zapata.

"Paulo."

"Yes, my Captain?"

"Keep your mouth shut."

The growl of the American engine mixed with the lament of the habanera on the radio:

> *What's the point of loving you*
> *if you no longer love me?*
> *We shouldn't dwell on a love forgotten.*

Twenty years ago Zapata had seen his dark magnolia in the rain.

> *Now I'm history.*
> *I can't come to terms with it.*
> *Like a piece of the soul*
> *wrenched heartlessly away.*

María Teresa's plaintive words were sharp blades slashing across Zapata's face. He was bleeding from humiliation when she added the final cut:

> *If only we could make all our dreams*
> *come true, you would love me like you did*
> *twenty years ago.*

Had it really been twenty years? Zapata thought that he still looked the same. The only thing different was that he dyed his hair and mustache black now. It wasn't that he was trying to hide his age, it was more that he was paying homage to how he had looked twenty years before. Time had stopped for him then. He didn't want to be a graying guy looking backward. He wanted to be forever who he was at that moment when he first saw her. So what if people didn't think the color of his hair looked natural? His intention was pure.

Always at the end of "Twenty Years," as its music trailed away, Zapata felt a hand rise up and grasp his heart in its fist. He wasn't a softy; he didn't wear his heart on his sleeve. How could he, since his heart was clenched in a fist that pulled him into the grave? He kept his feelings buried, out of sight. But always at the end of the song he added his own verse, one that he had scribbled down two decades before:

> *Dear darling of death,*
> *darts of memory pierce*
> *my tongue as startled swallows*
> *swoop over my grave.*

Zapata quickly checked himself, brought himself back to the present. Enough of reverie. He whispered to Bongo seated next to him.

"The President isn't safe."

"Hell," Bongo answered, "nobody is safe from the President."

"You should be careful. That kind of talk can get you into trouble."

"I've already got trouble. Why am I on this little joyride?"

"Police business."

"How do I know we're going to the morgue? You could be taking me to the Blue Mansion."

A rumba rhythm jumped from the radio and filled the car. Pedro and Paulo slapped out the beat with their hands on the metal dashboard. They were happy now. Pedro floored the gas pedal and the Plymouth shot deeper into the outskirts of Havana.

Bongo looked out the window. They were passing through the slums.

"Castro," Zapata whispered, "an old fox in a young fox's body."

"I heard he wasn't killed in the invasion. That he's shacked up with a hooker in Acapulco."

"Don't believe everything you hear."

"Or read in the papers?"

"Both."

"Why are you telling me this? It's none of my business. It's not my fight."

"It's going to be. It's going to be everyone's fight. Sooner or later you'll have to choose."

"Cubans have been doing that since the turn of the century. It doesn't make any difference what they choose because they always end up getting something they didn't ask for."

"This time is different."

Outside, Bongo saw a small boy standing in the dust as the car passed. The boy wore no pants, just a tattered T-shirt. His belly was bloated—ironically, from eating almost nothing. He turned back to the doorway of a shack with a roof of dried palm fronds. Something dangled from the crack of the boy's buttocks, a flashing silver thread. Bongo knew what it was.

Bongo turned back to Zapata. "I don't know why you think this time is different. Everything is the same as before."

"That's just the point," Zapata agreed. He too had seen the tapeworm that had grown so big in the boy's gut that it dangled out of his butt. "Maybe this time these people will listen. If they do, God pity you, God pity me."

"I have nothing to fear. I'm not political, you know that."

"There isn't any such thing as being non-political. You're a man, you've got a penis. You can make love with it or you can piss with it. It's your choice."

"I'm not pissing my life away."

"No. If anything you're fucking it away."

"Man's fate. You should know about that."

Zapata didn't say another word the rest of the way back into Havana.

Bongo was thankful for the silence. Of all the people in the world not to be talking to him about a wasted life it was Zapata. Zapata didn't have a life, he had a trap, a trap of his own making.

The tires of the Plymouth slapped pavement. They were no longer on a dirt road but on the highway heading into downtown Havana. The traffic thickened, people were crowded onto the sidewalks, the buildings became larger. The great dome of the Capitolio hovered above the skyline.

The Plymouth pulled up in front of the morgue. The morgue was like many buildings in Old Havana, Spanish Colonial, hundreds of years old, built in a grandiose manner and rising four stories above the street. In former times it had been a nobleman's mansion, a bank, a prison, a hospital. Now the high-arched windows were bricked in.

Bongo hated the morgue, its subterranean stone vaulted rooms parading off into dark recesses where cadavers were stacked up in cubicles. He hated the smell as he walked with Zapata down a long corridor. The air was clammy, not humid like outside but dank, like the devil's private wine cellar.

From the opposite end of the corridor, a man scuttled toward them. He wore a blood-spattered smock over his clothes, and his shoes were covered with chalky dust. He seemed to be some kind of netherworld crab. The Crab's laughter sprang from an oversized clown-red tongue, echoing against the stone walls. "Hah-hah-hah!"

The Crab stopped. "What can I do for you? Bake a cake? Break an egg? Hah-hah-hah!" He circled around Bongo and Zapata as if sizing them up for a casket. "Are you here for yourselves, or for a relative?"

Zapata showed his police badge.

The circling Crab raised his eyebrows. "Do you have an appointment? Hah-hah-hah!"

"I'm Humberto Zapata. You knew I was coming."

"Oh, so you are *Captain Secret*. Tell me, if your kind are so secret, why do you drive around in cars marked 'Secret Intelligence'? What's the sense in that? Hah-hah-hah!"

"I've got a corpse for you. Fished out of the ocean off of Playas del Este. I want a full autopsy."

"Oh, goody, I hope it's a big fish. Hah-hah-hah!"

"Outside in my car, in the trunk."

"A most welcome guest here. Plenty of room at the inn. Hah-hah-hah!"

"How long will it take?"

"This is our busy season, Christmas–New Year's holidays, lots of gruesome suicides and juicy car wrecks. But since you have an appointment, I can work all night and have the happy results for you by morning."

"Thanks for fitting it into your busy schedule."

"It's like President Batista's palace around here, everybody dropping in asking for favors. I do my job, I don't play favorites. Roll 'em in, check 'em out, stack 'em up, they're all equal to me. Hah-hah-hah!"

"You've got a customer in here that I called about earlier."

"I get so many calls. Impossible to keep track."

"The one with no ID. You had some people in who might have been the parents, but they couldn't make a positive identification."

"Oh, I remember. Say, that woman was good-looking, but did she puke when she saw the customer. Just puked and puked, rice and beans all over the floor. And the hubby was no help, bawling like a baby. A man shouldn't be emotional."

"I brought someone who might make the ID."

The Crab peered at Bongo. "You're not a sissy, are you? You're not a puker? If you are I'm going to give you a bucket to heave up in. Hah-hah-hah!"

Bongo assured the Crab, "I don't need a bucket." Then he looked at Zapata. What was he up to? A terrible thought came over Bongo, a wave of nausea. What if Zapata's demented game was that he brought him here to ID his own sister?

"If you've seen stiffs before"—the Crab winked at Bongo—"then let's be on our merry way."

The Crab led them through a maze of corridors into a bone-chilling room. He read the numbers stenciled on the doors of cadaver lockers until he came to the right one. He pulled the door open and tugged on a steel pulley. Out rolled a body covered by a rubber sheet.

"Here you are," the Crab announced. "Fresh from the oven!"

"Let's have a look," Zapata urged.

The Crab grinned at Bongo. "Don't get queasy." He grabbed the corner of the sheet and ripped it off like a magician displaying a marvelous trick.

Bongo stared in horror.

Zapata coaxed Bongo to speak. "Can you make the ID?"

Bongo heard words, but they weren't Zapata's. He heard the words spoken the night before by Mr. Wu, while sitting in the back of the Packard Victoria: *"Let's say you just got married, you had your honeymoon night, it was bliss, and the next day your wife disappeared. . . . You searched and searched but couldn't find her. . . . Finally the police called and said they had someone who might be your wife at the morgue and they wanted you to come and identify her."*

"Do you know who she is?" Zapata whispered.

"So you go there. It is a depressing place. You go into a cold room."

Zapata whispered louder, "Who is it?"

Wu's words rang in Bongo's ears: *"The police roll out a cart with a body on it. You close your eyes, because you don't want to see her once smiling eyes. They ask, 'Is this your wife?' "*

"Tell me!" Zapata demanded.

"You just stand there, you don't want to know. She's not breathing; she's dead. You are afraid to inhale her scent, afraid to breathe. But you must know the truth. What do you smell?"

Zapata nodded to the Crab. "He can't come up with anything. Roll this abomination away."

"What do you smell?"

"Cinnamon!" Bongo shouted. *"Cinnamon and jasmine!"*

"What?" Zapata was confused.

Bongo felt the tears that would sting his eyes if he cried, but he wouldn't, couldn't. The mangled flesh before him was blackened and burned. He was afraid to inhale the scent. But he knew what it had once smelled like.

"Who is she?" Zapata prodded.

"Mercedes!" The name exploded from Bongo's chest. "I can tell from the bits of satin dress. . . . It's what she was wearing last night."

Zapata gripped Bongo's arm. "Are you going to throw up?"

"No!"

"If you hadn't gone outside to get that orchid from Wu, you would have been at Mercedes' side when the bomb went off."

"So what?"

"Who would want to kill *you*?"

BOOK TWO

tropical alibis

1.

No Virgins

Sweet Maria's night job was at the Three Virgins Bar. It was a tough joint where every creep could crawl, every crippled thought could talk, and every fly on the wall could hear it all. Guys spilled the guts of their lies as beer foamed, whiskey flowed, rum drummed. If a man came in hard through the door everyone would mark him and take him down with a shouted challenge. Or they would offer to buy him a bottle of booze, drink it with him, then club him over the head with the empty bottle. If a tough man survived being marked in the Three Virgins, then walked out into the night watching his own staggering shadow, he'd never see the knife that twisted into him sideways with a shout in his ear, "You're not so tough!"

Don't act tough in a place where the sun has melted every promise, where every man's grandfather worked a lifetime of fourteen-hour days with a machete, clearing jungle and hacking cane for the reward of two fistfuls of rice and beans a day. At the same time his wife's or sister's skinny ass was being whipped in a breeding shed by an overseer who made sure that no slave wasted a second, that no wench went more than a month after grunting out a baby before being knocked up again so she could grow another cocoa colored kid.

Don't act tough in the Three Virgins, act sorry. Sorry as hell, crazy as hell, mad as hell, full of jism and half-baked reason. Never act like you have anything to teach another man, or anything to put over on him. Never act like the master. No way. That's a disaster. Better to scratch your balls through your pants and move on with your bad self. Move on with a grin and don't order a gin but a sugarcane aguardiente, then laugh and say that gin is shit for the white suckers, or their boot-licking golf caddies, pool cleaners, lawn cutters, car washers, all of them trying to act like overseers. Be a man whose arm still twitches from swinging a machete every day like his daddy and granddaddy before him. If someone else is buying, then it's okay to have a rum, the darker the better, black if they've got it, damn near the consistency of tar if you can get it, then slug it down, shrug the world off. Don't shrug the world off because it gets up on top and beats you down. Shrug it off because life's not worth a shit. And don't act tough. Take another swig of rum or aguardiente, give a laugh. Don't worry who's looking over your shoulder, whether it be an angel or a devil.

Bongo watched Maria serving drinks behind the bar counter. He was just about to order another rum when he heard whistling cat-calls. He spun around on his stool. Through the swinging doors came Guy Armstrong, dressed in white pants and shirt, his blond American features gleaming, a white tennis sweater looped casually over his shoulders, white plastic sunglasses set squarely on his nose.

The American moved through the room, parting the crowd of men as if they were mere waves making way for his grand cruise ship, sailing high, white and mighty right up to the bar, where his butt docked on a barstool, still stinging from all the slaps it had taken as it moved through the waves to its momentary safe harbor. Armstrong pulled out a wad of dollars and slapped them on the bar. "Maria," he called, "aguardientes for all of my amigos." And amigos he did have. They surrounded him like the gulls that follow a fishing boat to port hoping to feast on the knifed-out guts being thrown overboard or on the swill of the bilge floating to the water's boiling surface. It made no difference to these scavengers. Food was food, dollars were dollars, drinks were drinks, and they were being offered by a man who wasn't bothered by the surrounding rough hands that came pawing out of the air, trying to touch his green money, his white skin, to cop a feel between his legs or filch the fat wallet from his pocket.

Maria poured out shots of thick, sweet aguardiente to the sea of insistent hands around Armstrong. Her long black hair swished around her as she swiveled on high-heeled shoes. The shoes were red and glittering, like the sparkling red eyes of a snake writhing on the floor, or Dorothy's runaway shoes from the movieland of Oz, inexplicably here, in a waterfront dive on the edge of Havana Bay.

The surrounding frenzy grew more insistent. It wasn't Bongo's beat, these queer and not so queer fellows who would steer in any direction the money was blowing them. The aguardiente was having its effect. The floor swelled up and heaved. From the jukebox blasted an American voice. *"They'll be love letters in the sand."*

Guy Armstrong raised his aguardiente glass to the gang of admirers surrounding him in tight tank-top T-shirts that exposed their muscled arms glistening with sweat. Armstrong opened his mouth and lip-synched to the American voice pulsing from the jukebox, *"They'll be loooove leettteers in the saaaand."* Most of the men didn't understand the English words. They couldn't even write their own names in Spanish, since they'd been thrown into the bottomless pit of the labor pool before they were old enough to go to school. But they lip-synched along because the words were empty of meaning and easy to mimic, and because the alcoholic sugar of the cane fields was coursing in the blood history of their veins. As the night outside turned bluer-black, and the waves of the ocean pounded in furious spray along the stone-walled Malecón in the distance, it seemed certain that tonight at the Three Virgins some lucky soul's ship was going to come in, and maybe it would even come in twice.

Bongo glimpsed the edge of a two-dollar bill tucked into the top of Sweet Maria's bra, exposed above the skimpy ruffle of her low-cut blouse. Maria was covering all her bets. She crooned right along with the others as she worked her way down the bar, pouring out more shots from a fresh bottle of aguardiente. She stopped in front of Bongo, the bottle poised over his glass. Her low voice was flirtatious as she flicked her long black eyelashes. "How come you aren't singing, white boy?"

"It's not my beat."

"And what is your beat?"

Bongo's hands came up. He held them open-palmed over the glossy wood of the counter. His fingers came down in a flurry, beating out a fierce, complicated rhythm.

"I like you." Maria's sultry voice deepened as her eyelashes seemed to lengthen. She refilled Bongo's glass. "I've seen you before."

"We've never met."

"You can't fool Sweet Maria. You're the quiet type. I like quiet."

"I've never been in here. Must have me confused with someone else."

"No, we don't get many white ones. When we do, I remember. You've been coming here a lot lately."

"All of us white boys look alike."

Maria laughed. "That's right, when you're naked on a bedsheet you're all white as ghosts. You ever made love to a ghost?"

"I guess we've all made that mistake once or twice." Bongo finished off his drink. The sugar hit raced through his blood. Maria did look familiar, and not just from when he had been in the bar. Where had he seen her?

"Can you do that again?"

"Make love to a ghost?"

"No. What you just did with your hands."

"It was just noise."

"I know that beat, it's African. Where would a white boy learn how to do that?"

"I guess he would start by spending a long time in the dark."

Maria shook her head. "I don't believe you."

"Why not?"

"Because the sound you just made doesn't come from the night. It comes from the day. It comes from the African sun, from the *yuka* drum."

Bongo slipped his hands into his pockets. "Maybe you didn't hear what you thought you did."

"Oh, I heard it all right. Just what kind of a girl do you think I am, not to hear a sacred drumbeat?"

"I'm sure you're a good girl."

"That's right. And it's Queen Erzulie that makes me do bad things that are good for her." Maria crossed herself and touched the two-dollar bill sticking out of her bra.

Bongo winked. "Erzulie's going to make you do something bad right now?"

"She might." Maria leaned forward. She shook her long hair, it smelled like burning hemp. "Queen Erzulie makes me smoke cigars and drink rum. She makes me chase men."

Bongo looked over his shoulder. Armstrong was leading his fans in a new song from the jukebox.

"Is that what you're interested in?" Maria nodded to Armstrong.

"What?" Bongo feigned ignorance.

"The rich American? I'm surprised. You don't look the type."

"What the hell would make you think I am?"

"The way you look at him."

"Just curious."

"About what? What's he have that I don't?"

"You can't be serious."

"Okay, he's got white skin and money. It ain't only money, honey."

Out of the corner of his eye, Bongo saw Armstrong moving.

"I've got to go."

"Don't go." Maria placed her hand over his. "Sometimes Queen Erzulie makes me say bad things."

"I'm sure you're a good girl." Bongo pulled his hand away.

Guy Armstrong was off his stool and plunging into the crowd.

"A *very* good girl." Bongo slapped a peso tip down as he moved quickly away, not wanting Armstrong to get out of the bar before he did.

"You'll be back," Maria called, batting her eyelashes. "I know your kind. Sweet Maria will be waiting."

Outside the Three Virgins, Bongo waited in the Rocket convertible, its canvas top pulled up and windows rolled tight. He didn't want Guy Armstrong to spot him when he came out. Bongo lit up a Lucky Strike. He cracked a window, the cigarette smoke drifted out into the night. What was keeping Armstrong in the bar so long?

Bongo punched the glove compartment button and the lid dropped down. He pulled out a manila envelope and dumped its contents onto the passenger seat. In the dim light the photographed faces of three college girls smiled up. He ran his gaze over the faces, the

large brown eyes, the sweet curve of lips, the expressions of inno-
cence. He had examined the faces many times in the last week. His
interest went beyond the fact that the girls were friends of Mercedes'
and had been in the Tropicana on New Year's Eve. He was interested
because their mothers had come to his office; three weeping women
begging for his help in finding their missing daughters. They had been
to the police, who had taken money from them and promised to
investigate. Weeks went by without any word. When the mothers
returned to the police, they were told that their daughters had been
kidnapped and killed by terrorists. The police took more of their
money, claiming they would find the bodies. But there were still no
bodies. The grieving mothers believed Bongo could help; he understood how to investigate disaster, that was his job.

Bongo heard a car. A Chrysler Imperial limousine pulled up, its
headlights glowed like dragon eyes above the malevolent grin of the
slanted chrome grille. The deep throb of the Imperial's engine was cut
and three people climbed out. Bongo could tell right away they were
Americans, but not because of the car. Many Cubans had American
cars. They were obviously slumming it in a Cuban dive after a late
night at the casino. One of them was short, muscular and bald; he
moved with the square-shouldered forward lean of a boxer in the
ring. The other guy was big and blubbery, with a head like a watermelon clobbered by a sledgehammer, his face raw and red, and the tip
of his tongue dripped out one side of his mouth like a slobbering
Doberman. The woman was a big-breasted blonde, but not a blonde
like Mrs. Armstrong; this one was a peroxided dame. She tugged at
her short skirt as she hobbled on high heels. The Doberman growled
something at her as he watched the swell of her ass under the skirt
she had just yanked into submission. The woman's crispy voice sang
back to the Doberman, *"Chicks and ducks and geese better scurry,
when I take you out in my surrey."* The Doberman looked perplexed;
not knowing what to do, he slapped the bald man on the back of
the head. The bald guy turned around with a snarl. The peroxide
blonde giggled, the two men grunted at each other, and they all went
into the bar.

Laughter and excited shouts seeped through the thin wooden
walls of the Three Virgins. The front door flew open and two men

staggered out, but they weren't the two who had just gone in. The men had their arms around each other's necks, clenched in a rough embrace. Each gripped the long neck of a beer bottle, appearing ready to bash the other.

Bongo slipped the envelope with the photos of the college girls into the glove compartment and slid lower in the front seat. Over the top of the dashboard, he tried to get a clear look at the faces of the two men as they weaved in front of the bar. One of them, dressed in white, could be Armstrong. They both dropped their beer bottles, unzipped their pants and flipped out their dicks. They swung around, each with one arm still around the other's neck, laughing as they sprayed piss against the wall of the Virgins.

The bar door slammed open again and two more men stumbled out into the night. They swung around and unzipped their pants. "Charge on, team!" shouted the man in white. "Let's give this old wall a new paint job!"

The voice was definitely Guy Armstrong's. Bongo slid lower in the seat, completely out of sight. He heard mumbling and pants being zipped up, followed by footsteps and car doors opening and slamming shut. Engines started and tires spun out on gravel.

Bongo popped up from behind the dashboard and looked around. Two cars were speeding away in different directions, their red taillights winking through a veil of dust. Which car was Armstrong's?

Bongo turned the key in the Rocket's ignition, flicked on the headlights, and drove off behind a pair of red taillights. There was a fifty-fifty chance he had the right prey in sight. But he hung back. He couldn't afford to get close enough to the car ahead to see if it was the right one. He couldn't take the chance of being spotted. The car sped up. Bongo glanced down at the speedometer glowing in a green circle on the dashboard; a black arrow pointed to "80." He turned off his headlights, racing through the dark.

Bongo gripped the steering wheel with both hands. There was no moon and he couldn't see the black asphalt. He had to gauge the contours of the road by the red tracers of taillights ahead. The tires squealed. If he calculated wrong the Rocket would swerve onto the dirt shoulder and flip over.

Suddenly the glare of oncoming headlights beamed into Bongo's eyes. In the opposite lane another car was passing the car ahead. If the Rocket was far enough to the right, Bongo was safe; if the Rocket was over the invisible center line, the two cars would crash head-on.

Bongo had to think fast. Should he switch on his headlights to signal the oncoming car that he was there? If he did, he would give his position away to the car that he was following. He left the lights off. The rhythmic vibrations of the road pulsed through the Rocket's tires, its beat whirred up through the chassis. Through his grip on the steering wheel, Bongo got the beat. He felt where he was on his own song line as the onrushing car bore down on him with blinding headlights.

A wind-knocking *whoosh* whipped the air outside the driver's window of the Rocket as the other car blasted by. A sharp metal clang reverberated in Bongo's ear and the Rocket shuddered. Bongo held tight to the steering wheel. He glanced down to see the reflection of the other car in his outside mirror, but the mirror had been ripped off by the passing car. That was the metal clang he had heard.

Bongo looked up into the rearview mirror. He could see the car behind him in the illumination of its own taillights. The car screeched to a stop. Two men jumped out to see what their car had hit. Bongo recognized Pedro and Paulo, which meant that Zapata was inside. What was he doing prowling around at this late hour?

Bongo turned his eyes back to the road ahead. The car he had been chasing slowed down, turned off onto a side road, then zigzagged through dusty streets crowded with small houses. It stopped in front of a house. Bongo cut the Rocket's engine and rolled to a quiet stop a few houses away. He could make out the shape and make of the car he had been following. It was definitely Guy Armstrong's white Cadillac, as out of place here as a cruise ship beached on a mountaintop.

Armstrong got out and looked suspiciously around, as if suspecting that he had been followed. Then he rapped his knuckles on the car roof, and from the opposite side of the Cadillac emerged a young man with a slender build. He walked up to the house and unlocked the front door. Armstrong followed, closing the door behind him.

No lights came on inside the house. Bongo waited. Still no lights. He decided it was safe enough to get out and try to see something through the house's windows. Just as he opened the Rocket's door and stepped out, a car swerved around the corner in front of him, its headlights illuminating the street.

Bongo threw himself back into the convertible, lying flat on the front seat. He reached up to the glove compartment, popped it open, fingered under the manila envelope of photos, and pulled out his revolver.

The other car rolled alongside the Rocket, its engine rumbling.

Bongo twisted around on the front seat, lying on his back. He checked the gun to make certain it was loaded. He had a good view up through the Rocket's side window. If someone intended to jump him they were in for a surprise.

The car pulled forward, its engine was cut. Doors opened and slammed. Footsteps ran away.

Bongo inched his way up on the front seat until he had a view over the dashboard through the windshield.

He was surprised to see the two men who had joined Armstrong in pissing on the wall of the Three Virgins. They walked up to the front door of the house Armstrong had disappeared into. One knocked on the door. The door stayed closed. The man knocked again. The door cracked open. Armstrong's white face peered out, the two men quickly went inside. Armstrong closed the door.

Bongo waited three hours. No lights came on inside. He lit up his last Lucky and turned on the radio, keeping the sound low. He found a Miami station—only the Florida stations were on this late. Only the Americans worked and played twenty-four hours a day, never giving themselves time off, every moment was a job. A song drifted to a melodious end. The radio announcer came on, his voice intimate and wrapped in the folds of the night's inky darkness. "The next tune is by Miss Peggy Lee, so cuddle up next to your baby."

Bongo had no baby to cuddle up to. He gripped the handle of his revolver tighter and thought of Mrs. Armstrong. Peggy Lee was one of her favorites, along with Johnnie Ray. He remembered Mrs. Armstrong's blond hair cascading in front of his face and the scent of her perfume. Peggy Lee began to sing. Bongo was startled. It wasn't what he had expected. It sounded exactly like Mrs. Armstrong. The seductive tone spilled with creamy danger, knowing it had all the time in the world to find its mark, knowing it had the target all to itself, clearly in sight, inevitability just around the corner.

> *I hear you speak my name,*
> *softly in my ear*
> *you breathe a flame.*

The breathy voice panted into Bongo's ear.

> *Why quarrel without bliss*
> *when two lips want to kiss?*

The languid music seemed to be coming from the lips of a siren deep in the depths of the ocean, rising up in a lush tide. A watery darkness fell over Bongo and he floated away. He saw his sister holding out her hand to him in a flood, she was skinny and naked, only a child. She cried for his help as she clung desperately to a tree, her fingernails digging into the bark. The water was rising up far above Bongo's head, a deafening torrent, a liquid roar. His sister's mouth opened as she cried again for his help, but the water silenced her words. He swam toward her, past chickens and goats and turtles and sharks and dead people tumbling in the massive current. He tried to reach her, but he was a drowning boy in a drowning universe. He kicked his feet in the murky water, heading up. He kicked harder until his body broke the surface and he gasped for air, looking around. The flat surface of the water was everywhere; the earth was inundated. He gazed up. The sky was clear blue. The passing hurricane that had raised the waters had swept the heavens clean. Only a vast yellow sun was blazing, and from it came tumbling a giant white spider, falling straight into his face.

Bongo jerked awake in the front seat of the Rocket, gasping to get his breath back. The sun was beating down on the car. He sat up, grabbed the rearview mirror, and twisted it down to peer at his face. Was he visible or a drowned ghost? The mirror was fogged over with moisture. He swiped it clear with the back of his hand. His face was covered with sweat. He could still feel the white spider that had just been crawling on his skin. Then he remembered another face: the black face of the woman in white at the Tropicana, just before the blast. In his mind's eye he could see her ebony hand banging down on the table in front of Mercedes, crushing the spider. The face was Sweet Maria's. On New Year's Eve Maria's black face had been framed by a white bandanna and she wore no makeup. Stripped of her mask, she had looked completely different from the Sweet Maria who poured aguardiente behind the bar at the Three Virgins.

Bongo rolled down the window of the convertible, sucking in fresh air. Suddenly he was spooked, his body jerked involuntarily. Shadowy shapes surrounded the car. He thought he saw his sister and the three college girls. Then the shapes came into focus. Children encircled the Rocket, standing mute as they stared at him. How long had they been there?

Bongo rubbed his eyes and looked past the children. Guy Armstrong's Cadillac was gone, and so was the other car. The street was deserted. It was as if everything the night before had been a dream.

Monkey Shines was born on a street named bitterness, but he was an eternal optimist. He was a small man, his body was thin and hard, all twitching muscle and jangling bone. His skin was as black as the stain of indigo ink leaking from a fountain pen clipped to the white shirt pocket of a prosperous businessman. Shines wasn't prosperous, but he was industrious. This industry kept him moving all day long in the hot sun at his "office" beneath the palms on the steps of the marble José Martí monument in Parque Central. He sat hunched over on a rickety wooden box, shining the shoes of men who stood above him with one foot steady on the ground, the other foot propped up on the box. All day long the sun came and went over this scene, beating down on the larger-than-life marble figure of Martí, first father and first martyr of modern Cuba, his right hand outstretched before him, pointing toward freedom's future promise. No matter how hot it got, Martí remained vigilantly cool, despite his suit and long overcoat. Below him, carved in stone around his inscrutable perch, stood children, women and men, looking up in awe, or ahead with a resistant gaze.

Martí was the hero of all Cubans, and Shines had an honored spot at the great man's feet. He often imagined, just to keep himself going through the long hours of tedium, that he was shining the shoes of the great man himself. But never were the shoes he shined those of great men. Great men were no longer in Cuba. At best, the shoes Shines polished were those of important men of government, commerce or sport; at worst, they were those of elected criminals, small-time thieves or wife-beaters.

Shines never had to look up at the face or clothing of a customer to know what kind of a man he was. He intuited from the leather of the man's shoes, from the feel of the man's foot beneath as he rubbed on polish with his bare hands, whether a man was righteous or not. Shines could make conversation with men as he waxed their leathers without ever making eye contact, for he felt that if the eyes of a man were the windows to his soul, then his feet were the result of how he carried himself through the journey of life. The feet didn't lie, they were formed by where they had been, they couldn't hide their secrets.

Secrets were not hard for Shines to come by. Many of the men who stood above him considered him a shoe-shining machine that showed up ready for business at dawn as the red sun crept up over the immense Capitolio dome down the street. They assumed that there was no more brain between the two ears of Shines' shaved black head than there was between the ears of a black mule. These men would talk to their companions, if they had stopped by together for a quick spit shine, or to other men waiting for a shine, if they were getting a double-dip polish. Mostly the talk was about the weather, about sugar prices, about some undeserving cigar roller or canecutter who had won the lottery, about yesterday's baseball game at El Cerro Stadium. Sometimes the talk was about women, which ones were worth five minutes of a man's time to stick it to, which ones wanted it but pretended not to. The talk was never about wives; wives didn't seem to exist. But sometimes the talk was about big money and big deals, about political payoffs and personal back-stabbings. From all this talk, secrets would fall like coins onto Shines' shiny head, leaving their indelible imprint on his memory. Even in the shadowless glare of the tropical noon, Shines knew everything that was moving between men in Havana.

There were those with whom Shines would share these secrets, others to whom he would sell them, and some who would have to kill him before he would ever reveal a damn thing.

Shines had been feeling the feet of men in shoes since he was six years old. Six years old, working the streets with his battered little shoe box slung over his shoulder and bigger boys beating him up, stealing his meager tin of polish and smashing the box. But Shines was an optimist. He kept on walking the streets, tugging on men's trousers, grinning up at them, offering a shine. Shines learned early on that people don't give money to beggars to help the poor. They gave money to make *themselves* feel better. So young Shines offered free shines, an offer hard to refuse, and when the shoeshine was done, after a little polish, a lot of spit and ripping of the rag, the man would feel guilty and shove a coin into the offered hand of the skinny kid below him. Shines learned that there was money to be made off another man's guilt. No matter how high and mighty a man was, he felt guilty about something. A man might be wearing a fine suit and expensive shoes, but maybe he slapped his wife at breakfast because he didn't like the way she buttered his toast, or he kicked the family dog on the way out of the house, or he cheated on how much money he dropped into the charity basket passed around at church on Sundays. There were a million things, both large and small, that a man could feel guilty about.

Just as a fortune-teller peers into a crystal ball, Shines could touch a man's foot beneath his shoe leather and know where he had been and where he was headed. It wasn't the bunions that Shines felt, or the toes that were sometimes bunched or bent, that spoke to Shines. No, Shines could feel the *vibrations* of a man's soul in his foot, like the wind blowing through the top of a tree. When Shines didn't like the vibration he was feeling, he gave a short shine. When he liked the vibration, he gave a double shine and extra wax. And then there were the times Shines dreaded, when he felt no vibration at all. Then he knew he was shining the shoes of a dead man, a devil who had escaped from the grave, stolen the horse of another man's existence and was riding around on it. Or perhaps there was no vibration because Shines was shining the shoes of a man who was about to die but didn't know it.

Shines loved his job. It was good money, better than selling peanuts. He had once thought of selling lottery tickets, but he didn't have the connections for that; a guy needed to have a relative in the government or be a friend of racketeers, it was all the same thing. The problem with the lottery was too many hands were in the stew, taking all the meat out and leaving the seller with nothing but flavored water. No, that was not for Shines. He was an entrepreneur, an optimist, and Cuba was a great country that gave a man like him a break, a man who some said was slow in the head because of what had happened when he was a baby.

Shines' mother had been a rummy, and when he was three months old she had passed out once while breast-feeding him. Little skinny-assed naked Shines was alone in his mama's lap, his lips smacking on her nipple as he sucked, not for milk, but for air. His mama was suffocating him as she snored, her large breasts covering his tiny face. When the neighbors found him he was blue and had stopped breathing. They couldn't wake his mama up. She was dead, choked on her own vomit.

Baby Shines was spirited away by the neighborhood women, who delivered him to the altar of a Santera who consulted her Book of Shadows and determined the recipe needed to bring this humble soul back among the living. A spell was put on baby Shines. The Santera rubbed his small body with shark oil, blew cigar smoke up his nostrils, pried his lips open and breathed clouds of cinnamon-scented breath inside his mouth, then covered his face with a wet handkerchief soaked in the tears of a motherless woman. The Santera chanted to a horse beneath the sea; she uncovered Shines' face, then laid him down before a kid goat tethered to a stake. The goat licked Shines all over, and when it got to licking the baby balls between his legs, Shines' little chest heaved, his heart started to tick, his lungs began to work, and a crooked smile came onto his lips. The Santera slit the throat of the goat and its blood sprayed over Shines. The goat fell at the side of Shines, its feet twitching, its wide bulging eyes crossing over to darkness as Shines' eyes once again saw the light.

Shines was an optimist, he had come back from the dead. In his community he was considered a miracle. Even though he had no parents, he was always welcome at the homes of total strangers to share the meager food on their table. Women believed it was bad luck to turn their back on a miracle child, for if they did all their babies would be stillborn. Childless women were always happy to give Shines a scrap of clothing or a hug, hoping some of his once-upon-a-time magic would bless their wombs. But it appeared that the time Shines had spent over on the dead side of the world as a little baby had left him a touch slow in the head, or so people said. Others said he wasn't slow at all, just a kid without a mama and papa and nobody to teach him.

To Shines the feel of shoe leather beneath his fingertips held a kind of magic, because those skins had once housed souls, once belonged to the kingdom of animals. Now Shines kept them alive, kept them in proud shape, kept them ready for the journey of the man whose feet filled them. Shines thought it wasn't a man's feet that led him around, but rather the spirit of the animal in the skin of his shoes that determined his final destination.

Shines was bent right now over shoes that had obviously come up from a dark underworld. He had shined these particular skins many times. The man's feet didn't vibrate, they hummed. It was a harmonic sound, like songs murmured by the dead who have had their tongues cut out. The more Shines whipped his shoe-rag across the skins, the stronger the humming grew. This man was an *alabbgwanna*, a lonely spirit. He was a big spell and he wandered looking for the Goddess of Love. This man walked through Havana with an ax of rejection in his back and an arrow of loss shot through his heart. Shines felt sorry for him, though he knew that others feared him. This man was a restless spirit who wouldn't take any shit off any man, so Shines kept silent. Only when the man asked a question would Shines dare to speak.

"What kind of a woman would hire another man to follow her husband around?" the man asked in a whisper.

Shines rested his rag on the man's skins and gazed up at him. Behind the man was the brilliant sun, shooting spikes of light all around his head. The man's eyes were blacked out by the dark lenses of the silver-rimmed sunglasses he always wore, and a black mustache stretched across his upper lip like a burnt worm.

The man asked the question again. His voice remained low, a kind of hollow breathing, hard to hear in the noise of traffic circling and honking in the streets around the Martí monument.

Shines snapped his shoe-rag over the man's skins. On the middle finger of the man's right hand, which rested against his creased linen slacks, was a ring with a ruby as big as the eye of an angry octopus.

"Tell me. What kind of woman would pay someone to spy on her husband?"

"Well, Captain Zapata," Shines offered, "maybe the woman is trying to triumph over her enemies."

"And who might those enemies be?"

"Could be love devils . . . or political witches."

"Political witches?"

"There are all kinds of witches."

"I know."

"Sometimes witches get tangled up, and it's hard to untangle them, so you need to hire a spy."

"A kind of love spy? You're saying that love can become politics?"

"I'm saying sometimes love *is* politics."

"And what kind of man would take money to follow a woman's husband around?"

"A man who needs money," Shines said with enthusiasm.

"Or a man who wants the woman."

"Maybe he doesn't know how much he wants her yet. Maybe he is still dreaming. It could get worse if he wakes up."

"Let's say he wakes up. What then?"

"He might start doing stuff for her."

"What kind of stuff?"

"Stuff he normally wouldn't do. Could be a tragic story. Like that famous story that all my people know."

"There are a million famous stories your people know. How does your story end?"

"Here's how it *begins*." Shines bore down with his rag on the shoe propped up on the shining box as his words flowed. "A wife is being cheated on. She confronts her husband. He says she's no longer his *yerba dulce*. He leaves her. She goes to a Santera for advice. The Santera washes the wife's eyes out and she sees what to do. She goes to the husband's new house. In her hands she holds a white candle and a drained coconut shell. She knocks on the husband's door, but he won't open up to a spurned wife armed with weapons from a Santera. She beats on the door. When the husband shouts, 'Go away, witch,' she presses the coconut shell against the door, capturing his voice. She quickly plugs the hole in the coconut shell with the white candle. The husband's voice inside the hard shell of its prison screams for freedom. She races to a palm tree and digs furiously until she exposes its roots. She buries the coconut in the roots with only the white candle showing. She lights the candle. She doesn't have much time now. Before the candle burns down she must find a black chicken. She runs through the neighborhood. But all the chickens pecking in people's yards are white. She sees black goats, black rabbits, black pigs, and finally a black chicken. She chases it into a house where a man is sitting. She is panting, her dress soaked with sweat, and she screams that she must have the chicken. The man says that's impossible, the chicken is a member of the family. The wife shouts, 'I'll pay anything!' The man's children come in; the chicken is cackling, the sweating wife is shouting, the kids don't like it. The kids surround the chicken, begging their father not to sell their best friend, to sell it would be like selling one of them. The wife slips off her shoulder purse and dumps its contents before the man, an old comb, a few crumpled peso bills, and an ebony-handled knife. The man counts the bills. 'Not much here,' he says. He runs his thumb over the knife's ebony handle. 'This knife has led an interesting life.' The wife says, 'I can't sell it.' The man shakes his head. 'No knife, no chicken.' The children shout with glee and a little girl hugs the chicken to her. The wife pleads to the man, 'Sell me the chicken. It's a matter of life or death.' The man says, 'This is a holy chicken, it deserves a holy price.' The wife shouts, 'I'll give you my dress, too. It's not handmade, it's store-bought.' She grabs the dress, ready to pull it off. The man says, 'I don't need a dress. My woman left me long ago.' He looks at the wife standing before him. She has a very broad bottom and thighs like tree trunks, he envies her husband. The wife pulls off her wedding ring and hands it to the man. He gazes at the ring, she gazes at the chicken. The man slips the ring onto his little finger. The wife grabs the knife, snatches the chicken from the little girl's grasp, and runs from the house back to the palm tree. Beneath the tree, the candle in the coconut has burned down to the hole it was wedged in. Within seconds the hot wax will cave in, opening the hole and allowing the husband's essence to escape. The wife holds the clucking chicken by the neck against the palm's trunk. The bird's clawed feet scratch at the wife's arms. She plunges the knife into the chicken's breast. The bird squawks, then the surprised moan of a man bursts from its beak. The wife steps back. The pierced chicken is stuck to the palm. Everything has been done as the Santera instructed. The wife looks down. The wax in the hole of the coconut collapses inward. The hole is open. But it is too late for her husband's essence to escape back into his body. The spell has been cast."

Shines stopped speaking and took a deep breath.

Zapata said nothing. He gazed at the royal palms lined on both sides of the Martí monument like towering sentries.

Shines looked up at Zapata. "The day after the wife knifed the chicken her husband was found dead."

"How did he die?"

"Burned to death. He dumped gasoline on himself and lit a cigar for a farewell puff. Went out in a ball of fire."

"And the wife?"

"She got married to the man who sold her the chicken. But she could have married any man she wanted."

"Why's that?"

"After what happened, every man was afraid to resist her."

"You believe this story?"

"It happened."

"You think it could happen again?"

"A cheating husband can always go up in a ball of fire."

Zapata took a cigar out of his coat pocket, bit off the end, struck a match and lit up. He puffed on the cigar, smoke curling from the corners of his mouth like two question marks. He dug into his pocket, then handed Shines a peso.

Shines grinned broadly. "It's two pesos today. One for the shine, one for the story."

"That's expensive."

"It's a holy story."

Zapata reached into his pocket, then pressed another peso into Shines' open palm. "It's worth a holy price."

2.

The Pineapple Field

I hate this fucking bar."

"Then what are we doing here?"

"Being here is part of the job." Larry Lizard leaned back in his chair and locked his fat sausage fingers around the cocktail glass in front of him. He gazed contemptuously over at the long bar where people sat chatting and drinking on cushioned stools. Behind the counter, bartenders in tight short-waisted red jackets mixed concoctions in tall glasses. "Fucking ice-cube jockeys," Lizard said. "They act like they're checking test tubes for a polio cure every time they blend one of their pukey sugary daiquiris."

"What's the name of this place?"

Lizard squinted at Johnny PayDay and spit out the answer with disdain. *"Floridita."*

"Never heard of it."

"It's one of the smart places to park your ass in the old part of Havana. Socialites, rich tourists, politicians, show business people, famous writers, assholes like that come here."

"What about Joe Louis? He's not an asshole, but he's famous. Was Joe Louis here?"

"They don't let niggers in unless they're famous. Niggers know that, so they don't push it. Niggers don't push it in Cuba."

"Not like that place we were in last night. What was it called? The Two Somethings?"

"The Three Virgins."

"It's not swanky like this."

"It's a fucking pit."

"You said the Bad Actor would be there."

"Sometimes he is. You've got to understand Havana, it's not like other towns. Here the high people go to low places. Nobody gives a shit about appearances here except the middle-class types. Middle-class Cubans can be even more stuck-up than the Americans. The really rich Cubans and Americans, they stay mostly among their own, behind the walls of their villas or in their private clubs. Keep an eye open, though, and you'll see them come out to prowl."

"I've kept a bead on the Bad Actor for two weeks. He's done nothing unusual. He's just seedy, diddling that carrot-top teenager he's with. I didn't come down here to be a baby-sitter."

"You'll get your shot."

PayDay took out a PayDay candy bar and carefully unwrapped it. He bit off a chunk of the caramel slab and washed it down with a swig of beer. He had a lot to think about, he had to get the lay of the land.

"You see that guy over there?" Lizard nodded toward the end of the bar.

"The blond guy?"

"Yeah. The one with the white tennis sweater slung over his shoulders the way a dame would wear a mink stole. You remember him?"

"No."

"He was in the Virgins last night. He's a very rich guy."

"Looks like it."

"He's also a race-car driver. He's in the Big Malecón Race coming up. Races a Ferrari."

"A what?"

"One of those fast German cars or something."

"I'm from Detroit. I don't care about foreign cars."

"You'd better start to care. You've got a job to do during the Big Race."

"I'm itching for it. I want my pay."

Lizard nodded to the bar again. "What about the freckle-faced mulatto the blond guy is talking to? You recognize him?"

PayDay watched as the freckle-faced mulatto took an envelope from the blond guy and tucked it into his coat pocket.

"Never seen him before."

"He's famous here. One of the best pitchers in the Cuban League."

"I don't follow baseball, just the fights. Only boxing is real, the rest is just recreation; guys swinging bats, throwing footballs, racing in cars, all dipshits."

"Sports are important. Sports are for betting."

"That's the only good part."

"It's the sweet part. After the casinos and the prostitution, sports betting is the biggest moneymaker in Havana."

"I made money betting on Joe Louis. I could always pick the round."

"What makes you think that nigger was so clean? The Right Guys say Louis would throw his mother to the alligators. He threw that fight to the Kraut."

"Max Schmeling? No way. The Brown Bomber would never do a thing like that."

"The dough the Right Guys made off of betting that fight went into building the casinos in Havana."

"I don't believe it."

"I hope your aim with a gun is straighter than your line of thinking. Now, like I was saying about the Hurricane Hurler, it's your job to—"

A red-jacketed waiter, balancing a silver tray crowded with cocktail glasses, interrupted. "Can I bring you gentlemen some daiquiris?"

"Daiquiris!" Lizard banged his fist on the table. "Does it look like we're drinking fucking daiquiris? Bring me another Manhattan, and a beer for my friend, before I take a pink plastic straw from one of those glasses on your tray and stick it up your pink caboose."

"Sir, there's no reason to—"

Lizard shoved back in his chair and pushed his suit coat to one side, exposing the black handle of an automatic.

The waiter hustled away.

"Like I was saying"—Lizard leaned his chair toward the table again—"that freckle-faced mulatto at the bar is famous. He's a Sugar King."

"He owns a sugar plantation?"

"Baseball, man, baseball. The Havana Sugar Kings."

"I told you I wasn't interested in bats and gloves."

"What about the Yogi? You got to be interested in Yogi Berra, the great Yankee catcher? The whole world loves the Yogi."

"Sugar Ray Robinson. I like him."

"Another nigger fighter. You like to see niggers beating up white guys. What the hell kind of sport is that?"

PayDay ran his hand back and forth over the candy wrapper on the table. He stared at the word *PayDay* as if reading an inscrutable fortune cookie. What did he care about ballplayers and race-car drivers melting in the hot tropical sun? Nothing. But he did want to go out to the dog track. He could take his Betty along, she liked dogs. PayDay reached under the table and rubbed his dick through his pants. He was still sore from a passionate run he'd had with his wife in their room at the Nacional before Lizard called and insisted on meeting downstairs in the lobby.

"Yeah," Lizard continued, looking at the freckle-faced man at the bar, "that guy is the only redheaded mulatto in baseball. Father was Irish, mother was African. There were lots of Irish in Cuba early on. Just one block away there's a street named Calle O'Reilly. It goofs the American tourists up. They think, 'Where the hell am I? On a street in Boston with everybody speaking Spanish?' "

"So colored guys are allowed in here."

"Sure," snorted Lizard, "if they're famous. I'm beginning to think you're a nigger lover. I bet if Yogi Berra was black he'd be your best friend."

PayDay picked up the folded candy wrapper, then pulled it slowly between his thumb and trigger finger.

"The mulatto is called the Havana Hurricane Hurler, but his real name is Mick Stable. He's going up against our American League All-Stars this Sunday at El Cerro Stadium."

PayDay put his hand under the table and rubbed his dick again. It was itchy from riding his wife all afternoon and then not being able to take a shower after, since Lizard had been in such a hurry.

"The Right Guys want Hurricane to know which way the wind is blowing when he's on the mound Sunday. You know what I mean?"

"They want to make sure he's throwing in the direction they're betting."

"Not throwing too fast, not too slow. Just maintain the right point spread."

PayDay didn't like doing strong-arm muscle jobs that any goon could do. He was a specialist, he had worked too hard to get to where he was. But he was also a realist. He knew he was a new guy in Havana who had been brought in to do a big job. Maybe he was being tested. Maybe the Right Guys wanted to see if he was loyal. Maybe the Right Guys wanted to see if he could be trusted to handle a little job first.

PayDay scratched his itchy dick and said to Lizard, "I'm not a bone crusher. There's hoods who can do that."

"We can't crush the Hurricane's bones. We need his athletic skills. We can't mess with his real estate."

"So where do I come in?"

"We want you to teach him some respect. We don't want his mind to wander when he's on the mound Sunday in front of fifty-five thousand people."

"I know about respect."

"That's why I took you to the Three Virgins last night. Hurricane and the rich American are always hanging out together. I figured Hurricane would be there and I'd finger him for you. But Hurricane didn't show. Then I got a phone tip this afternoon that he was with Armstrong at the Floridita, piece of shit place that this is. I wouldn't be caught dead here unless it was business."

"Why didn't you tell me what was up last night?"

"Hurricane wasn't there so there was no need. Having smarts is like gas in a car, you don't need it until you've got someplace to go."

The waiter reappeared with a Manhattan cocktail and a bottle of beer on his tray. He set the drinks on the table and bowed. "Thank you, gentlemen."

Lizard tossed an American dollar on the tray. "That'll cover it. Now beat it."

The waiter stood immobile.

"What the fuck do you want?" Lizard growled.

The waiter smiled and still didn't move.

Lizard yanked a ten-dollar bill from his wallet and threw it onto the tray. "Bandit," he hissed. "That's more than your weekly salary."

The waiter's lips perked into a smirk, he pirouetted and strode off.

Lizard took a gulp of his Manhattan, sucking ice cubes into his mouth with the booze. He swallowed the liquor and crushed the ice between his teeth. "That Cuban Pete makes one ten-cent phone call to tip me that Hurricane is here with his pal, and he acts like he's set me up for a blow job from Marilyn Monroe."

PayDay heard the noise of Lizard's rant, but he wasn't paying attention. He was looking behind the bar at a mural depicting colonial Havana. On one side of the bay was a Spanish fort and lighthouse high on a cliff; on the other side was a small city encircled by a stone wall. It was a pretty scene because there were no people in it. PayDay knew it was different now, jammed with people who couldn't be trusted. Somebody could come out of the shadows to put a bullet in your head, or appear right in front of you, fully exposed in harsh sunlight, carrying on like it was life as usual, but there was nothing usual about it, murder was in the air. In Havana a man didn't have to watch his back so much as what was in front of him. The front action was where the play was, and it was always playing. Everything else was mere distraction.

PayDay glanced over at Lizard. After five Manhattans, Lizard had giant red-veined spiders clinging to each cheek. The spiders seemed to be moving around, angry, trying to get at one another across the bulbous bridge of Lizard's fleshy blackheaded nose.

PayDay wrapped his fingers around the cold neck of his beer bottle and took a drink. He smelled a sweet scent on his fingers; his wife's pussy, and something else. What was the other thing? Yes, Betty was always rubbing Pond's Cold Cream onto her skin, not spreading it just on her face but everywhere. Sometimes she would ask PayDay to help her smear it on.

Like this afternoon in their room at the Nacional, when Betty had come out of the shower. She sat in front of the dresser mirror and fingered cream around on her face in little circular motions that absolutely hypnotized PayDay. This was the best part about married life for him, being able to sit in bed with his back against the pillows while watching a naked woman rubbing cream all over herself. This is what guys who weren't married never got to have; slow moments with a dame who was all yours, a dame you didn't have to pay for, a dame who trusted you enough to let you watch her do all the secret girly stuff.

Sometimes Betty even left the door open in the bathroom when she took a pee. She'd call out through the open bathroom door, "Johnny, honey, would you bring me my hairbrush?" He'd bring the hairbrush to her as she sat on the toilet like a princess on a throne. "Johnny, honey," she'd coo, "would you mind brushing my hair?" "Yeah, doll," he'd say. And as he brushed with long slow strokes, she would arch her neck and her eyes would roll up toward him with a gleam and he would hear the stream of her pee splashing in the water. Standing next to her, he had to concentrate real hard not to get a woody. A woody would ruin it for her. A woody wouldn't be right. He had to grit his teeth and stroke her hair and concentrate to keep the blood from rushing to the head of his dick as she peed. These were special moments between a man and a wife, and PayDay was never going to give them up. Any guy who ever touched *his* wife, ever so much as bumped into her, he would do something awful to him, something so horrible that even PayDay couldn't imagine it.

This afternoon, after Betty had smoothed the cream onto her face, she got up from a silk-covered chair in front of the dresser mirror, took off her robe and lay down on the bed. "Johnny, honey," she cooed, "would you mind doing my back?" He rubbed the cool goo on her skin, slow, the way a wife likes it. When his palms ran up the hill of her ass he had to focus on not getting a woody, but when his hands came sliding down to the cushy bottom of the hill, he just couldn't help himself. "Oh, Johnny," Betty cooed, eyeing what he was up to after he dropped his pants, "you're so cute!"

PayDay sniffed the scent of his wife on his fingers as he drank his beer, wondering how long he was going to have to wait in this bar before Lizard gave him the sign to make his move. He wondered where Betty was now. Maybe she was at the hotel beauty parlor having her blond hair permed. Maybe she was in bed reading one of her movie magazines. He was so crazy about her that he couldn't give her enough, his woody just never went down. He considered himself one of the lucky ones. He had a wife he could count on.

A t that moment, PayDay was nearly right. Betty was lying on the bed in the hotel room waiting for the coral-pink polish on her toenails to dry. Between each of her toes was a big wad of cotton. She flipped through a movie magazine. There was a story about an actress who was going to marry a prince from some tiny country she'd never heard of: *"Can Grace Beat the Royal Jinx?"* There were lots of photos of actresses who had wedded royalty and none of the marriages lasted or they ended up in some kind of tragedy: *"On January 5th a starry-eyed Grace Kelly announced she would wed the world's most eligible bachelor, Prince Rainier of Monaco."* Betty chuckled. She had married the most eligible bachelor, Mister Johnny PayDay, and it had lasted. She flipped through more pages. *"The Most Intimate Interview Lucille Ball Has Ever Given! Lucille's Way to God."* This was serious, Betty thought. *"Lucy's a slapstick queen, a lovable screwball. Here for the first time are her innermost thoughts on faith and marriage, the unity between Desi and herself, though their faiths differ."*

This reminded Betty that the Lucy show was just coming on. She slid from the bed and hobbled across the rug to the TV, careful not to disturb her cotton-separated toes. The image of Lucy and her husband, Desi, having breakfast in their apartment flickered in black and white on the screen. Before long Lucy had tangled herself up in a vacuum cleaner hose and couldn't get loose. The look on Lucy's face was one of total bewilderment. Betty knew that look, she could feel it whenever her own face screwed into the same expression. It always happened when she was called upon to do something that Johnny normally took care of, like writing a check.

The phone next to the television rang. Betty picked up the receiver, expecting Johnny. Nobody back in the States knew she was in Cuba. Johnny always said it was important for her not to tell people where they were going. All businessmen have competition, Johnny had explained, it was better to keep things quiet.

But it wasn't Johnny's voice on the phone.

"Are you free, darling?"

"Who is this?"

"Can I come up?"

"You have the wrong number."

"No, I don't. It's you, my pet." The voice had an affected upper-class English accent, a singsongy swish of syllables. "My dove, you're not still angry with me, are you?"

"I'm not mad at anyone."

"Then don't be a naughty dolly. Come down here and meet me in the patio lounge."

"I can't."

"Why not?"

"Because Lucy's on."

"Lucy's down here too. She's on the TV behind the bar. She's got a vacuum cleaner hose wrapped around her neck."

"Johnny? Is that you? Are you playing with me?"

"I would like to play with you."

"If you're not Johnny I'm going to hang up."

"That would be a big mistake. Because then you won't get to meet Lucy."

"What do you mean?"

"Lucy's a friend, has been for years. Lucy and Desi have been on my yacht."

"You have a yacht?"

"And a house in Jamaica, and a house in Beverly Hills."

"Who *are* you?"

"A movie star. A very *big* movie star. Your husband's been trying to meet me for weeks. But he's too shy to approach me. I think he wants my autograph for you."

"You think so, really?"

"I know it."

"It could be true. My birthday is coming up. Maybe he was going to surprise me."

"Why don't you surprise him? I'll give you an autograph for *him*."

"That's kind of nice . . . I suppose. But how do I know you're telling the truth?"

"You don't, darling. You have to come down and have a peek.

And if I'm not a big star, you can disappear back into your rabbit hole."

"It'll take me a few minutes to get ready."

"I can wait. I can wait forever for a princess."

"I'll be right down."

It took Betty an hour to get herself ready. But after all, she was going to meet big Hollywood people; Johnny would want her to look her best. She checked herself out from all angles in the floor-to-ceiling mirror. Her chartreuse halter top plumped her breasts like two jiggling bowls of Jell-O. She wore her newest skirt, the one that flared out above the knees and had cute printed poodles prancing around it from front to back. Coral-pink toenail polish was the perfect finishing touch with her open-toed snakeskin spike-heeled shoes.

When Betty stepped out of the elevator into the grand lobby, all eyes were on her. She knew that look. It meant the women were jealous and the men were covetous as their eyes slid over her curves. She felt sexy and confident, hearing the *clickety-clack* of her spike heels on the tiled floor as she made her way in a dignified strut to the double doors leading out to the patio lounge. The doors swung open and two uniformed doormen bowed as she passed, as if she were a real princess, like Grace, the future Princess of Monaco.

Betty wasn't worried that the movie star might not be there. She knew enough about men to know that he would wait. Men hate to wait more than anything. It makes them furious. But they will never leave, because by the time the woman arrives, they know they've built up a certain amount of credit that can come in handy later, when she adds up the price they've paid to be with her.

The large outdoor patio seemed like the courtyard of a Spanish palace. Everywhere were ornate white wicker tables and chairs, occupied by elegant men in tropical suits and women in sophisticated summer dresses. Even though it was winter, even though it was January, it was warm, carefree and sensually humid; the air was perfumed with the scent of flowers blooming in giant red-clay pots.

"Darling! Over here!"

Betty knew an aristocrat's voice when she heard it, even though she had never met anyone aristocratic, unless you counted the judge who married her and Johnny in Atlantic City. But she had seen aristocrats in the movies.

Betty tried to focus among the tables, which seemed to float around her. She wasn't very good at seeing long distances, but it didn't mean she had to wear glasses. She considered herself way too young for that. And besides, it was her theory that blondes only looked good in sunglasses. Anything else was ridiculous, and she didn't want to look ridiculous. She wanted to be as up-to-date as the latest model of automobile rolling out of Detroit. No other woman in Havana was wearing a poodle skirt. They were all the rage in America, but she was the first, the only one to wear one here.

"Yoo-hoo! Right over here, princess!"

Betty had him in her sights now. A figure wavered in front of her, slightly out of focus on the far side of the patio. Behind him, rows of colored liquor bottles on an outdoor bar counter sparkled as the last shining slant of the sun dipped toward evening. Betty made her way to the man. He was deeply tanned and wore a white dinner jacket with no shirt underneath, his manly chest exposed; on his feet were expensive Italian loafers with no socks. Now, *this* was a movie star.

"My darling." He took her hand and held it to his puckered mouth beneath the slit of a mustache that dashed across his upper lip. He kissed her hand with a wet smack. "You were such a naughty dolly to have kept this jolly boy waiting so long! But, ah, my princess, I know how *delinquent* little girls can be."

Betty saw two cocktail glasses on the table. "Where's Lucy? Did she have to go to the little girls' room?"

"Lucy's not here. I just had her publicist on the phone. Maybe she can join us."

"Desi, too?"

"Desi, too. The publicist said Desi would love to meet you."

"Really?" Betty couldn't help but smile.

"Really, truly, madly, my precious." He gallantly slid a chair out and waited for Betty to be seated, then sat and gazed at her across the table. "You are"—his manly chest heaved—"more sublime close up than even I could have dared to imagine."

"How did you know what room I was in?"

"Everyone working here knows what room the most beautiful woman in the hotel is staying in."

"That's nice." Betty felt more comfortable.

"May I offer the princess a libation?"

"A what?"

"A cocktail."

"Oh, sure."

"Your desire is my command. It's right here." The man pushed one of the glasses on the table toward her. "A Banana Banshee, prepared to your high personal standard."

Betty brightened. "How did you know I drink Banshees?"

"I know many things. When I first saw you a few weeks ago at the pool, polishing the jewels of your toenails, I said to myself, I must get an invitation to partake of this sweet dish, this diva under the palms, this standard of American beauty that leaves her dark-skinned tropical sisters cowering in her shadow."

Betty sipped her yellow Banshee through a green plastic straw. The taste was cool and jungly. "What's a diva?"

"The brightest star in the heavens."

"That's nice." Through the straw Betty sucked the Banana Banshee right down to the bottom of the glass.

"May I offer you another libation?"

"A what? Oh, I remember. Yes, please."

He pushed the other full cocktail glass on the table across to her.

"What about you?" Betty asked. "Aren't you drinking?"

"With pleasure." From the inside pocket of his dinner jacket he slipped out a silver flask, unscrewed its cap and savored a long drink. "Ah, the best rum in the world. Only two people in the world have this rum. Me and the President."

"President Eisenhower drinks rum?"

"No, my jewel. President Batista."

"President who?"

"Our host in this fair country, President Batista."

"I didn't know Cuba was a country. I thought it was a state, like Puerto Rico, and there was a mayor or something who ran it."

"Would you like to meet the President? He's a close personal friend. You'll find no man a more charming puppy than Fulgencio Batista. The ladies quite like him."

"Batista, Batista, Batista." Betty let the name roll playfully off her tongue. She liked the sound of it.

"I can arrange the meeting."

Betty sucked on her Banshee. The rum made her giggle. "Batista goes bananas."

"Batista goes bananas?" He let the words trip off his tongue. "I like that. It's quite funny. Not only are you beautiful, you have a refined sense of humor. You are a political satirist."

"A what?"

"Funny, like Lucy."

"Where is she?"

"Enough about Lucy! Let's talk about *you*."

"I'm not very interesting."

"Oh, I think you *are*. I've watched you. I've asked myself, what is this jewel, this princess, this diva, doing with a little bald-headed fellow?"

"Johnny's my husband."

The man took a slow sip from his flask and leaned back nonchalantly in his chair. His white dinner jacket swung open, exposing more of his tanned chest; it was shaved bare. A gold chain encircled his neck with a heavy gold Spanish doubloon dangling from it. "You have a husband. Good. You can't have an extramarital affair unless you have a husband."

"Extra . . . marital? Is that like having an extra marriage or something?"

"You are as intelligent as you are beautiful and funny."

"Anyway, I'm married to Johnny."

"And what does the lucky Johnny do?"

"For a living?"

"He looks to me like a plumber, or a housepainter."

"He's a businessman and I'm a housewife."

"What kind of businessman?"

"I don't know. I've never asked him."

"Ah, you *are* the perfect wife. Too discreet to even inquire what your husband does for a living. Tell me, how old are you?"

"That's easy. Thirty-two."

" 'Thirty-two,' she says without hesitating! 'Thirty-two,' she trumpets without fear! I never date females that old. That shows how fearless you are, how special."

"This isn't a date." The smile fell off Betty's face and she was silent.

"Don't pout, my pet. I'm just playing. But seriously, let's talk about *amour*."

"There's a perfume called Amour, I think."

"My, how *intuitive*. I'm talking about that delectable perfume of the senses, that sizzle of the groins, that little drip of salacious saliva from the corner of Cupid's mouth."

"Who's Cupid? Where's Lucy?"

"Cupid, my darling, is an angel with a bow." He pointed a finger and stabbed it across the table, stopping it in front of Betty's breasts held up by the halter top. "An angel who lets fly the arrow of love straight to the heart of the matter."

Betty hiccuped. "I'd like another Banshee, please."

He snapped his fingers. A waiter ran up and placed another drink in front of Betty.

Betty bent over and put the plastic straw between her lipstick-ready lips.

"I have fought the wars of the heart, in hand-to-hand combat, from continent to continent," he said, watching Betty suck. "I am a five-star general of the battles of the bedroom. And I have lived to tell the tale."

Betty sucked harder, inhaling a flow of creamy yellow Banshee through her straw.

"You are either a dead pig," he said, "or a live frog waiting for a kiss."

Betty released the straw from her lips and sat up. "Huh? I don't get it."

"Would you like to win a kiss?" He leaned toward her. "A kiss from a prince that will transform you into a true princess?"

"Well, I don't know. I'd have to ask Johnny."

"You must be wearing sensational lingerie. Any woman who paints her toes like you, it's a dead giveaway that she's wearing delicious lingerie."

"Paints them like what?"

"Candy."

"Johnny never told me that."

"Husbands don't notice the small things. Lovers do."

The Banshees were making Betty bleary-eyed. She looked at the candle on the table burning between the two of them. Early-evening moths were diving into the flame, bursting in popping sparks.

"The truth is," Betty slurred, "I'm not wearing *any* lingerie."

Back in the Floridita, Johnny PayDay didn't know why the thought that his wife never wore panties or a bra came into his head. He hadn't really had enough of her this afternoon; he wanted more. He was irritated and bored, waiting for Lizard to give the go-ahead to bottle up the Hurricane Hurler.

The red spider veins on Lizard's cheeks had grown larger. He was still talking. In fact, he had never shut up.

"The problem is, some squares get lazy here, and you've got to teach a square a lesson. They think this is *mañana* land and the rules don't apply, because everything isn't American tidy. Say a square has a gambling debt, or a casino balloon floating over his head, or a drug habit he's got to pay off, and he walks away without paying off the float. When that happens, the Right Guys have got to send the lazy square back to school to learn his arithmetic. The square's got to be taught that Havana is no banana republic, that the casinos are owned lock, stock and barrel by the Right Guys. The rules of Havana are the same as the rules in Reno and Vegas."

"So when does school start for the Hurricane?"

"As soon as the square leaves, we follow him. When we get the chance we snatch him."

"What about his American pal?"

"If Armstrong gets in our way, we'll just have to move him."

"But what about the consequences?"

"There are no consequences. They make it easy for us down here. They've got a little war going on, a family spat. The government has a place where it plants dead bodies it kills by torture and assassination. It's called the Pineapple Field. You can always dump a body there, no questions asked."

"I thought you didn't want me to break anything."

"Yeah, just teach him a lesson. Put the fear of the Right Guys into him."

"Got it. And Armstrong, do I shoot him to move him?"

"No. Armstrong's important to the Right Guys. All their money is down on him to win the Big Race."

"Armstrong's on the inside? He's fixed?"

"Sweeter than that. He's being used. He's got things he wants kept on the hush-hush, so he'll walk the line. Last year he came in second at the Big Race. This year we've got a racer who's going to block the pack so Armstrong can win. That way we haven't touched the winner. He's clean and our money is clean."

"Message received." PayDay looked over at the bar. Armstrong and Hurricane were paying up. "They're leaving."

"Let's move."

Across the flame of the candle on the table on the patio of the Hotel Nacional, Betty watched the aristocratic actor sway from side to side, as if he were caught in a heavy wind. He was swaying because she was on her fifth Banana Banshee. She tried to hold him in one place with her eyes, but she wasn't having any luck, even though he was talking straight at her.

"Now, some rums are young, they haven't been corked up long in a bottle, so when you let them out to play they're like frisky puppies, all rough-and-tumble. Then you've got your old granddaddy rums, stately and low-down smooth, easygoing, never showing you their true colors, though all the while their sophistication gnaws off your nerve endings, eats away at your inhibitions. Here"—he reached his silver flask out to Betty—"take a lick of the granddaddy."

Betty hesitated, not because she didn't want to taste it but because she was starting to see double; there were two silver flasks, and she didn't know which one to take. She took a chance and grabbed one, the right one, and figured that meant she wasn't so tipsy after all. She tipped the flask up and took a swallow.

"How do you like old granddad?"

Betty was speechless. The fire of the rum seared her tongue, burning right down into her gut. She didn't know if she'd ever be able to talk again. All she could do was grin like a mute clown, a clown crying big tears with streaks of purple mascara running down her cheeks.

"Did I ever tell you"—the man leaned close, the fire of his breath was in her crying face—"that I was adopted?"

Betty shook her head in a no. She looked on the table for a glass of water to put out the fire in her belly, but there was none. The waiter placed another Banana Banshee in front of her; she gulped it down.

"It's true. I was adopted, a little foundling just like Moses in his basket. All the facts about my life were made up by the movie studio, none of them are true. I'm not an English gentleman. I'm an Irish bastard. And I wasn't raised in British upper-class boarding schools. I went to rattrap public schools in the Siberia of California's San Fernando Valley. On the weekends I went to the movies. The thing I learned was that if a fellow had a gentrified English accent nobody messed with his porridge, everybody paid him respect and was happy to have him around. And the English gent never had to work, all he needed was a trimmed mustache, a full cocktail glass and a clever sense of humor. People invited him to their parties, let him lounge at their swimming pools, drive their cars, stay in their houses, all for free. Being an English gent works with Americans. But you can't get away with it in Britain, there they know that if you were born a gent with money, have been to the right schools, you're probably an asshole."

Betty nodded enthusiastically, even though she didn't believe a thing. She knew this was being made up to put her at ease. She knew he really *was* an English gentleman. She hadn't told him yet, but she had seen him in a musical, and there was no faking the way he moved and talked on the stage, a true-blue English gentleman. The lyrics of something he had sung smoldered up from the fire in her belly, and she sang, *"I have often walked down this street before. But the pavement always stayed beneath my feet before. All at once am I several stories hiiiigh."*

He arched an eyebrow. "Let's talk about you and artichokes."

"Artichokes?"

"The vegetable *art-e-choke.*"

"We don't have them in Detroit."

"Bright green, hard and big as a baseball. You boil it, peel the leaves off and eat the soft bottom. At the center there's a purple heart with spikes around it. I never ate the heart because my adopted father said it was bitter. He would take a knife and cut the spikes away and pop the heart into his mouth like a slimy snail. One day, long after he died, I ordered an artichoke at the Beverly Hills Hotel. I cut off the sharp spikes surrounding the slimy heart and popped it into my mouth. I went out of my mind."

"You should have listened to your father. He didn't want you to have a bitter experience."

"It wasn't bitter, it was divine, splendor on the tongue. The son of a bitch had lied to me my whole life so *he* could eat the best part."

Betty winced. "That's not nice. But at least he adopted you."

"Do you know why I'm telling you this story?"

"No."

"Because it's about *you*."

"I've never eaten an art-e-choke."

"It's not about the artichoke. It's about how people pretend to protect you from *bad* things in life, because in fact they want to keep those *bad* things all for themselves."

Betty was completely lost.

"Don't you see? That's the lie about marriage. They preach that fidelity is the sweetest part, that you're being saved from a bitter alternative. When in fact, right there in front of you the whole time is the sweetest part, the heart of the matter . . . *infidelity*."

"Johnny bought me a high-fidelity record player. I've got all the big Broadway shows on records."

The man leaned conspiratorially close. "I don't mean *that* kind of fidelity. I mean monogamy is bullshit."

"There are some good things."

"Like what? Just give me one good example of why I should *not* put some sugar in your bowl."

Betty didn't hesitate. She sang, "*A lady doesn't wander all over the room and blow on some other guy's dice. So let's keep the party polite.*"

"Ah, you she-devil. You're singing from *Guys and Dolls*! I can match you." He sang in a booming baritone, *"Luck let a gentleman see how nice a dame you can be. Luck be a lady with meeeee."*

"It's the wrong game with the wrong chips. Tho' your lips are tempting, they're the wrong lips."

"But they're such tempting lips, that if some night your freeee . . ."

"It's all right with meeeee!"

"I knew you'd come around! My delicious songbird!" He took Betty's hand into his.

"Come around to what?"

"You and me, sweet pea. It's time. Let's go to my suite at the Capri. It has a mirror next to the bed."

Betty didn't say yes or no. The Banshees were running amok in her head, she couldn't think clearly. "Why would I want to sleep on a mirror?" she asked. But no answer came back. She felt herself being lifted from the chair and whisked away. Everything was wobbling, people were swimming past her in murky water. Was she already in the mirrored lake of a bed?

Betty recognized the bright tiled floors of the Hotel Nacional. Swimming straight for her across the tiles was a redheaded teenager with a fierce sunburn. Even though the teenager was underwater, Betty thought she was going to burst into flame.

The teenager jabbed her finger into the bare chest of the man in the white dinner jacket. "Daddy, why did you keep me waiting so long?"

"Daddy got distracted."

"Baby has to go potty and she has nothing to tip Señorita Pee-Pee with. It's the señorita who keeps all the potties clean and shiny for baby's naked bottom to sit on."

With her brain in a Banana Banshee buzz, Betty couldn't follow the conversation. She managed to say, "I've got to pee too. Some-times I let Johnny watch me pee. That's the best part about being married . . . you don't have to close the bathroom door."

"She's loaded to the gills," the teenager said in disgust to the man. "Look at her, she's old enough to be my mother. What's wrong with you?"

"Mother." Betty heard the word through the haze. "Is this your daughter?"

"My daughter?" The man kissed Betty on the cheek. "I knew you were a naughty dolly."

"Is that it?" the teenager demanded. "Are you screwing this old lady?"

"What old lady?" Betty looked around. Was someone else there?

"Gimme the potty money." The teenager stamped the heel of her shoe into the man's foot. *"Now!"*

He opened his wallet and took out a five-dollar bill.

The teenager grabbed the money, spun around, and marched down the hallway, turning left through the door marked LADIES' LOUNGE.

Inside the lounge a toilet attendant sat behind an ostentatious imitation Louis XVI desk. She was a dignified woman in a prim dove-gray uniform with a no-nonsense air about her, as if she were a schoolteacher, or the appointment secretary in the outer office of an important international diplomat.

The teenager snapped, "Listen, Señorita Potty-pot, I'm not here for a pee. I want to powder my nose."

The attendant slipped open the top drawer of the desk and took out a plastic compact.

The teenager threw her five-dollar bill down and snatched the compact. She walked across the room and stood before a mirror above a marble sink. She opened the compact and speared a dab of white powder with a long fingernail. She raised her fingernail and held it beneath her nose. Watching her reflection in the mirror, she snorted the powder, the expression on her face corkscrewing into a grimace as the white bite flew up her nostril. She took five more hits out of the compact, her eyes growing wider and more startled after each snort. Suddenly, reflected in the mirror, she saw the bare-chested man in the white dinner jacket behind her. She shouted angrily, "What are you doing in here? This is for ladies only!"

He grabbed her skinny shoulders and spun her around. "You dumb cow! I told you to wait for me back at the Capri. Why did you show up here and ruin it?"

"I was bored. The only thing on TV is that stupid Lucy show."

"This is too important to mess up!"

"You're not my leading man. You can't tell me what to do. Do you want me to call my mother in Cleveland and tell her what's *really* going on?"

"Your mother knows, goddamn it! What do you think I'm *paying* her for?"

"My own mother," the teenager howled. "She's been taking money the whole time and not *splitting* it with me."

"You ungrateful bitch." He smacked her in the face.

The teenager fell back against the marble sink. A trickle of blood smeared her mouth. She looked shocked; her lips trembled. Then she quickly smiled at him. "Kiss me, I'm bleeding."

"You turn into a hooker when you're doing blow."

"You got me started. You like it that way." She hiked up her skirt, sliding her white bottom up onto the marble counter. She raised her bare legs, scissored them around his waist, and pulled him to her.

Reflected in the mirror behind them, the uniformed toilet attendant sat at her desk, her face expressionless.

The man gripped the teenager by her ankles.

The teenager wiggled her naked bottom on the slick marble beneath it. "Come on, Daddy, let's play house."

He yanked her legs open and hissed into her face. "Will you shut the Christ up! I told you, the bald-headed husband of that dumpy bleached blonde out there has been following me for weeks. I don't know why, but I know that in this town *anybody* following you around is dangerous. I told you to stay out of my way until I could get the truth out of that bimbo; fuck it out of her, or beat it out of her."

Traveling along the Malecón in his Chrysler Imperial, Lizard kept both hands on the steering wheel as he followed Armstrong's white Cadillac Eldorado.

The Eldorado's convertible top was down and the warm evening sea breeze blew through Armstrong's blond hair. Next to him, the wind skimmed over Hurricane's buzz cut. The two seemed not to have a care in the world, turning their heads only to glimpse the action caught in the car's headlights of couples fondling each other as they leaned against the Malecón's stone seawall.

Lizard barked at PayDay, seated next to him, "Light me a ciggy, would you? They're in the glove compartment."

PayDay popped open the glove compartment and took out a pack of Camels. He knocked free a cigarette and lit it up from the glowing tip of the lighter he pulled out of the dashboard. He handed the Camel over to Lizard.

Lizard mashed the cigarette between his fat lips, smoke leaking from the sides of his mouth as he spoke. "Why don't you have a ciggy yourself?"

"I don't smoke. I prefer my PayDays."

"That kiddy shit is going to rot your teeth."

"I've got good teeth. Don't worry about my teeth."

"Where do you think these two birds ahead of us are going?"

"I don't know this town. All the street signs are in Spanish."

"Yeah, that's stupid. The Americans are the ones who kicked the Spanish king's ass out of here. You'd think after that the Cubes would print everything in English. All the hookers here speak English, that's a big motivator for the whole country to get in line. If you're gonna fuck a guy you've got to at least be able to count in his language."

"Damn right."

"It's only obvious."

"Damn right."

"Hey, when we finish our work with these birds tonight, what do you say we go to the track and bet the dogs? You said you liked to bet dogs."

"We'll have to stop and get Betty first. She gets lonely at the hotel all by herself."

"You really *are* pussy-whipped."

"If you've got to be whipped, it's best to have a pussy do it."

"Not for me, brother. I say, you keep your wife and kiddies in one place, your pussy in another place, and *you* do the ass-whipping."

"We might not be able to make it to the track tonight, if these guys in front of us don't step on it."

"They're headed for Miramar and the swanky Country Club part of town. That's where these rich birds go. They're like goddamn homing pigeons."

"What if they end up at one of their homes? What then?"

"Then everything has to be done faster. Wham, bam, thank you ma'am. We get Hurricane into our car and we're off to the races."

"Got it."

"You know, if we don't go to the dog track later, we can hit the Three Virgins."

"It's not my kind of place."

"It might be." Lizard gummed the stub of the cigarette in his mouth. The tobacco was almost burned down to his lips. "You never know what life has in store for you. Life is not always gonna serve your eggs sunny-side up."

"I like my eggs scrambled."

"There you go. That's what I mean."

"Watch it! Those guys ahead are turning left!"

"Don't get your panties in a twist. I grew up driving getaway cars and chase cars before I even had a driver's license. Driving's a piece of cake here in Cuba. They drive on the same side of the road as we do, not like in England."

"You've been to England?"

"Yeah. I had to do a job there once. Shitty food."

"Where do they drive in England?"

"Crazy limeys are on the wrong side of the road all the time. A miracle they don't kill themselves. And they all *dress* on the wrong side."

"What do you mean, dress on the wrong side?"

"The side of your crotch you wear your dick on. In England, they hang it on the wrong side."

"How do you know?"

"I told you. I've been there. I seen it— What the fuck, where are these birds headed now?"

"Making a quick right. Stay on them."

"Goddamn, these guys are going into the Nacional!"

"Yeah." PayDay looked through the windshield at the avenue of palms leading to the high-arched hotel lobby entrance, where snappy attendants in crisp uniforms stepped forward to greet arriving guests.

Lizard stopped behind the Cadillac. "Get ready to snatch Hurricane."

"Armstrong's not getting out. He's staying in the car."

"Makes it easier. When he pulls away, act fast."

A uniformed attendant opened the passenger door of the Cadillac. Hurricane stepped out and waved good-bye to Armstrong. The Cadillac drove off.

"What's this! I don't *believe* it!" PayDay nearly choked on his words.

With the Cadillac out of the way, there was a clear view up a broad staircase leading to the lobby. At the top of the stairs stood Betty with a man in a white dinner jacket at her side.

PayDay banged his fist on the dashboard. "It's the Bad Actor!"

"Goddamn!" shouted Lizard. "Don't mess up my car!"

"I'm going to kill that Hollywood creep!" PayDay screamed.

Lizard grabbed PayDay by the knot of his necktie. "Don't go apeshit on me! Take care of business! Get Hurricane!"

PayDay's chest heaved, his breath shot out in short bursts, he was ready to explode. He jerked out his automatic and checked that it was loaded.

Lizard barked into PayDay's face, "You're a professional man! Don't fuck it up!"

The hotel attendants opened both front doors of the Chrysler at once, bowing and saying in unison, "Welcome to the Hotel Nacional, luxury under the sun."

PayDay jumped out and in two long steps he was up the staircase and nudging the gun into Hurricane's ribs. "Turn around. No sounds. Into the Chrysler."

Hurricane was blasé, as if he had been expecting PayDay. He turned and headed toward the car, leaving PayDay standing alone.

"Johnny!" Betty shouted with delight. "Honey!"

The Bad Actor, next to Betty, saw PayDay facing him with the gun. "Holy shit," the Actor groaned, his face draining of all color. He took a step and stood behind Betty for protection, then he backed up through the door into the lobby and ran.

"Honey!" Betty stumbled down the steps, crashing into PayDay. "I'm so glad you're here."

"Yeah-yeah, baby." He put his arm around his wobbling wife. "Let's go for a ride."

The terrified attendants watched as the three climbed into the backseat of the Chrysler and the door slammed closed. The Chrysler peeled off in a screech of tires.

As they sped away, the glowing green lights from the Chrysler's dashboard reflected on Lizard's face. So many things had just happened to piss him off, he didn't know where to start first. "You don't bring your goddamn drunk wife on a job!"

PayDay ignored him.

Hurricane interjected calmly, "I knew somebody would be coming for me. You want to shake me down for my tab. But if you hurt me, I can't pitch on Sunday. I don't pitch, there's no fix."

Lizard reached up and twisted the rearview mirror, so that his face was reflected in it and everyone in the backseat could see the rage in his green, glowing expression. He growled at Hurricane, "Maybe we won't need you, asshole. Maybe the All-Star game will be rained out. Then we won't have any need to put up with your spitball bullshit."

"You guys don't scare me." Hurricane gave a cocky grin.

PayDay shoved the gun barrel deeper into Hurricane's ribs. "Keep your fly-trap shut."

"Johnny, honey," Betty trilled with oblivious good cheer, "where are we going?"

Hurricane spoke coolly to PayDay. "Why don't you answer the little lady? Tell her we're going on a nice picnic."

PayDay pressed the gun so deep into Hurricane's ribs that it made the other man wince. "This is no picnic. Wipe that smirk off your face or I'll blow your tonsils out through your ears."

"Johnny, honey, who are these people? Did somebody say this is a picnic?" Betty's head lolled from side to side, her dilated eyes rolling.

PayDay wanted to know what the Bad Actor had done to her. Had he drugged her? The Bad Actor was a dead man.

Lizard barked at PayDay. "Would you tell your daffy dame to put a lid on it?"

"Don't worry," PayDay said. "I know how to do my job." He turned his face to Hurricane in the headlight glare from a passing car.

Hurricane didn't like what he saw in PayDay's face. He reached into his shirt pocket and pulled out a thick envelope. "Here"—he handed the envelope over—"take this. I just came into a small inheritance from a sick aunt who passed away."

PayDay handed the envelope back.

"Why not take it?"

"Because after I kill you, it's mine anyway."

A band of sweat broke out across Hurricane's forehead. For the first time he was worried. He appealed to Lizard in the front seat. "Would you tell this gentleman to accept the money? That's what you're shaking me down for, isn't it? You want me to settle my white-lady bill."

Lizard shot Hurricane a glare in the mirror. "I don't give a shit about you and your cocaine habit. Do we look like a couple of goons who are going to bust your balls over money? This is bigger than that. This is your *life* on the line."

"What do you want from me?"

"Nothing. We're the ones doing the giving."

The Chrysler headed beyond the outskirts of Havana, where the sprawl of the city had not yet laid claim to open fields. The car sped along a highway lined with the silhouettes of wild palms, turned and roared down a road fenced by rows of high-spiked cacti, then spun off onto a dirt trail and stopped. Lizard cut the engine but not the headlights. Dust roiled up around the car.

"Where are we?" Hurricane craned his neck as he tried to peer through the dust.

"Last stop." Lizard smiled into the mirror.

Hurricane stared out the windshield. The thrust of headlights cut through thinning dust into a field. Creatures in the distance were captured in the light, their eyes reflecting red.

Hurricane jerked with a start as Lizard hit the car horn, spooking the red-eyed creatures; they darted away into the darkness. Suddenly Hurricane knew what the creatures were—rats, scurrying among bones and skulls.

"Oh, God, this is the Pineapple Field," Hurricane moaned. "You guys have the wrong man. I'm not political. There's not a political bone in my body. This is a mistake. I'm an athlete."

"No mistake." PayDay rammed the tip of his gun sharply into Hurricane's side. "Shut up and get out."

"No."

"Yes!" PayDay shoved the gun harder into the ballplayer's ribs.

Lizard got out from the front of the car, yanked the back door open, and pulled Hurricane out. He unbuckled Hurricane's pants belt and slipped it off, then tied his hands behind his back with the belt.

Hurricane pleaded, "Don't kill me. I've got a wife and kids."

Lizard snarled, "Jesus didn't have a wife and kids but they killed him anyway. You ain't no better than Jesus. You're just a cokehead ballplayer."

"I never do blow when I'm on the mound."

"What the fuck do I care? This ain't your last confession." Lizard yanked Hurricane by the shirt, pushing him into the field.

Hurricane stumbled forward, stopping at the front of the car, afraid of stepping on bones.

"Keep walking," Lizard demanded.

Hurricane turned, his face illuminated by the headlights. "I get it. You guys are government goons. You guys are with Batista. Well, *fuck you*. You'll never win."

PayDay got out of the car and stood next to Lizard. "He's peeing in his pants and ranting anything just to save his ass."

"Yeah," Lizard sneered. "Flush the turd down the toilet."

PayDay stepped over to Hurricane and pointed the gun in his face.

Hurricane looked defiantly at PayDay. "You'll never beat us."

"Turn around."

"That's the kind of cowards you Batista lackeys are, you only shoot men in the back." Hurricane turned his back to PayDay.

PayDay jammed the gun under his belt. He took out a handkerchief, knotted it, and slipped it over Hurricane's head and eyes, blindfolding him. "Start walking."

Hurricane marched into the field, the car headlights beaming into his back.

PayDay aimed his gun and fired.

Pow! Pow! Pow! Pow! Pow!

The bullets smacked the skulls on the ground around Hurricane. The skulls shattered, bones went sailing. Then there was dead silence.

Hurricane, to his surprise, was still standing.

"Down on your knees," PayDay ordered.

"I'll die standing up!" Hurricane shouted. "Go ahead and shoot!"

PayDay walked up behind Hurricane. He took off his necktie, balled it up, reached around and jammed it deep into Hurricane's mouth. "When the Right Guys ask you to do something, you do it. The Right Guys don't ask twice." PayDay kicked Hurricane behind the knees.

Hurricane fell to a kneeling position. He waited for the shot in the back of his head. He heard footsteps, then the sound of a car driving off. He didn't know if both men had left. Maybe one was still there, ready to kill him. He remained on his knees, blindfolded and gagged, his hands tied, expecting the worst.

O n the drive to Havana, Betty woke up in the backseat of the Chrysler. She raised her head from her husband's shoulder, where it had been resting.

"Honey," Betty asked, "were there fireworks at the picnic? I heard fireworks. Did I miss the show?"

"Don't worry, doll."

"What about Lucy? Where's Lucy?"

PayDay didn't know any Lucy. He figured he already had a problem with the Bad Actor horning in on his wife, and now there was a *Lucy*. This whole problem was much bigger than he'd originally thought, but he had to stay cool. "Lucy couldn't make it to the fireworks. Lucy says hello."

Betty smiled and rested her head on PayDay's shoulder again, dreamily singing, *"Luck, let a gentleman seeee, how nice a dame you can beeee. Luck, be a lady with meeeeee."*

Hurricane was a ballplayer, a pitcher, a hurler on the mound, he was used to playing in a field of dreams, not kneeling in a field of death. He had been kneeling so long that his knees were numb and his legs cramped. He wondered if he would be able to walk again, much less pitch. Rats rummaged through the scattered bones surrounding him, gnawing on remnants of flesh. The high-pitched gnawing unnerved him, it was as if the rodents' sharp incisors were biting into electrical wires. It was enough to drive a man crazy, especially a blindfolded man. The gnawing of rats stopped at the sound of heavy steps approaching. The rodents clattered away.

The steps came closer.

Hurricane thought the goons had come back. Maybe he would be better off if they killed him now, because his arms had been twisted up and tied behind his back for so long that they had no feeling. If he survived this, he might not be able to pitch again. How many hours had he been kneeling here?

The steps stopped.

Something big and wet slapped Hurricane's cheek; an animal's tongue. As the tongue explored his face a sickly sweet scent breathed from a mouth that had been eating decayed human flesh.

The animal moaned, its sharp teeth probed the soft flap of Hurricane's earlobe. Sweat dripped down Hurricane's cheeks as the teeth bit into his ear. He smelled his own blood.

Hurricane heard other steps approaching. The animal beside him released his ear. A threatening growl ripped from the animal's chest.

The approaching steps stopped.

There was silence, then more steps, and all around Hurricane barking went up. He was surrounded by dogs.

A rank scent lifted from the fur of the dog next to Hurricane. It was the smell of an animal prepared to defend its prey against intruders.

The surrounding dogs kept up their barking, running in a tightening circle. The air exploded with lunging fury, vicious snarling and the gnashing of teeth, followed quickly by pathetic moans as life bled out of dogs.

Hurricane didn't move. His shirt was soaked with sweat. His head baked in the sun. Above him, the air beat with the wings of buzzards.

A dog's labored panting came close. The sickly sweet breath was again in Hurricane's face. The winner of the fight was claiming its reward.

Hurricane tried to move his cramped legs, to get up and run, but he couldn't.

The dog snarled, sensing Hurricane's urge to flee. Its bony snout punched him in the face like a fist.

Hurricane waited for the canine's teeth to bite into him. Then he heard a car approaching, bones crunching beneath its tires as it rolled to a stop. The engine was cut, the doors flung open.

The dog next to Hurricane sniffed the air, trying to gauge the threat.

The bang of a gun sounded, bullets whizzed by Hurricane's head, the dog next to him yelped and crashed to the ground.

"Pedro, you got the mother's whore! Good shot!"

"Damn right I got it! These graveyard bitches are eating the devil's meat!"

"Look at all the other dead dogs. Bloody as hell. Must have been a big fight."

"Maybe they were fighting over this guy here."

"You think we should untie him?"

Hurricane was relieved, the men were speaking Spanish, they weren't the American thugs who had left him there. He wanted to call out, to tell them who he was, but his mouth was gagged. He tried to move toward them, but his knees wouldn't work.

"We can't untie him. Someone left him here for a reason."

"You're right. The Captain sent us to do a job. He'll be pissed if we don't follow orders."

Hurricane stopped trying to move toward the men. They were talking about a captain. That meant they must be government, they must be Batista goons. He heard the trunk of the car open and the men grunting as they lifted something heavy.

"Don't drop her, Pedro."

"What difference would it make? "

"It's bad luck to drop a dead body."

"Who says?"

"My Santero."

"Maybe he's right."

"Never wrong."

"This one is the prettiest. Great tits. Long legs."

"Pedro, do you think anyone will . . . find out?"

"Jesus, Paulo, we strangled her, and you're worried someone might find out we fucked her first?"

"I'm worried about the Captain. He said not to do that."

"So who's going to tell the Captain? We killed all three girls."

"At least we gave them a good send-off."

"Yeah, who wants to die without a last fuck?"

"I think it was love I saw in their eyes, not just thanks for the fuck."

"Women are funny that way, especially when they're young."

"Is this a good spot to leave her?"

"Good as any."

"Let her down easy."

"It's done. Let's get the other two."

Hurricane heard the sound of two more bodies being lifted out of the car trunk and laid on the ground. Then he heard what he didn't want to hear.

"What about *him*? You think we should shoot him?"

"It's not in the orders. You know how the Captain is about following orders."

"But this guy heard us talking."

"So what. He's blindfolded. Whoever left him here to die will come back and finish the job. If the dogs don't get him first."

"Yeah, he's dog food. Chomp-chomp, lick-lick."

"Let's go. This place gives me the creeps."

"Not me. We've been out here so many times, I'm getting used to it."

"I'll never get used to it."

"This job has its ups and downs. We have our fun, and the pay's good."

"You're right. Beats going through life with a tapeworm hanging out of your ass."

The trunk lid clanged shut, the car doors slammed closed. The car drove away. A cloud of dust mixed with acrid engine exhaust drifted over Hurricane.

Maybe the two goons were right, Hurricane thought. Maybe the American thugs were coming back to finish him off. He heard buzzards overhead, flapping their wings as they lowered in the sky. He waited for them to land and tear into his flesh with their beaks.

In the hot sun, Hurricane's brain boiled with hallucination. The bones and skulls surrounding him rose up; resurrected skeletons jerked like marionettes in a profane dance to searing Zombie music. The Papa Drum and Mama Drum were angry, unleashing the heated beat of a knife-wielding Sorcerer to slice open mysteries. The dancing chorus of bone-clanking skeletons heralded the souls of those in the field of death who had been brutalized, raped, tortured, shot, electrocuted, strangled. A percussive rhythm swayed the earth in a tide of sorrow as a thousand skeletal hands reached up and grabbed the sun's shining orb, crushing it. The sun's boiling innards spurted out, showering terror from the sky.

Behind Hurricane's blindfold all became darkness. He was woozy from the blistering heat, but he *did* hear music. Was it the music of hallucination, or had he died of heatstroke and crossed over to the final realm? He heard the swoon of a woman's voice passionately recounting her sorrow:

> *We shouldn't dwell on love forgotten,*
> *like a piece of the soul*
> *wrenched heartlessly away.*
> *If only we could make all our dreams*

come true, you would love me
like you did twenty years ago.

Hurricane knew the song, "Twenty Years." He knew the singer, María Teresa Vera, her mournful voice floating on a simple melody sketched by a three-string guitar. He thought he was dead in heaven and María Teresa was singing just for him. He started to weep, then his weeping became uncontrollable sobbing. He was a strong man, an athletic man, but the song exposed him for the soft emotional fruit that he was.

Hurricane cried himself empty. María Teresa's voice was still there. It wasn't coming from paradise, it was close and tinny; it came from a car radio. When had the car arrived? Had the American thugs come back to finish their job? Had Pedro and Paulo returned to kill him because they realized he had heard their names?

A car door slammed shut and the singing stopped. Footsteps walked across bones to where the three bodies had recently been dumped. The footsteps started again and came to Hurricane. He heard a rustling sound; something was being taken out of a pocket. A gun? There was a soft tapping, then the scratch of a match being struck. The scent of phosphorus and tobacco wafted in the air.

A man's voice asked, "You want a smoke?"

Hurricane bobbed his head up and down in a yes.

A hand reached down and pulled out the necktie stuffed into Hurricane's mouth.

Hurricane's tongue had been jammed up in a bent position at the back of his throat for so long that he could barely move it. His mouth was parched, he needed water, not nicotine. "Wa . . . wa . . . water."

The man ignored his request. "You've got red ants crawling all over your face. They're having a ball, wiggling their legs like they're playing drums on your skin. Can't you feel them?"

Hurricane couldn't feel them, his face was too numb and swollen, but he realized he had heard their drumming.

"I've been coming to this field for weeks," the man continued. "You're the first live person I've seen. Somebody didn't finish the job on you."

Beneath Hurricane's exhaustion, terror returned. Maybe this man had come to finish him off.

"I wonder if you had a hand in killing those three girls over there?"

Hurricane shook his head.

"But you might know who dumped them? Those bodies are fresh."

Hurricane didn't know who this man was, whose side he was on. He didn't like the questions the man was asking, so he said nothing.

"You know, when a guy is tied up and blindfolded, he's in no position to bargain."

Hurricane felt the metal tip of a gun barrel press against his forehead.

"Who killed those girls?"

Hurricane spluttered, "Not me!"

"Why are you out here like this?"

Hurricane took a chance. "Some guys kidnapped me and dumped me. I swear, I had nothing to do with those girls. I was tied and blindfolded the whole time."

"Yeah, sure, you're just an innocent redheaded lamb."

"Do you know who I am?"

"I've seen you before."

"Let me see who *you* are. Do that, and I promise I'll give you answers."

"I thought you didn't have answers?"

"You haven't asked the right questions."

The man grabbed the handkerchief tied around Hurricane's head and pulled it free.

Hurricane blinked his eyes. All he could see was white glare. He stared down, away from the sun, and focused. He saw polished two-toned spectator shoes, above them a pair of linen trousers held at the waist by a thin alligator belt, a blue knit shirt beneath an unbuttoned tropical sport coat. Hurricane took in the man's handsome face.

"I know you. I saw you playing the drums New Year's Eve at the Tropicana. You're King Bongo."

Bongo removed his sunglasses. He wanted Hurricane to see his eyes, he wanted Hurricane to know that he meant business. "I've been coming here on the chance that my sister's body might turn up."

"I know the Panther. Untie me and I'll talk."

Bongo shoved his gun back into its shoulder holster, reached behind Hurricane, and jerked loose the belt that was knotted around his wrists.

Hurricane pulled his hands free and rubbed his raw wrists. "Thanks."

"What about my sister?"

"She's safe."

"Does Zapata have her?"

"Is that what you think?"

"That's how Zapata acts."

"He's trying to find her too."

"Where is she?"

"I swear I don't know."

"And you don't know who killed those three college girls over there?"

"Oh, God!" Hurricane tried to get up and fell. There was no feeling in his legs.

Bongo pulled him up and supported him as they walked through the bones, stopping in front of the bodies of three naked women in their early twenties. Purple rope burns ringed the smooth necks of the women.

Bongo asked, "Who did this?"

"I was blindfolded. I heard two guys, but I don't know who they were."

Bongo glared into Hurricane's bloodshot eyes. "You're lying."

"I'm not. What would I have to hide?"

"Why someone left you out here like this."

"It wasn't a political reason, it was personal. It's Havana, that's how it goes."

"Yeah, Havana."

Hurricane's cockiness was beginning to flow again. "Hey, pal, give me a lift back into town."

"If you tell me why you and the Armstrongs left the Tropicana on New Year's Eve just before the bomb exploded."

"We were headed to another club. What's the crime in that?"

Bongo yanked his gun from its holster. "You're going to have to do better than that!"

"Saint Lazarus," Hurricane blurted. "The cripple with the dog. Follow him."

"Why?"

"He knows the way to your sister."

"How do I find Lazarus?"

"Ask the White Spider Woman."

3.

Perfumed Dreams

The Crab scuttled along the morgue's stone corridor beneath flickering fluorescent lights. He stopped in front of Bongo.

"Hah-hah-hah! Good to see my favorite mourner. You've been coming here every day. Today is your lucky day."

"Might be my *unlucky* day, if you have who I'm looking for."

"You're looking for so many, all beautiful young women. Tell me, just between us, have you tasted all of them? You've shown me their photographs, what fruit!"

"I'm not involved with them in that way."

"So humble, hah! But you should eat fruit when it's young. When it's ripe the peel is close to the meat, when it's old the skin is falling away, hah!"

"I'm not here on a shopping expedition. You phoned and said you had something for me."

"Fresh produce. Right this way."

Bongo followed the Crab through a maze of corridors and into a bone-chilling room. Iron cadaver casements were stacked up along the walls to the ceiling. The Crab opened the door of a casement and rolled out a sheet-covered body.

Bongo feared the worst.

"I think this is what you're looking for." The Crab stripped the sheet away. "She's in her twenties, a real beauty. Sorry about the face."

Bongo looked at the corpse. The Crab was right, it was a beautiful female body, and the right age. The face had been smashed in, unrecognizable. Bongo breathed a sigh of relief. "It's not her."

"Maybe it is. Why don't you smell her? The first time you were here you made an identification just by *smelling* the body."

"I'm telling you, it's not her. The one I'm looking for has white hair."

"Black girls don't have white hair."

"The one I'm looking for does."

"Well, then"—the Crab shoved the corpse back into its cold cradle—"we'll just have to keep our hopes up. Every day there is a new crop."

"Speaking of that, I've got some for you."

"Finally."

"But you have to go and pick them up."

"Hah! Now you're talking."

"They're the other three young women I was looking for. The college girls."

"You don't get a discount on three."

"They're in the Pineapple Field."

"I don't pick up in there. Too dangerous."

"What would persuade you?"

"Money."

"You'll get it. The mothers of the girls are on their way here."

"Let's go."

The Crab led the way through another maze of corridors and stopped before a door marked PERSONAL EFFECTS.

"Hah. I have something here from the fish you and Captain Zapata brought in."

"Don't act like you're giving me a present. I paid twenty-five bucks for you to give it to *me* instead of to Zapata."

"There wasn't much left, hah, after the sharks finished snacking."

"Did Zapata try to impound it as evidence?"

"Of course. But it's yours."

The Crab opened the door and switched on overhead lights in a room filled with dank humidity and rusting filing cabinets. He opened a creaking file drawer and rummaged around, extracting a brown paper package bound tightly with coarse twine. He read the label, "Havana, John Doe, number nine hundred and eighty-three." He tossed the package to Bongo. "Hah, now you have all his worldly belongings!"

Bongo tucked the package under his arm and walked out. At the end of the corridor he saw three women entering the morgue. As he got closer, he could see that their faces were streaked with tears.

The women stopped. One asked, "Where are our girls?"

"I'm sorry," Bongo answered in a subdued voice. "They haven't been brought in yet. I just found them this morning."

"Where?"

"It's better if you don't know. They'll be here this afternoon."

The woman collapsed with a sob. The other two pulled her up, supporting her as she gasped. Regaining her composure, she asked in a whisper, "Were they . . . hurt? Hurt in some evil way?"

"No," Bongo lied. "The end was merciful."

The mothers clung together, the blood draining from their faces.

The Crab stepped around from behind Bongo. "Don't worry, ladies. When I deliver them for burial, they'll look as innocent as the day of their first Holy Communion."

"Keep quiet," Bongo said to the Crab under his breath.

"But I'm the maestro of makeup."

Bongo glared at the Crab, shutting him up.

One of the mothers pulled a wad of cash from her purse and handed it to Bongo. "We promised to pay you the other half if you found our daughters."

"Please know I did everything to find them, before—"

The mother choked back tears. "You don't have to explain. We understand."

Bongo handed the money to the Crab. "Here's your fee to bring in the young ladies."

The Crab clutched the bills to his chest. "I know what to do."

"Do it," Bongo ordered. He turned to the mothers, nodded respectfully, and headed for the door.

One of the mothers called after him in a pleading voice, "Find the monsters who did this to our children."

Bongo turned to look back at the mothers. "You have my word. I'll find the monsters."

The Crab spit out a sarcastic laugh. "Hah-hah-hah! You won't have to look hard. In Havana the monsters will find *you*."

In Havana the monsters will find you. The Crab's words haunted Bongo as he steered the Rocket up the steep La Rampa of Twenty-third Street, past the massive steel skeletal construction for the new Havana Hilton Hotel covering an entire city block, past tree-shaded Coppelia Park with its kiosks of ice cream vendors, balloon sellers and strolling families. The air hummed with the noise of shiny new American automobiles. Tree-lined sidewalks were crowded with shoppers loaded with merchandise from chic shops and modern department stores.

The Rocket's convertible top was down as Bongo zoomed through this sun-stunned, palm-laced paradise. Where would monsters hide in all this modern gleam? Bongo tried to put the idea out of his mind. He was a man on the way up, who wanted to play the lighter side of life with its spontaneous music and heady possibilities of chance. He was too young to be thinking like an old guy who knew all the crooked moves, anticipated all the disasters. But as the Rocket's engine propelled him into brighter light, he knew that invisible monsters *were* all around, even in the backseat, along for the ride, rattling their sabers like Spanish conquistadores, cracking their whips like plantation overlords, waiting for brutal times to roll again.

Bongo couldn't shake the feeling that he was being followed. He watched the cars behind him, reflected in the rearview mirror. He drove across the intersection of Avenue of the Presidents. He was heading in the opposite direction from where he really wanted to go. He couldn't take the chance that someone might be dogging him.

He thought about Mrs. Armstrong. She had telephoned him that morning. He heard her voice starting the conversation.

"Meet me at the California Shoe Store in central Havana."

"Why a shoe store?"

"Be there at four o'clock."

"You think it's safe to meet in public?"

"I have nothing to hide."

"I do."

"Don't worry about my husband. He's playing tennis at the Pan Americas Club."

Bongo replayed the short conversation in his mind as he drove alongside the Colón Cemetery, glimpsing its forest of white-marble saints, crucifixes and angels.

At the Almendares River, he crossed the concrete bridge arching above the green crawl of water. He looked down. On one side of the river was a muddy slope where a tangle of tropical vegetation nearly hid the squalor of battered wood and rusted tin shacks in the shantytown of El Fanguito, Small Mud. On the opposite shore was an untouchable world of privilege, imposing houses commanding the high ground, castles for the bourgeoisie. Bongo knew what it was to live in view of them. He had spent part of his childhood in El Fanguito, where excrement and wasted spirits seeped into the damp earth with the same fetid stink of hopelessness. It was a stink that didn't wash off, that success couldn't dissipate.

The familiar odor of El Fanguito floated up, making Bongo's nostrils twitch as he crossed the bridge. He gunned the Rocket's big engine, but no car could outrun the stink of memory.

Past the bridge, Bongo wound down toward the river, driving by lush gardens surrounding sprawling houses. Before one of the gardens was a high pink stucco wall with spikes of scarlet bougainvillea cascading over it. A driveway entrance cut into the wall, but was blocked by a closed gate. Bongo pulled to a stop and peered through the gate's iron bars, up to a stately Spanish Colonial building with high-arched windows. Parked in a motor court were Buick Rivieras, Lincoln Continentals, Chrysler New Yorkers and Cadillacs. One of the Cadillacs was a white convertible Eldorado.

Bongo turned off the Rocket's engine. He heard the hollow *thwack* of tennis balls being hit behind high green hedges. Tennis wasn't his game, two people smashing balls at one another until somebody won. He preferred the moves on a dance floor, which required that two people *merge* into one rhythm in order to win.

A uniformed guard came down the driveway from the far side of the gate and slipped a strapped rifle off his shoulder.

Bongo started the Rocket.

The guard aimed his rifle. "Stop!"

Bongo turned the engine off.

"What were you looking at?" the guard demanded.

"Admiring the architecture."

"There's no stopping. This is a private club."

"I didn't see a sign that said that."

"This says it." The guard poked the rifle barrel between the bars of the gate.

"That's a language I understand. I'm on my way."

"Wait, is that a Rocket Eighty-eight you're driving?"

"It's a 1955, two hundred horses under the hood."

"Don't move."

The guard opened the gate and stepped up to the Rocket. His gaze ran covetously over the slick red-and-white Naugahyde upholstery. His eyes riveted on the clear plastic center of the steering wheel, ostentatiously etched with the Oldsmobile insignia of conjoined North and South American continents. He whistled with appreciation.

"You must be sucking on the bribery bottle to get a car like this."

"I'm not in the government."

"How'd you get it, then?"

"Insurance."

"You're a repo goon?"

"I *sell* insurance."

"Insurance guys don't make any dough."

"I sold car insurance to a bartender at the Jockey Club in Oriental Park. He bet the ponies, but his touts were no good. He couldn't keep up the payments on the car, so I got it."

"That right?" The guard leaned over to admire the padded red dashboard and the radio's sparkling chrome dials. His rifle clanked on the driver's door. "You ever take her out on the new autoway and open her up real good?"

"Sure. Watch your rifle. She scratches easy."

"If I owned this beauty, I'd drive around Havana with the top down and wait for the girls to jump in, like fish into a boat."

"I'd rather have that," Bongo pointed up the driveway to the white Cadillac Eldorado.

"Fat chance."

"Who owns it?"

"An American."

"What's he do?"

"You know Americans, they don't have to do *anything*. Those guys have it made, going from one club to another. Life's a big party, tennis, dancing, swimming, eating."

"What about the Cadillac American? What's he doing here now?"

"Mr. Armstrong? Same thing every Tuesday and Thursday. Tennis. Arrives at four and plays for an hour."

"Then what?"

"Home to the little lady, I guess."

Bongo glanced at his wristwatch: 4:10. He started the Rocket. "Got to go." He backed up, almost knocking the guard over.

"Hey," the guard shouted, "maybe you could come back and give me a ride sometime!"

Bongo kept driving, retracing his route. Crossing over the Twenty-third Street Bridge again, he glanced down, remembering when the world below had blurred in the fury of a hurricane and everything flooded, leaving dead bodies in the trees and his father washed far out to sea.

When Bongo reached the Malecón, he merged into the traffic streaming along the ocean's edge. He sped past Torreon de San Lazaro, the seventeenth-century stone watchtower overlooking a cove where invaders had once landed from an armada of ships, storming ashore to plunder the fabled Pearl of the Antilles.

He then passed the monumental General Maceo, cast in bronze on a rearing horse. It had taken twenty-four bullets from the Spanish in the war for independence to kill this military titan. Now he was an inspiration, eternally prepared to ride into battle. The monument blurred as Bongo turned off the Malecón toward the towering concrete drabness of the Hotel Deauville, then drove up Galiano Avenue, a posh promenade of elegant apartment buildings, shops, restaurants and theaters, all showcased by flamboyant tropical foliage.

Bongo didn't want to leave the Rocket on the street where someone might recognize it. At Concordia Street he abruptly turned into an auto garage of perforated mortar-block walls resembling a giant wasp nest. He parked, took from the trunk the paper package that the Crab had given him, and exited onto the busy sidewalk. He looked both ways, to make certain no one was tailing him, then walked quickly until he reached a narrow, two-story building with its interior exposed through a glass facade. Above the doorway was a sleek aluminum sign: CALIFORNIA. The word shimmered, conjuring a world of exoticism. Bongo entered.

Inside, glass globes suspended from the ceiling rained brilliant light onto display cases populated by plastic molds of women's feet. The feet, cut off at the ankles, were provocatively fitted with high-heeled shoes, their varied upper strappings exhibiting an artistry of binding and thinly disguised functionality.

Despite the air-conditioned atmosphere, Bongo felt hot and uncomfortable. Elegantly dressed saleswomen around him stood motionless, their eyes gazing vacantly. This wasn't a place for a guy to be, even if he did love the mystery of feminine ways.

"May we be of assistance?"

The question floated in the chilly air. Bongo looked around to find its source, but the women, stationed strategically throughout the vast monotoned space, didn't break from their robotic conspiracy of non-emotional display.

Bongo didn't want to say Mrs. Armstrong's name. "I'm here to meet someone."

A woman's voice answered. "Of course, as we don't cater to gentlemen."

"She's American."

"Ah, why didn't you say so?" One of the women broke from her inanimate rank of haughty commerce. "Madam is upstairs. Follow me."

The woman turned and walked as if in a trance, up a staircase that appeared to have no visible supporting structure, just slick wooden steps ascending into midair and ending on a broad mezzanine. Mrs. Armstrong was seated on a low-slung suede sofa. A pretty shopgirl knelt at her feet.

"You're just in time." Mrs. Armstrong waved to Bongo. "Come here and help me choose."

Bongo ran a finger under the collar of his shirt. Even in the chilled air he was getting hotter. "I don't know anything about shoes."

Mrs. Armstrong raised a slender white finger with its pointed pearl-colored nail, and motioned for him to come closer.

There was no place for him to sit, except next to her on the plush sofa.

She smoothed her hand across the suede seat. "Come and sit here. You're just like a man, nervous to be surrounded by so many women."

Bongo sat down, breathing in her intoxicating perfume. The closeness of her body created an urgent velocity. He felt a centrifugal force pulling him toward her. He placed his hands on the leather seat, trying to get a grip.

Mrs. Armstrong stretched out a leg in front of her. She was wearing high-cut linen shorts; the length of her leg, from the lower thigh to the tip of her toes, was exhibited in flawless white-skin glory. "How do you like it?"

Bongo admired the outstretched piece of anatomy. He cleared his throat and admitted the obvious. "Perfection."

"Really?" Mrs. Armstrong turned her foot, getting a different angle on the leather strapping of a sandal that was wrapped in an open pattern from her toes to her ankle.

Bongo thought her foot looked like a glorious white fish held in netted bondage.

"I'll take these," Mrs. Armstrong announced, "in all three colors." She turned to Bongo. "What do you think? Shall we try on evening shoes?"

"Evening shoes?"

Mrs. Armstrong turned back to the shopgirl. "I want to try on all of your Italians."

"Of course, madam."

When the shopgirl was out of sight, Mrs. Armstrong's expression changed from one of high-spirited informality to business. "What have you to report?"

"Well, you were right. He's playing tennis now, at the Pan Americas Club."

"How do you know?"

"I saw his car there."

"Did you see Guy?"

"No, but the car—."

"What kind of investigator are you? You saw the car, but not him? How do you know *he* isn't following *you*?"

"The guard at the club told me he was there."

"Don't take a guard's word for anything. They make more money in bribes for telling lies than they do from their regular salary."

"If you know so much, why did you hire me?"

"Look. I don't need to verify that my husband is playing tennis at Pan Americas Club, golf at Biltmore Country Club, or skeet shooting at Luyano Hunters Club. These things I know. I want to find out whom I'm losing him to. Give me my money's worth."

"Do you know a bar on the waterfront called the Three Virgins?"

"Cute name. Never heard of it."

"Not such a cute place. It's a rough trade bar on the docks, frequented by sailors, laborers, occasional thrill-seeking tourists. It's not one of your country clubs. He's a regular there."

"Here comes the shopgirl. Let's stop talking about this?"

The girl knelt at Mrs. Armstrong's feet and began opening shoe boxes.

"Oh, my," Mrs. Armstrong sighed, "look at all these Perugias and Ferragamos. Amazing, so modern. I didn't see these styles in New York or Paris."

"I'm not surprised," Bongo said. "Havana's more sophisticated than most people think. Did you know more Cadillacs are sold here than in any other city in the world?"

"More than Beverly Hills, more than Monte Carlo? I don't believe it. How do you know?"

"Insurance. It's my job. I see all the statistics."

"Well, Mr. Statistic"—Mrs. Armstrong stretched a leg out again, a white, shapely offering—"why don't you kneel down there among all those shoes and find me the magic glass slipper?"

Bongo nodded toward the shopgirl. "It's better we leave you in the hands of an expert."

Mrs. Armstrong moved her face close to Bongo's. Her blond hair was held back beneath a silk Hermès scarf. Her perfectly proportioned ears were exposed, their lobes pierced by diamond clusters cut in the shape of dazzling flowers. Her blue eyes sparkled, her pink lipstick gloss shone, her seductive voice spilled with creamy danger. "Don't you want to be my Prince Charming?"

"You don't need a magic slipper." Bongo looked into her eyes. "You already are a princess."

"Oh, listen to him." Mrs. Armstrong smiled at the shopgirl. "He doesn't know that even a princess can use another pair of Ferragamos." She pointed to a pair of black-and-gold velvet pumps. "I'll try those first."

"Excellent choice, madam." The shopgirl raised her prize catch from its sea of satiny tissue paper and held it up, its needle-tipped heel resting in one upturned palm, its open-toed front balanced on her other palm.

"What's it called?" Mrs. Armstrong pursed her lips with delight. "Mr. Ferragamo always gives his creations such naughty names."

"The Velvet Gold-Caged Pump. We are the first store in all of the Americas to have it."

"Slip it on. I need it."

The shopgirl placed a hand behind Mrs. Armstrong's heel and negotiated the black-and-gold concoction onto the offered foot.

Mrs. Armstrong pivoted on the sofa seat, arched her back and raised her leg higher, taking the final fit of the shoe.

The shopgirl was enraptured by the white foot strapped into gold and black velvet.

Mrs. Armstrong smiled into the girl's eyes. "The princess has her slipper. Hurry, put the other one on before I turn into a pumpkin."

The girl nodded conspiratorially, slipping the other shoe into place.

Mrs. Armstrong stretched out both legs to admire the shoes that caught her feet in their perfect net. Her silk panties were exposed beneath her linen shorts.

The shopgirl blushed at the flash of silk.

Bongo was intrigued. He looked back and forth between both women. He noticed that beneath Mrs. Armstrong's lacy blouse, her nipples were hard and pricked at the thin material. It was unusual that a woman like her wasn't wearing a brassiere.

"Oh, my, I'm late," Mrs. Armstrong exclaimed, looking at her diamond-faced wristwatch. "My husband will be home before I am. I must run." She winked at the shopgirl. "Ring up the Ferragamos."

The girl slipped the velvet shoes off Mrs. Armstrong's feet, cradled them back into their cardboard nest, and hurried off.

Mrs. Armstrong swung quickly around to Bongo. "Give me the package."

"Package? What are you talking about?"

"Don't be coy. If it's not for me, who's it for?"

Bongo glanced at the brown paper package that he was holding. "It's not for you. It's personal."

"So, you have another girlfriend?"

"My girlfriend was killed in the Tropicana."

"Ah, I get it. It's one of your precious orchids. It's one of those *Dear Mirandas*."

"*Vanda dearei*."

"Oh, yes. You said there was only one in Havana."

"Lost in the Tropicana blast. I had it in my hands for a brief moment."

"That's like briefly having a girl in your arms."

"I had the right girl in my arms that night at the Tropicana. Her name was Mercedes."

"Mercedes and Vanda, your two lost loves. Your two eternal flames."

"No flames left. Everything's up in smoke."

"Sounds heavenly."

"You really don't give a damn about anyone but yourself." Bongo nailed her with a hard look. "I'll give you back your lousy money. Go find out who your husband's cheating with on your own."

Mrs. Armstrong stared silently with icy blue eyes.

Bongo's fingers started tapping on the stretched leather seat. It was a fast, hot-blooded rhythm, a volcano steaming.

Mrs. Armstrong placed her hand over his, as she had that day in his office, stopping the rhythm. "When you get nervous you start drumming."

"I'm not nervous." Bongo glared.

"Listen, Drummer Boy. Keep the money I gave you. I'll hire another investigator."

"Such an American. If you don't get what you want from some-one, you buy it from somebody else. Just like you buy elections and countries."

"I don't care about politics."

"What do you care about? Besides shoes?"

"Love."

"What do you Americans know about love?"

"We understand the *economics* of love. To really sell a torch song, you've got to be willing to light yourself on fire."

"So you've been burned. Your husband is cheating on you. Now you have your money's worth."

"And if you stay on the job, you'll get your money's worth."

In a flat voice, Bongo sarcastically quoted the Peggy Lee song he had heard on the radio. *"I hear you speak my name, softly in my ear you breathe a flame."*

"Don't get cute."

Bongo continued more sarcastically, *"Why quarrel without bliss when two lips want to kiss."*

"I see I'm influencing your taste in music. What about Johnnie Ray? Have you heard him?"

"I don't give a *damn*."

"You will. It's not his hit song, 'Cry,' that I want you to hear. It's 'Gee, but I'm Lonesome.' "

"Sounds complicated."

"The most profound thoughts are corny."

"Not in the Latin world. Love is about life or death, like war."

"That's what I'm talking about."

The shopgirl reappeared with Mrs. Armstrong's purchases,

wrapped like gifts in red paper with blue bows. "We've put the items on your charge account. Thank you, madam."

Mrs. Armstrong took the packages and turned back to Bongo. "Answer me something personal. What do you think of them?"

"Them?"

"The Ferragamos."

"You really want to know?"

"The honest truth?"

Bongo held his tongue. He knew better than to come between a woman and her taste in fashion.

"Come on, answer. This isn't a complicated crossword puzzle."

"You could walk on razor blades with those shoes, and you wouldn't bleed."

"My, how romantic."

Mrs. Armstrong shifted her attention to the shopgirl. "Honey, what's your opinion?"

The shopgirl didn't want to get in the middle. She smiled and kept her mouth shut.

"You Cuban girls are so tongue-tied when there's a man around," Mrs. Armstrong scolded. "Let me warn you about Havana men like this Romeo here. If you give them the chance, they will cut your heart out and throw flowers in the hole."

The shopgirl was stunned.

Mrs. Armstrong continued sweetly, "Honey, the next time I come in here, can you get them to turn the air-conditioning down? The cold makes my nipples so hard it takes hours to thaw them out."

The shopgirl blushed deeper than when she had seen Mrs. Armstrong's panties.

Bongo glanced at Mrs. Armstrong's blouse, her hard nipples stabbing like ice picks at the thin lace.

Mrs. Armstrong got up. "Got to run."

Bongo watched her walk away. She seemed to float down the floating staircase, a vanishing vision of charming venom.

The shopgirl began gathering up the scattered pairs of shoes that Mrs. Armstrong had tried on and discarded.

Bongo said, "Tell me about the shoes the lady bought."

"Which pair, sir? The lady bought several."

"The gold-and-black Italian jobs."

"The Ferragamos?"

"Yes. Do they come in other colors?"

"Besides the Velvet Gold-Caged Pump, there's also the Velvet Silver-Caged Pump."

"I'll take the silver."

"What size, sir?"

"Same size."

"I'll have them wrapped and waiting downstairs."

The girl walked off with a load of stacked boxes in her arms and descended the staircase. Bongo admired her shape from behind and the way her hips swung. She looked like she could definitely dance.

He gazed around. New female customers had arrived while he was talking with Mrs. Armstrong. They had the same smug pout of entitlement on their lipstick-glossed lips that Mrs. Armstrong had. Bongo wanted out.

He headed down the staircase and the shopgirl met him with a fancy wrapped package.

"How much?" Bongo asked.

"Twenty pesos, sir."

Bongo let out a whistle. "Twenty pesos? That's my rent."

The shopgirl smiled. "Mine too."

Bongo opened his wallet and pulled out a twenty. "Here, thanks." He started for the door.

"Sir, you forgot your shoes!"

He turned around. "And I forgot to ask your name."

"Mercedes," she brightened. "Like the car."

"*Mercedes*—that name has a special place in my heart. Well, my dear Mercedes, those are not my shoes, they're yours. You deserve them, after what you were put through."

"But I thought you and the lady were . . ."

"No!" Bongo laughed. "We're not. *You're* the one I'd like to dance with."

"I *am*?" She blushed a lovely pink.

"I'm never wrong about rhythm."

"Thank you."

Bongo winked, then slid his business card under the package's blue ribbon. "Come dancing with me sometime." He swung the glass door open and headed outside.

"I will," she called after him, "and I'll wear the shoes!"

Bongo stepped out onto the sidewalk in front of the California Shoe Store. After having been cooped up in icy air-conditioning he was mugged by the reality of tropical humidity bearing down. For a moment, he was disoriented by the fast movement of the crowd and the glaring sunshine. He lit up a cigar and paused to collect his thoughts. He didn't know if he had been fired by Mrs. Armstrong and he didn't give a damn if he had been. Her curt aloofness was making him feel something he had never felt before. It was a cross between desire and repugnance. He didn't know if he wanted to sleep with her or if he wanted her the hell out of his life. Christ, he couldn't even bring himself to think of her as Elizabeth. It was always *Mrs. Armstrong,* a chilly, impenetrable shield. And what if she wasn't joking about her husband's not playing tennis at the Pan Americas Club. What if he was tailing him instead? The only true thing to fear in life was a jealous husband, who could quickly become a cuckolded coward with a license to kill.

Bongo took a meditative puff on his cigar. He had less than an hour before meeting Mr. Wu in Chinatown, and Mr. Wu didn't like to be kept waiting.

Bongo held the Crab's package closer to his side, fearful that someone in the passing crowd might know its contents and jostle it away from him. He turned and headed up Galiano Avenue, as if returning to where the Rocket was parked. But he kept going past the garage, walking fast, turning right at Virtudes Street. In a few blocks he was in a different world. Women strutted provocatively in tight dresses that clung to every curve. Their lipstick-smeared lips called out taunting offers. "I'll unzip your cigar and smoke it for five pesos.

Only ten pesos for my ripe papaya. Fifteen pesos for the caboose."
The taunting made Bongo think of Mrs. Armstrong. This world was
a million miles from her world, but there was something similar
about the solicited price of things, where the line blurred between the
barter for emotions and the blunt offer of sex.

A very short man with slicked-back brilliantined hair and dressed
in a cheap white suit fell into step beside Bongo, waving the women
away with a cane as if shooing flies. The man strutted along—what
he lacked in height, he made up for with cockiness.

"Mister, what you looking for?"

"Nothing." Bongo held the package tighter under his arm and
quickened his pace.

"That's what they all say."

The man tried to size Bongo up. "Maybe you need a young one?
These nags are all too long in the tooth."

"Not interested."

"Twelve years old? Interested now?"

"No."

"Okay, a virgin. Ten years old."

"Forget it."

"A real virgin, not one who fakes it with a tomato in her pussy."

"I'm sure it's your sister who's for sale."

"How did you know?"

"Guys like you have a hundred sisters."

"Only one, a little watermelon with no seeds. Come on, she's
close by, a baby asleep in her crib."

Bongo growled, "Shove off."

"Hey, you're not American. You could pass for one, but your
Spanish is too good. My mistake, *hombre*. You get the local
discount."

"Your sister is half price?"

"How about an eight-year-old? Young man like yourself needs
green fruit. Half price, only ten *cocos*."

"*No!*"

"Damn, you're a hard sell. Americans are easy. But I have a hard
time even selling blow jobs to Cubans."

"Why's that?"

"All the loving women on this island. A man's not going to spend money in a restaurant when he can get the same meal for free at home."

Bongo stopped. "Do you have any midgets?"

"Midgets?" The short man leaned on his cane and scratched his chin.

"Yeah, midgets. Little people your size."

"My size?"

"I hear little guys like you have really big dicks."

"That's what you're looking for?"

"About your size."

"Go to hell, you bumhole pigeon!"

The short man turned angrily away and stalked off, slashing his cane threateningly at the women along the street who were laughing at him.

One of the women called to Bongo, "You're a clever one, you pissed off the little dick! How about I light your cigar for free?"

Bongo blew her a kiss and waved her away. His eyes were already taken by a sign that read: THE FIRST UNCENSORED MOVIE HOUSE IN THE WORLD. SEE IT TO BELIEVE IT.

The sign was above a green lacquered door. Next to the door was a movie poster in a glass case. Beneath the glare of sunlight bouncing off the glass Bongo could make out the image of a blond woman, naked from the waist up, hiding the swell of her full breasts with a strategically placed plastic beach ball. Across the poster's top, bold red letters declared: "*Brandi Barr and Her Girlfriend at the Beach!* Last Day!"

What made Bongo walk through the green door and buy a ticket was not the promise of Brandi in a frolic with her friend, rather, it was the face on the poster. The high forehead, classically arched eyebrows and aristocratic nose of the face were eerily familiar.

The theater was a claustrophobic room reeking of tropical rot. An air conditioner churned the moldy atmosphere, its clanky motor competing with a metal rattle from the movie projector. A mumbling and fumbling came from men seated on shabby chairs. Bongo sat down at the end of an aisle. There was a sigh from the men as a naked redhead on the screen became entwined with a boa constrictor, a bigger sigh as a naked brunette cavorted intimately with a donkey.

The projector's light was cut and the screen went black. Boos went up from the men. The screen flashed back to life and the men cheered at a projected title: *Brandi Barr and Her Girlfriend at the Beach*. Suddenly a larger-than-life Mrs. Armstrong was on the screen. She was naked, strutting across a sandy beach in high-heeled shoes with a plastic beach ball tucked under her arm. She stopped, waved, thrust her breasts up. The men stamped their feet and whistled for the blonde to do more.

Bongo couldn't believe what he was seeing. Was it *his* Mrs. Armstrong? He scrutinized the body on the screen, observing every curve and feature, even the three tantalizing beauty marks on the left breast. Maybe it was just his imagination that was transforming all blond females into Mrs. Armstrong.

The giant Mrs. Armstrong kept waving, all of her fleshy assets jiggling. Then it became clear what she was waving at. The men were thrilled and let out a series of panting grunts as if they were humping up a hill. From the far side of the screen another woman appeared, younger than Mrs. Armstrong, pert and pretty, her skin giving off an amber glow. She too was naked, wearing only high-heeled shoes. Her heels poked holes into the sand as she walked forward with a bright smile, the *identical* smile of the pretty shopgirl in the California Shoe Store.

In a smoothly provocative motion the nude Mrs. Armstrong raised her arms high into the air, the beach ball balanced in her hands, then let it fly. Her young friend stretched her arms out and caught it. Then, with a tantalizing wink at the audience, she swiveled her hips and threw the ball back. Mrs. Armstrong leapt up, her back arched, her pelvis thrust out as she caught the plastic globe in midair.

"Shut the fuck up!" an angry voice yelled out from the back of the theater.

Down in front of the screen two men were in a heated discussion. They paid no attention to the demand from the back for silence.

Another man behind Bongo shouted, "For Christ's sakes, can it! We're trying to jack off in here!"

The two men in the front row didn't quiet down; their voices grew louder.

Next to Bongo, a man leapt from his seat. "Get the fuck out of here, you faggots, before I cut your balls off!"

The loud men in front fell silent, left their seats and raced up the aisle past Bongo. Once again Bongo couldn't believe his eyes. It was Guy Armstrong and a Cuban, the same Cuban Armstrong had left the Three Virgins with the night Bongo had followed them to the house.

Bongo waited a few minutes, then walked out into the lobby.

The ticket seller behind the lobby counter wore a guayabera shirt stained under the arms with yellow rings of sweat. The sweat stains were the same color as his teeth when he opened his mouth to grin at Bongo. "You're leaving before the best part. You can't believe what goes on between those babes and the ball."

"I'm sure every man in there would like to be that ball."

"Why don't you go back in? You can't imagine what they do in the hot sand."

"I can imagine."

"Only in Havana is there a theater like this. First of its kind in the world."

"I think a few other places have it by now."

"Like where?"

"Miami, New York, Amsterdam, Paris."

"Why the fuck would a man travel that far, when he could see it here in Havana?"

"Good logic."

Bongo checked his watch. He had to choose between following Armstrong or meeting Wu. He swung open the green door and stepped out in time to catch a glimpse of Armstrong and the Cuban as they turned the corner at the end of the next block. Bongo followed them, staying far enough behind so that he wouldn't be spotted. When the two men got to Flogar's department store they stopped under the massive brick overhang of the entrance. Whatever it was they were talking about was becoming more intense. They entered the department store, disappearing among the shoppers.

There was no time to follow the men in such a crowd. Bongo

crossed San Rafael Street and kept walking back up Galiano Avenue, quickening his pace. When he passed in front of the California Shoe Store, he stopped and glanced through the window to see if he could catch sight of the pretty shopgirl. She was inside, smiling at a woman trying on a pair of shoes. She was not at the beach with Mrs. Armstrong.

Bongo walked the maze of Chinatown's narrow streets. Chinese men were pushing carts loaded with vegetables, fruits and fish. Chinese women were selling bright toys, kites and lychee nuts. Canaries trilled from bamboo cages, noodle shops were filled with customers sipping from porcelain bowls. Laughing children darted in and out of the tiniest spaces.

Bongo stopped in front of a brick building with a sign above the door: WHITE ORCHID LAUNDRY. He entered a steamy room lined with stone basins. Scalding water funneled into the basins from overhead pipes. Chinese women, with bandannas tied around their heads, stood on elevated platforms above the basins, stirring clothes in soapy water with long paddles. Beyond the basins was an open courtyard strung with ropes from which clothes hung in the sunlight. Between the rows more bandanna-headed women took down dry clothes and hung up wet ones in a never-ending cycle of labor.

Bongo walked along a row of wet clothes to the far side of the courtyard. He stepped through a low doorway and entered a semidark warehouse where bulging sacks of rice were stacked. People were sitting or lying on many of the sacks. A slurred female voice called out. "Hey, Bongo-boingo-buddy!"

Bongo tried to find the voice among the shadows. Chinese men were making hollow sucking sounds as they inhaled opium through long-stemmed pipes. An old, thin Chinese woman moved among them in clouds of smoke, smoothing the foreheads of those in a stupor, refilling the pipes of others.

"Boingo, bingo, bongo, come join the party!"

Bongo gazed further into the dim light.

"Over here, drummer boy."

Bongo moved among the shadows, between listless bodies sailing on their pillows of rice.

"Keep coming, Mr. Investigator. You're almost home."

Bongo rounded a wooden support column to find Sailor Girl slouched on a pile of rice sacks with two uniformed American sailors. Her jaunty sailor's cap tilted off to one side of her head as she sucked on the slender mouthpiece of an opium pipe. She coughed, then offered the pipe to Bongo. "Do you want a magic puff?"

"I don't ride the tiger."

Sailor Girl's eyes rolled. "I'm not riding the tiger, the tiger's riding me."

One of the sailors laughed. "Baby, that tiger ain't riding you, it's eating you, gobbling up your little titties and licking out your brain."

"Licking my brain," Sailor Girl moaned. "That's what it feels like." Her head lolled from side to side. "Last time I saw Bongo he was making love to a goddamn orchid or something. Should have come dancing with me instead of almost getting his head blown up in the Tropicana."

"Blown *off*," one of the sailors corrected. "His head blown off."

"Goddamn it," Sailor Girl slurred, "don't correct me. Without that uniform you're just a hick with an eighth-grade education. What do you know about blown-off, blowed-off, blown-up? You can just blow me."

"Now, how am I going to *do* that?" the sailor smirked.

"Use your imagination," Sailor Girl laughed. "Pretend I'm your boyfriend here."

The sailor laughed back at her. "I don't have to pretend."

Sailor Girl leaned close to Bongo and fluttered her eyelashes. "You see my eyes?"

"Beautiful," Bongo answered. "Big as soup plates."

"Trouble is, sailors don't want my beautiful eyes," Sailor Girl said sadly. "They want a boy in every port, a rooster in every pot." She squinted at Bongo as if he were a mile away. "Say, where's your cute girlfriend? The one you were dancing with New Year's Eve?"

"Blown up," Bongo answered.

"Blown up? The whole world's about to be blown up in an

atomic blast. So don't be a party-pooping square and give me back that pipe."

"You're holding it," Bongo said.

"Oh . . . yeah." Sailor Girl looked down, then lifted the pipe and sucked at the stem. The low-burning coal in the pipe bowl glinted. Smoke seeped from Sailor Girl's lips as she spoke. "Like . . . I . . . was . . . saying . . ."

"She's flying," one of the sailors said, pulling the opium pipe out of Sailor Girl's limp hands. He winked at Bongo. "Sure you don't want to join the party?"

"Must be my lucky day," Bongo answered. "Everyone's asking me to join their party."

"We give rain checks," the sailor said.

"But we prefer cash," the other sailor chimed in.

"No, thanks." Bongo shook his head.

"We're shipping out tomorrow."

"Fucking Korea," the other sailor added.

"The girls there aren't as cute as the Cuban bunnies," his pal offered.

"But the boys are more beautiful," his friend countered.

"Brother, you can say that again. Bee-yew-tee-full."

An angry voice boomed from the shadows. "Bongo, you're late for your appointment. Mr. Wu doesn't like late."

Ming came out of the shadows and stood in front of Bongo. He was wearing a purple suit and a wide purple tie with an embroidered snarling dragon, the same combination he wore at the Tropicana on New Year's Eve. Bongo had heard that the Chinese were superstitious about colors.

Ming said sternly, "I've got to frisk you."

"You know I'm packing. I'm always packing."

Ming reached under Bongo's coat and slipped the gun from its shoulder holster. "You'll get it back."

"When?"

"When Mr. Wu is finished with you."

Sailor Girl fluttered her eyelashes, attempting semiconsciousness as her head rolled from side to side. "Wu's who? Wu who?"

"She's gone," Bongo said to Ming.

"When was she ever here?" Ming answered.

Ming led the way out of the darkened warehouse and into a room hissing with steam. Chinese workers were bent over hot clothespresses, perspiration dripping off their faces as they repeatedly slammed iron lids down on wet laundry.

Ming looked over his shoulder at Bongo as he kept walking. "Too bad about your girlfriend. But Mr. Wu told you not to be in the Tropicana."

"Then why the hell didn't he tell me what was going to happen?"

Ming stopped, turned and faced Bongo with his broad, muscular body. "Don't curse when using Mr. Wu's name."

"I wasn't cursing, I was swearing."

"It's disrespectful."

"Listen, Ming, I know fourteen families control everything in Chinatown. I know what Mr. Wu's position is, but it's not like I'm going to have an audience with the Pope. So lighten up and don't be so goddamned Charlie Chan sensitive."

"Fuck you."

"Man, that's the fifth offer I've had today!"

Ming poked his finger into Bongo's chest. "You're in Chinatown now. No disrespect."

"Not a disrespectful bone in my body."

A sour expression spread across Ming's face. "Answer me something."

"Yeah."

"When you're in a Chinese restaurant, do all the waiters look the same?"

"Now that you mention it, yes."

Ming sniffed with disdain. "When I'm in a Cuban restaurant, all you assholes look the same to me."

"What about when you're in an American restaurant?"

"I've never been to America."

"You wouldn't have a problem there. The waiters wear name tags telling you who they are."

"Really?"

"Maybe Chinese waiters should wear name tags, that way we'd know who was who."

"Who gives a fuck about who their waiter is?"

Ming turned around and led the way up a circular staircase that rose from the middle of the pressing room. The staircase spiraled higher and higher, ending at a small door.

Bongo was panting for breath. He had to give up smoking Lucky Strikes; they weren't so lucky for his health.

Ming knocked on the door, then pointed at his watch. "You have ten minutes with Mr. Wu. No more."

"I thought I had thirty."

"You did, but you were twenty minutes late."

"I had a good reason. Mr. Wu would understand."

"Mr. Wu understands everything. You understand nothing."

"You know, Ming, you remind me of that Chinese Kwan Kong guy."

"*Saint* Kwan Kong."

"Yeah, the one who was ambushed and beheaded. When a monk found the guy his body was running around in circles, screaming, 'Where's my head? Where's my head?'"

Ming placed his index finger on the knot of his dragon tie and cocked his thumb on the underside, then quickly pulled his hand down the length of the tie. The silk slicing between his fingers sounded like a knife slitting a throat.

Bongo opened the door into a jungle of orchids beneath a glass roof crisscrossed with wood lathing that provided shade from the sun. Piped up from the laundry below, steam vented into the room with a hiss, then was caught in a cold blast from a battery of air conditioners. The hot and cold air swirled together into a humid mist. Mr. Wu stood in the midst of lush blooming exotica; the sweet mash odor from the smoldering cigarette at the end of his long ivory holder mingled with the perfume of cinnamon, vanilla and gardenia.

"Greetings, my wandering friend." Mr. Wu spoke without looking up. His head was bowed toward a crimson bloom, his nostrils twitching at its aroma. His chest puffed up beneath his long blue silk tunic. He pulled back with an odd smile, remaining at a discreet distance, as if fearful that his scrutiny might frighten the flower. He moved cautiously to the swollen bloom of the next orchid, maintaining his air of deference as he surveyed the specimen from different angles, not allowing his gaze to become licentious. "We cannot expose our male irreverence to these creatures," Mr. Wu said. "Otherwise they will droop and die. They are like women, wanting their beauty admired, not raped with a leer."

Mr. Wu's rapture had a hypnotic effect on Bongo, his streaming words were like an ancient incantation: "Chao Shin-Kem wrote the first book on orchids in the twelfth century. He was from Fukien Province, China's intellectual center and the heart of orchid culture. Shin-Kem instructed how orchids must be revered, for gazing at their beauty is to experience universal sexuality. If man loses his respect and beauty denies him, then man is worse off than before he knew of beauty's existence. All else will fade to pale. If that happens, man's torment will be beyond measure."

Bongo inhaled the perfumed air. He thought he could still smell the delicious *Vanda dearei,* its scent imprinted in his memory.

"Have you ever," Mr. Wu asked, "loved so much that after you lost that love your life itself was lost, and you became a burnt-out shell, a walking, talking dead man?"

"No, I can't say that I have," Bongo answered. "My philosophy is to not get too close to that precipice."

"All of those men down there in the rice warehouse, sucking on pipes, sucking on what you call foreign mud, they have lost the beauty once glimpsed. They are dead. Nothing can fill the hole in their hearts."

"You've got some other customers down there who I don't think have hearts."

"Healing medicine is for all," Mr. Wu sighed. "That is our custom, rich and poor are equal, all entitled to the same medicine."

"I saw Americans downstairs. You get many?"

"White Americans prefer cocaine. Cocaine is just a tourniquet, merely covers the wound. Opium fills the wound with dreams. So the Americans we get are mostly black."

"Why's that?"

"You know what they say, no matter how long the Chinese have been in Cuba, they're still homesick. Those Chinese you see in the warehouse, their pipes are filled with dreams of China. The black Americans, their pipes are filled with dreams of Africa."

"How come I don't see any black Cubans in the warehouse?"

"Ah . . ." Mr. Wu rose from the flower he was admiring and faced Bongo. "That's because in Cuba the black ones secretly kept their African religion, they have their own dreams."

"And the black Americans?"

"In America, the black ones only have the white religion. They smoke the wrong dreams. So they need our pipes."

"Speaking of dreams," Bongo said, "thank you again for the *Vanda dearei.*"

"I told you not to take her into the Tropicana." Wu shook his head sadly. "She never should have been in such a place. It's a tragedy she's gone."

"There are worse tragedies." Bongo remembered Mercedes' smiling face as she waved to him for the last time.

"She was unique. Don't think there will ever be another."

"I don't." Bongo still saw Mercedes' smiling face.

"Men make that mistake, they always think there will be another. But each beauty is unique and can never be repeated."

"Amen to that, Mr. Wu."

"Now, my dear wanderer, why are you here?"

"I brought you something." Bongo handed Wu the brown package that had been tucked beneath his arm.

"Is it a gift, or a payment for debts owed?"

"I need your help."

"Will it cost me?"

"No."

"Then let's have a look." Wu set the package on his potting table. "Will it blow up in my face?"

"No harm will come to you."

Wu slipped a blade under the thick twine binding the brown paper. "This is tied well. Is it money?"

"No."

Wu sliced the twine and began unwrapping the package. "Three layers of paper. What can be so precious?"

A salty, nauseating stench wafted up. Wu let go of the wrapping and turned his face away in disgust.

Bongo pulled at the remainder of the wrapping, trying not to inhale any more than he had to. A balled-up gray cloth object lay on the table.

Wu scolded, "You shouldn't have brought this here. This is a place of beauty."

"I didn't mean any disrespect."

Bongo carefully spread the gray ball out. It was a piece of clothing, faded and torn.

Wu held his nose. "What is it?"

"The underpants of shark bait."

"That's not funny." Wu pinched his nose harder. "You're insult-ing me."

"I paid the Crab at the morgue a bribe to get this."

"You wasted your money."

"These are the underpants of a murdered man."

"Why bring them here?"

"They might have something to do with downstairs."

"The warehouse?"

"The laundry."

"I don't understand."

Bongo turned over the frayed waistband, exposing the faint inky outline of a number. "I need to know which laundry customer had this number."

Wu bent closely to examine the mark. "Impossible to make out."

"Try."

Wu picked up a large silver-handled magnifying glass, the one he used in the most intimate moments of trying to agitate his reluctant orchids into reproducing. He peered through the magnifier. "It's not a mark from one of the Chinatown laundries." He squinted for better focus. "Nor is it a downtown Havana mark. It's farther out, past Vedado, way out in the Country Club area."

"Then a laundry there would know who the number belongs to?"

"If I find the right laundry, they will have a record. We Chinese keep good records, better than lawyers."

"Once I get the name of the dead man who was wearing these, I can try to find his murderer."

"Don't forget the business I'm in. I know everyone's laundry. I know all the secrets in Havana."

"Please help me on this, and—" Bongo hesitated. He wasn't cer-tain he could trust Wu.

"And?"

Bongo took a chance. "And also help me find beauty."

"Go on."

"My sister? Where is she? You said you know all the secrets."

Wu laid the magnifying glass down on the table. He wrapped the package back up. The air cleared.

"Ah . . . the Panther, the beauty that rivals the orchids." He took Bongo by the arm. "Come with me."

Wu guided Bongo down a row of long-stemmed orchids whose heads were bowed from the weight of bright flowered crowns. He spoke softly as he walked. "In his first book, Chao Shin-Kem wrote the story of only twenty orchids. He knew nothing beyond his village. He wasn't aware that orchids account for one out of every ten flowering plants in the world. There are twenty-five thousand *different* species of orchids, our dear Cuba alone has more than two hundred natives. What's fascinating is that the orchid spends its life living off of another plant, a host; it can only survive with symbiosis. That's why orchids have so many guises. Some are marble-smooth like the testicles of a young boy, others are pendulous and hairy like the swinging balls of a bull, some have penises, narrow as pencils or fat as cigars. And then there are all the lady orchids, exposing their most intimate parts, their fleshy petals spread, their labia excited and sometimes gorged with fluorescent colors." Wu stopped abruptly.

A spectacular orchid towered before the men, spicing the air with a lush gingery and gardenia scent.

Wu whispered conspiratorially, *"Angraecum sesquipedale."*

"Unbelievable," Bongo marveled. "It's as tall as a person."

"She is."

"But what does she have to do with my sister?"

"She is more than just a perfumed dream," Wu said with gravity. "Gaze upon this beauty and see if you can find your own life within hers."

Bongo wondered, why all this Chinese inscrutability? Why all these tests of his patience? Why didn't Wu just say what he knew about the Panther? Bongo examined the plant; its magnificent trunk of a stalk thrust high, from its top exploded riotous fleshy tendrils that cascaded in a colorful fall back to earth, where the tendril tips tenaciously dug into soft soil to re-root.

Wu asked, "Have you ever seen such blooms as these on an orchid?"

"Never." Bongo bent closer. "They are the size of human hands. And there are so many of them, budding out of the trunk, blooming off of the tendrils."

"What does their white shape look like?"

"Spiders. Enormous star-shaped white spiders."

"And?"

Bongo's mind flashed to the banyan in the Tropicana that he was sitting under with Mercedes, the tree that the white spider had fallen from. Suddenly he saw the black woman swathed in white, her hand coming down to smash the spider.

Wu watched the expression change on Bongo's face. "You are *there*."

"Where?"

"On the road to finding the White Spider Woman. She will lead to your sister."

"How do you know about the Spider Woman? You weren't in the Tropicana that night. You were outside in your car with Ming."

"I know everyone's laundry." Wu smiled. "I know everyone's secrets."

4.

Everything Shines

I'll tell you what you can't get in America anymore."

"What's that?" Johnny PayDay asked.

"A fucking shoe shine worth a shit," Lizard said. "It's the end of civilization when you can't get a decent shine. Only two places left where a man can get shined right, here and Mexico City. It's only greaser bean-farters and nigger boys who can get the job done." Lizard peered down at the shaved head of Monkey Shines as he rapped his shoe-rag across shoe leather. "Ain't that right, nigger?"

Shines didn't answer.

"I forgot," Lizard laughed. "These black Cubans don't speak English like our niggers, they only speak Spanish."

Shines understood English. Having shined shoes for thousands of hours in the hot sun, he had been all ears and picked up languages, the basics anyway. That's how he'd been able to get ahead, that's how one day he would make his fortune selling lottery tickets to tourists.

Broadway Betty stood next to PayDay. She wore a short zebra-print skirt and a cobra-print halter top; it was what she thought of as her jungle look. "Johnny, honey, can I buy some peanuts?"

PayDay pulled out his wallet and handed Betty a dollar. "Here, babe. And get me some too, peanuts taste better down here."

Betty headed toward a crowd of boys standing in the cool shadow of the José Martí monument. Long strings of peanuts were looped around the boys' necks. They shouted at the glamorous customer and jostled each other, trying to prove who had the best nuts.

Lizard nodded his head in approval at the competition. "These Cubes are natural-born hustlers. Who says all they can do is cut cane and roll cigars?"

"I never said that."

"I didn't mean *you*. Cuba's got a future with hustlers like this. You know the difference between Cuba and the States?"

"What?"

"The nigger problem."

"There's lots of black ones here too."

"Yeah, but here the niggers all think they're Spanish."

"How'd that happen?"

"The Cubes gave them Spanish names and only let them speak Spanish. After that, they fucked the hell out of their women. Smart, huh?"

PayDay pulled out a candy bar and carefully peeled down the wrapper. He took a bite, watching his wife in her tight zebra skirt, surrounded by boys who were shaking strings of nuts at her. He wondered, had she gone to bed with the Bad Actor? PayDay had asked her, but she insisted that the Actor had been a real English gentleman, and promised to introduce her to Lucy and Desi so she could get their autographs. "Where did you say the Actor lives?"

"Like I told you a hundred times," Lizard said, "he has a place at the Hotel Nacional to keep up appearances, and a secret penthouse at the Capri where he can pop underaged cherries."

"Is the Capri penthouse on the roof?"

"No, the roof's got a swimming pool."

"A swimming pool on a roof?"

"It's something. At night you can skinny-dip under the sky."

Lizard looked down at the black bobbing head of Shines as he worked wax into shoe leather with his fingertips. "That's right, boy, wax it up."

Lizard turned back to PayDay. "There could be a nigger problem here one day. Real niggers could take over, not just house niggers like President Batista. That's one reason the Right Guys got involved in local politics."

"Does the Actor—"

"Forget about him until your job is done."

"I'm itching to do it. Then I'm going to whack the Actor."

"You can't touch him unless the Right Guys say you can! Like I told you, the Actor's an inside-out guy, working both sides. When the time's right, he'll outlive his usefulness and the Right Guys will feed him to you."

"I'll eat him alive." PayDay swallowed the last of his candy bar, folded the wrapper and slipped it into his pocket.

"The thing that's twisted about the niggers here is"—Lizard continued his cultural appraisal—"they've got a queer religion. They've got a Saint Joan, or Saint Barbara, or something like that, and she changes into another god; they call it a Shango or a Chango. Now, here's the funny part, this Shango-Chango is a *guy*. So if you think about it, the niggers are worshiping a cross-dressing, cigar-smoking, rum-sucking, rumba-ass transvestite."

Shines' rag *swick-swack-swick*ed as he bore down in a fury on Lizard's shoe, hoping that the friction would set the leather on fire.

PayDay turned around to watch Betty. He could watch his wife for hours. Every little way her sweet body moved excited him.

Lizard interrupted PayDay's reverie. "Would you stop ogling your wife's ass like you're a teenager with a boner caught in his zipper?"

"We aren't teenagers. We're married."

"You really are a sucker. The reality of marriage is, the woman doesn't want you. What the woman wants is a kid. And she'll let you fuck her every which way to Sunday to get it; in the cunt, the ass, the mouth, the ears, and if that's not enough, she'll cut you a new hole to fuck her in. After that she doesn't need you, you're finished, the great embarrassing fuck that gave her what she wanted. The joke is, her kid, the little angel, wasn't born in heaven, but in a sperm-spewing hell where she made you fuck like you had a gun to your balls and a hot poker up your ass."

"Betty doesn't want kids."

"Phew-wee, man! They *all* say that until their kid clock goes off like a stick of dynamite in an empty oil drum."

"Betty means it. We've been married seven years."

"Don't forget that seven-year itch, pal. It's the same for women as for men, except women itch in a different place."

PayDay imagined Lizard as a corpse with a PayDay candy wrapper stuffed in his mouth.

Lizard gazed down at Shines with an expression of admiration.

"Would you look at this one go, like a house on fire. He just can't do enough to please a customer."

"He takes pride in his work."

"Nah. He's in it for the tip," Lizard snorted. "Now listen to me, before your precious bride comes back. Do you remember when you're scheduled for the job?"

"Three past three."

"Right. And what hotel room? "

"Top floor, out of the elevator, turn right, end of hall, last door."

"Yeah, and don't forget, the race is always timed to the minute. Three past three is when the lead car passes by. Everybody will be distracted."

"It'll go off as planned."

"Big bonus for you if it does."

"I'll settle for the other half of my dough."

"Listen, the Right Guys are so powerful, nobody can move a blade of grass without their permission. You pull this job off and there will be something bigger for you. Guaranteed."

"What's bigger than a President? A Pope?"

"Not a bad idea."

"So what's bigger? What's the idea?"

"A bigger country, a bigger president."

PayDay looked down nervously at Shines. Lizard had a big mouth, and a big mouth leads to a big downfall.

Lizard grinned. "I told you not to worry. Monkeys like him can't even read a comic book in Spanish, let alone speak English."

"I've got the details. Let's cut it."

"Here comes your wife, anyway. What's she doing with those strings of peanuts wrapped around her neck?"

"She's having fun. She's on vacation. Relax."

Lizard wasn't relaxed. Betty's buns looked great wrapped in the tight zebra skirt, and her big boobs flounced beneath the flimsy halter top. She looked dumb and blond and oblivious, just the way Lizard liked it. He wanted to slap the sultry pout on her lips and jump her bones. He remembered seeing her coming out of the Nacional with the Actor, stumbling on her high heels, her skirt hiked up. Lizard was ready to bet anything that that slick Hollywood shit had been fucking her so hard that it woke up the Pope in Rome, fucking her so hard that the penguins in Antarctica felt the ice shake beneath them. Just by the way she was walking now, it was clear she had been fucked up one side and down the other. Lizard would fuck her harder than the Actor. That was the best thing about his job, he got to fuck *everything*.

Betty flapped the wreaths of peanuts slung around her neck in front of PayDay. "Look at what I got for your dollar!"

"That's great, babe."

"You could have bought twice as many for fifty cents," Lizard snorted sarcastically. "You got poked by those Cuban Petes."

The Cuban boys had followed Betty, hoping to make one last sale.

Lizard snarled at them, "Get the fuck out of here!"

The boys all pulled back, except one, who held a bucket of pineapple slices in ice.

"I love that shit," Lizard barked. "Give it to me." He grabbed the bucket and shoved a dollar at the boy. The boy snatched the bill and ran away.

Lizard slurped a pineapple slice, smacking the cold yellow fruit between his duck-bill lips. Splashes of juice rained down onto his shoes.

Shines wiped off the syrupy drops as they fell onto Lizard's shoes, attempting to preserve the gleam on the leather he had worked so hard to achieve.

Betty smiled at PayDay. "Hon, those kids are so cute."

PayDay nodded. "Glad you got what you wanted."

"Know what I want now?" Betty cooed.

"What's that, babe?"

"To eat Moors and Christians."

"Eat *what*?"

A cruel gurgle came from Lizard's throat as he choked and spit out a half-chewed piece of yellow goo. "Moors and Christians," he blurted. "That's just beans and rice shit, cooked in pig lard. It'll give you a fat ass. You want a fat ass like a Cuban mama?"

Betty didn't think Cuban mamas had such fat asses, most of them were teenagers anyway, they looked sweet. But she wasn't going to answer Lizard. Instead, she encouraged her husband. "Hon, buy me some Moors and Christians."

PayDay shrugged. "I don't know where to go."

Lizard butted in. "Not all the restaurants serve it. In the Right Guys' restaurants we've got Italian pasta, not Cuban slop."

Betty gave her husband a helping smile. "My guidebook says that the Floridita restaurant is right around the corner and that famous people go there. Maybe we'll see someone famous eating Moors and Christians?"

"All right, babe," PayDay said. "I'll take you."

Betty took his arm. "Let's go have lunch."

"Wait a minute, sister!" Lizard jabbed a finger in front of Betty like a mad traffic cop stopping a line of cars. "The Floridita's a piss-hole filled with wall-to-wall tourists, trust-fund babies and pretend big shots. Me and PayDay are going to the Hotel Plaza to have some oysters and continue our man talk. This is no holiday, this is business."

PayDay could definitely see Lizard as a dead man with a PayDay candy wrapper shoved in his mouth. He gave his wife a mournful look. "Sorry, babe."

Betty frowned, then quickly brightened, giving PayDay a kiss on the cheek. "I'll go to the Floridita and eat some Moors and Christians. Don't worry about me. I love this country, everybody's so cute."

PayDay grinned. "I'll bring you back here someday when it's not all work."

Lizard nudged PayDay approvingly. "Now you're talking, pal. Bring the little lady back when it's all play." He turned to Betty. "You'll like that, won't you?"

Betty looked Lizard right between the eyes and trilled one of her Broadway show tunes. *"From this happy day, no more blue songs, only whoop-dee-do songs, from this moment on."*

Lizard scratched his head and looked at PayDay. "What the fuck is she crooning about?"

PayDay didn't answer.

"Girly," Lizard said to Betty, "just go away. I've got to talk to your hubby."

Betty gave PayDay another peck on the cheek. "See you back at the hotel, hon." She walked away with a little wiggle in her zebra skirt.

Lizard fished out a quarter from his pocket, flipped it in the air with a flourish, caught it in his open palm and slapped it into Shines' upturned hand. "Here you go, boy."

Shines stared at the silver coin.

Lizard advised PayDay, "I never tip these guys, ruins it if you do. We don't want to dampen their entrepreneurial spirit."

"Sometimes a tip is a good thing."

"Not here. It'll put ideas into their heads. Next thing you know they'll have egos bigger than French waiters. Come on, let's go over to the Plaza."

The two men walked across the square, past a group of men shoving and shouting, preparing for a fight.

PayDay asked, "What's going on?"

"That's the so-called hot corner of the square. It's where these Cubes come to talk about their true passion, and it ain't women or politics, it's baseball. Baseball's more of a life-and-death blood sport here than bullfighting is in Spain."

"So what's to argue about?"

"*Everything,*" Lizard smiled.

"Like what?"

"Like whether or not Hurricane threw yesterday's game. Whether he's a national hero or a cokehead on the take."

"They could be right either way."

"Chumps."

In the hot corner fists started flying, honor was on the line.

"About the Big Race hit"—Lizard lowered his voice and looked around suspiciously to make certain he wasn't being overheard— "the President won't be seated in front of the *Maine* monument."

"Where's he going to be?"

"In front of the Nacional. The Right Guys wanted it kept secret until the end. Not even you could know."

"Is the shooter still going to be in the same place?"

"Yeah."

"Then nothing's changed for me."

"One thing. No fucking candy bars."

"What do you mean?"

"Don't leave one of your goddamn PayDay wrappers rammed into the shooter's mouth after you finish the job."

PayDay smiled a fake expression of sincerity. "You've got my word on it."

Monkey Shines watched the two Americans as they walked off across the square, almost getting themselves mixed up in a fistfight over baseball in the hot corner. Shines glanced down at the thin slice of silver in his palm; twenty-five cents for an hour's worth of work. That big American had kept talking and talking and Shines had kept shining and shining, and all he was left with was twenty-five cents and no tip. Shines tucked the coin into his pocket and grinned. He might have been born on a street named bitterness, but he was an eternal optimist. He wasn't going to let anything get him down. Life was good, and he had the only shine spot beneath the great Martí, the father of the country. All the other shiners had to work the sidewalks or in the stone arcades. He was in the center of everything. He liked watching kids hustling strings of peanuts, eager guys offering lottery tickets, and old fellows playing dominoes as they talked about life in Spain. He liked to hear the portable radios that were tuned to heartthrob love songs, big-band rumbas, baseball games at El Cerro stadium or horse races at Oriental Park. Shines especially loved the names of horses being shouted as they raced: General Fang, Mysteria, Brass Kid, Captain Flares, Dancing Doctor, Guerra Fria. Those names were a magic carpet offering adventurous rides. What great battles had *Captain Flares* fought? How cold was the war of *Guerra Fria*? What mysterious worlds did *Mysteria* haunt? The radios also played the news. When Shines heard a captured rebel in Cienfuegos say that Cuban men shouldn't be on their knees shining shoes, Shines shook his head in wonder. What was that rebel talking about? Nobody would join people who thought like him, he was fighting a lost cause, because being a shoe shiner was a noble tradition. Shines was grateful for the fact that he *had* work, and that his work was in the heart of Havana.

Shines was grateful that, if he had the money, he could travel anywhere. And if he didn't have money, he could still say whatever he wanted, as long as it wasn't against the government. What freedom! It was a crime that some were trying to tear this all down, to smash what Shines could see all around him—people moving freely, doing business, buying whatever magazines and newspapers they wanted, listening to whatever they chose on the radio. Shines didn't want revolutionaries telling him what to believe. He loved his job and where he was, right on the Prado with its palatial buildings. Shines was in the center of the world, he was the architect of grandiose dreams.

Colorful parrots flew overhead, circling the Martí statue. Shines looked up and waved as the birds flew toward the immense Capitolio dome, then he bent back to his work. A steady stream of customers propped their feet up on his battered shoe box. He prided himself that he could observe the world of men without raising his head as he shined. Shoes told the story of the famous fight for love and glory. When the shoes had their laces undone, their leather tongues started wagging. When the shoes weren't talking, they exposed revelations deep in their leather grain, like the creases of destiny in a hand. The shoes of Havana passed under the spell of Shines' rag. He shined politicians, thieves, priests, pimps and even the great Cuban boxer Kid Chocolate. But it made no difference if he was shining a bishop or a canecutter, every man got the same elbow grease, the same respect.

Shines didn't have to go anywhere to keep up with important news, the news found him, for not only did the shoes of the customers talk, their owners talked too. He heard that Cuba's Labor Ministry was purging Communists from the Telephone Company. He heard that President Batista had been named honorary chief of the Sheriff Air Patrol of Florida. He heard that the new 1957 Pontiac was the greatest road car in history and it could be seen at Villoldo Motor Company at Calzada and Twelfth Streets in Vedado. He heard that two innocent passersby, an elderly man and a young woman, were seriously injured by a bomb blast at the corner of Concha and

Fabrica. He heard another bomb went off at the Trust Company of Cuba Bank. He heard that the great Negro singer Nat "King" Cole was coming to the Tropicana. He heard that Little Cyclone, the pet dog of the Magoon Fire Station, who had been to every important fire in Havana for twelve years, died beneath a speeding car and was buried by a forty-man honor guard at Saint Francis of Assisi pet cemetery. He heard that one hundred young Cuban beauties were competing to be Carnival Queen, and they would parade in skimpy bathing suits before judges. Shines heard so many things, a river of information washed over him. And to think the rebel on the radio wanted to liberate him from his job. He would rather die first.

Life was good. Shines made up for the money he had been cheated out of by the loudmouthed American who had stiffed him. He sat with his head down and his rag poised over the box waiting for the next man. But the shoe that slid onto the box now belonged to a woman, a spike-heeled shoe in three different colors of leather. This would require some real finesse and the steady hands of a surgeon.

A honey-coated voice floated down to Shines from above.

"You do women, don't you?"

The fact was, in Cuba, women didn't get their shoes shined in public. It was considered unseemly for a woman to expose her leg on a shoe box, and no husband or boyfriend would tolerate his woman's feet being touched in such an intimate way by another man. But it wouldn't be proper to turn a lady's request down, even if the request was improper. And since the request was made in English, perhaps that meant the code of impropriety didn't apply. Shines stared at the shoe on the box, its top slit provocatively, exposing vulnerable white skin. Above the slit was an elegant ankle with a thin gold chain around it.

The woman's voice floated down again. "Do you speak English?"

Shines felt his tongue was tied in a knot and he struggled to untangle it. "*Gracias*. Thank you much. English, yes."

"Good. I wore these shoes dancing on New Year's Eve. They're Ferragamos, I adore them. Don't you think the turned-up toe tip looks like the turned-up nose of a snobby boarding-school girl? It's called the Oriental-toe, only Salvatore Ferragamo does it, he's a genius. Wearing Ferragamos is like being in an Italian opera and Caruso is singing just to you, sublime. Have you ever had your hands on Ferragamos?"

Shines tried to unwind his tongue to answer, but she didn't wait.

"So, on New Year's Eve I was dancing at the Tropicana, and you know how people are, they don't watch where they're stepping, especially if it's a rumba. My poor little Oriental-toes took a terrible beating. I couldn't bear leaving them in a dark closet crying because they were no longer pretty. They deserve another chance to dance. Don't you think?"

This time Shines had his tongue unraveled and was prepared to answer, but she beat him to it.

"I'm on my way to meet my husband at the rooftop lounge of the Sevilla Biltmore Hotel. I don't like the bar downstairs, just stuffy Brits with sunburnt faces. We're going to watch the cannon-firing ceremony across the bay at the old fortress. *BOOM! BOOM!* I love those big guns thundering over the city, makes me feel like I'm back in Colonial times. Isn't that fun?"

Shines thought, no, it wasn't fun if your people were brought here in chains. And besides, the cannons always frightened the parrots in the trees along the Prado, sending them screeching into the sky. He wanted to tell her that he had never been to the Sevilla Biltmore. Even if he had the money to go there, he wouldn't be allowed in, he was the wrong color. But his most pressing problem about color now was how to shine this woman's shoes, since he didn't have any gold, blue or red polish. Maybe, with some spit and fancy rag work, he could work what color was left in the shoes back up, raise it from the dead so the shoes could dance again.

"Are you going to shine me or not?" the woman asked.

Shines slid his rag gently across one of her shoes; he didn't want her to think he was trying to feel the delicate outline of her toes underneath.

"Oh, that feels good," the woman said as Shines' rag slipped back and forth across the leather with more force. "I'm sure you'll bring them back to life."

"I'll try."

"That's nice that you're talking. I was beginning to think you had just fallen off of the sugarcane train."

Out of the corner of his eye, Shines could see that the men and boys in the park were transfixed by the sight of a woman having her shoes shined in public. It was their lucky day, two spectacles in just hours—first the American woman in the zebra skirt, and now this. Above his head Shines heard the silk swish of the woman's dress hem as it swayed from the vibration in her body caused by the rhythm of his shining.

"I love this time of early evening," she sighed. "This purple light is gorgeous."

He wanted to look at her knees, but he didn't dare look higher than her ankles. He was a professional man and had his standards.

"And I love the way the light makes the Capitol over there look like it's on fire. They say your Capitol dome is bigger than ours in Washington. Is that true?"

Shines didn't want her to know that he wasn't well traveled, he'd never been out of Havana. But he knew his job, and his main concern was to keep her from seeing him use spit instead of polish on her precious shoes. He nodded a distracting hip-hop-bop of his head as he raised one hand to his lips and cupped a cap of spit into his palm. He slapped the palm onto the shoe, massaging spit into leather, giving a shine slicker than an American dime.

"What kind of man would take money from a woman to spy on her husband?"

The abruptness of the question caught Shines by surprise. He recalled that Captain Zapata had asked him a similar question, but he couldn't answer the woman the way he had answered Zapata; he couldn't speak of triumphing over love devils, that was men's talk. Maybe, if he didn't answer, she would change the subject.

"I used to fly every year to Rio for Mardi Gras. But one time a friend of mine from Newport said, 'Oh, you must go to Carnival in Havana, it's ever so much more authentic.' And that's how I met my husband. We fell in love in the middle of all that wonderful dancing. Do you make lots of money during Carnival?"

Here was a place Shines felt he could speak, but he kept his voice low and humble, as was his station.

"During Carnival people drink and dance. They forget to pay for their shines. I don't make any money."

"That's terrible."

"Carnival is when you let your angels and demons out to play, that way they'll be happy for the rest of the year."

"You're a smart one."

Shines didn't know how to react to a compliment from an elegant woman, it wasn't in his experience. He smelled a fragrance coming off the skin of her bare legs. Roses and vanilla? Honey and money? As he shined he felt beneath his fingers something ill-defined, preventing him from reading the foot's vibration. This had never happened before. When it came to the human foot, Shines was a diviner, he could tell where a person stood in the struggle between good and evil. But not now. These feet had been places Shines couldn't imagine, and perhaps they had never touched the ground at all.

"You're so smart. I'd like to adopt you."

Shines wanted to shout, "You want to adopt me! Where do I sign the papers?" But he didn't.

"So answer me. What kind of man would take money from a woman to spy on her husband? I know you know the man I'm talking about. I saw you shining his shoes once, you were talking up a storm. You two must be good friends."

"I'm good friends with some customers, not so good with others."

"What kind of man? Answer."

"A man who knows he's the *right* man for the job."

A slight breeze picked up the silk hem of the woman's skirt and fluttered it above her knees. She reached down and pulled the hem lower, her hand passing near Shines' face. On one of her fingers was a wedding ring with a diamond the size of a dove egg.

It was then that Shines understood his difficulty in divining the essence of the life journey that the woman's feet had traveled. Hers was a privileged life with rules of its own making. Her morality was not something that could be found spelled out in a book or preached in a church. She was like a cloud reflected on the water's surface; try to grab the cloud and it would disappear into the water. Shines was incapable of finding the good or the evil in her.

"I don't think," the woman continued, "that those ears of yours miss a thing. I believe you hear all the secrets. Will you share some with me?"

No, Shines was not going to betray King Bongo. He knew that's who she had been talking about. Anything he said about Bongo might be taken the wrong way. Silence on the matter was how to defend his friend.

The woman leaned forward, her mouth close to Shines' ear in a whisper. "You're honorable to protect your friend."

Shines was hoping that her lips would remain close, but they didn't. She straightened up.

"Oh, my, look at those beautiful Ferragamos! Now they can go dancing again!"

The sudden compliment thrilled Shines.

The woman reached down and touched his smooth head with her cool white fingers. The setting sun spiked golden rays around her body. Above her shoulder, perched high on a corner tower atop the baroque Gallego Building across the street, was an enormous bronze angel. The angel's wings spread above the woman and they both flew into a shimmering heaven and disappeared. From the clouds above fluttered down a perfumed American ten-dollar bill.

Zapata stood hidden in the inky blue shadows beneath the stone arches of the Gallego Building. He watched as a woman walked away from Shines and stopped for the traffic before crossing Neptuno Street. Cars screeched to a halt in front of her, male drivers eyed her covetously and whistled, others honked their car horns, demanding the way be cleared so that they could have a better view of the beautiful blonde standing on the curb in a pair of very high-heeled shoes.

Zapata was disgusted. It was the kind of spectacle that gave the impression that all Cuban males were just excitable boys who couldn't keep their pants zipped up.

The woman strolled down the Prado, then disappeared into the Sevilla Biltmore Hotel. Zapata stepped out of the shadows and crossed the boulevard over to the square of Parque Central. Beneath the José Martí statue, he placed his foot up onto Monkey Shines' battered shoe shine box.

Zapata asked, "She tipped you big?"

Shines could barely conceal the grin on his face. "Who?"

"The rich American you were shining. Quite a show, the way she had her bare legs exposed, the sun shining right through her flimsy dress so that every man could see the outline of her body. Cheap American stuff."

"She's not cheap. She paid me ten dollars for a shine. That's more than I make in a week."

"No husband should let his woman shame him in public like that."

"He's American. They have different ideas."

"I'll tell you the different idea. He would rather spend his nights at the Three Virgins than at home."

"You mean her husband is *that kind*?"

"He is. There's not a cat peeing or a dog licking his balls in this town that I don't know about."

Shines shook his head in disbelief. "How could any man resist her? She's so beautiful, like an angel."

"She's an angel, an angel with balls of steel."

Shines still felt the touch of her fingers on his head, and he had her ten dollars in his pocket. She would always be a celestial being to him.

"Rich ones like her are cold as ice, they'll turn the page on a man's life without thinking twice."

"You know everything, Captain."

"I know that her husband's being a regular at the Three Virgins is not the whole story. Something more is going on."

Shines wanted to know what more was going on, so he kept quiet.

"Can I ask you something personal and intimate?"

"Certainly, Captain."

"Why the hell aren't you shining my shoes?"

"Sorry." Shines took out his rag and wax and set to work.

"So you think Mrs. Armstrong is beautiful?"

"Like a religious vision."

"She's not to my taste." Zapata made a sour sound with his lips. "Too white, reminds me of chicken. Why eat chicken every night if you can afford to eat Black Angus steak?"

Shines looked up. "Who's Angus? Is she pretty?"

"I discovered early on that the blackest girls are the best. Those girls are originally from sugarcane country. Love from them is the sweetest."

Shines' head bobbed up and down, he was into the rhythm of the shine. "That's right, Captain. Closer to the sugar, sweeter is the lovin'."

"I can't figure why an intelligent man, one who could have any woman, would break his teeth on a concrete cupcake like that Mrs. Armstrong."

"I can't break my teeth on her. My teeth aren't even real." Shines opened up with a grin that wrapped over his gums, exposing the jagged line of his ill-fitting dentures.

"I didn't mean you. I meant King Bongo."

"Ah . . . King Bongo. He loves all the ladies, and *they* love him."

"Is that so?"

"I've never seen a woman who could pass him by."

"Mrs. Armstrong is passing him by."

"She's married. So maybe she doesn't have the right rhythm for him and they can't dance."

"A woman like that doesn't need rhythm."

"Everybody needs rhythm."

"What did she say to you?"

"About King Bongo?"

"About anything."

"Nothing special."

"That woman doesn't waste her time. She got a shine because she knows you're the number one rumor man in Havana."

Shines held his rag suspended over Zapata's shoe. "She said she wanted to adopt me."

"Bullshit!"

"That's what she said!"

"They have no shame, these Americans. Telling shoe shine boys they want to adopt them. What kind of arrogant crap is that?"

Shines ripped his rag into Zapata's leather again. "She could have meant it."

"Shines, when your mama passed out and nearly smothered you when you were a baby, she ruined the part of your brain that knows the score."

"I know the score."

"You do? Then tell me, who won yesterday's ball game?"

"Hurricane was throwing a no-hitter into the top of the ninth, we were ahead one to nothing."

"And?"

"*Swish-swish*, the Hurricane's fastball slices the first two batters in half."

"Then what?"

"Three batters get on base, the next, *whoosh*, a home run. We lost four to one."

"No, that wasn't the score."

"It was. I heard it with my own ears on the radio."

"The real score was that the game was fixed."

Shines stopped his rag dead center on the toe of Zapata's shoe. "Impossible!"

Zapata laughed. "You'll never know the score, even when it's right in front of your eyes."

Shines didn't like what he was hearing. More than that, Zapata was talking more than usual, which meant there was trouble ahead. Shines kept his head down.

"Did Mrs. Armstrong say anything about her husband?"

"Only that they were meeting at the Sevilla Biltmore."

"What about Hurricane? Did she mention him?"

"She's an American, she doesn't know anything about Cuban baseball."

"The score, Shines, the *score*. Hurricane was with the Armstrongs on New Year's Eve."

"The only thing she said about that night was what shoes she was wearing."

"When I hauled Hurricane in for questioning this morning, he immediately said he didn't do it."

"Do what?"

"Fix the game that he lost."

"That's bad. Real bad."

"In Cuba, that's the same as raping a nun."

"Worse."

"I told Hurricane I'd believe he didn't throw the game if he told me why he had been with the Armstrongs. He said they were just friends, out for some New Year's fun."

"Maybe it's true."

"I called him a redheaded lying mulatto and said I was booking him for throwing a game for the Right Guys."

"Santa Barbara, protect us all!"

"Then I reminded him that he just happened to be speeding away from the Tropicana in the Armstrongs' car moments before a bomb exploded, a college girl was killed, and the Panther disappeared."

"What did he say?"

"That he didn't know the girl and he had no idea where the Panther was."

"Hurricane's a national hero. He's not mixed up in bombings and disappearances."

"Shut up and pay attention. You don't know the score."

"Yes, Captain."

"I informed Hurricane that if he knew where the Panther was and didn't tell me, I was going to walk him onto the pitcher's mound in front of his fans, stick my gun in his ear and blow his brains out."

"Wheeew!"

"That loosened his tongue. He told me about the cripple."

"Cripple?"

"He said to follow the crippled beggar with a dog at Carnival."

"Cripple with a dog . . . that's Saint Lazarus."

"But which one? Carnival is crowded with guys dressed in rags like Lazarus, walking mangy dogs on ropes and praying for everything from a syphilis cure to forgiveness for murder."

"Too many Lazaruses."

"Too many. So I pulled my gun and shoved it in his ear. He said he didn't know who the right Lazarus was, but that the White Spider Woman knew."

"You spared his life?"

"Do you know how many women dressed in white gowns and bandannas run around this town acting like they're the goddesses of the White Spider?"

"Hundreds."

"Thousands."

Shines' hands began to tremble. "So you shot Hurricane?"

"I gave him a week to come up with better dirt, or he's a dead man."

"That's a relief, since he's the starting pitcher on Thursday."

Zapata lit a cigar, took a puff, then said in a confidential tone, "You have the rumor ear. I need answers."

"I won't hold back."

"Without me, you wouldn't have the best shoe shine spot in Havana. I keep the other shiners away from here."

"You're my protector."

"Then tell me about the Panther."

Shines stopped shining, sweat beaded on his bald head. He glanced up. "Some shoes walking the streets . . . they whisper that the Panther still dances."

"That means she's alive. Where?"

"It's whispered that she dances for the crippled saint."

"Saint Lazarus! A saint is taking care of her?"

"Yes. But like you said, there are so many of them."

Zapata angrily flipped his cigar away. "And only the White Spider Woman can lead to the right one. Around we go in a circle." He reached under his coat, slipped his revolver out and pressed its barrel against Shines' sweating head. "No more mumbo jumbo. Who is the White Spider Woman?"

Shines felt the gun, ready to explode a bullet into his brain.

"Who *is* she?" Zapata demanded.

Shines forced his tongue to move before it was too late. "She works at the Nacional."

"Her name!"

"I don't know."

"What does she do?"

"A maid."

"The White Spider Woman is working as a maid in a pricey hotel? More mumbo jumbo. I don't believe any of it." Zapata pressed the barrel harder. "Give me some truth."

Shines saw his terrified reflection in the glossy shine of Zapata's shoes. Then his reflection disappeared as his own tears of fear splashed onto the shine. He had to come up with something big. "The Americans!"

"The Armstrongs?"

"No! Two men! I shined their shoes. They were with a woman in a zebra skirt. They talked!"

"Unless they talked about something serious, like assassinating the Pope, it's not enough to save you."

"They *did* say something about the Pope . . . and about the President, how everyone would be distracted when it happened at three past three."

"Three past three, when? What day?"

"The day of the Big Race."

"Did you catch where the Americans are staying?"

"They mentioned the Nacional and the Capri."

"Right next to each other, and on the route of the race. What did the Americans look like?"

"One was bald like me, short and mean-looking. The other guy was big, really ugly, with a flat face, but thick lips like a duck."

"That sounds like Lizard."

"Not a lizard, lips like a duck."

"Larry Lizard, does special affairs at the Nacional. He's got a wife and three kids, seven different aliases, arrest warrants in the U.S., Puerto Rico and Dominican Republic."

Zapata removed the gun from the base of Shines' skull and slipped it back into its holster. He pulled a peso from his wallet. "Here's for the shine."

"Thanks, Captain." Shines took a deep breath. "One other thing. I tossed the coconut shells last night, all four of them."

"I don't believe in that saints-and-devils circus."

"I asked about *you*."

Zapata laughed sarcastically. "My fate, I suppose?"

"The shells don't tell about fate. The shells don't tell good or bad. They speak of a flow, a journey like a river."

"Where does the river lead?"

"All rivers lead to love."

Zapata laughed with deeper sarcasm. "Are you going to start singing a love song?"

"The shells say, you don't have to fear other men. Other men will not be able to kill you. Only love can kill you."

"Now you *are* singing a love song."

"The shells say, the steel arrow of lost love has rusted in your heart and filled your soul with gangrene. Unless the arrow is removed, it will kill you."

"So my fate is foretold. Sing on, my friend."

"The shells say, it takes an arrow to remove an arrow."

BOOK THREE

tropical truth

1.

Knockout Muse

King Bongo sped his Rocket convertible under the gleaming white arch spanning the entrance drive to the Tropicana. He drove up the palm-lined road, parked and walked into the casino. At night the casino had the allure of adventure and a promise of winning the hand of Lady Luck; by day it was completely different. Bongo passed between green-felt gaming tables abandoned like rafts on a sea of red carpet. He followed a ramp down into the vast open-air cabaret. In the tropical trees and twisting jungle vines, unlit bulbs were connected by a tangle of electrical wires. The illumination that transformed everything at night into a colorful spectacle was gone, replaced by a flat daylight that revealed forlorn theatrical artifice. Between the rows of empty tables, a lone man was sweeping up trash from the previous night's show.

Bongo called out, "Say, have you seen the Giant?"

The man stopped sweeping. He cocked a hand over his eyes to get a better view. "I know who you are."

"Is that so?"

"Yeah. I'm the parking attendant at night. You're the famous tango dancer, Carlos Guardel. You were wearing a powder-blue tuxedo on New Year's Eve and snazzy two-tone spectators from Argentina."

"Good memory."

"You left the cabaret and came back in with an orchid. Then everything exploded."

"Besides me, who else do you remember from that night?"

"Are you kidding? There were hundreds of people in and out. I told the police what I remembered. As a matter of fact, one of them had been here that night. Zapata was his name."

"When did Zapata leave the cabaret on New Year's Eve?"

"Only minutes before you came back with the orchid. I don't forget a thing like that."

"And the two guys with him?"

"They left at the same time. But Zapata returned the next day to ask me questions."

"Did you mention anything that was out of the ordinary before the bombing?"

"Everything is out of the ordinary at the Tropicana."

"True enough. Have you seen the Giant today?"

"You're not a cop, are you?"

"No. Insurance."

"The big man isn't here. But Fido's around. You want me to find him? He might know where the Giant is."

"Thanks."

"No problem, Mr. Guardel. No problem at all." The man hurried off.

Bongo pulled down one of the chairs stacked on a table and sat. Before him was the immense show stage, where his sister had slithered down from a towering palm and had been transformed into a magnificent Panther, dancing to a powerful beat of *bata* drums as she was pursued by hunters. Where was the beautiful jungle cat now? What stage was she dancing on? What cage was she locked in?

Bongo gazed around the amphitheater. Everything from New Year's Eve was still vivid. Zapata, seated at his table with two bodyguards. Mercedes, waving to her college friends, above her a spider dropping from a glistening thread. The woman in white hissing, *"White spiders are bad luck, especially tonight."*

Bongo could see it all, but what was it he *wasn't* seeing? Everyone that night, except Mercedes and the Judge, had told him to leave.

"King Bongo, my man! King of Kings!" A hulk of a man leapt onto the stage. He was dressed in a suit and his shaved head gleamed. He fell to one knee, placing a hand over his heart like a crooner trying to put over a sappy song. The huge gash of his mouth belted out,

"*I drove along the Malecón; got my pay today, hoping tonight to get some play.* Hah! You remember that?"

Bongo smiled. "A Fido original."

"Could be a hit. What do you say we slip a rumba under it? It could take off bigger than Beny Moré."

"Never going to happen."

Fido bounded off the stage and slapped Bongo heartily on the back. "Come on, pal, why so glum?"

"Among other things, I'm trying to find my sister and it keeps getting more complicated. I've got one guy in a Pineapple Field telling me to follow a cripple with a dog. I've got another guy in an opium-orchid nirvana telling me to go ask the White Spider Woman. What's it add up to?"

"Illusions, man. Cuba is an island of illusions."

"So let's not talk illusions, let's talk business."

"Business is the biggest illusion of all," Fido laughed. "Bigger than love."

"No illusion is bigger than love."

"You sure are in a sour mood. Did you run over a Chihuahua in your Rocket?"

"A Great Dane."

"Then you've got the big blues."

"I don't know what I've got. All I know is that I've been so distracted that my business is going to hell. I need to sell some insurance."

"Can't help you there. You've already insured my house and car. The only thing not insured is my balls." Fido winked. "But you know, your small outfit couldn't handle that job."

"True. Only Lloyd's of London could insure something so colossal."

"Damn right." Fido roared with laughter.

"I'm looking for the Giant. After the bombing, he's sure to want to up his coverage."

"The Giant's not here. He's out running around town with the King."

"The King?" Bongo asked good-humoredly. "I thought I was supposed to be the King."

"Nat 'King' Cole, the great American bolero singer. He's doing a show here tonight."

"You can help me by putting in a good word with the Giant. He respects you. Tell him, if the Tropicana gets hit with another hurricane like the one of 1944, this whole place will end up at the bottom of the ocean between here and Miami."

"I already told him. You know I'm always trying to be of assistance. You've helped pull me through many hard times."

"That's between friends. We're Cubans, we don't owe one another."

"I owe you big. If it wasn't for you, I wouldn't be happily married with three kids."

"It's easy to call a punch in a love match, if you're watching the fight from outside the ring."

"I'm a fighter, and I didn't see the punch coming."

"A man in love never does."

"Fighting is about the only thing the Giant listens to me about. I told him to bet on a sixth-round knockout in the Niño Valdes fight. Sure enough, in the sixth Niño hooked the big German's chin, then smashed his liver."

"It was a bloodbath."

"The Right Guys were betting the German to go down in the third. I said no, Niño will keep it going to show his stuff, he wants the Americans to see that he's ready to fight their best. He's going to be the first Cuban heavyweight champion of the world, it'll be like the good old days when Kid Chocolate was champ."

"Good days."

"I'm looking forward to those days. Cuba back on top."

"It'll come. Right now I'm trying to get on top of my own life. What do you know about White Spider Women?"

"They're all over the place, religious women. Some days they're protecting the spiders as gods, other days they're smashing them like devils. Depends on what the saints tell them to do."

"There was one here New Year's Eve, just before the bombing. She said she knew who I was."

"So? Damn near everyone in Havana knows who King Bongo is."

"She knew I was half black. Very few people know that. And she was very black. People that black are not allowed in here."

"That's right. If they're blacker than me they don't get past the door, unless they're part of the show."

"Then you must have known her. You must have let her in."

"No."

"Who, then?"

"If I'm distracted and someone makes it past me, they still have to get by the Judge. He stops everyone before they go into the cabaret."

"So the Judge let her in."

"Or she paid him off."

"What time does the Judge come to work?"

"Should be here soon, to get ready for tonight's show."

"I'll wait."

"You look worried."

"I think I know who this White Spider Woman is. The Judge can tell me for certain."

"Who is she?"

"She works at the Three Virgins."

"What are you doing *there*? It's not the side you dress on."

"Part of the job."

"Now you're selling insurance to pie boys and pudding men?"

"Not exactly."

"Be careful, a pretty man like you, they're going to want to get you in a corner."

"I can handle it. What does rattle me, though, is that someone is shadowing me all the time."

"You're just paranoid. These are spooky times. Read the paper— bombings, arrests, missing people, unexplained murders."

"Someone *is* tailing me."

"Who would want to waste their time following you?"

"Zapata maybe? He thinks I'll lead him to my sister."

Fido looked over Bongo's shoulder. "Look who's here."

Bongo turned around, half expecting to see Zapata, but it was Ming.

Ming called out, "Bongo! I knew you'd be here."

Bongo whispered to Fido, "Maybe it's Ming who's been following me."

Ming stepped in front of Bongo. "Mr. Wu wants you to know that your laundry has come back."

"My laundry? Oh, yes, of course, the *laundry*."

"The number matches to a customer who lives in the Country Club district."

"Those must have been very expensive underpants."

"Made by Brooks Brothers in New York."

"What's the customer's name?"

"Guy Armstrong."

"That doesn't make sense. Unless there are two Guy Armstrongs. It's a common name in the States."

"There's only one Guy Armstrong in Havana. He and his wife have all their laundry done under the same laundry ID number."

"What's the wife's name?"

"Elizabeth," Ming answered, irritated at being quizzed. "Like the queen of England."

"Okay, I'm not doubting you. But the reason it doesn't make sense is because Guy Armstrong is alive. He wasn't the one fished out of the ocean wearing those underpants."

"Mr. Wu doesn't make mistakes. He thinks the dead man and Armstrong were lovers, they got out of bed in the dark and mistakenly put on each other's skivvies."

Fido laughed. "That could never happen to a straight man. I couldn't get my little lady's undies around my wrist, let alone my waist."

Ming ignored Fido. "One more thing, Bongo. Mr. Wu wants you to know that hidden beneath the skivvies there was a tattoo on the guy's ass."

"I have a feeling," Bongo said, "you're going to tell me his ass was tattooed with 'Guy Armstrong Forever.' "

"No, it said, 'I love María Teresa Vera.' "

"What the hell are you talking about? Is this a joke?"

Ming tugged on his dragon tie, cinching the silk knot tighter around his neck. "Mr. Wu doesn't joke."

"The Crab didn't tell me about any tattoo, and I paid him."

"You paid him for the skivvies, not for the tattoo."

"Who paid him for that information?"

"Mr. Wu. He doesn't want you to keep running around in circles like Saint Kwan Kong the headless monk."

"Well, I am running in circles. Who would expect a stiff to have 'I love María Teresa Vera' tattooed on his ass? She's our greatest singer, but she's ancient, born in Guanajay back in the last century."

Ming shrugged. "I don't care when she was born. It's not my music."

"I thought you people considered yourselves to be more Cuban than Chinese," Bongo said. "I thought you loved Cuban music."

"Not me. I like American stuff, Fats Domino, Elvis, Johnnie Ray."

Bongo laughed. "Who are they compared to Beny Moré?"

"You just don't get it," Ming snapped. "Especially Ray, he's better than Beny. Listen to 'Soliloquy of a Fool.' Ray beats himself up over what a dope he is about love and life, he pukes his heart out. It could be your theme song."

"Thanks for the classical music lesson."

"There's nothing more for me here," Ming said with irritation. "I've delivered your dirty laundry." He spun around and left.

Bongo and Fido watched Ming walk away.

Fido said, "That guy's got a twelve-ton chip on each shoulder."

"Tough, too."

"I never mess with Chinese. They don't fight fair, they've got all those jujitsu moves. Not like in the boxing ring, where you can only kill by following civilized rules."

"Listen, I'm going outside to wait for the Judge. Maybe he'll have the answer I'm looking for."

"The Judge, have an answer?" Fido looked at Bongo skeptically. "You're on your own there. They don't call that tight-lipped onion the Judge for nothing."

"I'll see what I can do to peel the onion."

Bongo stepped outside through the Tropicana's swinging glass entrance doors. He tapped out a Lucky Strike from its pack, lit up, then strolled along the stone path leading to the fountain of the muses. He knew that the Judge would have to walk by the fountain on his way inside.

A car pulled up the drive, obscured by a wall of jungle plants. The car stopped and someone got out. Bongo stamped out his cigarette and waited, expecting the Judge.

A young man appeared on a path leading through the jungle plants. Bongo recognized him. He was the same young man whom Guy Armstrong had left the Three Virgins with late the night that Bongo had followed them to a house.

The young man walked up to Bongo, sniffing the air. "You've been smoking?"

"That's right."

"Mind if I have one?"

Bongo tapped two Luckys from the pack, handed one to the young man and popped the other between his lips.

The young man asked, "Can I have a light?"

As the young man leaned over Bongo's Zippo lighter, Bongo noticed his long dark eyelashes, like a woman's.

"Nice lighter," the young man said. "What's that engraving?"

"U.S. Navy. It was my father's."

"How long have you been here?"

"About half an hour."

"Here by the fountain?"

"No, first inside."

"Was Hurricane in there, the baseball player?"

"No."

"I was supposed to meet him."

"The only ones inside are Fido and the guy sweeping up."

"No one else?"

"A Chinese guy, but he left."

"Did anybody pass by the fountain since you've been here?"

"You're expecting somebody besides Hurricane?"

"Just him."

The young man looked up at the eight naked marble muses posed provocatively around the fountain. Water flowed from beneath their bare feet, spilling into a circular pond. "When this is lit up by colored lights at night, the muses look like they're dancing."

"I've seen it."

"I come here every chance I get. It's best when nobody's around and I have them to myself."

"A man alone with beauty."

"You ever been to Madrid?"

"No."

"In the Prado Museum, they have Goya's *Naked Maja*. You know the painting?"

"The nude lying on a sofa?"

"That one. She has luminous white skin and a mysterious smile that will stop your heart."

"I suppose."

"I went to Madrid just to see her. I got to the Prado early. It was still dark and I was first in line. When the doors opened, I ran through the corridors. The *Maja* is kept in a small room. For three minutes, before the crowd showed up, I had her to myself, it was just the two of us. You know what that was like?"

"I have an idea you're going to tell me."

"*Heaven.*"

"That's how it is with women, first the heaven, then the hell."

"I'm an art student at the university."

"When it's open. The government is always closing it down."

"My classes have been suspended, so I have time to admire these beauties."

"Sorry you don't have them to yourself."

"Do you know their history? Interesting story."

Bongo looked up at the muses. Some were turned inward, displaying gracefully arched backs and curved buttocks, others looked outward, shoulders thrust back and breasts tilted up, their faces ecstatic. "No, I don't know their history."

"They used to be at the old Casino Nacional across town. That place was palatial, before it was torn down. The muses were in the casino's beautiful garden. Even though they were based on Greek mythology, they came to represent Lady Luck for all the gamblers of Cuba."

"That's a big job."

"They were sculpted by an Italian named Aldo Gamba. He fell in love with one of the models he was using, a French woman. He gave his whole heart and talent in capturing her every curve, mood and gesture. Then tragedy."

"She left him?"

"How did you know?"

"You said it was an interesting story."

"He shot himself."

"Another good man down."

"The shot missed. But the powder burns of the gun blast blinded him."

"At least he survived."

"Long enough to die in a Nazi concentration camp. He was a Jew."

Bongo gazed up at the voluptuous beauties. "I'll never look at them the same way again."

"But Gamba had his revenge. In Greek mythology there were originally nine muses. When the French model left Gamba for another man, he smashed her statue to dust, destroying her chance at immortality."

"And then there were eight," Bongo smiled. "Let's have another Lucky, for Gamba." He tapped out two more cigarettes.

"To Gamba." The young man grinned. He reached for a cigarette, then stiffened. "A car is coming."

"I hear it. So what?"

The young man threw the cigarette down.

A car door slammed on the other side of the jungle foliage. Footsteps sounded.

A man appeared at the far end of the path, walking stiffly, dressed in a tuxedo.

"The Judge," Bongo said. "I was waiting for him."

"So *that's* the Judge."

The Judge walked up to Bongo and fixed him with a hard stare. "What are you doing here? Trying to sell insurance to this gullible youth?"

"No. Did the check I gave you on New Year's Eve clear?"

"It would have been your balls if it hadn't." The Judge turned and jabbed his elbow into the young man's side. "Don't ever get insurance from this guy's rinky-dink outfit. Stick with a big American company."

"I'll remember that," the young man said.

"The only good thing about this guy is his sister." The Judge smirked. "She is, or was, the sexiest broad in all of Havana. Black with white hair, damnedest thing you've ever seen. And when she danced, looked like a whirl of tar and white feathers. Fascinating."

Bongo brought up his fist to smash the Judge, just as the young man pulled a gun from his pocket and fired into the Judge's face.

The Judge pitched backward into the fountain.

The young man aimed the gun at Bongo. "If it weren't for your sister, I'd shoot you as a witness." He slipped the gun back into his pocket. "When the cops come, say you got here just after he was shot. You'll be okay."

The young man turned to leave.

"Wait. Where's my sister?"

"I can't tell you." He disappeared back along the path and into the foliage.

Fido ran up to Bongo in front of the fountain of the muses. With Fido was the lanky Hurricane Hurler. Bongo hadn't known that the two men knew each other.

Fido looked down at the Judge floating in the water. His face broke into a big grin. "The Judge is having his last dance with the muses."

Hurricane eyed Bongo accusingly. "You shot him."

Fido looked slyly at Bongo. "Nobody will blame you. The trash that came out of his mouth."

"I wish I *had* shot him," Bongo said.

"Then you saw who did it?" Hurricane asked.

"Of course he didn't see the murderer," Fido said. Then he glanced at Bongo. "*Did* you see who did it?"

"I was getting into my car, heard a gunshot, came back here and found the Judge at the muses' feet."

"Maybe you caught a glimpse of the murderer running away?" Hurricane asked.

"I saw nothing."

Fido grinned. "See no evil, hear no evil."

"That's about it." Bongo pulled out his pack of cigarettes. "You fellas care for a Lucky?"

The men lit up and smoked in silence. They contemplated the Judge's floating body.

From behind the fountain a cluster of nearly naked women stepped tentatively out from the mass of jungle plants. They wore feathered headdresses, and gold glitter sparkled on their bare breasts. They moved like a flock of exotic birds, cooing among themselves, then their voices took on a fevered pitch as they grew bolder, prancing around the fountain.

Bongo sensed a competition between these proud black Tropicana showgirls and the marble-white muses.

More people ran up, pushing in for a closer look as they shouted questions, eager for details.

Bongo surveyed the growing crowd, hoping to spot the Giant. After all, this killing proved that the Tropicana needed more insurance. He didn't see the Giant, but he heard a car pull up on the other side of the plantings.

Within moments Pedro and Paulo came running up the path and pushed their way to the fountain. They were thrilled to have such a large audience, and to see the fleshy charms of the Tropicana showgirls exposed in broad daylight.

Pedro shouted with bullish authority, "This area is under control of Captain Zapata of the Special Police. You will all be asked to remain and give your names and a statement."

Paulo chimed in, "We will also need your addresses." He was hatching a scheme to visit the showgirls' homes for further investigation.

Zapata strolled up the path, wearing his usual linen suit and Panama hat, the image of the crowd reflected in the black lenses of his sunglasses. When he stopped, the black lenses reflected the white muses of the fountain. He ran his finger slowly along his pencil-thin mustache as he looked down at the Judge floating in a pond of blood.

The crowd waited for Zapata to speak. When he did it was in his customary whisper. "Did anyone witness this?"

A person in the crowd meekly asked, "Sir, will you repeat that? We can barely hear you."

Zapata turned and faced the crowd. "Did anyone see the *killing*?"

No one answered.

Zapata asked again, *"Anyone?"*

No one broke the silence.

"In that case," Zapata said, "give your statements to my men. I want to know how each of you came to be here."

An agitated showgirl shifted her weight from one high-heeled shoe to another. "What about us? We've got a show to put on."

Zapata looked sternly at her. "So do I. Do as I've ordered."

Pedro and Paulo whipped out their notebooks, ready to get all the vital information from the girls.

Zapata slowly turned his head, surveying the crowd. His sunglasses reflected the image of Bongo. "What are *you* doing here?"

Bongo walked up to Zapata. "I came to sell insurance to the Giant."

"Can he verify that alibi?"

"The Giant's not here. I was headed home."

"I'll talk to you later, at the station."

"The station?"

Zapata sneered, "You think we should meet instead at Chez Morito for steaks?"

"That's a stuffy Vedado restaurant. How about Charley Sing's in Chinatown? Great chop suey."

"Always the smart guy."

"I just know my restaurants."

"You're a suspect."

"Since when *haven't* I been, in your book?"

"You're on page one."

"I'm hoping to write the last page."

"Only *I* can write the last page to your story."

"We'll see about that."

"Is that a threat?" Zapata asked angrily. "If it is, I'll lock you up in the same dungeon where your slave ancestors were kept."

"I've always been your threat," Bongo smiled wryly. "You know that. And what's more important, *she* knows that."

"If it wasn't for her, I wouldn't have saved your skinny nine-year-old ass after the hurricane. You'd be dead."

"I don't owe you for that. You got what you wanted."

"Yes, I got her." Zapata slowly drew a finger across the line of his black mustache, then growled, "Get out of my sight before I finish it."

Bongo didn't move until he had the last word. "I know the truth. She's escaped your cage. Now you don't have her. You have *nothing*."

Bongo turned his back on Zapata. He pushed his way through the crowd and walked along the path to the parking lot. Before he could open the door of the Rocket, four cars raced up and men jumped out. Photographers popped off flashbulbs as reporters shouted questions.

Bongo shouted back, "What are you *doing*? I'm not the story! The story is the muses!"

"Muses?" a reporter asked. "What muses?"

"The ones that are dancing on a dead man!"

The men took off running.

Bongo, what are you doing here? The Virgins isn't your kind of joint. Have you gone over to the other side?"

Bongo swung around on his barstool toward the voice behind him.

Sailor Girl stood grinning from beneath her jaunty sailor cap, two new boyfriends at her side.

"I haven't gone over to the other side." Bongo winked. "I'm still staying on my side of the bed."

"Too bad. You had me excited there for a moment. You see these cute boys?" She pinched the muscled arms of the two men on either side of her.

"Hard to miss."

"Hard and crisp and taste like animal crackers."

"Enjoy your picnic," Bongo said, turning back toward the bar.

Sailor Girl grabbed his shoulder, eager to fill him in. "These guys are Russian merchant marines. They don't speak a word of English."

"Convenient."

"They just sailed in on a big cargo ship." Sailor Girl leaned in close to Bongo's ear. "The ship's carrying rockets and ammunition for the bearded boys in the mountains."

"Probably just carrying pickles and pig knuckles."

"Hah. My Russians have all the pickles and pig knuckles a girl could want."

"I'm glad you're getting the best of the foreign exchange. Not to change the subject, but—"

"You want to know what boy toy I use on them?"

"No."

"A big black dildo."

"Why black?"

"That's the only color they have in Havana. They think all dicks are black."

"Interesting theory."

"It's like Henry Ford said: 'You can have any color Model-T car you want, as long as it's black.' "

"Maybe Ford has the dildo market cornered in Havana."

"We Americans have *everything* cornered."

"To change the subject, I was going to ask if—"

"You know what I like about sticking it to men?"

"You don't have to send flowers after."

"I like it that they scream out what they want. Not like women, who never tell you what they want when you're laying them, expecting you to be a goddamn mind reader. Men are like a car on the road, honking to get your attention."

"You Americans are so romantic."

"Some of us, anyway."

"I wanted to ask you about a bartender here."

"I knew it. You *have* gone over to the other side."

"Sweet Maria. What do you know?"

"You have good taste. She's creamy and tart, like mango pie."

"Tell me more."

"She's my competition."

"She hasn't been around lately."

"She's not working here anymore."

"Where can I find her?"

"She lives out past the Rancho Boyeros airport, in Rincón. She complained what a long bus ride it was, especially since she had two jobs."

"Where's the other job?"

"The Hotel Nacional. She's a maid."

"She must work the day shift, since she was always here at night."

"I suppose."

"What part of Rincón does she live in?"

"By that church where all the cripples go to get cured. Saint Lazarus or something, it's called."

Bongo gave Sailor Girl a kiss on the cheek.

"A kiss from the King! I must have pushed the right button."

"You did."

"You want to come with us to the Mocambo Club? It's air-conditioned. If there's no air-conditioning in a place when I'm dancing, I take my shirt off so I can cool my titties. But some people are offended when I act like one of the boys. Pricks."

"Can't join you. I've got a date."

"So, you're finally dating after what happened to your girlfriend."

"It's not that kind of date."

Sailor Girl leaned close with a big smile. "Don't lie to me. I can tell you're ready to date again."

"Maybe."

"I'm your girl."

"I'll take a rain check."

"Rain check?" Sailor Girl laughed. "It never rains in Havana when you expect it."

"Don't expect it."

Outside the Three Virgins, Bongo put the Rocket's top down, climbed in and started the engine. He turned the car onto Avenue de Paula, a mambo serenading him on the radio. He drove along the city's oldest paseo, a souvenir of Havana's four-hundred-year-old seaport heritage, past vast shipping docks, curving around the Point of San Salvador and the stone remains of a Spanish castle that once guarded the entrance to the city. From across the bay, the cannons of La Cabana thundered through the salty air. He checked his watch. Nine o'clock. He was late from talking to Sailor Girl, but he had needed her information. He pressed harder on the gas pedal, hitting the straightaway of the Malecón, passing the Maceo monument. On either side of the road men labored in the evening shadows, erecting bleacher seating for the next day's Big Race.

Bongo sped by the giant bronze eagle perched atop the *Maine* monument's marble pillars, then zoomed through the tunnel beneath the Almendares River and up onto the grand twelve-mile promenade of Fifth Avenue, divided down the middle by a manicured display of exotic plantings. After several miles he cut away from the avenue, driving past streets of impressive homes and well-dressed people strolling beneath the glow of streetlamps. He turned the Rocket through two granite columns and followed a drive to the front of a sprawling Mediterranean-style building. A man hurried out.

Bongo stopped the Rocket and ordered the man to get in.

"Sir, this is the Biltmore Yacht Club. Don't you want me to park your car?"

"We'll park it together."

"That's an unusual request."

"It's the way I like it."

"If it's your pleasure, sir." The man got in.

"Where do you park the cars?"

The man pointed through the windshield. "That direction, sir."

Bongo drove behind a stone wall and passed several rows of gleaming American automobiles.

"Sir, you may park where you like."

Bongo kept driving. He turned along another row of cars and stopped behind a white Cadillac Eldorado convertible.

"Sir, there's no room to park next to Mr. Armstrong's automobile. Perhaps we can drive on a little farther."

"Get out."

"Out? Here?"

"Now."

The man got out.

Bongo handed him a peso.

"But I didn't park your car."

"You earned it."

Bongo stepped on the gas. He drove back through the granite columns, following the road to where it split into two directions around the expanse of a golf course surrounded by mansions. Suddenly he hit the Rocket's brakes, skidding up behind a long line of cars stopped before a wooden road barricade.

"Damn," he muttered.

He looked at his wristwatch: 9:30. He didn't have time to wait while cars were searched and IDs were checked. He honked his horn. A soldier with a rifle walked toward him and shined the beam of a flashlight into his face. "What's the hurry?"

"I've got an emergency."

"Do you live up ahead in the Country Club?"

"No, but I've got a hot date waiting for me there."

"So what's the emergency?"

"She won't stay hot for long."

"Get out of the car. Let's see your ID."

Bongo got out, pulled his wallet from his pocket and then dropped it.

"Pick it up," the soldier demanded.

Bongo picked the wallet up and slipped out a ten-peso bill. "This must be yours," he said.

The soldier grabbed the ten. "I have to search you. Nobody gets into the Country Club without a search. Hands on your head and turn around."

Bongo did as he was ordered.

The soldier patted Bongo down. He felt the holster under Bongo's jacket and slipped the gun out. "It's going to be a long night for you if you don't have a permit."

"I have one."

"Show me."

Bongo opened his wallet and pulled out another ten. "Here's the permit."

The soldier took the ten and peered at it. "This permit has expired."

Bongo took out another ten and handed it over.

"Everything's up-to-date," the soldier said, "for *now*. You'll need to come to central headquarters next week for an extension." He handed Bongo back his gun.

"What's the trouble? Another bombing?"

"There's been a threat against the President."

"That's not unusual."

"This one's more serious. Something big is supposed to happen tomorrow. Weren't you stopped at any roadblocks before this?"

"No."

"You're lucky. Everything's screwed down tight. You'd better get going before your luck runs out."

Bongo got back into the Rocket and headed around the long line of cars. Two soldiers removed the barricade blocking the road and waved him through. He took the right-hand split in the road, driving past mansions, each becoming bigger and more imposing, boasting their classical pedigrees with elaborate Greek and Roman architectural details. Only one was constructed with no reference to past glories, sustained instead by a streamlined boldness. Bongo stopped in front of its steel gate. The gate magically swung open. He continued to a block-long, one-story-high monolithic wedge of concrete pierced by rows of round windows lit from the inside, giving the illusion of a recently landed spaceship.

Bongo parked the Rocket and got out. As he approached the house, outdoor lights mysteriously switched on, illuminating human-size shrubs in ethereal topiary shapes.

He walked up to an aluminum door arched into the flat concrete facade. He raised his hand to knock, but the door swung open by itself.

A young woman in a short yellow sundress stood at the beginning of a long hallway.

"I'm King Bongo. Sorry I'm late. But there was a roadblock and—"

The woman turned away and walked down the hallway. Bongo assumed he should follow, and as he did he noticed that the walls and floor were made of a material he had never seen before, a modern plastic meld with the shine of glacial ice. He could see his reflection in it, and also the reflection of the pretty woman as she led the way. He liked the way her hips were swinging; she definitely had the rhythm. He planned to slip her his business card before he left.

The young woman opened a set of glass doors and stepped into a large room bare of any furniture except for two sleek sling-back metal chairs with a round Lucite cocktail table between them.

"Would you like a cocktail?" the woman asked.

Bongo took in her brown hair and eyes. She had the Latin loveliness that he was partial to. "Do you have Hatuey?" he asked. "I'll pay."

A slight smile curved her pretty lips. "No need."

"And a glass of ice, and a lime."

"One slice of lime or two?"

"Three."

"Four," she said, and left.

Bongo looked around. On the walls were large paintings of children's faces floating behind sheets of clear plastic. The children appeared to be on the verge of howling with laughter or weeping inconsolably, as if they had witnessed something hysterically funny or had been raped. Their unsettling eyes were large as plates, ballooning over tiny mouths the size of sparrow eggs.

The singing of a sultry female swelled into the room. It was the voice of the American, Peggy Lee, sounding like a silky zipper sliding open a velvet dress. Bongo looked around, but he could see no speakers anywhere in the room. The voice floated, disembodied.

The pretty woman returned. She set a plastic tray on the cocktail table, and poured a Hatuey beer into an ice-filled glass. She left before Bongo had a chance to say a word or offer her his card.

He sat back in the low-slung chair and took a swig of the drink. Beer and lime tingled in his mouth as Peggy Lee sang:

> *Just when I think you're mine,*
> *you try a different line and*
> *baby, what can I do? . . .*
> *I went to school and*
> *I'm nobody's fool . . .*
> *until I met you.*

The singing stopped.

Mrs. Armstrong stood silhouetted in the arched doorway. Light shimmered through the silk of her champagne-colored dress, a diamond choker glistened around her neck. "You've got a lot of courage to come here when my husband isn't home."

"You're the one who called and invited me."

"Not this late."

"There was an army roadblock."

"You braved the army just to see me?"

"To ask some questions."

"That's interesting, since I'm the one who invited you."

Bongo could smell her, that singular, odd aroma of roses and the scent of a new car's leather upholstery. She came toward him. Her blond hair was swept up and away from her face, exposing her symmetrical features, like an elegant figurehead on the prow of a ship.

"Why are you looking at me like that?" she asked.

"Like what?"

"Like I'm an object."

"If you were, you'd be too expensive for me."

"Don't play the poor boy and act like you only have two choices with the rich, marry them or—"

"Shoot them."

"Since you can't marry me, you'll just have to shoot me."

"I thought there might be a third choice."

"The wealthy don't allow alternatives." She sat on a chair across from Bongo. She no longer looked like the proud figurehead of a ship. She looked like a giant precious gem in the window of the world's most expensive jewelry store. She was changing before his eyes, not allowing him to get a grip.

"I have an alternative," Bongo said. "I have information on your husband."

Her frosted pink lips curved up, forming the same high arch as her perfectly plucked eyebrows. "Tell me."

"I suppose I can trust you."

"You suppose *you* can trust *me*!"

"Your husband is at the yacht club, just like you said he would be."

"Of course. Guy always goes out with his crowd before the Big Race. They drink all night, then get behind the wheel in the morning. They're crazy, these racers."

"Perhaps you asked me here because you want to insure your husband's life before tomorrow's race?"

"I don't need any money if Guy dies."

"Then why would he take out a policy on *his* life and name *you* as the beneficiary?"

"How do you know that?"

"He took the policy out with me."

"When?"

"Right before the first of the year."

Bongo studied her blue eyes for a reaction, but her gaze remained unchanged.

"Your husband seems to have mysterious habits, one of them being his friendship with Hurricane Hurler."

"Hurricane's just a friend."

"Are you certain?"

"Guy is a sportsman. He prefers the company of other sportsmen."

"Sportsmen who dabble in dangerous politics?"

"If Hurricane is involved in politics, that doesn't mean Guy is."

"I have to explore all the angles. Hurricane has information about my sister. Maybe you do too."

"That's preposterous. I've only seen your sister once, onstage at the Tropicana on New Year's Eve."

Bongo studied her blue eyes again. They were direct and unafraid. He needed to rattle her cage.

"Are you aware that your husband plays both sides?"

"He's not a gambler."

"That's not what I mean."

"What *do* you mean?"

"You remember when we were in the shoe store, I mentioned a rough bar on the waterfront called the Three Virgins."

"You said Guy was a regular there. That's preposterous."

"A man your husband was involved with at the Virgins was found dead."

"What's your proof of Guy's involvement?"

"The dead man was found wearing your husband's underpants."

"What! Is this some kind of monstrous joke?"

"The laundry number on the underpants was assigned to your husband's name."

"There must have been a mix-up."

"There was a tattoo on the dead man. I went to all the tattoo parlors in Havana. I found out the man's identity."

"And?"

"He was a part-time university professor who made extra money picking up Americans at the Three Virgins."

The color drained out of Mrs. Armstrong's face. She stared coldly.

Bongo gave her cage a harder rattle.

"There's another fact, even *more* serious."

"More serious!" Mrs. Armstrong exclaimed. "What could be more serious than a wife finding out what you've just told me?"

"Murder."

"Just because Guy's underclothes were found on a dead man doesn't make him a murderer!"

Bongo leaned forward, determined to shake her loose.

"The professor was fished out of the ocean. His torso was pierced by a metal bar."

Mrs. Armstrong said flatly, "There's no proof Guy is guilty."

"There's no proof he's innocent."

She glared, the blue color of her eyes intensifying, as if a cold sea were rushing in.

"I need Johnnie Ray."

"What?"

She stood and left the room.

Bongo picked up his glass from the table. The ice had melted and the beer was flat, but he drank it anyway. The sound of singing jolted him. Johnnie Ray's voice blared into the room from the invisible speakers, skinning a song lyric like he was scraping his own skin off with a razor blade:

> *If your sweetheart sends a letter*
> *of goooooodbyyyyeee*
> *it's no secret you'll feel better*
> *if you crrrryyyyyy*

The tears of lament spurted from a torn heart.

> *When waking from a bad dream,*
> *go right on and crrrrrrrrrrryyyyyyyyyy!*

The song ended. There was silence in the room, then a motorized whir. On hidden rollers, one of the walls rolled back, exposing a shimmering blue light reflected from a rectangular swimming pool outside. Standing at the distant edge of the pool was Mrs. Armstrong, a pink towel wrapped around her.

Johnnie Ray's voice filled the air again with a different swoony suicidal swan song:

> *Sooooothe me with your caressss*
> *sweeeet lotus blossoooom.*
> *Help me in my distresss!*

Mrs. Armstrong smiled at Bongo from across the blue chlorine glow.

> *You alone can bring my loverrrrr*
> *back to meeeee, even thooough*
> *I know it's just a fantaasssyyyy!*

Bongo didn't have many rules when it came to women, but one rule he did have was no married ones. But Mrs. Armstrong wasn't married in a real sense; he knew the truth about her duplicitous husband. He stepped outside to the pool, facing Mrs. Armstrong.

Johnnie Ray wailed, a saxophone gasped, a trumpet wept.

> *Knooock me clear ouuuut*
> *sweet lotus blossoooom!*

At the far end of the pool Mrs. Armstrong reached up and undid the knot of the towel. The towel dropped to her feet. The water's vaporous haze reflected off of her smooth white flesh. She untied the bun of her hair. It shimmered down over her bare shoulders and breasts.

She dove into the blue water.

Bongo kicked off his shoes, pulled off his clothes, and stood at the pool's edge.

Mrs. Armstrong surfaced in the water beneath him. She floated on her back, her arms spread, water caressing her. Her blond hair spread out like a halo.

Bongo gazed at the revelation. If he took the plunge, he didn't know if he would return. He dove in.

Watery bubbles burst around Bongo's submerged body, then a silken skin was next to his. He raised his head above the surface. Mrs. Armstrong's arms were around his neck. His hands cupped her breasts, her legs wrapped around his waist. The perfume of her breath came fervently into his face. "You don't know how long I've waited. How long I've been without."

"Then I don't feel guilty."

"Neither do I."

Their lips met in a rush that tumbled their bodies back beneath the water.

From hidden underwater speakers, Johnnie Ray cried out a gut-wrenching plea:

> *You alone can bring my loverrrr*
> *back to meeeeee,*
> *even though I know it's fantaaasssyyy!*

Bongo held his kiss with Mrs. Armstrong. When he opened his eyes he was still underwater. He could see through the liquid haze to the glass wall of a belowground observation grotto. On the other side of the glass was the young woman in the yellow sundress, watching. He was suddenly reminded of the pretty salesgirl from the California Shoe Store, the one he thought he saw magnified larger than life on the movie screen, with only a plastic beach ball between her and Mrs. Armstrong's naked bodies.

Bongo tightened his hold around Mrs. Armstrong's waist and pushed with her to the surface.

They burst through the water. Mrs. Armstrong's arms clung to his neck. "What's wrong, darling?"

"I need to see if one of your breasts has three beauty marks."

"There's plenty of time for that." Mrs. Armstrong laughed in a sultry voice. "Just shut up and love me!"

Her lips came onto his with a crush as Johnnie Ray's words rushed in:

> *Knooooock meeee clear ouuuut!*

2.

All Bad Actors

From the broad expanse of the Hotel Nacional's rooftop, two five-story turrets soared into the sky, suggesting a majestic castle in medieval Spain. When out at sea, fishermen looked to the turrets to guide them safely home in both good weather and bad.

Beneath the red-tiled roof of the east turret, Zapata took in the far view through a pair of binoculars; from the Morro fortress at the mouth of the bay to the shipping docks lined with cargo-lifting cranes, to the oil-storage tanks dotting the cluttered industrial horizon. In the middle distance, the Capitolio's white dome dominated central Havana, and from there an unbroken line of high-rise office and apartment buildings marched to the sea. Closer in was the raw beginning of the new Hilton, a towering, block-long steel skeleton destined to be Cuba's largest hotel. Nearby, on the rooftop of the recently completed Capri Hotel, tourists floated on their backs in the swimming pool, staring at a sun-white sky, unaware of the overlayered centuries of construction and conspiracies surrounding them.

Zapata trained his binoculars on the roadway of the Malecón. It was empty and lined with a crowd waiting for the cars of the Big Race to come speeding into view. Zapata tipped the binoculars up. Stationed on the rooftops of the buildings facing the Malecón, army sharpshooters aimed rifles at the crowd, ready for trouble. Only the rooftops of the Nacional and Capri hotels were free of obvious marksmen. Zapata himself commanded the Nacional, and across from him, by the Capri's rooftop pool, some of the lounging tourists were actually his own men. Zapata's tip from Shines was that the assassin would be firing from one of these two hotels. His strategy

was to catch the gunman in the act, then torture the truth out of him
as to who was behind the conspiracy. He glanced at his watch. 2:45.
According to Shines, the hit was scheduled for 3:03. Eighteen minutes to go.

Directly below Zapata, on the top floor of the Nacional, Sweet
Maria stepped out of the elevator. Dressed in her maid's uniform, she pushed a cart of sheets, towels, mops and brooms.
She stopped at the end of the hallway before the last door on the right.
She opened the door with her master key and switched on the
light. The departed guests had had a real party the night before. The
blankets on the bed were twisted in knots, the ashtrays overflowed
with cigarette butts, empty rum bottles were scattered across the
floor.

Maria pulled opened the drapes and pushed up the window to let
the stale air escape. In the garden below, excited spectators waited in
a viewing grandstand. Beyond them, across the empty roadway of
the Malecón, was the glittering sea. Maria inhaled the tropical air
and sighed, grateful to be living on such a lovely island.

She went to the bedroom closet. Leaning at the back was a rifle,
just as planned. She took from her apron pocket two gloves, a white
one with shiny buttons and a pink suede one. She pulled them on,
then picked up the rifle and cradled it in her arms.

In a suite one floor below, Johnny PayDay gazed at his face in the
bathroom mirror. He slapped Old Spice cologne onto his cheeks.
He hated the smell of the stuff, rotten limes and nun farts, but
his wife loved it. He picked up a tube of Wildroot Cream-Oil Hair
Tonic from the countertop and squeezed the goop into his palm. He
slapped it onto the shiny pate of his bald head and rubbed hard until
the white slime disappeared. Betty didn't like him to go out without a
good dose of hair cream on his dome.

He walked into the bedroom. On the bed was a leather shoulder
holster with a gun. He slipped the holster on and cinched it, so the
gun was snug against his ribs. He put on his sport coat and knotted
his tie, ready for work. He went to the open window. Noisy chatter

floated up from people crowded into the grandstand below. PayDay shook his head in disdain. To him racing was stupid, just guys in cars going fast. He didn't watch racing or bet on it. It wasn't like boxing, where two guys are caught between the ropes and only one will walk away. *That* was sport.

He took out a PayDay bar, carefully removed the slick wrapper and slipped it into his pocket. He popped the slab of candy into his mouth and chewed. Nuts and caramel slid thickly down his throat. He kept his eyes on the grandstand below; to shoot someone there from this distance would take a true marksman. He knew of only one rifle in the world that could throw a bullet that far and still be lethal—a Czech rifle made for Russian Army snipers. Its recoil could knock a man flat on his ass. The Commies had some good modern hardware, but PayDay was old-fashioned, with a penchant for the close and personal. Given a choice, he preferred a knife across the throat.

King Bongo stopped the Rocket beneath the arched entrance portico of the Nacional. The usual parking attendants were not there. He left the car and walked into the lobby; it was deserted. He rang the bell on the reception counter. No one came. He rang louder. A man appeared from a back office. His lapel pin read, "Concierge."

"Sorry, sir. Almost everyone is outside watching the race. Are you checking in?"

"I'm looking for a girl."

"Aren't we all." The concierge grimaced. "The cliché of life."

"She works here."

"This is a proper establishment. We don't have working girls here. I suggest you try some of the lesser-known hotels."

"I don't mean *that* kind of girl. I mean a maid."

"We have many maids, more than any other hotel in Havana."

"Her name is Maria."

The concierge tried to hide a laugh behind his hand.

"What's so funny?"

"Half the maids in the hotel are named Maria. Maria Teresa, Maria José, Maria Antonia, Maria del Mar."

"I don't know her last name. Statuesque, long black hair, brown eyes, long eyelashes."

"That describes *all* of our Marias."

"She works nights at the Three Virgins Bar."

The concierge wrinkled his nose in disdain. "I doubt if any of our Marias would also be employed in such a place."

"She is. She's a poor girl, lives out in the Saint Lazarus district."

The concierge made the sign of the cross piously in front of him. "God bless Lazarus. I make the pilgrimage to his shrine every year. He cured the boil on my mother-in-law's face. He makes miracles."

"This makes miracles too." Bongo opened his wallet, took out a crisp five-peso bill and laid it on the counter.

The concierge eyed the bill. "Sometimes miracles do happen."

"Check to see which Marias are working and what rooms they're assigned to."

The concierge placed his hand over the bill and slid it discreetly into his palm. "I'll be right back."

Bongo turned around. In the expanse of the extravagantly tiled lobby, dark-suited men had appeared, pretending to read newspapers through their sunglasses. Bongo wondered why the secret police were inside, instead of outside, protecting the President from his adoring countrymen?

The concierge returned with a clipboard holding a sheaf of papers. "Let's start on the top floor and work our way down."

"Good idea." Bongo took out a notepad and pen.

"On the top floor we have one Maria working. No Marias on the next floor. Two Marias after that, and—."

"Give me the room numbers of where each Maria is right now."

"Certainly." The concierge read through all the pages, giving Bongo the information, then looked up. "That's the end. Twenty-nine Marias in all."

"Thanks." Bongo slipped the notepad and pen back into his coat pocket.

"Anything for dear old Saint Lazarus." The concierge winked. "By the way, there was someone here earlier looking for a Maria."

"Why didn't you tell me? What was his name?"

"He didn't give one."

Bongo took out another five and slapped it on the counter. "What did he look like?"

"Average height, pencil-thin mustache. Linen suit, straw hat, sunglasses. Kind of a dandy but shifty, like a guy in a bad detective movie."

"Did you find his Maria?"

"I gave him the same list I gave you."

"What then?"

"He took the elevator up."

"And?"

"He never came back down."

I n the penthouse suite of the Capri, the Bad Actor soaked in a massive marble bathtub fit for a Roman emperor. He had a lighted cigarette at the end of a holder clenched between his teeth. His hair was plastered down by a tight black hairnet, and white cold cream was slathered on his face.

Within view of the open bathroom door was a heart-shaped king-sized bed. Sitting cross-legged in the middle of the heart was the red-headed Teenager, wearing nothing but a pair of cotton panties printed with laughing pink elephants. She kept putting her thumb under the elastic waistband, pulling it back and then letting it snap against her pale skin with a smack. Her golf-ball-sized breasts were two-thirds nipple, the same strawberry color as her hair. Her gaze was riveted on the television set in the corner. Tears welled up in her eyes, formed and fell, hitting her sharp chin, bouncing off a strawberry nipple and landing on the bedsheet in small damp spots.

The Bad Actor talked around the cigarette holder clenched in his teeth, so his words had the tinny ring of an old-time bandstand crooner singing through a cardboard megaphone. "Why so gloomy?" he asked.

"Timmy's lost Lassie," the Teenager whined.

"For Christ's sake, it's just a show about a mama's boy and his kiss-ass dog that never pees on camera."

"Don't talk about them like that."

"It's all phony made-up crap."

"It's not. These are true stories."

"TV is only a baby-sitter for kids like you."

"Hah!" the Teenager blurted. "What about Milton Berle? Uncle Miltie's a grown-up?"

"If you call a guy who comes out at the end of every show in a woman's dress a grown-up."

"You're just too old for me. God, what are you? Forty, or something? They shouldn't let people live so long."

"Well, *you* almost killed me last night. You damn near bit my weenie off."

"You weren't paying attention to me."

"I've had things on my mind. I've been distracted."

"The big man."

"My bearded friends in the mountains aren't doing so well. I've got to send them more money."

"I thought you were broke."

"I am. That's why I'm here. I can always squeeze a little juice from the Right Guys or the President."

"Squeeze all you want, see if I care. Look! Lassie's come home! She's licking Timmy's face!"

"I hope she's not a biter."

"Pig."

"Turn the channel to the race."

"Why don't you just get out of the tub and look out the window? It's right there."

"I need my beauty soak."

"You're such a bully." The Teenager got up, flicked the TV channel to the race and flopped back on the bed. "When are we going to get out of this dump? You promised we could go back to Jamaica. I like it better there. All the servants speak English."

"I told you, I need to squeeze some juice. Then the yacht sails back to Jamaica."

"So get squeezing."

"What do you think I've been doing here for the past weeks? But it's getting dangerous, everybody's playing sides, so I've got to play *all* the sides. And there's that bald guy who's been shadowing me. I've still got to fuck the reason why he's tailing me out of his bimbo wife."

"Is that the only reason you're interested in her?"

"Yeah. I don't want anybody but you. You're prime, at least until you turn sixteen."

"Pig!" The Teenager plucked a pillow from the bed and hurled it through the doorway. It fell with a splash into the bathtub.

The Bad Actor howled with laughter, then threw the soggy pillow back.

The Teenager whined, "I want to go to the pool. I want to get some sun on my titties."

"Lean out the window."

"That's not funny."

"I told you, my little strawberry polliwog, we *can't* go to the pool. We've got to stay in the room until four o'clock."

"But Daddy Poo-Poo, *why*?"

"Because an ape named Lizard told me something is going to happen around three o'clock that wouldn't be good for my image, that I should lay low until four."

"You care more about your public image than making me happy," the Teenager pouted.

"You want to come in here and play with my froggie?"

"No!" She grabbed the soggy pillow and held it against her skinny chest. "I'm on strike!"

"Turn up the TV volume."

"Stinker Daddy Poo-Poo! What a bully!" The Teenager flounced off the bed with a groan and cranked up the volume, staring resentfully at the screen. Race cars rounded a curve on the Malecón, then the camera panned to the grandstand in front of the Nacional. "There's your *friend*." She puffed up her cheeks, pretending to vomit. "The one from dinner last night who tried to feel me up under the table."

"The President, yeah. The Right Guys will have touted him on the race. He'll be flush with money. I'll squeeze more juice out of him." The Actor slid a fresh cigarette into his holder, careful not to get it wet. "Did my polliwog let the Prezy-whezy feel anything under the table?"

"You told me not to wear any panties to dinner."

"So what did the Prezy feel?"

The Teenager pulled the elastic band of her panties back, then let it slap her skin so hard that an angry red mark welled up. "Wouldn't you like to *know*?"

Leaping Larry Lizard was having a great day, seated in the President's grandstand in front of the Nacional. There was more than just a race going on. History was about to be made. He checked his wristwatch, then glanced up to the hotel's top floor, to the window where the Right Guys had told him Sweet Maria would be. It was a long distance to shoot, but he knew the perfect weapon was in her hands. Maria's hands could work all kinds of magic, Lizard got a throbbing boner just thinking about it. Too bad she would no longer be around after PayDay finished her off. But she deserved to go. She was just another dirt-poor sugarcane kid who'd landed in the city hoping for a better life, but she made the mistake of falling for a radical university boy, who seduced her with visions of equality, free education and housing, then trained her to be a crack shot with a rifle. Lizard checked his watch again. The President and Maria had only minutes to live.

Lizard heard the distant roar of race-car engines. The people crammed into the grandstand shouted with excitement, especially Broadway Betty, seated next to him. He already had a boner from thinking about what Maria's hands could do; now it danced wildly in his pants as he pictured what he wanted to do with Betty. He was no longer pissed off at PayDay for bringing the blond bimbo along on the job. He eyed her knees peeking out from beneath the edge of her poodle skirt as she sat scrunched up between him and a Cuban Pete whose lips smacked away at a torpedo cigar. Lizard hated the way these Cuban Petes were with cigars, like Frenchmen with wine bottles, sucking like pathetic baby pigs. Lizard knew this Cuban Pete was one of the President's bodyguards. The President was sitting high up in the grandstand surrounded by more bodyguards, and he looked fatter than ever with a bulletproof vest padding out his white suit coat. Lizard had no respect for the Cubes. It was only a matter of time before the island became the forty-ninth American state and all the Cubes were shipped back to Mexico, or wherever they swam over from.

"They're coming!" Betty shouted with a thrill.

"Yeah." Lizard cocked his head, pretending to watch for the racers but really trying to get a closer look at the bimbo's breasts, quivering like two bowls of vanilla pudding in an alligator-print halter top. It occurred to Lizard that if this ditsy dame dressed with alligator and poodle prints on her clothes, she must be something unusual when caught between the sheets. He was just the gator to bite her puppy puss. His nostrils flared at her musky poodle scent, the dame was in heat. He wanted to bang her in front of the whole world, bang her as hard as he knew the Bad Actor must be banging her. But the Bad Actor's banging days were soon to end. The Right Guys had found out he was betting all four corners of the table. No one gets away with that unless he owns the table. Only the Right Guys owned it, and nobody owned *them*. The Actor's last big bang was going to be Betty, or that carrot-top teenager with dick-cutting braces on her teeth.

"They're getting closer!" Betty shouted. "Oh, my, what a roar!" She pressed her knees together, the poodle skirt flounced up to her thighs.

The cigar chomper handed Betty his binoculars.

"Thank you." Betty smiled.

She raised the binoculars to her eyes, her lips circling into a provocative O.

Lizard was pissed at the cigar chomper, trying to work his greasy Latin chivalry. He grabbed the binoculars out of Betty's hands. "Here, let me have a look!"

"Thanks," Betty purred sarcastically.

Through the binoculars Lizard could see a blur of speeding cars rounding a distant curve of the Malecón.

"I told you they were coming." He handed the binoculars back to Betty, thinking he would be generous.

Betty passed the binoculars back to the Cuban. "Thank you. *Moocho-grassy-ass.*"

The Cuban smiled. "You're quite welcome, Señora."

Lizard was really pissed now. The Cuban Pete was still pretending to be a gentleman, when all the Cube wanted was to dive under Betty's poodle skirt and start yapping at her pussy like a Chihuahua.

Lizard could play the Cube's game. He offered up a chivalrous ploy to Betty. "Your husband's going to be tied up after the race. Come into town with me and I'll treat you to some Christians and Moors."

Betty didn't answer.

"How about the Floridita?" Lizard leaned close and breathed heavily into Betty's ear. "I'm the guy who can take you there."

Betty turned and gave Lizard a smile with her candy-red lips. Looking straight at him, she sang with knife-edged sweetness, *"I get too hungry for dinner at eight. I like the theater but never come late. I never bother with people . . . I hate."*

Sweet Maria ran her hand affectionately over the wood stock of her rifle. A brass plate at the stock's base was stamped with the word CZECHOSLOVAKIA. She wondered what the word meant. It wasn't Spanish, and she couldn't imagine how to pronounce it. But the rifle had a fine balance; she could intuit its straightforward inner workings. It excited her that with the squeeze of a finger she could ignite a deadly velocity. She leaned her cheek against the polished wood, as if it were the naked thigh of a lover. She peered through the sight scope mounted above the long barrel, and her view of the world expanded with pinpoint magnification.

Below the hotel window, Maria saw the grandstand in the garden facing the Malecón. She scanned the crowd through the rifle scope, stopping at the sight of a blond woman in a halter top and poodle skirt seated next to Larry Lizard. Maria aimed the rifle at Lizard's heart. She puckered her lips and made a loud pop. If only she could squeeze the trigger—but she was stalking bigger game. She swept the view of the scope over the crowd and sighted on the President. He was no longer the bright young bull who offered Cuba hope. His face was puffed from rich food and smoothed from pampering, his slack cherubic expression was the familiar mask of all despotic Latin American death angels. Maria targeted the red carnation pinned on the white suit coat above his heart. The roar of approaching race cars was in her ears.

In the long moment before Maria pulled the rifle's trigger, she thought of the bearded young saints in the mountains. She thought of the cries of starving children in the night. She thought of the sorrows of women selling their lives as underpaid laborers, selling their sex for less than the price of a fishhook.

She thought about the film *Las Mujeres Madan,* a movie she had seen at the Teatro Fausto, about a mythical island of women. For her the film wasn't entertainment, it was a revolutionary tract. The women were all sexy, tough and smart. They could sing and dance. They had their own army. They wore uniforms of cute shorts belted by holstered pistols, tight blouses, and caps tipped at racy angles. They were experts with weapons, even machine guns, which they squatted behind in dangerously pretty poses, taking aim at any man who threatened their island paradise. These valiant females could kill with their looks as well as their weapons. Maria understood that revolutions can be made for selfish reasons, as well as idealistic ones. She checked her wristwatch. It was 3:01.

She remembered what she had been taught: safety off, target in sight, remain calm, steady pull on the trigger. But she always added something of her own—a wiggle of her ass for good luck.

From the grandstand below, a voice boomed from loudspeakers that a Maserati, driven by an Italian, was leading the pack, followed by a Ferrari, driven by the American, Guy Armstrong. The crowd was on its feet, shouting into the deafening roar of the approaching machines.

Maria prepared her shot. She wiggled her ass. Steady. Calm. She sighted the rifle on the red carnation.

The brightly colored cars roared in front of the grandstand. The Maserati swerved right, allowing the Ferrari to speed by. The Maserati swung back into the center of the roadway, blocking the other cars from catching the Ferrari.

From her window, Maria firmly pulled the trigger. The shot skimmed over the President and angled down at the Malecón, smashing through the Ferrari's windshield.

The windshield shattered into Guy Armstrong's face. He clung to the steering wheel, struggling to control the skidding car, his eyes clouded with dripping blood. The side of the Ferrari scraped along the Malecón's stone wall, striking a trail of sparks. The Ferrari flipped and exploded in a thundering fireball that sent it over the wall and out to sea.

The recoil of the rifle shot was so powerful against Maria's shoulder that it knocked her to the floor. She pulled herself up and looked through the open window down to the grandstand. The President was surrounded by a wall of bodyguards. Beyond the grandstand, the fireball of the Ferrari sank into the sea with a great hiss. "Mother of God," Maria moaned, "forgive me. I have shot my *compañero*!"

Maria hid the rifle beneath sheets stacked on her cleaning cart. She pushed the cart out into the carpeted hallway and walked quickly away.

At the opposite end of the hall, the elevator door opened, revealing two men inside.

Maria recognized them. She decided to keep pushing the cart.

King Bongo and Johnny PayDay stepped out of the elevator at the same time.

Bongo spotted Maria. "Finally!"

PayDay looked suspiciously at Maria, then hurried past her.

Maria batted her eyelashes innocently at Bongo. "What's going on?"

Bongo glanced down the hall.

PayDay stopped in front of the door to the room Maria had just vacated and pulled out a gun.

Bongo pushed Maria and her cart into the elevator.

PayDay flung open the door to the room and rushed in. No one was there. He looked out the window down onto the garden. There was a clear view of the grandstand, now empty. "Shit!"

Bongo and Maria stepped out of the elevator into the hotel lobby. Maria rolled the cart before her as Bongo held her arm in a tight grip. Around them, panicked people ran in all directions, except for a circle of men listening intently as Zapata spoke. The circle broke up, the men raced off in different directions. Zapata saw Bongo and headed for him.

Bongo whispered to Maria, "Don't let him see your face." He began kissing her.

Zapata walked up and jabbed Bongo in the back. "What are you doing?"

Bongo turned his head. "What does it look like I'm doing?"

"That's just like you. Making out like a teenager at a time like this."

"Any time is a good time." Bongo flashed a smile.

"I don't have time for this. I'll get to you later." Zapata stepped into the elevator, punched a button, and the door closed behind him.

Maria turned her head up to Bongo. "Thanks."

"I didn't want him to get his hands on you. Let's go."

"I've got to put the cart away. I'm responsible for it."

"No tricks!"

Bongo followed Maria as she rolled the cart across the tiled floor, dodging running people.

She stopped outside a door marked LADIES' LOUNGE. "I have to leave the cart inside."

"Hurry before Zapata returns."

"That was some kiss." Maria winked. "I'll be right back."

She rolled the cart into the lounge, the door swinging closed behind her.

Inside the lounge, Señorita Pee-Pee was waiting. She locked the door behind Maria, pulled the hidden rifle from beneath the sheets on the cart, and buried the weapon under stacks of towels in a storage closet.

Maria stepped to a mirror in front of a marble sink. She plucked off her fake eyelashes, ran water into the sink, scrubbed her makeup off with soap, then pulled off her long dark wig, exposing the thick matted kink of male hair.

Señorita Pee-Pee handed Maria a man's blue suit and a pair of brown men's shoes.

Maria kicked off her pumps, pulled off her maid's uniform and unstrapped her padded bra, exposing a skinny male chest. "I hate it when I'm *not* a woman anymore."

"You're still a woman," Señorita Pee-Pee offered sympathetically. "Did it go well?"

"I missed."

"We'll get him next time."

Maria put on the man's suit and shoes. She looked at her male reflection in the mirror and sighed with exasperation. "No style."

"They'll be looking for a maid. Only we know that Maria is really Joseph."

Maria swung around defiantly. "Nobody can say a sweet Maria didn't have the balls to shoot a president."

Johnny PayDay had his escape route planned in advance. Lizard had shown him a secret door that opened up behind the bar and onto the sunbathing deck next to the swimming pool. From there it was an easy stroll through a garden gate and down the street to the Capri. PayDay opened the secret door behind the bar. He walked around the pool alongside splashing swimmers and got to the garden gate just as another man did. The man was thin, wore a blue suit and brown shoes. PayDay could swear he knew the face. Then he recalled, on his way to the shooter's room, he had passed a maid. This guy's face had the same features.

PayDay held his hand on the gate. "Do I know you?"

The man lowered his head and answered in a baritone voice. "*No hablo* the English."

PayDay opened the gate. He watched the man walk away. The guy had a decidedly feminine sway to his hips.

PayDay went straight to the Capri, walked in under its swooping concrete overhang, passed the reception desk, and waited with a crowd in a hurry to return to the safety of their rooms. He wedged himself into a packed elevator, rode to the top floor, got out and knocked on the penthouse door.

A girl's voice called from behind the door, "Who is it?"

"Complimentary champagne for the film star."

"Oh, goody."

A man's voice growled at the girl, "Don't open it. We don't know who it is."

PayDay banged the door open and pointed his gun at the Teenager standing directly in front of him.

"Daddy," she screamed, "someone's here to kill us!"

PayDay pushed inside, slamming the door behind him. "Shut up and get on the bed."

The Teenager sat, her bony knees banging together as she shivered with fear.

The Bad Actor continued to soak in the marble tub, his face slathered with cold cream, the hairnet plastered on his head. He called out nonchalantly, "The wallet's in the second dresser drawer. The Rolex is on top of the TV. Take them and beat it."

PayDay walked into the bathroom.

"Oh, shit, it's *you*!"

"Yeah, the *husband*."

"I didn't touch a hair on her head. Take the wallet, there's some dough in it, and the watch is solid gold."

"You movie pricks think you can buy the world. I'm not here to take anything. I'm here to *give* you something."

"What?"

"This." PayDay put the tip of his gun barrel to the Actor's lips. "Why don't you suck on this. That's why you actors are so well paid, isn't it?"

"That, and we eat a lot of concrete pussy too."

The Teenager screamed, "Daddy, don't talk to him like that! Can't you see he's going to blow your brains out!"

The Actor's eyes widened in surprise at PayDay. "Would you really dare to kill a movie hero?"

"In my movie"—PayDay clicked off the gun's safety—"you're the bad guy who dies in the end."

The Actor slid under the water, as if he could hide there. He saw the gun aimed down at him. His cheeks puffed up, bubbles escaping from his mouth as he tried to hold his breath.

"Don't let him drown!" the Teenager pleaded.

PayDay reached into the water, grabbed the Actor by the ears and yanked his head up. He could see behind the Actor's ears a white crisscrossing of scars where the skin had been slit and pulled up by face-lifts. From beneath the Actor's hairnet, black hair dye trickled down.

Tears came into the Actor's eyes. "Dear boy! Don't let me die like this! What will my fans think?"

PayDay shoved the gun barrel deep into the Actor's mouth.

The Actor pissed with fear, a yellow cloud escaping from his limp pecker into the bathwater. The cloud grew larger, creeping above the Actor's waist to the water's surface.

The scent of piss pierced PayDay's nostrils. It wasn't like his wife's sweet pee, when she sat enthroned on the toilet while he brushed her hair. No, this had the stink of a rancid fart from a dragon's asshole.

PayDay pulled the gun out of the Actor's mouth.

The Actor moaned, "I didn't fuck your wife."

"I know that."

"How do you know?"

"She told me you didn't."

"And you believed her?"

"If I didn't, you'd be dead."

"Never trust a dame, especially if she's your wife."

"Shut up, you idiot!" screamed the Teenager. "He's giving you a chance!"

PayDay pressed the gun to the Actor's temple. The sweaty drip of hair dye splashed like black tears into the yellow bathwater.

The Actor tried to squirm away from the gun. "Wait! I know Judy Garland! I can get you a blow job from Dorothy of Oz! That little girl can whistle while she works!"

Before PayDay could answer, the door banged open.

Leaping Larry Lizard stood framed in the doorway, his gun poised, the slab of his face purple with rage. He kicked the door closed behind him. "What the fuck are you doing? First you fuck up on the shooter, now you fuck up on this!"

"The shooter wasn't in the room," PayDay said. "There was only a maid in the hall."

"The maid *was* the shooter, asshole! And you were warned *not* to shoot this dickhead yet!"

The Actor croaked and slipped lower in the water. "Pleeeease!"

"Now you *have* to shoot the prick, he knows too much!"

"What about the girl?"

"Her too! No witnesses!"

"Yeah, okay." PayDay turned his gun toward the bed.

The Teenager pulled her bony knees up to her skinny chest. "Oh-my-God! Oh-my-God! I'm too young to die!"

PayDay took aim at the Teenager. In a split second he jerked the gun to the left, ripping six bullets off into Lizard's face, pulverizing it into a mess of flesh and bone. Lizard's body thumped back against the door and slid to the floor.

The Teenager screamed as PayDay aimed the gun at her again. "Oh-my-God! Oh-my-God! I beg you, no!"

PayDay walked over to the Teenager and handed her his gun. She held it, trembling, confused.

PayDay reached down and picked up Lizard's pistol.

The Teenager swung her gun at PayDay and pulled the trigger: *click-click-click.*

PayDay grinned. "It's empty." He turned Lizard's gun toward the Actor in the tub. "But this one isn't."

The Actor sank completely beneath the water, an eruption of bubbles churning up above his terrified face.

PayDay blasted away.

The wall behind the bathtub shattered, tile fragments flew through the air.

The Actor couldn't hold his breath any longer. He popped his head above the water, gasping for air in gulping sobs.

PayDay kicked Lizard's body away from the door. He leaned down and placed the gun in Lizard's limp hand. Then he took out a PayDay wrapper from his coat pocket and shoved it into the hole where Lizard's mouth had been.

PayDay turned to the Teenager. "Tell the cops Lizard broke into the room and tried to rape you. But you shot him. Say the gun in your hand belongs to the Actor."

The Teenager's face was white with fear. She pointed to the Pay-Day wrapper protruding from the bloody pulp on the floor. "What about that? What's it mean?"

PayDay ran his hand over his bald head and grinned. "So the Right Guys will know . . . they can take this island and shove it. Me and my little lady are on the next plane out of here."

3.

Love and War

King Bongo looked through his office window. The late-afternoon clouds that had earlier piled up on one another and pummeled Obispo Street with rain had cleared, and evening's purple shadows were beginning to fall. Bongo dialed the telephone on his desk. On the other end of the line, he heard the clamorous din in the Three Virgins Bar. He shouted into the mouthpiece to make himself heard.

"Is Sweet Maria there?"

"No" came the annoyed reply. "Stop calling here. She won't be back."

"She could change her mind."

"She won't." The line went dead.

Bongo wearily rested his head in his hands, thinking about how Maria gave him the slip at the Nacional. When she hadn't come out of the ladies' lounge, he pounded on the locked door until a Señorita Pee-Pee opened it. He asked where the maid was. The señorita insisted there had been no maid. The señorita was dressed in a drab hotel dress, she had the demeanor of a school principal, not of someone who would work in such a menial position. Behind her desk was a locked door, but she refused to open it. Bongo dropped a peso into her gratuity bowl. Without a word, she handed him a key. He unlocked the door and stepped out, surprised to be overlooking the sunning deck of the hotel swimming pool. He saw Zapata's men, Pedro and Paulo, demanding to see everyone's identification papers. Bongo quickly stepped back inside the lounge and locked the door. He knew that Maria was long gone.

Bongo dialed the phone on his desk again. This time, the voice of a young woman answered.

"Armstrong residence."

Bongo recognized the voice; it was the pretty woman in the sundress. "Sorry to bother you. Is Mrs. Armstrong back from the funeral yet?"

"I told you earlier, she won't be back until late. Then she's packing to return to New York."

"Tell her I have something for her."

"You already asked me to do that."

"You won't forget?"

"I don't forget messages."

"Thanks. I appreciate it."

The woman cut the connection.

Bongo suspected that Mrs. Armstrong was there and dodging him. He had gone out to her house, but the automatic driveway gate that had once magically opened for him no longer would. The grounds were patrolled by private security cops, so there was no point in trying to go over the fence.

Bongo glanced down at the newspaper on his desk. The front-page story was an even bigger event than Guy Armstrong's having gone over the Malecón wall in a ball of fire. The article was about a famous American actor who, on the day of the Big Race, had saved his niece from being raped by an intruder at the Capri Hotel. The newspaper sported a photograph of the actor, grinning beneath the dash of a clipped English mustache. He was quoted as having been in a heroic life-or-death struggle with the intruder before gunning him down, barely managing to save the virtue of his niece, who had been cowering in the bathtub. What kept the story alive was that all three of the players were Americans and that the dead man was an employee of the ritzy Nacional. There was a grisly shot of the victim, the face blown mostly away, and an ill-defined object was jammed into the mangled mouth.

The phone rang, jarring Bongo from his thoughts.

He picked it up. There was heavy breathing, then a click, then silence. This was the third time in the past hour that someone had called and then hung up.

Bongo decided he'd had enough for one day. He locked up the office and walked down the stairs. He stepped out onto Obispo Street and strolled up to the Ambos Mundos Hotel. Inside the open-air lobby an old gentleman, wearing a straw bowler hat and a once fashionable suit, tinkled out a slow bolero on a piano. Next to the piano player a skinny black girl in a pink starched dress scraped a soulful tune from a violin. At the long mahogany bar, there was the usual contingent of white female tourists, sitting on stools, leggs crossed, sipping cocktails through colorful plastic straws. The women gave Bongo the once-over. He smiled back but his heart wasn't in it. He walked away, turning the corner onto narrow Oficios Street, crowded with centuries-old noble mansions that were now sub-divided among numerous families. Above the weathered doorways, stone-chiseled heraldic coats of arms were nearly worn away by time, and from the rusted balconies laundry hung. The scent of roasting chicken, boiling pork and steaming rice and beans drifted from open kitchens, where women bent over hot stoves and bare-armed men in T-shirts read newspapers. Walking this street, between groups of laughing children kicking balls, always sank Bongo into murky memories. He was reminded of when he had a family in El Fanguito, until that day when the river rose up in a hurricane fury, ripping his father away and delivering his sister into Zapata's arms.

Bongo turned the corner into San Francisco Plaza and stopped at the Fountain of the Lions. The slouching white-marble beasts were gathered around a gurgling waterspout. Across the plaza, inside the Baroque Church of San Francisco de Assisi, the crypts held the bones of conquering Spanish lords. Pigeons landed on top of the church's spiraling tower, which once was the highest point in the city, the high-est man-made point in *all* of the Americas.

Bongo crossed over to Teniente Rey Street, following it until he emerged onto Plaza Vieja, Havana's Colonial heart. Here, all the architectural splendor that the spoils of a raped land could afford had been imaginatively conjured. The buildings were supported by soaring Pantheonic columns, but the modern-day President and his men had transformed the plaza's center into a parking lot; the begin-ning of a plan to demolish Old Havana, from the simplest adobe hut to the most eccentric Baroque palace, replacing all with towers of steel and glass.

Bongo felt he was the last man walking through a delusional dreamscape. When he got close to his apartment, he always stopped to read the bronze plaque that was Havana's oldest traffic sign: CALLE DE RICA, IN MEMORY OF HIS EXCELLENCY THE COUNT OF RICA, SENT BY HIS MAJESTY TO RESTORE THIS CITY. YEAR 1763. The count had smashed an occupation by the English and again brought the iron fist of Spain down on the island. Bongo wondered what leader would arrive next, on a white horse or on the wings of a white dove, to declare the city his. Maybe it wouldn't be a man leading an army this time, but an invasion of greenback U.S. dollars, infiltrating every bank and every pocket, billions of capitalist ghost bullets striking at the heart of every citizen. Bongo didn't consider himself immune; such seductive bullets were hard to dodge.

Bongo's apartment was in a once majestic five-story mansion built for Spanish royalty. He unlocked the old iron gate that guarded the mansion's patio. Surrounding the patio were tiered terraces crowded with potted plants, bicycles, and clattering refrigerators. Bongo climbed the tiled steps of the staircase to the top floor, unlocked his door and stepped inside. He took a deep breath, gazing out over a field of flowers.

Orchids were everywhere, fragile beauties and robust specimens, in small pots and giant urns, in bookcases, on the floor, on tables and window ledges. Bongo didn't have Mr. Wu's teeming jungle of rarities, but he was proud of his brood. Among the exotica his phone was ringing. He grabbed it.

"Hello?"

No answer.

"Hello?"

The line clicked and went dead.

Bongo was certain someone was tracking him. Sooner or later, he'd find out who it was. He decided not to worry about it. He poured himself a glass of rum and walked out onto the rooftop terrace. He took a swig and breathed deeply, the alcohol's tingling sensation in his nostrils mixed with orchid perfume. What he wanted to smell most was the scent of cinnamon and vanilla, the provocative drift of his *Vanda*. He couldn't get her fragrant memory out of his mind, especially after he drank a second rum and the memories of New Year's Eve rushed in. Then his heart clenched in a fist of pain, leaving him with nothing but sorrow over a dead girlfriend and a lost sister. He poured another rum; damned if he was going to let self-pity get the better of him.

He gazed out across the skyline. The buildings of Havana were streaked with lavender light and the atmosphere was charged with the mystery of oncoming night. Across the rooftops, he could see the life-sized Mercury perched on the dome of the nineteenth-century Commercial Exchange building. The bronzed god had turned an ethereal green with age, but he remained eternally young, one foot raised as he prepared to fly off in his winged helmet. Bongo raised his glass in a salute to Mercury. The race goes to the swift.

Below him, Bongo could see the Luz Docks. An American cruise ship was berthed, its profile illuminated by glittering lights strung the length of its deck. Beyond the ship, a ferry chugged through the water toward Casablanca. From this distance, Casablanca had the look of a medieval town, rising up in rowed streets of whitewashed houses. On Casablanca's summit stood an unfinished marble statue of Christ, fifty feet high and headless, caged within steel scaffolding. Finished, he would be taller than the Christ overlooking Rio. He had one arm raised to the sky in what was intended as a benevolent blessing to the people of Havana, but since the arm had no hand, the gesture seemed bluntly hostile. One day the Christ would be completed and take his place in the record books as the largest sculpture in the world created by a woman. Bongo raised his glass in praise to the headless wonder. Behind Bongo a loud commotion erupted.

Zapata's men, Pedro and Paulo, barged through the unlocked apartment door, knocking down orchids and stomping them underfoot as they charged toward Bongo, their guns drawn.

Bongo shouted at the blundering bulls, "Don't hurt the flowers!"

Pedro and Paulo grabbed Bongo's arms, twisting them up behind his back. The glass of rum in his hand flew over the terrace railing and shattered in the street below.

"Don't give us any trouble," Pedro growled.

"I'm not, but those orchids are innocents. Don't rough them up."

"We wouldn't dare to hurt your little friends," Paulo mocked.

"Nice of you boys to telephone earlier and say you were coming," Bongo said.

"No wise talk." Paulo jerked Bongo's arm up painfully.

Pedro pulled Bongo's gun from its holster. "Forget about this." He threw the gun to the floor.

"Let's get going," Paulo urged. "We're late."

"Yeah," Pedro agreed. "If orchid boy had stayed at his office we'd be right on time."

Pedro and Paulo handcuffed Bongo and hustled him out of the apartment, down the stairs and into the backseat of Zapata's black Plymouth.

Bongo waited for them to get in, then asked, "Where to, friends? The police station, or the Blue Mansion?"

Pedro turned from the front seat and knocked Bongo across the mouth with the back of his hand. "I told you, no lip."

Bongo tasted blood.

Paulo started the Plymouth and steered it into traffic.

"Put on some Beny Moré," Pedro said.

"I'll see if I can find some." Paulo spun the radio dial, hunting through a jumble of voices and music. "Shit, no Beny. How about this?" He stopped on a station with a pathetic whiny voice singing about a little white cloud that cried.

"What's that crap?" Pedro asked.

"That American guy, Johnnie Ray."

"You know I can't understand English. Kill that canary."

Paulo changed the station. "How about *this*?"

"That's more like it! Beny himself, the Barbarian of Rhythm!"

"Rumba, rumba, rumba!"

The Plymouth sped through the narrow streets of Old Havana and then onto the broad boulevards of central downtown. When the car approached the police station, it did not slow down. The Plymouth swerved onto the Malecón, roared along the oceanside highway, past La Rampa, past Vedado, through the tunnel under the Almendares River and up onto Fifth Avenue. The Spanish-style clock tower loomed ahead, the black hand pointed to 9. The Plymouth turned toward Miramar Beach and pulled up before an ornate two-story mansion, plastered an intense indigo blue and surrounded by bright green bayonet-pointed cacti.

Pedro and Paulo pulled Bongo out of the Plymouth and marched him up to the mansion's entrance. A guard with a rifle swung open a massive wooden door. Pedro and Paulo pushed Bongo inside, past the marble foyer, through a series of rooms with half-finished walls, exposed electrical wires and tilted posts propping up ceilings. The deeper into the mansion the men went, the gloomier it became, each room more unfinished than the last, until they emerged into what was intended to be the mansion's kitchen. A white porcelain sink ran the length of the room's back wall. The sink and wall were spattered with blood.

Pedro and Paulo pushed Bongo down into a chair at a wooden chopping-block table. Above the table, a cord hung down with a lighted bare bulb casting a sharp glare.

Zapata stepped into the room and stood in front of the blood-spattered sink and wall. He wore his linen suit, Panama hat, and dark sunglasses. The line of his mustache seemed straighter than ever in the harsh glare.

He pulled out a chair and sat across from Bongo, his intimate whisper of a voice laced with menace. "There's a Panther loose."

Bongo didn't answer.

Without looking up, Zapata commanded Pedro and Paulo. "Get the others."

"All at once, sir?" Pedro asked.

"The woman first."

"Yes, sir," the two men said in unison, hurrying off.

Zapata took out a snub-nosed revolver and set it on the chopping block. "The Panther is special to many people," he whispered. "But for us, she represents more than life. Don't you agree?"

"You brought me to your torture palace just to ask me that?"

"I brought you here because you are in the center of things. Many fingers point to you."

"There's not anyone that you *don't* suspect."

"Especially you. I always suspected that she loved you more than me."

"She *never* loved you. You saved her and she was indebted. That's different."

"I plucked her little body from the floodwaters. I took her home and sponged the mud from her flesh. She quivered back to life in my hands. I *created* her."

"And you left me in the mud to die."

"I thought you were dead. You were just a pathetic white thing, barely breathing."

"She was—"

"A goddess cub, a cat child."

"Tell me"—Bongo leaned forward, staring into the opaque orbs of Zapata's sunglasses—"how long were you spying on my family from your house across the river?"

Zapata sighed heavily, then caught his breath and whispered, "It was fascinating, like watching a play. The hovels offered little shelter, so life was carried on outside. I studied it all, like it was my personal anthill."

"It was a sad place, shit ran in the streets, kids were covered with open sores. What kind of anthill is that?"

"The best kind, a colony of desperation."

"Poverty can also have its nobility."

"I could see your sister pissing in the mud. I could see your father copulating in the mud."

Bongo struggled to free his hands from the handcuffs. He wanted to choke the life out of Zapata, but the circles of steel cut into his flesh and he bled.

Zapata's hollow whispering continued, "I watched *everything,* day after day, through my binoculars."

"And you never did anything to help. You just watched."

"There are some things that cannot be helped."

"They weren't things. They were people."

"The way your father used to stand you and your sister together, dressed only in your undershorts, and slap your shaved heads like they were drums as people with real instruments gathered around and joined in. It went on for hours, into the night. In the light of fires I could see you and your sister, standing still as statues. Amazing. The bongo beat being played on your skulls traveled across the river to me."

"I'm glad you enjoyed the show."

"And then the hurricane crashed across the cane fields and the Almendares swelled up and tore through the pathetic shacks of your mud town. I spent days after, searching among the jagged stumps of ripped-up trees hung with the bodies of animals and people."

"I know the story."

"At the mouth of the river, where the sea churned brown from the mud that had washed into it, I found the two of you twisted together, one black one, one white one."

"You left me there to die and took her."

"Of course I took her. A man doesn't need another *man.* I could give her *life.*"

"Or keep her in a cage for twenty years."

"The only escape from the cage is death."

"You've killed every man that ever got close to her."

"Except you. But your time is coming. That's why I took you to see the miserable shark bait speared through the chest. That will be your fate."

"He was one of my sister's lovers?"

"That's why I had his ass tattooed. He was a university professor, they're all subversives. I eradicated a piece of leftist trash, and a personal irritant. Two birds, one stone."

"The professor may have been a leftist, but he *wasn't* her lover. When he was fished out of the ocean he was wearing underpants that belonged to the American who died in the Big Race. The professor and Guy Armstrong were lovers. You killed the wrong guy."

Zapata's lips quivered into an ironic smile. "Ah, my dear boy, you are so wrong. The professor wasn't the lover of Guy Armstrong. He was the lover of your sister, and *Mrs. Armstrong.*"

"Impossible."

"The professor was often at the Armstrongs' house when the husband was gone. He just happened to put on the wrong underpants one night in the dark after he was finished with her."

"I don't believe it."

"I've had the Armstrong house under surveillance for months. The husband wanted us to think he was just a rich cream puff who liked cheap sex with our Cuban boys. It was all a pretense. Armstrong was behind the plot at the Big Race to kill the President. He used his wife's money to destabilize our little island. His kind are the most despicable, idealists dressed in Brooks Brothers suits, Cadillac commies."

"Mrs. Armstrong . . . she was part of this?"

"She's ignorant of politics. But she did know her husband wasn't a homo. They had, shall we say, an active bedroom life."

Bongo was silent. The words that Mrs. Armstrong had once breathed into his ear flamed in his mind. *"You don't know how long I've waited. How long I've been without."*

From outside the room there was a clanging, then thuds, then scuffling.

Zapata ignored the sounds. His lips moved below his mustache. "Sometimes, when I see you in a certain light," he whispered, "you look so much like your sister that it's hard to tell you apart. She is the blackest of the black. You are white, but your heart is that of a black."

Bongo pulled at the steel cuffs cutting into his bleeding wrists. He spat out his words. "Sometimes, when I see you in a certain light, you look *almost* human."

Zapata didn't answer. He remained motionless, his eyes hidden behind the glare of sunglasses.

The silence between them was broken by shouting and footsteps, then the door was flung open. Pedro and Paulo burst in, pulling a handcuffed woman, forcing her to stand before the blood-spattered sink behind Zapata.

Zapata did not turn to face the woman. He directed his whisper at Bongo. "Do you know her?"

Bongo looked at the woman. It was Señorita Pee-Pee from the Hotel Nacional.

Zapata whispered more insistently. "Do you *know* her?"

The woman didn't seem frightened. She wore a drab hotel uniform dress, but held her head up in noble defiance.

It was obvious to Bongo that Zapata already knew who she was, that he was fishing for more information. Bongo betrayed nothing by stating, "She's a Señorita Pee-Pee. She works in the ladies' lounge at the Nacional."

"How do you know she works *inside* a ladies' lounge? That's not a place a man would go."

Bongo had no intention of telling Zapata that he had followed Sweet Maria into the lounge, where he met Señorita Pee-Pee.

"I didn't say I was in the lounge. I was in the hotel, trying to sell insurance."

"What about the hotel maid I saw you kissing? Were you selling her insurance too?"

"Whatever it takes to close a sale."

Zapata tilted his head toward Pedro and Paulo and ordered, "Get the others. Close the door behind you." He waited until the two men left, then turned to Bongo. "Did you know that during the Big Race, someone tried to shoot the President from the Nacional? They missed and struck Armstrong's windshield instead. That's why he crashed."

"It's news to me."

"Of course, you were too busy trying to close insurance deals with maids and pee-pee girls."

"It's not an alibi, it's how I make my living."

"So your visit to Mrs. Armstrong's house the night before her husband was killed was—"

"—just business. Sometimes I have to go to the clients."

"And I suppose you just happened to be at the Tropicana on business when the Judge was murdered?"

"As a matter of fact, I was. Ask Fido, ask the doorman. I was there to sell insurance to the Giant."

"The same as you had been on New Year's Eve?"

"That was one reason, yes."

"And you just happened to be called away New Year's Eve only minutes before the bomb exploded?"

"A series of coincidences."

"You know I don't believe in coincidence."

The door slammed open. Pedro and Paulo herded in three hand-cuffed men and stood them before the long sink with Señorita Pee-Pee.

Zapata remained facing Bongo. "Do you know these men?"

The men were beaten and bloodied. The big black one with the shaved head was Fido; he grinned at Bongo with his smashed lips. Next to Fido was the mulatto, Hurricane, his pitching arm broken at the elbow and hanging limp. The third man was white, his face cratered by festers from burning cigarettes that had been stubbed out on his flesh. His blood-caked eyelashes were long like a woman's. Bongo recognized him, it was the student who shot the Judge.

"I know them."

"They are your friends?"

"Fido is a friend."

"And a good one he is. He refused to say anything bad about you."

"He doesn't deserve this."

"Leave it to me to decide who deserves what."

The student coughed. A purplish fluid gurgled up and trickled from his split lips.

Zapata reached across the table and pulled the pack of Luckys from Bongo's shirt pocket. He tapped out a cigarette and lit up. His black sunglasses lenses reflected smoke rising into the air. "There are no secrets anymore. What do you have to say?"

"How about a smoke?"

"That's all you have to say?"

"What else? You're a man who doesn't believe in coincidence?"

"You're right. Take this pack of Lucky Strikes, for instance. They're the only brand you smoke. At the fountain of the muses, where the Judge was shot, there were butts of freshly smoked Luckys. Your fingerprints were on them."

"Where did you get a copy of my fingerprints?"

"You forgot. When you registered your gun, it's the law. We have an extensive archive of prints—union workers, university people, journalists. We even have the pawprints of cats that screw in the night."

"My prints on some cigarette butts doesn't make me a murderer."

"No, but they might make you an accomplice. You and your friend Fido."

"Accomplices prove nothing, if you don't have a murderer."

"Ah, but we do." Zapata looked at the snub-nosed revolver that he had placed on the table before Bongo. "That is the murder weapon."

The student behind Zapata coughed blood again.

"After I matched up the prints on the cigarette butts to their owners," Zapata continued, "it was just a matter of finding a gun registration with the same prints. Which one of these handsome fellows behind me do you think is the owner of the murder weapon?"

"None of them."

"If that was the case, I wouldn't have invited you out to this splendid abode. Do you know who this mansion was being built for?"

"No idea."

"A high public official who wanted to be even higher, so he was secretly working with those who want to overthrow our government. That's how it always works out. There are no pure revolutions, only tainted humans."

"It's not my game."

"It's everyone's game now, no one is on the sidelines." Zapata picked up the gun and aimed it between Bongo's eyes. "Shooting me isn't going to accomplish anything."

"We'll see." Zapata stood up and turned around. He stepped to Señorita Pee-Pee, his voice intimate, as if he were a lover. "You are special. I will save you for dessert." He moved to Hurricane.

"You bastard!" Hurricane shouted.

Zapata ignored him and moved to the student.

The student tried to speak, but blood gurgled from his lips.

Beneath his mustache, Zapata's own lips formed the crescent of a smile. He moved to Fido. "I suppose this isn't your gun either?"

"I don't need a gun to kill a man. I can do it with my bare hands."

Zapata walked back to the student. "I found this gun in your house. You killed the Judge. He worked for me."

The student tried to spit in Zapata's face, but his bloody lips only twitched.

Zapata shoved the gun barrel between the student's teeth and pulled the trigger.

The blast reverberated as the back of the student's head spattered against the wall above the sink and his body fell at Zapata's feet.

Zapata stepped in front of Hurricane. "Backstage at the Tropicana, on New Year's Eve, you smuggled the bomb in, hidden in a basket of flowers. You gave the basket to a dancer as a gift. The plan was for her to place it on my table. The explosion was timed for midnight. If the Judge hadn't warned me, I'd be dead. Because of that, you set the Judge up to be executed by the university student."

"You can't kill me, I'm a sports hero."

Zapata leveled the gun at Hurricane's face and pulled the trigger. Hurricane slumped to the floor. Zapata looked down at the body. "Now you're a dead leftist punk."

Zapata casually sidestepped up to Señorita Pee-Pee. He nuzzled the gun barrel against her blouse, aiming at her heart.

"You've got it wrong," Señorita Pee-Pee declared firmly. "It's not your mansions we want. We want our dignity."

Zapata circled the outline of her breast with the tip of the barrel.

"When I searched the Nacional after the assassination attempt on the President, I found the rifle that was used. It was hidden beneath towels in the closet of your lounge."

"Next time we won't miss."

Señorita Pee-Pee stared fearlessly at Zapata as he drew back the trigger. The blast knocked her against the wall, her eyelids twitched, her eyes rolled up, she slid to the floor.

Zapata swung around, leaned across the table, pointing the gun at Bongo's forehead. "Tell me where the Panther is!"

Bongo could see his face in Zapata's sunglasses. He stared at his own reflection without saying a word.

The only sound in the room was Fido's mournful sobbing at the carnage surrounding him. Blood was spattered on his face and pooling at his feet.

Zapata pressed the gun barrel into Bongo's forehead and hissed, "You are my bird dog. Go scare up the bird." He yanked the gun away. "And take your dumb boxer friend with you, before I change my mind and dump you both in the Pineapple Field."

Mrs. Armstrong came toward Bongo across the terrace of the Hotel Sevilla rooftop bar. She wasn't dressed like a grieving widow. She wore a sleeveless sheath of shimmering silver silk. Her long blond hair swung with the same rhythm as the hem of her dress swishing at her knees. She glided through the crowd as if the beam of the full moon overhead was her own personal spotlight.

Bongo stood up at his table and pulled a chair out for her. The familiar scent of roses and new car leather hovered in the air.

"Thank you for coming," Bongo said with polite formality. "It must be a trying time."

Mrs. Armstrong sat down. "I've packed everything up and closed the house."

He waited for her to continue, to say something about the death of her husband, but she didn't. He asked, "Where are you going?"

"Palm Beach. It has Cuban weather without the Cubans."

"If all you Americans left, we would have Cuba without the Americans."

"I suppose."

"My condolences about your husband. The reason I asked you to meet me has to do with him."

"It does? Oh, yes, I forgot." She opened her purse. "I still owe for the job you did." She pulled out her checkbook.

"That's not what I meant. Given what's happened, you don't owe me anything. We're even."

"I always honor my obligations." She quickly wrote a check and handed it over.

"Do you have time for a cocktail?"

"Not really."

Bongo raised his hand and snapped his fingers. A white-jacketed waiter appeared. Bongo said, "Bring the lady whatever she wants."

"I'll have a Cosmopolitan," Mrs. Armstrong said.

"And I'll stay with what I've been drinking, rum and Coke."

"Yes, sir." The waiter bowed and left.

"It's just like you to drink *that*," she said with disdain.

"Rum and Coke." Bongo smiled. "We Cubans have a sweet tooth. It's the heat."

"Rum and Coke, half Cuban, half American, like you."

"Right now I feel only Cuban."

"That means you're stuck with antiquated traditions."

"And you're stuck with your pursuit of a tomorrow that never comes."

"Americans are about progress." Mrs. Armstrong's frosted-lipstick mouth tightened. "That's why we are different."

"I'm becoming aware of how different we *really* are."

Bongo looked at the diamond pendant hanging from a gold chain around her neck, its strategic sparkle was directly above the swell of her breasts. He remembered the cool feel of her breasts in his hands.

The waiter returned, served the drinks and left.

Mrs. Armstrong raised her cocktail glass to her lips, her smooth white arms glistening in the moonlight.

Bongo still didn't know if there were three dark-starred moles on her left breast. The night he had tried to see them, the vaporous haze of the swimming pool water, and his impatient desire, had prevented him from getting a clear view.

She set her cocktail glass down with a sharp clink. "What are you staring at?"

Bongo couldn't reveal that he was trying to look down her dress, to finally determine if she was the naked blonde he had seen on the movie screen.

"I was, ahh . . . just admiring your pendant."

"Guy gave it to me." She caressed the diamond with her slender fingers. "It was a wedding present."

"Generous."

"He was generous with what he had."

"So I hear."

"What do you mean by that?"

Bongo didn't want to speak ill of a man to his widow.

"Answer me," she demanded. "What do you mean?"

"Nothing. Forget it."

"I don't want to."

Bongo pulled out his Luckys and his Zippo. "I was wondering," he said, lighting up, "do you by any chance have three moles on your breast?"

"What!"

"On your *left* breast?"

Mrs. Armstrong blushed. She glanced around to see if anyone had overheard, then looked back at him. "What if I do?"

Bongo smiled, but said nothing.

"Should I open the top of my dress right here in public? Would that satisfy your curiosity?"

"I'm not asking that."

"Then what are you asking?"

"Who *are* you?"

Mrs. Armstrong lowered her voice. "You should know, since you *had* me."

"I'm not sure that I *did*."

Bongo couldn't tell her that he thought he had seen her in a theater in a blue movie. Or that he had seen her husband in the same theater, arguing with the now dead university student. For Bongo, she remained more of a mystery than her husband. At least there was a possible explanation for her husband's having been in the theater with the student. Perhaps they were secretly plotting against the government. What more innocuous place to meet than in a darkened movie theater filled with guys watching raunchy stag films?

Mrs. Armstrong leaned across the table, the bright diamond orb swinging between her breasts. "If it wasn't me you had, then *who* was it?"

"I think I'm the one who's been had."

Bongo stared at the diamond glittering provocatively. He recalled her slippery body in his arms in the water, her breath coming into his mouth as she kissed him. *"You don't know how long I've waited. How long I've been without."*

Mrs. Armstrong gave a curt smile. "I think I know what's on your mind."

"I don't think you do."

"Someone from the government visited me after Guy's accident."

Bongo's spine stiffened. "What was his name?"

"Zapata, like the Mexican revolutionary."

"Zapata, like the lake in Cuba."

The waiter reappeared. "May I offer another round?"

"No," Mrs. Armstrong said. "I'm about to leave."

"And the gentleman?"

"I'll have another rum and Coke. Hold the Coke."

"Right away, sir." The waiter bowed and left.

"This Zapata character," Mrs. Armstrong continued, "he told me Guy was not who he appeared to be. He said when Guy was a student, he dropped out of Harvard to fight the fascists in something called the Lincoln Brigade."

"You would have known if he had."

"I knew that Guy left Harvard for a year to knock around Europe."

"Some knocking around, fighting in the Spanish Civil War."

"Zapata also said that Guy was involved in trying to overthrow the Cuban government, that he had a perfect cover, being married to me."

"He was hardly someone you'd think had Communist tendencies."

"Who said he was a Communist?"

"Many who fought against Franco were."

"No, Guy was an idealist."

"Not to Zapata."

"He said Guy was using my money to fund his activities. I never asked Guy how he spent my money. He had expensive hobbies—race cars, polo ponies, yachts."

"Overthrowing governments, that's some hobby."

"You're being sarcastic. You think he was a dilettante meddling in affairs down here."

"Hardly a dilettante. He thought everything through with great care."

"What do you mean?"

Bongo reached inside his coat pocket and pulled out an envelope. "This is why I asked you to meet me here."

Mrs. Armstrong opened the envelope and pulled out a check. Her eyes widened in astonishment. "What is *this*?"

"A half million dollars."

"For what?"

"It's from my insurance company. Your husband took out a life insurance policy with me shortly before he died. You're the sole beneficiary."

"I don't understand. Why would he want me to have another half million? He knew I didn't need it."

"I think that's why. He wanted to show you he could give something back. He wanted to show that he loved you."

Mrs. Armstrong fell silent.

Bongo saw something he had thought he would never see. From the blue sky of her eyes, two tears fell.

"The rich," Bongo said, "get richer."

Mrs. Armstrong raised her wet eyes and glared with contempt. "And the poor get *poorer*."

She put the check in her purse, snapped it shut and pushed back her chair.

"One last thing." Bongo stubbed his cigarette out in the ashtray. "I know you don't think I'm a very complicated crossword puzzle."

"That's right."

"So help me with *your* puzzle. Zapata told me about the university professor."

"What university professor?"

"The one Zapata killed because he was my sister's lover. The one you were screwing behind your husband's back."

Mrs. Armstrong sat very still, barely breathing.

"Everything about you is a lie," Bongo said. Then he twisted the knife. *"You don't know how long I've waited. How long I've been without."*

Her blue eyes took on a starkly strange expression. He didn't know if she was going to scream or hit him.

"I wanted you," she said coldly, "and I *had* you."

"Simple as that?"

"Simple American efficiency."

"Such a cruel culture."

"The professor was a two-timer. No one does that to me. I saw you on New Year's Eve at the Tropicana playing the bongos. Then I saw your sister dancing onstage. The two of you were fascinating, the exact opposite of each other, yet identical."

"So I was the revenge on your lover?"

"Yes."

"And having me follow your husband was a ruse?"

"You got paid, in more ways than one."

"Jesus!"

"Jesus had nothing to do with it. It's love and war." Mrs. Armstrong stood up. "Have a nice life in paradise."

Bongo watched her walk away, untouchable in her sunny-with-money world, where no shadow of regret lingered. He thought, it really is true about the rich: marry them, fuck them, or kill them.

4.

Asylum

Along the Malecón the chaos of Carnival ruled. The night shook with a rumba roar and throbbed to a conga beat as outrageously flower-bedecked floats rolled down the broad boulevard, surrounded by thousands of gyrating people. Men in leopard thongs swung immense lanterns before them, prancing defiantly with iron slave collars around their necks. Nearly naked females, draped in provocative strips of velvet, satin and sequins, dueled one another with tricky dance steps. Giant papier-mâché gods and devils danced duets to the thrill of cheering spectators.

Bongo watched the dancers and floats passing by in raucous procession, celebrating freedom from a colonial enslavement that still stung with the harsh memory of its whip. All the neighborhood and religious organizations of Havana were parading. This was the night that the true royalty of the people, the Queen of the Carnival, reigned supreme.

Black men on white horses galloped in front of Bongo. Huge plumes of white peacock feathers nobly crowned the heads of the men, their skin sparkled with gold glitter. Chasing the men was a twenty-foot-tall slave master in a white suit and white top hat. The monster stomped along as women cursed it and children screamed in panic, then he stopped, throwing fistfuls of candy at the suddenly gleeful onlookers.

The crowd's hysteria grew and Bongo knew that royalty was close. A marching band came into view, blaring the beat of an infectious rhythm. Behind the band, the Royal Float glided forward. Atop it, on a throne surrounded by hundreds of orchids rioting with exotic blooms, was the voluptuous Queen in a strapless sequined gown, waving and blowing kisses to her cheering subjects.

Behind the Royal Float emerged a line of women in billowing white dresses and white bandannas around their heads. The women chanted a shrill chorus: *"He who plants the seeds of love will harvest love,"* as they swept the street ceremoniously with palm fronds, preparing the way for men paying homage to Saint Lazarus. The men wore tattered rags and held on to leashed dogs that symbolically guided the way from the world of the dead to the living. The men shouted promises of penance for their sins and pleaded loudly with prayers for miraculous medical cures.

Bongo pushed through the crowd to get closer to the women in white. He fell into step with them as they sang and swept, trying to get a clear look at their faces. One of them looked up from her sweeping.

"It's *you!*" Bongo shouted.

The woman dropped her palm frond and ran. Bongo chased after her, but he lost sight of her in the crush of people. He kept going until he broke free of the crowd and a side street opened up. At the end of the street, he saw the woman running. When he got there, she was gone. Three streets branched off in different directions. Bongo quieted his heavy breathing, listening. Footsteps echoed back from one of the streets. He ran in that direction, following the street as it narrowed between dilapidated Colonial houses, then passed beneath a stone arch and abruptly ended.

Bongo stopped, staring out at the flat water of the bay. Wedged in among shipping docks was a weather-beaten wooden shack. The tinny sound of jukebox music came from inside, scratching at the night. He took a deep breath and walked toward the shack.

Bongo threw open the door into the Three Virgins. The usual throng of muscular men in sleeveless T-shirts sized him up; some tried to block his way, others tried to catch his eye with a challenging stare. He only had eyes for the woman in white sitting at the far end of the long bar. He pushed onto the stool next to her.

Sweet Maria turned to Bongo. She was breathing hard and sweating. She gulped beer from a glass, then wiped foam from her lips. Her voice was sultry deep. "Honey, you must really want me."

"I do."

"You were giving such a good chase, I thought, why not let the poor boy catch me."

"You've been hard to catch."

"Don't think you're the only one trying. That viper with the mustache has been after me. He went door to door in my neighborhood, threatening people. But they wouldn't talk."

"I knew they wouldn't. That's why I didn't go."

"You never would have found me there."

"So why let me catch you now?"

"I know what you're after."

"What?"

"Your sister."

"Yes."

"I don't know a thing."

Bongo opened his coat, exposing his holstered gun. "I thought maybe I could impress you."

Maria batted her eyelashes. "That doesn't impress me."

"What?"

"Your rod."

"You've seen bigger?"

"You can't imagine."

Bongo smiled. "That's not what I had in mind." He reached inside his coat, unbuttoned a pocket and pulled out a glass jar. He set the jar on the counter.

The color drained from Maria's face.

"This spider is from the Tropicana," Bongo said in a flat voice. "You didn't kill it on New Year's Eve. It's come back to take its revenge and give you the bite of death."

Maria stared at the large white spider inside the jar, its gnarly legs attempting to climb up the glass wall. She hurriedly made the sign of the cross. "Santa Barbara, save me."

"You can't outrun this spider. It will get you, unless you tell the truth."

"I can't tell you where she is."

"Look closely." Bongo held the trapped creature up in its glass prison in front of Maria's face. "Tell me, is this spider crying or smiling?"

Maria stared in horror at the tropical albino spider larger than a tarantula. She pleaded, "I tried to warn you of what was going to happen. I knew you were your sister's brother."

"Is it crying or smiling?"

"Every New Year's Eve, Zapata takes the same table at the Tropicana to watch your sister dance. He sits with his back to a banyan tree so no one can shoot him from behind. Only his two goons are at the table, protecting him against assassins coming from the front. Your sister brought the basket of flowers with the hidden bomb to his table before her show started."

"My sister! Christ, I never suspected her!"

"Neither did Zapata."

"What went wrong?"

"A dancer who was jealous of your sister, she told the Judge something was going to happen to Zapata. The Judge got Zapata out, but the bomb was still there. We didn't want innocents hurt, so one of our people brought the basket to another table and defused the bomb beneath the flowers."

"Who did that?"

"Mercedes. But she didn't disconnect the right wires. Minutes later the bomb exploded."

Bongo stared intensely at the white spider struggling inside the glass. In his mind's eye he saw Mercedes standing in her shiny gold satin dress, jasmine blossoms woven into the braided crown of her hair, her smile joyous as she waved to him across the room to join her. He still heard the crowd, chanting the countdown to the midnight blast that shattered his world.

Bongo shook his head, scattering the terrible memory. He gazed at Maria. "This is your last chance." He screwed off the jar lid and flipped the jar upside down. The enormous spider thumped onto the top of the bar. "Answer me. Is this spider crying or smiling?"

"Don't let it kill me."

"Where's my sister?"

The spider pumped up on gnarly legs and crawled toward Maria. She froze in fear.

Bongo brought his fingers down around the spider, forming a cage. In a blur, his fingers began drumming.

"Stop!" Maria pleaded. "Don't drum that rhythm!"

"You know it?"

"It's the rhythm of the sorcerer! It's the serpent's tongue, it's the evil call in the blood!"

Bongo's fingers flew faster, confusing the creature in its confined space. "If my fingers miss and crush this spider, its spirit will crawl into the mouth of your dreams and poison you."

"Your sister's not smiling!" Maria gasped. "She's crying!"

"Where?"

"In the asylum of Saint Lazarus."

"Which one?"

"Saint Lazarus of the Lepers."

"Lepers! Why with the lepers?"

"No one would think to look there."

Bongo stopped drumming. He scooped up the spider, placed it in the jar and screwed the lid tight.

Maria's eyes filled with tears. "I didn't betray anyone, did I?"

"No. You're a good woman."

"You really mean that? You really think I'm a *woman*?"

"The best kind."

Maria placed her hand on Bongo's cheek and tenderly caressed him. "Be careful, honey. Zapata wants you dead."

Tropical dawn streaked the sky as Bongo aimed the Rocket up a road ascending a steep hill. At the summit, he cut the engine and got out, standing before an old circular fountain surrounded by angels. The angels resembled gargoyles more than celestial spirits, their granite faces and wings knocked off long ago. Bongo turned and gazed up at the high stone facade of a seventeenth-century convent, its window shuttered. The convent's thick wooden door bristled with iron spikes. Bongo pulled a rope hanging next to the door. A bell clanged, but the door remained closed. He yanked the rope harder; still no one came. He went back to the Rocket and honked its horn. After the sharp blast all was quiet again, with only the gurgle of water spouting from faceless angels.

Bongo looked back at the monolithic stone convent. He knew his sister was inside. He decided to crash the Rocket through the formidable door. As he turned to get into the car, the convent door creaked open on iron hinges. A specter appeared in the doorway, draped in a gray cloak, the top of its head covered by a tall conical hat with a wide brim flaring out like the wings of a prehistoric bird. In the shadow of the brim, lips murmured, "This is an asylum. Honor the silence."

"I'm looking for a young woman. She was brought here New Year's Day."

"There's no one here like that."

"I'll see for myself."

Bongo pushed past the specter and into the convent. More specters rushed at him from long hallways, the winged brims of their hats flapping as they surrounded him.

A specter stepped forward. "Stay out! This is a holy place of healing. Saint Lazarus protects us."

"I understand," Bongo answered respectfully. "I too am a faithful follower of Saint Lazarus. I have prayed to the saint for a cure."

The specter gazed skeptically at Bongo. "What promise of penance did you declare, for the saint to cure you?"

"I promised Saint Lazarus that if he delivered my sister to me, I would kill the devil of darkness."

"To kill is a mortal sin resulting in eternal damnation."

"Yes, that is the highest penance of all."

The specters all turned their backs against Bongo, murmuring urgently, their heads bobbing beneath the flapping brims of their hats. They suddenly fell silent. One of them turned. "What you say is true. But we cannot allow you to commit a mortal sin in the name of a promise to Saint Lazarus. You must leave."

"I can't leave, I've come too far. Sweet Maria sent me."

"*Sweet Maria!* Why didn't you say so? Come with me!"

The specter spread the arms of its cloak and appeared to sail away down the corridor.

Bongo followed. He heard soft moans from behind some closed doors that he passed, from behind other doors came giddy, ironic laughter. A strange scent clung in the air, the mingled odors of sterilizing alcohol, burning cloves and rotting oranges.

The specter stopped before a door, and from the folds of its cloak withdrew an iron key.

Bongo shouted angrily, "You keep her locked up!"

"For her own safety."

"But she's trapped inside!"

"On the contrary, the world is locked out."

"*Give* me that." Bongo grabbed the key. "You aren't going to lock *me* up! Besides, how do I know she's even *in* there?"

"That depends on whether you truly *believe* in Saint Lazarus."

The specter turned and glided away.

Bongo unlocked the door and stepped inside, closing the door. The tiny room was empty except for a cot against a stone wall. Through the slot of a narrow doorway was a small garden. Among the flowers stood a figure dressed in a flowing, bridelike linen gown. The figure slowly turned. Bongo heard bold laughter, a familiar sound he had known since childhood.

Bongo stepped into the garden. His sister came toward him, her head and face covered by a gauzy veil. Her laughter became more insistent, washing over him, almost hysterical. Maybe she had been undone by all that had happened to her, perhaps she had gone mad. He wanted to take her into his arms, to hold and protect her. But she could be dressed this way to hide something hideous, a scarring disfigurement from the Tropicana bombing. Or maybe she was a leper.

She stopped laughing.

Bongo took her in his arms.

"Oh, thank you," she sighed. "I was afraid that if you thought I was a leper you wouldn't hold me."

Bongo would not allow himself tears. Together they could survive, together they were one. Her breathing deepened. Bongo felt her strength surge as she gave herself up to who they were together. Bells began ringing.

"Those are the bells for morning prayers," she said. "We're supposed to go into our cells and pray. But we will talk, like we did as children." She took his hand and led the way back into the cell and closed the door.

In the enclosed space there was the odd scent that Bongo had smelled earlier. He didn't know if the scent was coming from this cell, or if it had permeated everything.

His sister sat on the cot against the wall. She pushed the veil above her face. In the dim light, he could only see the whites of her eyes and the white flash of her teeth as she smiled.

She asked, "Can you see my face?"

He couldn't see her ebony skin. Perhaps she was disfigured and would only reveal herself in darkness. "I can't see very well in this light."

"Come sit next to me."

Bongo sat close to her on the cot. She lowered her veil, obscuring her face.

"You're still beautiful," he said.

"My skin is not falling off. I'm not a leper."

"It wouldn't make any difference to me if you were."

She reached her hand out from beneath the linen gown.

Bongo took her hand and kissed it, not caring if it was scarred from a bomb blast or disfigured from disease.

She held his hand tightly. Ever since they were children, her black hand in his white hand had seemed to him a beautiful miracle.

"You don't have to worry," she assured him. "I'm not hurt at all. I don't have a mark on me."

"Then why are you dressed like this?"

"The nuns wanted me to look like the others. There are some here"—her voice trailed off—"who must be covered."

"But you have nothing to hide."

"Oh, but I do. If I'm here, and dressed like this, it is difficult for people to find me."

"I've found you." Bongo squeezed her hand. "I'm going to get you out of here."

"But I don't want to go."

"I can protect you."

"I *am* protected."

"By prehistoric nuns?"

"And others."

"Who?"

"You wouldn't understand."

"I understand they aren't here *now*."

Bongo got up and walked across the room to a shuttered window. "What does this look out onto?"

"The entrance."

Bongo pulled the shutter open. Through the dusty glass he had a view of the faceless angels around the fountain. On the inside of the windowpane flies buzzed and knocked themselves against glass, trying to escape.

"Are you expecting someone?" she asked.

"Yes." Bongo drummed nervously on the glass. "Do you remember diving for coins when we were children?"

"I remember *everything*."

"Try to forget the bad parts."

"I can't."

"People grow up."

"They don't outgrow the color of their skin."

"What do you mean?"

"I'm a *black* person."

"You're talented and intelligent. You can have the life you want."

"If you were dressed in my skin, you'd know different."

Bongo drummed his fingers harder against the glass, aiming for the flies. He knew they had come here because of the odd, sickening stench. He heard the tapping of his sister's foot behind him. She was keeping time to his drumming.

"If you were in my skin," she continued, "you would see through the lie. You would see that this island is a prison. Most of us are still slaves."

Bongo kept drumming.

Her voice rose. "The masters want to get their white hands on me, to treat me as their private Cuba."

One of Bongo's drumming fingers pinned a fly, crushing it against glass.

"There is no one to liberate us," she continued. "We must fight to liberate ourselves."

"That's why you were willing to plant a bomb in the Tropicana?"

"*Yes!*"

"Innocent people, even your own brother, were at risk."

"No one is *exempt*. I could have been killed too."

Another fly died under the furious beat of Bongo's drumming.

Behind him, her tapping foot kept his rhythm as she talked urgently.

"If we can't wake up the world to our condition, then we must wake up our countrymen."

"And bombs in public places are the alarm clock?"

"If that's the only way to blast people out of their complacency!" she shouted with conviction. "I will bomb the casinos, the offices, the restaurants, the theaters! I will destroy all the government goats sucking off the bottle of greed! You don't see this country as I do!"

"I'm not blind. I see the poverty. I see the kids with tapeworms hanging out of their asses."

"That's the least of it. People are so poor they're eating boiled fleas." She laughed, the same ironic laugh he heard earlier. "Two fleas for a family of eight."

"Average people are doing better than they did in General Machado's day."

"Better isn't good enough, when the average wage is only a hundred and fifty pesos a year. That's not even *half* of what a person makes in the *poorest* state in America."

"Your university professor taught you well."

"I didn't need him to see the truth. I lived it as a kid. You know that."

Bongo smashed another fly beneath the flurry of his fingers. He remembered sleeping on a dirt floor, lice crawling on his scalp, the scent of shit reeking up from open mud trenches, the festering sores on his sister's skin, the pus running from her infected eyes, he couldn't keep the flies from covering her face. He stopped drumming. Dead flies were tattooed across the glass window. He stared at the smashed black bodies oozing white guts, as if they posed a question. "They don't bleed, do they?"

His sister was silent. She studied the tattooed design littered across the window. "No," she said softly, "they don't. But neither do ladybugs."

Bongo was startled by her words. They made him feel like he did as a kid, that she was the one who was more aware of life's harsh realities. He remembered his father's hands beating in a rhythmic slap on both of their shaved heads. He heard his father's song: *"The Bongo has two heads, man and woman, hate and love, war and peace! Those heads are always at odds! The Bongo is the same drum!"*

Through his father's singing, Bongo heard his sister calling from the far side of the room.

"I will always love you, but we must separate."

A flood was rising to tear them apart. Bongo struggled to reach her before it was too late. He finally got to her. He held her. She opened her mouth to say more, but so many tears flowed beneath her veil that they flooded her mouth, flooded the floor, flooded the room, flooded the world. In the torrent, turtles, sharks and dead people tumbled, it was impossible to resist the current.

Bongo was again a drowning boy in a drowning universe, and his sister was being ripped from his side. He grabbed her hand tightly and kicked his feet in the murky water, fighting the roaring crush of gravity. He heard his sister's voice. "I have to leave you! I have to cross over to the other side!" He kicked harder, rising up, breaking the surface and gasping for air, his face pressed to the window of his sister's cell. Outside, the sky was clear blue, and beneath it a black Plymouth drove up to the fountain of faceless angels. The car's back door flew open. Zapata jumped out. Bongo felt his sister's hand slip from his. She was gone.

Zapata stood in front of the fountain of faceless angels, gazing up through his dark sunglasses at the convent's steep stone facade. He ran a finger over his mustache, his lips curved in a smile. He had to admit that he never would have thought of looking for her here. He glanced over at Bongo's Rocket and his smile became bigger; the bird dog had flushed the bird.

Pedro and Paulo walked up behind Zapata and stood next to him.

"Captain," Pedro said nervously, "maybe it's not such a good idea to go inside. They say the nuns here are the cruelest in Cuba."

"That's right," Paulo added. "They're left over from the Spanish Inquisition and dress like witches."

Zapata spoke quietly. "Pull the bell rope so they know we're here."

"Paulo," said Pedro, "you do it."

"Not me," Paulo whined. "They're all lepers in there. I don't want to have my fingers and toes fall off."

"If you two don't do what I ordered," Zapata said, "I *will* shoot your fingers and toes off."

Paulo walked reluctantly to the massive door. He glanced from side to side as if expecting a witch to come zooming at him on a broom. He turned to Zapata. "Nobody's home. Let's get going."

"Pull the damn rope," Zapata demanded.

Paulo grabbed the rope, but before he could pull it the door swung open and the specter of a nun appeared in a cloak and a winged hat.

Paulo leapt back with a yelp.

Pedro made the sign of the cross and shouted, "Jesus, save us!"

"Shut up," Zapata hissed.

Pedro tried to regain his composure. "Sorry, Captain."

"Sister," Zapata said, "I have reason to believe a fugitive is hiding here. May we come in?"

"Who are you?" the nun asked.

"Police. Special Police."

"No one is here, except for the dying and the humble servants of Saint Lazarus."

Zapata pointed at Bongo's Rocket parked next to the fountain. "Do the humble servants of Saint Lazarus drive red convertibles?"

The nun began to close the door.

Zapata stepped forward and grabbed the nun by the arm and pushed her into the foyer. "You know who I've come for! Where is she?"

Beneath the winged brim of her hat, the nun's face contorted with pain from Zapata's twisted grip. "Only the sickest are here."

"I'm looking for the Retinta, the blackest of the black. There's only one like her, because she has white hair."

"We have many black ones here. They are all God's children."

"Damn you!"

Zapata twisted the nun's arm violently. It broke with a loud crack as she cried out and fell to the floor.

The nun's cry echoed in the foyer. More nuns came running, the wings of their hats flapping.

Zapata pulled his gun.

The nuns stopped, cowering close together.

Zapata grabbed one of them. "Come with me!"

"Captain," Pedro called, "what about us?"

"Stay here. Don't let anyone leave."

"Yes." Pedro smiled. "We'll keep these chickens in their coop."

Zapata ordered the nun, "Get moving. I want the white-haired Retinta."

The terrified nun nodded, then led Zapata down a long corridor and stopped before a door.

"Please don't hurt anyone," the nun pleaded.

"Unlock the door!"

The nun glanced at the nail above the door. There was no key hanging there. "Mother Superior has the key."

"Where is she?"

"You broke her arm."

"Go get the key. Don't try anything funny. If you do, I'll let my two men loose on your girls. You know what men like that do to virgins, don't you?"

The nun nodded, terrified, then hurried off and quickly returned with a key.

Zapata shoved the key into the lock; it wouldn't turn. "You gave me the wrong key! Damn you!" He tried the key again. "Wait a minute! It's already unlocked!" He pushed the door and it swung open.

Zapata stepped into the shadowy room with a bare cot against one wall. Through the crack of a barely open door he glimpsed a shrouded, bridelike figure in the garden outside. He pushed open the door and emerged into sunshine so bright that, even behind sunglasses, he was momentarily blinded. His eyes began to refocus as the shrouded figure turned, and a flash of light flared from its center with an explosion.

The bullet struck Zapata with the same pain he had felt twenty years before, when an arrow flew from the sea and pierced his heart. He raised his hands to his heart, as if an arrow were really there. He grasped for the arrow's shaft, trying to pull it out before it did fatal damage. Finally, he had it, he had the arrow of pain between his hands. He pulled it as hard as he could, but it refused to come out. He pulled harder. A torrent of blood spurted from his heart. In the red haze, Zapata whispered, *"Nobody understood the perfume of your belly's dark magnolia."*

The arrow fell from Zapata's hands. He was released. He pitched forward, falling at the feet of the shrouded figure.

King Bongo hurried down a long corridor, turned a corner and stopped. Shouting and running toward him were Pedro and Paulo, their guns drawn.

"You shot the Captain!"

"You bastard!"

Bongo reached instinctively to his shoulder holster, but it was empty. He had given the gun to his sister, before she crossed over to the other side.

Pedro aimed his gun at Bongo. From behind Pedro, a blast sounded and a magnum force bullet slammed his head and blew out through his face, scattering blood and bone.

Paulo turned to see where the blast came from. Before he could fire at the assailant, four bullets thudded into his chest, spinning him around in a headlong crash.

Behind the two dead men lying on the floor stood the towering figure of Fido, his gun still aimed.

"Where's Zapata?" he demanded.

"Dead."

Fido looked down at the blood pooling around Pedro and Paulo on the floor, then grinned at Bongo. "I told you I owed you. It was me who has been following you all along, sticking right to your shadow."

"Thanks."

"Like you said, we help each other, that's the Cuban way. Where's your sister?"

"Gone. I could no longer hold on to her."

Fido nodded sympathetically. "The rising tide of change has taken her."

"The tide has flooded everything."

"Our whole country."

"We'd better get out of here. The police, and the *army*, will be looking for us."

"Don't worry. The nuns won't say a word. I'll take the three stiffs to the Pineapple Field."

"They'll make a good meal for the devil dogs."

"Top-quality government meat," Fido laughed.

"So long, pal." Bongo walked away down the corridor.

Fido shouted after him, "No matter how much the tide changes, the country will always need you! You've got the rhythm! You're the King of the Bongo! Without music, we die!"

Bongo stepped through the convent's doorway into sunshine. Birds chirped in the palms, water gurgled from the faceless angels into the fountain. The red Rocket gleamed in the light. He felt he could aim the Rocket at a new universe. Life had changed forever. Anything was possible.

A yellow Packard Victoria roared up the drive and stopped in front of Bongo. The front window rolled down. Ming leaned his face out.

"Hey, headless wonder!"

"What do you mean?"

"King Kwan, that's been you all this time, a headless swordsman swinging away."

"I don't get it."

"Hop in, Mr. Wu will tell you."

Bongo opened the Victoria's back door and climbed into an interior of supple leather and polished wood.

Mr. Wu reclined in the corner on embroidered cushions. He was buttoned up tight in a silk tunic, a skullcap on his head, his ivory cigarette holder between his lips. He took a deep pull on the cigarette, exhaling a cloud of blue smoke.

Bongo closed the door. "How come you always know when to show up?"

"I told you, we Chinese know everyone's laundry."

"So you knew where my sister was the *whole* time?"

"The *nuns* did her laundry, not *me*."

Bongo heard a laugh, he looked up. Ming's face was reflected in the rearview mirror above the front seat.

"I told you," Ming laughed again, "Johnnie Ray's 'Soliloquy of a Fool,' that's the one. The guy beats himself up over what a dope he is about love. Pukes his heart out. A real tearjerker."

"Yeah," Bongo said cryptically, "a real tearjerker. I'm crying right now."

Mr. Wu released another column of smoke from his lips as he spoke. "She's crossed over. You've lost her again."

"It's the way she wanted it."

Wu looked through the window at the parked black Plymouth. "Now that Zapata is out of the way, the nuns will no longer be doing your sister's laundry. She's needed elsewhere. She's a brave girl."

"She always was."

"You've lost your twin, but I have another twin for you."

"What do you mean?"

"I lied, when I said there was only one *Vanda dearei* that made the journey from China to be with you. The truth is, she had a sister, and I secretly kept her." Wu snapped his fingers.

Ming reached down onto the seat next to him, then held up a splendid orchid. The plant's proud green stalk shot up from a clay pot, its flamboyant purple bloom filling the air with the scent of vanilla and cinnamon.

Wu sighed. "She's the exact twin of the one you lost."

Bongo took the orchid. Her weight in his hands was solid, the lush fragrance of her bloom beckoned. "She's gorgeous."

"Be good to her. I don't want her to blow up in your face."

"That will never happen again. I'll protect her."

"She's the last, and she's in your hands."

"I know how valuable she is. I will repay you."

"Promises made, promises to be kept. There will be time in the future to repay. Revolution, like Rome, is not made in a day."

Bongo quickly turned to Mr. Wu. "Revolution?"

"Yes." Mr. Wu grinned.

The truth was as obvious as the bloom of the flower that Bongo held in his hands. He answered his own question with a shout. *"Revolution!"*